THE MARRIAGE BREAK

Claudia was born in Dublin, where she still lives and works an author and actress. She's a *Sunday Times* top ten bestselling author in the UK and a number one bestselling author in Ireland, selling more than three quarters of a million copies in paperback alone.

To date, Claudia has published sixteen novels, five of which have been optioned – three for movies and two for TV. She's currently hassling producers for a walk-on role and is hoping they might even let her keep the costumes for free.

CLAUDIA CARROLL

The Marriage Break

avon.

Published by AVON
A division of HarperCollins*Publishers* Ltd
1 London Bridge Street
London SE1 9GF

www.harpercollins.co.uk

This paperback edition 2020

First published as *Will You Still Love Me Tomorrow?*
in Great Britain by HarperCollins*Publishers* 2011

A catalogue copy of this book is available from the British Library.

ISBN: 978-0-00-835598-2

Typeset in Minion by Palimpsest Book Production Limited, Falkirk, Stirlingshire
Printed and bound in the United States of America by LSC Communications

19 20 21 22 LSC 10 9 8 7 6 5 4 3 2 1

Huge thanks to Marianne Gunn O'Connor, amazing agent, amazing lady, amazing pal.

Thanks to Pat Lynch, for all his endless patience and tireless hard work.

Thanks to the incredible team at HarperCollins Avon, it's such a pleasure to work with the 'A' team!

Special thanks to Claire Bord, for all her incredible thoughts and suggestions and for being the kind of editor you basically dream about working with.

Thanks to everyone else at Avon, especially Caroline Ridding, Claire Power, Charlotte Allen, Kate Bradley, Sammia Rafique and Keshini Naidoo. I owe you all such a debt of gratitude for everything you've done and are doing. And somehow chatting to you ladies never, ever feels like work!

Huge thanks to the legend that is Moira Reilly, what would any of us do without you? And to Tony Purdue too, who works so hard, here in Dublin.

A very special thank you to a very special lady, Vicki Satlow in Milan who does such Trojan work selling the translation rights to my books.

Finally to all the readers out there who've been kind enough to write from far and wide to say nice things about my books; in these cash-strapped times, I feel constantly humbled that anyone would shell out their hard-earned cash to buy something that I've written.

But please know it means the world to me that you're enjoying the books, and thank you.

For Frank Mackey, with love.
This is your year Frankie and don't forget it!

Oh, life is a glorious cycle of song,
A medley of extemporanea;
And love is a thing that can never go wrong;
And I am Marie of Romania.

Dorothy Parker,
Not So Deep as a Well (1937)

Prologue

Thoreau said that the mass of men lead lives of quiet desperation. Course he wasn't to know it, but he was actually talking about me.

Falling in love is easy, you see; any idiot can do it. It's falling out of love that's hard.

It takes courage, brinkmanship and a certain degree of recklessness, not just with your own heart, but with someone else's too. Someone else whose whole existence once meant more to you than your own ever did.

And if you've ever sat across the kitchen table from the person you're supposed to be living happily ever after with and wondered where in hell the spark went . . . well, then you'll know exactly what I'm going through right now.

I'm looking silently across the breakfast table at Dan and trying to pinpoint when exactly we first became such a disconnected couple. And I just don't get it. When did we first start swapping 'I' for 'we'? Dan and I used to be able to have unspoken conversations together. We used to finish each other's sentences. We used to finish each other's food. For God's sake, there was a time when we'd even skip breakfast altogether in favour of an extra hour, tangled up together in bed, making love in a daze of exhausted pleasure.

Now I'm wondering if I sat here dressed like Lady Gaga, singing all the words and doing all the moves from the 'Telephone' video, might he even look up from his *Times'* Sudoku puzzle? Because the sad truth is this: like wearing nappies as a baby, or the lost City of Atlantis . . . any love life we once shared is little more than a hazy memory now, as we sleep side by side, like stone figures on a tomb.

The thing about this house though, is that avoidance is generally considered to be a good thing. A sign of deep maturity and awareness. We both know that we're in a minefield and have been for the longest time; so on the very rare occasions when we find ourselves alone together, we sidestep any embarrassment by just tiptoeing carefully around each other. On the principle that if you don't acknowledge or talk about a thing then it'll just quietly go away all by itself.

Trouble is that all this living in denial is physically starting to give me heartburn and I honestly think I'll scream if I don't get to articulate what's going on inside my head. Which is that the current state of our marriage is a steady beep emerging from a heart monitor showing a clear, straight line.

We have officially flatlined.

I take a sip of tea and unconsciously stare over at Dan, my mind in whirling, agonising turmoil but he's too engrossed in the paper to even notice.

Honest to God, if you were to look at us from the outside, having a civilised breakfast, utterly comfortable in silence, you'd swear our lives were perfect. Dan and Annie, Annie and Dan. Even our names go together. We've been together for almost half of our lives, which I know makes us sound like one of those silver-haired, middle-aged couples with porcelain veneers that you'd see in an ad for stair lifts, and yet we're not. Both of us are only twenty eight. But I can barely remember back to a time when we *weren't* a couple.

At fifteen, he was my first boyfriend, I was his first girlfriend, and now, at an age when most of our old pals from our old life in the city are just beginning to think of settling down and getting married, here's me and Dan like the Mount Rushmore of couples; utterly unchanged from the outside, even after all these years.

Dan reaches out for another slice of toast, but then his tanned, handsome face crinkles with worry as he catches my eye.

'All right, love?'

I nod back, but stay firmly focused on the Pop-Tart in front of me.

There's so much that I need to say to him and I haven't the first clue where to start.

I want to tell him that even though the day has barely started, I already know exactly how it'll pan out. It'll be virtually identical to yesterday and the day before and the day before that. I'll spend the morning working at a job that I don't particularly like for next to no money, just to get me out of this house but most importantly of all, to keep myself busy. Because busy is always good. Busy means less time to think.

And on the way there, I'll probably meet one of our neighbours, Bridie McCoy, who'll chat to me in minute detail about that most gripping and urgent of subjects – her bunions. Like she always does. Then, when I get to the local book shop where I've got a part-time job, my boss will joshingly ask me the same question that she always does, day in, day out. Now that I'm pushing thirty, and now that Dan and I have moved from the city into his family's big country house, when exactly are we planning to start a family? And I will do what I always do: an adroit subject change by asking her whether she fancies Jaffa Cakes or HobNobs with her mug of tea this morning. Never fails me.

Then by the time I get back home, Dan's mother will have dropped in, letting herself in with her own door key like she always does. She'll comb through room after room, lecturing me on how the good table in the dining room needs to be polished daily, or else, my particular favourite, the correct way to clean out the Aga in the kitchen. And I will smile through gritted teeth and remind myself that The Moorings is really her house, not mine, so, in fairness to her, she's entitled.

Then later on in the afternoon, Lisa Ledbetter will make an appearance to the soundtrack of thunderclaps and a cacophonous minor chord being bashed out on an organ in my head. She'll charge in and do what she always does: sit at the kitchen table drinking coffee while moaning about her husband's recent redundancy. Like this was a state of events he'd brought about on purpose with the sole intention of annoying her. Lisa, by the way, is a local gal and old friend of Dan's from when they were kids growing up together. We're roughly the same age and its received wisdom around here that she and I are each other's greatest pals.

But let me dispel that notion right now and tell you that any real friendship between us is a complete and utter myth. Lisa, you see, is a funny combination of needy, vulnerable and demanding; one of those people who's fully prepared to allow everyone around her to do everything for her.

Babysitting, cooking meals for her and her kids; you name it. From time to time, she even lets Dan help out with her household bills. And has absolutely no problem doing this, either.

So I'll sit and listen and sympathise and nod my head at appropriate moments, like I always do. All while mentally steeling myself not to allow her to suck all the life and energy out of me, like she always does. If people can be divided into either drains or radiators, then Lisa is most definitely a drain. So much so that I've silently nicknamed her The Countess Dracula.

Later on Jules, Dan's flaky younger sister, will breeze in, raid the fridge and then make a little cockpit for herself around the TV, surrounded by beer, nachos and last night's leftovers. She's just dropped out of college and doesn't seem particularly bothered about finding something else to do, like, God forbid, looking for an actual job or anything. But she's all the time in the world to flake out in our living room, watching all the afternoon soaps, back to back. Exactly like a lodger, except one that doesn't pay any rent.

Don't get me wrong though, this will actually be the brightest part of my day, mainly because I like Jules. She's by far my favourite person round here. Otherwise I wouldn't have any real friends here at all, just people who don't hate me. Jules is dippy and quirky and fun to be around, like she's got too much personality for one person yet not quite enough for two.

So you get my drift. Dan's family and friends just come and go as and when it suits them.

Like weather. Or bloat.

But it's all part of the joys of small town country life, it seems. And here, in the tiny Waterford village of Stickens (its real name, look it up if you don't believe me . . . makes me feel marginally less bad about calling it 'The Sticks'), privacy is an utterly unheard of concept. Honestly, if I as much as sneeze leaving the house one morning, by lunch-time at least three well-intentioned locals would have called to ask how my terrible bout of swine flu was.

No secrets in Stickens.

In fairness to Dan, he grew up here so he knows everyone and thrives on the humdrum, everyday minutiae of village life. He's the local vet, by the way, just like his father was before him and in turn, his father was before him too. And it's a pure vocation for Dan: he loves, loves, *loves* his job and is one of those people who can't for a split second understand why anyone would possibly want to do anything else.

But when his dad passed away over three years ago . . . well, that's when the trouble all started really. Dan inherited this crumbling old family manor house where the surgery is, which was way too big and unmanageable for his mother to live in anyway. So she and Jules moved into a smaller apartment in the village, which meant that there was nothing for us but to move from our old, happy life in Dublin and settle here, into Dan's family home. It wasn't just the right thing to do; it was the *only* thing to do.

Thing about Dan, you see, is that he's officially The Nicest Man On The Planet. Everyone says so. It takes time, trial and error to creep into his affections, but once there, you're there for life. Anyway, after his father died, naturally he was anxious to be as close as possible to his mother and sister, both of whom he continues to support financially. A bit like a one-man welfare state.

8

But that's Dan for you; helping others is his Kryptonite.

We'll make this work, I had said to him supportively at the time, even though it effectively meant putting my own acting career on hold, as we packed up our independence in the city and got ready to move. Sure as long as we're together, we can make anything work, I said reassuringly. And if a job comes up for me, I'll just do the long commute back and forth to Dublin.

Because our marriage comes first. Doesn't it?

But, like I said, that was well over three years ago and since then, the goalposts have shifted. Considerably. For starters, I'm finding it far, far tougher than I'd ever have thought, hauling myself up and down from Dublin every time there's a sniff of a job. So to keep myself busy, I've done just about every gig in The Sticks that comes my way. Given the odd drama workshop to kids in the local school, worked part-time at the local florist's, you name it, I've given it a whirl.

But the hard, cold fact is that I've been treading water rather than really loving what I'm doing, knowing in my heart that if it's acting work I really want, then I need to be in the city, where all the big job opportunities are. Not to mention where all my old friends are. We stay in touch, of course – we text and phone and email and Skype is my new best friend . . . but it's just not the same as seeing people all the time, is it?

I'm constantly begging/pleading/nagging my old pals to come and visit, even just for a weekend, and in fairness, most of them have done at one time or another. But the thing about The Sticks though, is that it doesn't exactly offer all that much in the way of nightlife. Apart from a couple of pubs where the average age profile is about eighty and the main topic of conversation among the sages of the snug is still the Civil War, there's not a whole lot else on offer.

Bear in mind that you're talking about a tiny village where the main tourist attractions are a Spar newsagents and a large clock in the middle of Main Street, so, unsurprisingly, repeat visits from my Dublin buddies tend to be few and far between.

But it does my heart good though, to keep in touch with our old circle. I love hearing all my girlfriends' tales from the city, of how well they're all doing in their careers and most of all, hearing their stories direct from life at the great dating coalface. And even if their romances don't go exactly according to plan, at least they're all out there, having fun/ breaking hearts/ having their hearts broken in turn/picking themselves up and getting back in the race . . . just like you're supposed to be doing at our age.

Sometimes I'll see them all looking at me, like I'm some prematurely middle-aged housewife in a Cath Kidston apron with matching tablecloths and they'll say, 'But you're *married*! Why aren't you at home, getting fat?'

And I'll want to tell them the truth; that the whole reason I got married was to grow old *with* someone and not *because* of them. But instead, I'll smile and laugh and make a joke and say that Victorian virgin brides in arranged marriages saw more of life than I did before I walked down the aisle. Then they'll all jolly me along by reminding me that I got lucky, because I didn't just marry a great guy, I married the holy grail of men, didn't I?

And the heartbreaking thing is that it's all true – I did.

It's just that the grass is always greener on the other side of the M50 motorway, that's all.

10

I often think that life here is far, far easier for Dan, who's surrounded by his family, along with friends he's known since he was in nappies and has grown up with. Some people live a life that's already been planned out perfectly for them, as inescapable as a circle. And that's Dan and he's perfectly content with that. But the truth is that after three long years here, the claustrophobia is slowly starting to get to me. It's like every time I glance in the mirror I see a woman who looks like it's raining inside of her. Crushed under the weight of my own future.

Because I have deep grievances with my life here that over time, feel like they've barnacled permanently onto my skull. In spite of all my super-human efforts to fit in and to be a good wife and half-decent daughter- and sister-in-law . . . I swear to God, there are days when I physically feel like I'm being smothered. That I can't breathe. That I'm slowly being asphyxiated as surely as if someone had tied a plastic Tesco's bag over my head.

Worse still, that I'm going to go to my grave with an unlived life still in my veins.

Even the clinking sound of Dan's coffee mug as he rests it on a saucer is almost enough to make me want to scream. There's so much I need to talk to him about and yet we're sitting here in total silence. Like an old married couple that ran out of things to say to each other years ago.

Another, tacked-on worry pops into my mind unbidden; is this what we're going to be like twenty years from now? Because as far as I can see, that's the road we're headed down. Rare enough that we even get to eat a meal together given the eighteen-hour days he's been working for as long as I can remember. Rare enough that we get time alone together at all, given that his family still consider this to be

11

their home and just breeze in and out whenever it suits them. Not to mention his work colleagues, who treat our house as a combination of a twenty-four-hour free canteen-cum-low-grade hotel. But to think that we're wasting this precious opportunity to talk, really talk, with him rattling away at the shagging paper and me restlessly glowering off into space . . .

Dan looks up and catches my eye again. A tiny sliver of hope; he used to know my mind nearly better than I did myself.; time was when he could read my subconscious as easily as an autocue. Maybe, just maybe, he's noticed that his wife is slowly drowning right before his eyes and will throw me some kind of lifeline. Maybe, after all my fretting and stressing, he and I are something that can be fixed after all . . .

'Annie?'

'Yes?'

Come on, Dan, come on . . . meet me halfway here . . .

'You won't forget to pick up that fungicidal cream from the chemist for the cat's ringworm today, will you?'

I do not befeckinglieve it.

Brilliant. Just brilliant.

When I don't answer, he tosses the paper aside and for a split second looks at me again; really looks at me this time, his soft, black eyes now full of concern.

'Everything OK?'

And like the moral coward that I am, I back down.

To be polite, I freeze frame a watery smile onto my face and even allow the grin to reach all the way up to my eyes.

'Everything's fine.'

But I'm lying.

Everything is so *not* fine.

WINTER

Chapter One

OK, two things you need to know about me: firstly, I'm really not the sort of person to mortgage my entire future on a whim. Secondly, if life in The Sticks has taught me anything, it's this: the lower you keep your expectations, the less likely you are to get let down. And above all, do not, repeat, *do not,* expect miracles to happen in this neck of the woods. Long and unbelievably boring conversations with Audrey, my mother-in-law, about the correct way to make a poinsettia entirely out of icing for the Christmas cake, yes, but miracles . . . no, sorry, love. 'Fraid not. Not in this neck of the woods.

So when the phone calls start coming from about eleven-thirty in the morning onwards, you'll get some idea of how utterly, unbelievably staggered I am by this bolt from a clear blue sky.

I'm up a ladder in the dusty back room of our local book shop, stacking shelves with copies of a hot, new young adult series which we're hoping will bring in some badly-needed footfall over Christmas. Because considering it's only a few weeks off, business is worryingly quiet and so far this morning I've already had the owner, Agnes Quinn, who's been around for approximately as long as the Old Testament, explain to me that she's really very sorry but she just doesn't think there'll be a job for me here after the holidays.

Not her fault of course, she was at pains to explain, people just aren't spending cash in the same way that they used to . . . more and more people are buying books online now . . . Amazon are squeezing her out . . . rents are too high . . . recession is still having a massive knock-on effect . . . blah-di-blah . . .

I know the story only too well and sympathise accordingly. Try not to worry, I say positively, and look on the bright side. Yes, business is slack I gently tell her, but just think, it'll give you more time to work on your own book. Her round, puffy cheeks flush at this, as they always do whenever she's reminded about her as-yet-unfinished magnum opus. It's a cookbook, by the way. Agnes has spent the last three years eating her way through her granny's recipes with a view to publication.

'Anyway, I'm sure you won't miss working here, will you now, Annie, love?' she twinkles knowingly at me from where she's standing over by the till, surveying a shop floor so empty it might as well have tumbleweed rolling through it. 'Because it'll mean you'll have far more time to spend up at The Moorings with your in-laws, won't it?'

I do what I always do: smile, nod and say nothing.

Then she rips open another cardboard box that's just been delivered and sighs disappointedly, 'Oh, look at this. More books.' In much the same manner as someone who'd been expecting petunias.

Anyway, just then I feel my mobile silently vibrating in my pocket. I ignore it and quietly get back to stacking shelves. Audrey, most likely, ringing from my house to whimper down the phone at me, in her frail, reed-thin,

16

whispery, little-girl voice, like she does every day, even though she knows right well that I'm at work and therefore not supposed to take personal calls.

OK, three possible reasons for her ringing: a) she wants to have a go at me, in her best passive-aggressive way for still not having put up the Christmas tree yet; b) she's having one of her little 'turns' and needs me home urgently, even though I'm at work. Not that she doesn't have a daughter of her own at her permanent beck and call, who's unemployed and therefore has far more time on her hands than I do. But somehow, it's always, always me she'll call, like I'm some kind of nicotine patch for her nerves.

Or worst of all, point c). Whenever Audrey runs out of things to guilt me out about and yet feels the need to use me as a kind of emotional punch bag, she'll have a right good nose through the house when I'm not there, then pick on me for making some supposed change to The Moorings behind her back. Any minor shifting around of furniture or rearranging of china on the kitchen dresser by the way, all fall under this category and if I even attempt to deny said change, she'll usually resurrect one of her favourite old gripes. Namely the fact that I had the outright *effrontery* to strip the flowery wallpaper from our bedroom wall and paint it plain cream instead. Not a word of a lie, when I first brought her upstairs to proudly show off my handiwork in all my newly-married innocence, honest to God, the woman's intestines nearly exploded. The local GP had to be called, sedatives had to be administered and to this day, I still haven't heard the last of it.

This, by the way, would be the one, single decorative change that I've made since moving into the house; the first and the last. How could I have even thought of doing such an insensitive thing? I'll never forget Audrey whimpering at me, laid prostrate on our sofa like Elizabeth Barrett Browning having an attack of the vapours and glaring accusingly at me with her pale, fishy eyes. No messing, all the woman was short of was a hoop skirt, a cold compress on her forehead and a jar of smelling salts. Not only had I completely destroyed the look of that whole room, she sniffled . . . but did I even appreciate that the wallpaper had been there since she first came to The Moorings as a bride?

Ohh . . . way back in the early eighteenth century, most likely.

The Moorings, I should tell you, is a vast, seven-bedroomed crumbling old mansion house; relentlessly Victorian, with huge, imposing granite walls all around it – exactly the kind of location that film scouts would kill to use on an Agatha Christie-Poirot murder mystery and decorated in a style best described as early Thatcher. Which is a crying shame, because with a bit of TLC and if I was really allowed to get my hands on the place, I know it could actually be stunning. I often compare it to Garbo in a bad dress; you can see the bone structure's there, if you could only strip away all the crap. All the house's features are intact and perfect: the coving, the brickwork, the stunning, sixteen-foot high plastered ceilings, but layered in a blanket of someone else's old-fashioned, long-faded taste. With the result that I permanently feel like I'm a guest in my own home.

From the outside though, it's so scarily impressive that the very first time Dan took me here, aged fifteen, I remember joking to him that it was half posh mansion, half the kind of place you'd go to get your passport stamped.

And he laughed and little did I think it would one day be my home.

Trouble is that ever since Dan's father died, Audrey, Queen Victoria-like, has pretty much wanted the house to remain exactly as it was when he was alive – a living mausoleum. Right down to his boots in the outside shelter which are still in exactly the same place he'd always left them. And his favourite armchair, that no one is allowed to sit in, *ever*, just where he liked it to be – in the drawing room, right by the window.

Grief does funny things to people, my Dan, Dan Junior, gently reminded me after the whole wallpaper-gate debacle, so of course I apologised ad nauseam and solemnly vowed not to do anything that might bring on a repeat performance. Nothing to do but bite my tongue and support Audrey for as long as she needed. Let's both just be patient with her, Dan said to me; together we'll help get her though this.

Course that was around the same time that he buggered off to start working eighteen-hour days and started communicating with me via Post-it notes stuck on the fridge door, telling me not to bother waiting up for him, that he wouldn't be home. And of course, Jules was in college at the time and just couldn't have been arsed doing anything.

Leaving me alone, to handle Audrey all by myself.

You try living inside a memorial with a mother-in-law who still considers it to be her home, a husband who's never around and who, when he is, barely bothers to speak to you anymore.

Go on, I dare you.

Anyway, back to the book shop, where my mobile keeps on ringing and ringing and still I keep ignoring it, wondering for the thousandth time if Audrey has any conception of basic office etiquette – that you can't take phone calls when you're supposed to be working. But then, that's the kernel of the problem; she doesn't consider what I do to come under the banner heading of 'work'. No, in her book, being a vet like Dan is an actual hardcore, proper 'job', what I do is just arsing around. Just in case, God forbid, I got any kind of notions about myself.

By lunchtime, business is so slack that poor, worried old Agnes tells me I can finish up early for the day. In fact apart from a lost backpacker sticking his head through the door looking for directions and Mrs Henderson waddling in from across the street, not to buy, but to give out that she can't pronounce the place names in any of Stieg Larsson's books, we haven't had any other footfall the entire morning.

Mrs Henderson, by the way, is something of a crime book aficionado and she drops into the shop pretty much every day to tell us the endings of whichever thriller she's stuck into at the moment. Well, either that or to describe all the twists and red herrings, and then to tell us exactly how she saw them coming from miles off.

Anyroadup, between one thing and another, it's just coming up to one o'clock before I even get a chance to check any of the messages on my mobile.

To my astonishment, not a single one of which is from Audrey.

A Dublin number, one that hasn't flashed up on my phone, since, oooh, like the George Bush administration. One Hilary Williams. Otherwise known as . . . drum roll for dramatic effect . . . my agent.

OK, the CliffsNotes on Hilary: firstly, she wasn't exactly a fan of my decision to move to The Sticks. In fact, she's a sixty-something, bra-burning, first-generation feminist of

20

the Germaine Greer school and the very idea that I'd sacrifice a budding theatre career to, perish the thought, actually put my marriage first, was almost enough to have her lying down in a darkened room taking tablets and listening to dolphin music.

Secondly, her nickname is Fag Ash Hil, on account of the fact that she smokes upwards of sixty a day and climbing. She's the only person I know who actually went out and organised protest marches *against* the smoking ban, and among her clients, it's an accepted rule that you don't even think about crossing the threshold of her office without at least two packs tucked under your oxter for her.

Hence she normally sounds deep, throaty and gravelly, a bit like a man in fact, but . . . not today. Four messages, in a voice designed to wrest people from dreams and all rising in hysteria till by the last one she sounds like she's left Earth's gravity field and is now orbiting somewhere around Pluto.

'Oh for GOD'S SAKE, ANNIE, why are you not returning any of my calls?! Can you please stop please stop role-playing Mrs James Herriot from *All Creatures Great and Small* and kindly get back to me? Like . . . NOW?'

This is delivered, by the way, like an edict from the Vatican. I listen to what she has to say, call her back toot suite . . . then hop straight into my car.

And faster than a bullet, I'm on the long, long road to Dublin.

Sticking to the speed limit, it generally takes the guts of three hours to get from The Sticks to Dublin and believe me the drive is not for the faint-hearted. It's motorway for a lot of it, but you still have to navigate a good fifty plus miles before that on narrow, twisting, secondary roads that would nearly put the heart crossways in you. Anyway, anyway, anyway, fuelled by nothing more than adrenaline, I manage to a) drive at breakneck speed, b) not get caught by the cops and c) even beat my own personal record of getting to the city in under two-and-a-half hours flat, with my foot to the floor and my heart walloping the entire way.

I finally arrive in Dublin late in the wintry afternoon, avoiding the worst of the rush-hour traffic and miraculously managing to find a space in a handy twenty-four hour car park, right in the middle of town and conveniently close to Hilary's office. In my sticky, sweat-soaked, heart palpitation-y state I amaze myself by even remembering to pick up a few obligatory packets of Marlboro Lights for her.

'Annie, get your arse in here and sit down!' is her greeting, which might sound a bit harsh, but coming from Hil, can actually be taken as a term of endearment. I obediently do as I'm told and head inside, dutifully handing over the cigarettes as we air kiss.

It's been over three years since I set foot in this office and at least a year since we last spoke, so it's comforting to see, in spite of my being out of circulation for so long, that precious little has changed round here. Hil still has the same grey spiky hair, the same grey trouser suits, same matching grey skin tone. Same sharp tongue, same short fuse. Oh and she still chain smokes like it's food.

And another thing, with her there's never small-talk of any description. Never a hello-how-are-you-how's-your-life-been. Hil, you see, favours the Ryanair approach to her work: no frills, no extras. Time is money so it's always straight down to business. She plonks down behind her desk, dumps a thick-looking script down in front of me, then leans forward so she can scrutinise me, up close and personal.

'Good, good,' she nods, taking in my appearance as thoroughly as a consultant plastic surgeon while lighting up at the same time.

'Ehh . . . sorry, Hilary, . . . what's good?'

'You still look the same way you do in your CV headshot. Living the life of a countrified recluse hasn't altered your appearance that much. Which at least is something.'

All I can gather from that comment is that she half-expected me to clamber into her office dressed in mud-soaked wellies with straw in my hair, brandishing a pitchfork and looking exactly like Felicity Kendal from *The Good Life*. And while ordinarily that mightn't be too far off the truth (The Sticks isn't exactly Paris during fashion week), at least, thank God, today I'm out of my normal jeans and woolly jumper and am in my best shop assistant gear: a warm woolly coat, a wraparound dress and a half-decent, non-mud-stained pair of boots.

'No,' she growls, still scrutinising me. 'You still look like the same old Annie Cole. Which is good news. Which is exactly what we want.'

She's got black and white pictures of all her clients dotted round the office walls and through the haze of smoke I manage to make my own photo out. Taken over four years ago, but apart from a few more wrinkles and a few extra pounds . . . no, I'm not really all that much different. Same dark skin, same long, dark, centre-parted, wiry hair that needs enough hairspray to put a dent in the ozone layer just to get it to lie down flat . . . same everything.

Funny, but looking at my own photo always reminds me

of how alike Dan and I are, even the way we look. We both have the identical eye colour: deep brown, which turns straight to coal black when either of us are worn out or exhausted. We could almost pass for brother and sister. Or as Jules puts it a bit more cruelly, I look like him dressed in drag.

Ouch.

'OK, down to business,' says Hilary, sitting forward and balancing her fag on the edge of an ashtray. 'You're familiar with Jack Gordon's work, no doubt?'

'THE Jack Gordon? Are you kidding me? Yes, yeah, of course I am, he's completely amazing,' I blurt out, wondering where this could possibly be headed.

Jack Gordon, by the way, would be one of the youngest and hottest theatre directors in town; so unbelievably successful that you'd almost think the legal firm of Beelzebub and Faustus had a contract on file with his name scrawled on it in suspicious looking red ink. I'm not joking, actors nearly impale themselves just to get a chance to *audition* for him, never mind work for him. But then Jack's reputation goes before him and boy, does he have the Olivier awards hanging out of him to prove it. His productions are always cutting edge, razor sharp and invariably the talk of the chattering classes. In fact, probably the only thing that's slowed down the guy's progress over the years is the deep drift of bouquets and laurels that he's had to wade through.

The theatre world's Alexander McQueen, in short.

'Then have a read of this,' says Hilary, tossing a bound script over to me.

I look at the title of the play, *Wedding Belles*. By a new playwright whose name I'm not familiar with.

'It's a comedy-drama and a smash hit to boot,' Hilary goes on. 'Set in a health spa where a group of women of different ages and all from the same family go for a hen weekend, because the protagonist is getting married. It opened at the National back in October, during the theatre festival and is still packing them in.'

Now a distant bell begins to ring.

'Yeah, that's right . . . I remember reading some of the reviews when it first opened,' I tell her, excitedly grabbing hold of the script and flicking through it.

Fag Ash Hil just raises a Vulcan eyebrow at me, like she's shocked that we actually do get paper deliveries down in The Sticks and don't just communicate with the outside world via carrier pigeon. But I don't care, because by now I'm on the edge of my seat with anticipation, wondering what all of this can possibly have to do with me and with my little life. The show is already up and running so it's not like I can go and audition for it, now is it? Aren't I already a few months too late for that?

'The curtain goes up at seven-thirty sharp tonight. I've already managed to wangle a house seat for you, and I need you there,' says Hilary, pulling so deeply on her fag that it's like the breath comes from her toes. 'Then you'll go back to bog-trotter land . . .'

For the sake of diplomacy, I let that one pass. Mainly because I know only too well that as far as Hilary is concerned, if you're based anywhere further than a thirty-mile radius from Harvey Nichols, chances are you live in a mud hut and spend your spare time either milking cattle or else throwing stones at the neighbours. When you're not worrying about the new taxes on cider, that is.

On she goes: '. . . where you'll spend the rest of the night studying that script like your life depended on it. Then tomorrow afternoon . . .'

'But, Hilary, I don't understand . . . none of this makes any sense . . . I mean, the show is already cast and in production . . .'

'If you'd let me finish, I was about to explain that the leading actress has literally just given notice to the producers that she's pregnant and will have to drop out of the show very soon. In a matter of weeks, as it happens. It seems that she's almost four months gone and unfortunately for her, the pregnancy can't be disguised any more. Plus, as you'll see when you read the script, her role is quite a physical one, so she's been advised by her doctors to drop out of the show as soon as possible. For the health and safety of the child, naturally.'

'Pregnant?' I repeat stupidly.

'Which is where you come in. Jack Gordon remembered seeing you in a production of *Twelfth Night* years ago. Of course that would have been before you decided to take early retirement and disappear off into the professional wilderness . . .'

Again, I bite my tongue and let that pass; I'm *waaaaay* too keyed up right now to bother defending my life.

'. . . And he thinks that you might possibly be right to take over the role . . .'

'He *WHAT*? He actually said that?' I almost yell, stunned that the mighty Jack Gordon even remembered me in the first place.

'So maybe if you'd shut up for two seconds together, I could get to tell you the really good news. Jack is only seeing three actresses this week to audition them for the part. And you, my dear, are one of the lucky three.'

For the first time since I arrived here, I'm completely shell-shocked into silence.

After I leave Hilary's office, I somehow stagger to a Starbucks, find a quiet corner and desperately try to calm down, even though my heart's palpitating so fast, I almost feel like I should be breathing into a paper bag. I grab a mug of coffee and start reading through the script, with trembling hands and eyes that won't even focus properly; I'm that all over the place.

The play, by the way, isn't just amazing, it's an absolute cracker. A wow. It's rare enough that you find half-decent parts written for women these days, but this one really is like the gold standard. It's an all-female cast, five women in total, ranging in age from a teenager right up to a woman in her mid-fifties. And the part I'm up for, fingers, toes and eyeballs crossed, is the bride-to-be, aged twenty four, the exact same ludicrously young age I was myself when I got married.

I'm not just saying it, but it really would be a dream role, it's got everything. Highs, lows, thrills, spills and a twist that never in a sugar rush could you possibly see coming. A show that lulls you into a false sense of security . . . then gives you a swift, sharp punch right to the solar plexus. Starts out as pure farce and ends in tragedy.

So not all that different to my own marriage, when you come to think about it.

In fact, I'm so utterly engrossed in reading it that before I know where I am, it's already past seven pm. So I race for the National theatre, which is right in the dead centre of town and thankfully only a short sprint away. I call Dan on the way, of course, knowing full well that I'll only get his voicemail. At this time, he'll still be out doing farm calls, so I leave a hysterical message explaining what's happened and faithfully promise to be home right after the show. The full story, I figure, can wait till we're talking properly. Face to face. So he can't get away from me, or tune me out, or else start talking about bovine diarrhoea.

Course by now there's about four missed calls from Audrey wondering what could possibly have happened to me/where am I/do I realise this is her pension day and that she needs to be driven to and from the post office? But I don't get back to her, deciding instead to postpone the guilt trip till tomorrow. This is one fire I'll just have to pee on later.

I swear to God though, even just being back inside the theatre does my heart the world of good. Like the little actress that's been dying inside me for years suddenly gets an adrenaline shot right to the bone marrow. I've worked at the National many times before and it feels beyond exhilarating to be back and to see everyone again.

Tom, the gorgeous front of house manager is straight over to me, giving me a big bear hug and welcoming me back so warmly that I almost get a bit teary. Then the box office girls all squeal when I stick my head in to say hi and tell me it's like old times seeing me back. Like this is the set of *Hello Dolly* and somehow I've morphed into Barbra Streisand for the night.

And the play is only mesmerising. Hilariously funny, but in the blackest way you could imagine, yet packing such a mighty powerful punch that judging from the look of the audience around me, leaves people reeling by the final curtain. The cast takes an astonishing three standing ovations and I'm pretty sure I'm the last person to leave the auditorium; I just want to stay here, soak up the atmosphere and not break the magical spell that's been woven round us all.

Even better, a very old pal of mine going back years, an actress called Liz Shields is in the cast too, so I text her to tell her I'm here and waiting in the bar to say hi to her. Ten minutes later, she bounces out from her dressing room, still in all her war-paint, with her swishy blonde hair extensions and wearing her usual 'rock chick' gear of leather and denim. Looking like a young Madonna and Christina Aguilera if they were to step out of the matter transporter in *The Fly*, if you get me.

I'm not joking you; Liz yells out my name so loudly that half the bar turns round to take in the sideshow.

'Holy Jaysus, Annie bloody Cole!! Come here and givvus a hug! Have you any idea how much I've missed you?!' So we hug and squeal and kiss and I can't tell you how beyond fab it is to see her again.

Liz and I trained in drama school here in Dublin together, ooh, way back in Old God's time, and from the day we met, we just clicked. She's completely wild and mad and fun – one of those people that you could start off having a normal night out with, like say, grabbing a few drinks in town . . . then you wake up the following morning in Holyhead. And by the way, that Holyhead story is no exaggeration and I should know; it happened on my hen night.

Anyway, we grab a table, order a vodka for Liz, a Coke for me and settle down into a big catch-up chat, yakking over each other just like we always used to. Juggling about five different conversations up in the air simultaneously.

'So what did you think of the show?' she asks excitedly,

'and by that of course I mean, what did you think of me? Go on, rate me. And none of your plamassing either; be inhuman. Be vicious.'

'Easy, eleven out of ten,' I giggle back at her, loving the banter and not realising just how much I've missed it. For a split second not even being able to remember the last time I actually *laughed*.

'Feck off, eleven out of ten sounds insincere.'

'Right then, nine point nine if it'll make you believe me! Seriously, Liz, do you even know how amazing you were out there tonight? Honest to God, girl, you'd be magnetic if you stood on the stage reading out instructions to an IKEA flat pack sofa . . . but in a show as good as this? You were bloody mesmerising! Only the truth, babe.'

She playfully punches me, then yells over to the barman: 'What's keeping our drinks, Ice Age?'

Pure, vintage Liz. I give her a completely spontaneous hug and then tell her the real reason why I came to the show all by myself tonight. Well, they must hear her shrieks all the way back in The Sticks. I honestly think that she's more excited about my audition than even I am, if that were possible. Bless her, she even offers to ring up another one of the cast to get her to say her magic, foolproof novena to Saint Jude, to guarantee I land the part.

'So tell me then,' I ask, fishing for the one scrap of information I'm burning to find out. 'What's he like to work with? The mighty Jack Gordon.'

Liz sucks in her cheeks and thinks before answering.

'Jack is . . . it's hard to say . . . I don't really know him, even though I've known him for years. He's like nine parts genius to one part knob, if that makes sense. Hard to please. Never happy with the show, even on nights when we take three standing ovations, one after the other. Never happy with anything. Apparently the National are putting him up in some five star hotel in town and he walked straight into it and said, 'what a dump.'

My heart shrivels at this, suddenly nauseous at the thought that I have to audition for him tomorrow.

'Oh and he's having a fling with one of the box office girls here in the theatre,' Liz continues. 'A young one barely old enough to have seen all the episodes of *Friends*. And he treats her like complete shite, if you ask me. Always saying he'll call her and then not. Inviting her to dinner after the show then not turning up and leaving the poor kid standing here on her own, with the rest of us all looking at her mortified. And afraid to bitch about him to her in case it all gets back. So in short: beware. Jack's a guy who's very good at saying things that he doesn't mean to people, then trampling on them to get what he wants. And because he's lauded as the wunderkind of the theatre world, he gets away with it.'

Just then, the drinks arrive and the two of us automatically get into an 'I'm getting this/no, feck off, I am' tussle over who pays. 'Anyway, do you realise,' Liz says, mercifully changing the subject, 'that if you do land the gig, we'd end up playing best friends? I mean, come on, Annie, how incredible would that be?'

I glow a bit, for a split second, allowing myself to believe that the fantasy might really come true. And then I remember the full details of the job, spelled out carefully to me by Fag Ash Hil in her office earlier. The massive, full extent of the commitment involved, in the unlikely event of things going my way. In other words that, no matter how overwhelmingly thrilling the thoughts of doing the gig might be, fact is, it still comes with the most massive price tag attached.

Anyway, there's no time to dwell on that because meanwhile Liz has already buzzed onto another major catch-up topic, as she brings me up to speed on her love life.

'So in unrelated news,' she says, laying into the vodka, 'I'm still single. In fact, since I last saw you, I've had a total of about thirteen flings, roughly about the same number of shags and only one actual bona fide boyfriend. Crap, isn't it? Oh and by "boyfriend", just so you're clear, I actually mean, "guy who I saw for longer than a single weekend". Although, to be honest, he was one of those blokes who basically would have gone home with a gardening tool. And by now I've gone on so many blind dates, they should consider giving me a free guide dog. In other words, Annie, I still have a massive radar for emotionally unavailable guys with low self-esteem. Commit-twits. Half the time they don't even have jobs either. So there you go. But, in a way, isn't it reassuring to know that some things don't change? You got lucky and meanwhile, I'm still out there chasing after nut-jobs.

'Anyway,' she breaks off, waving to the barman to send over another vodka, 'like I always say, if Matt Damon was single and if he wasn't famous and if he lived and worked in Dublin and if he knew me . . . I'm highly confident that we'd be dating, you know.'

'That's an awful lot of ifs, babe,' I giggle.

'Easy for you to say. Cos let's face it, you married the only decent guy left in the entire northern hemisphere.'

I say nothing, just shake my head and smile quietly to myself, remembering fondly back to all the long, long nights we'd spend dissecting every aspect of Liz's dating history, then putting it all back together again.

'But if pressed on the subject by well-meaning but irritating relations, here's what I always say,' she laughs, knocking back the last dregs of her vodka and suddenly putting on a posh, cut-crystal English accent, '"One of the reasons I've never married, in spite of quite a bewildering array of offers, is a determination to never be ordered around." Go on, Annie, I challenge you to name that one.'

This, by the way, is a game we've been playing ever since drama school – the Quotation Game. One of us throws out a line from a well-known play or movie, and the other has to guess where it's from. And inevitably, with her sharp brain and her great memory for trivia, Liz wins.

'Ehh . . . Glenn Close as the Marquise de Merteuil in *Dangerous Liaisons*?' I ask, gingerly.

'Ten out of ten! You never lost your touch, babe. Anyway, enough about me. Tell me some of your news.'

'News? From Stickens? Are you kidding me? I wish.'

'Oh come on, hon, how's that gorgeous big ride of a husband of yours? How's your perfect married life in rural bliss?'

This is my cue to lie of course, not let the side down, smile brightly and say that everything is wonderful, lovely and perfect. All the while thinking to myself that seeing as how I'm in Dublin anyway, I might as well scatter the ashes of any sex life we once might have had into the River Liffey.

'. . . which neatly leads me onto my next question,' Liz says, munching on an ice cube from her empty vodka glass, just like she always used to. 'If all goes well at your audition tomorrow and if you land the part, do you think Dan will be OK with . . . well, . . . you know. With everything. With the whole package, I mean. It's one hell of a commitment.

I mean, when you think about it, it's something that could rock far less stable marriages then yours, hon.'

I look sheepishly across the table at her and take a sip of my drink.

'The thing is, you see, Liz . . . he doesn't know.'

It's ridiculously late, almost two thirty in the morning before I'm finally pulling into The Moorings' massive gravelled driveway, then tip-toeing up the main staircase to our bedroom. I almost have a mental map in my head now of the floorboards that creak versus the ones that don't, so I creep in a ziz-zag pattern all the way upstairs, so as not to wake Dan. Honest to God, if you saw me, you'd swear I was off-my-head drunk, even though I was on nothing stronger than Diet Coke for the whole night.

It's nearly pitch dark when I skulk into our bedroom, but I can still make out Dan's huge, muscular silhouette, faintly red in the alarm clock light. He's got the duvet covers flung off him, his thick dark bed-head is all skew-ways, and he's wearing only a T-shirt; as ever, his hulking, six-foot-two frame taking over about ninety per cent of all available bed space. Plus he's sleeping like he always does, in the shape of someone who's just been washed up on a beach. Totally out for the count and utterly oblivious to the sword of Damocles that's potentially hovering over both our heads.

Half of me is bursting to wake him up and tell him all, but the cautious half wins out; I just can't. He's worn out and exhausted and it would be mean. It'll have to wait till the morning, simple as that.

Weird thing; it's as though I'm looking at him and really seeing him clearly for the first time in ages. Noticing things I'd either blanked out about him or else completely taken

34

for granted. His broad-shouldered, toned, fit body for one; trim and in fantastic shape from all the sheer physical exertion his job involves. The gentle sounds he makes whenever he's in a really deep, exhausted sleep. His musky smell and the heat from his body, the sheer, pulsating warmth of him. All the joshing and messing we used to have way back in earlier, happier days, about how permanently freezing I am and about how he's like a big, giant, human comforter, perfect for snuggling up to at night. Like I'm the air-conditioner in the summer and he's the electric blanket in winter.

I get undressed as quietly as I can, trying my best to ignore the anxiety-knot that's solidifying into what feels like a tight ball of cement right in the pit of my stomach. God, even just thinking about The Major Chat he and I are going to have to have at some point tomorrow is enough to get my heart palpitating all over again. What Dan might say . . . how he might react, what he might feel . . . or worse, what he might not bloody well feel at all.

My head is starting to thump with worry now, as I pull on a pyjama top and slip quietly into the comforting, dull warmth of the bed beside him. Because whether I like it or not, no amount of sugar glazing can disguise the fact that our marriage is on dangerously shaky ground and has been for a long, long time.

And now, here I am.

Potentially about to throw a hand grenade into it.

How Dan and I first met

Everyone I knew envied me growing up. Everyone. But I spent my entire youth shooting down the myth and telling anyone who'd listen that all resentment of my childhood was completely and utterly uncalled for. Thing is, my mother was, and still is, a diplomat, working for the Department of Foreign Affairs. Posted to Washington DC at the moment, as it happens, which is a massive promotion for her. For me though, it means I get to see and spend time with her an average of about once every twelve months if I'm lucky . . . but that's a whole other story, ho hum.

Anyway, the thing about me was that I pretty much spent my formative years being brought up single-handedly by Mum as a lone-parent family. She and I, *contra mundum*.

My mother, by the way, embodies all the best qualities of Churchill, Henry V, Joan of Arc and Joanna Lumley. An incredible woman, your mother, is what everyone says about her and they're dead right too.

My father, who I often think was intimidated by such a high-octane success story as Mum, had walked out on us when I was very small and now lives in Moscow with his new wife and my two little half-brothers who I've never met and most likely never will. I harbour him no ill-will though; it can't have been easy for him, forever playing Bill Clinton to her globetrotting, ladder-climbing, hard-working, ambitious and ultimately far more successful Hillary. And believe me, my father ain't no Bubba.

So I grew up with Mum and spent my childhood being shunted abroad from one overseas posting to another, trailing around country after country in her wake. Funny, but I often think that one of the first things that attracted me to Dan was his background; so completely normal and ordinary, with parents who were still very much a couple, an adorable kid sister and everyone happily living together under the one, permanent roof.

The perfect nuclear family.

By contrast, people constantly used to tell me how exotic my upbringing was. How glamorous. Jammy cow. You're so lucky. Talk about living the high life and pass me the Ferrero Rocher while you're at it, Madame Ambassador.

OK, time to dispel the myth. You see, back then Mum was never posted to any of the glitzy or cosmopolitan capitals like say, Paris, Buenos Aires or even Monaco. No, not a bleeding snowball's chance. In fact, by the time I hit secondary school, I'd already lived in Lagos, Nigeria, East Timor and not forgetting all the bright lights, excitement and glamour of Karachi, Pakistan. So in other words, we were a bit like gypsies, only legit.

It was a nomadic, rootless upbringing, one which left me with a deep, lifelong yearning to lead some kind of settled, normal, family life. Preferably in a place where you could actually drink the tap water and leave the house without a police escort.

Plus, by the tender age of fourteen, I'd already been to no fewer than five different international schools; an experience which left me shy, a bit introverted and with a lifelong terror of change. Always the new girl, always the outsider and it was always the same old pattern: no sooner was I slowly beginning to be accepted among my peers and gradually starting to forge new friendships, than it was time for me to be uprooted and shunted off to yet another school, in yet another far-flung country with yet another set of language barriers, thrown headfirst into a group of yet more strangers.

Anyway, by the time I turned fifteen, my mother was allocated to a new posting, this time to Georgetown, Guyana, South America – a city noted for many things but sadly, not for its wealth of half decent schools. Trouble was that by then I was at the 'exam age' with the Leaving Certificate hovering scarily on the horizon and of course, Mum was desperately anxious that I get the best education going.

Which as far as she was concerned, could only mean one thing: boarding school. Back home in Ireland. Anyway, aided by my grandmother in Dublin, who was only dying to get her sole grandchild back on home turf, they finally hit on a suitable school: a co-ed by the name of Allenwood Abbey in County Westmeath. Not too far from Dublin airport, so I could still get away to visit Mum on the long holidays, and yet close enough to where my granny lived, so I could visit her on the weekend exeats.

To this day, I can still vividly remember the sheer terror of arriving at Allenwood for the first time, a full week after term proper had started on account of a delay in leaving Pakistan. I remember driving up the miles-long, tree-lined driveway from the school gates all the way up to the main building, flanked by my mother and grandmother, both of whom kept trying to sell the school's strong points to me, like a pair of estate agents high on speed. Mum in Hermès and pearls, Gran in tartan and support tights. Me in the back seat, crouching down as low as I could, silently praying that no one out on the playing fields would notice the new girl arriving, then write me off as some attention-seeking git with a bizarre 'make-an-entrance' fixation. Not only conspicuous for being the new girl but feeling like I might as well have a neon sign over my head screaming, 'look at me! Step right up and get a load of the freak arriving. Oh what a circus, oh what a show!'

No question about it; I felt shitty in about ten different ways.

Anyway, the three of us were ushered through an entrance hall that could almost have doubled up as a cathedral and down a vast stone corridor into the headmaster's office – one Professor Proudfoot. I'd never in all my years seen anything like him. He actually wore a proper black, swishy cape and looked a bit like a medieval king, with snow white eyebrows overhanging his wrinkled face, like guttering on a huge building.

Professor Proudfoot then insisted that as I was a late arrival, it would be best by far if he brought me straight down to my new classroom right away. Plenty of time for me to meet my dorm-mate, Yolanda, and to do all my unpacking later on.

Vivid memory to this day: hugging Mum goodbye, the smell of her Bulgari perfume. Me looking into her face, trying to gauge whether she was as upset as I was, but her make-up was so thick, I couldn't get a read. Then squeezing Gran and getting the same smell you somehow always got from her – strong peppermints mixed with weedkiller. (Gardening is her God and Alan Titchmarsh is her Jesus Christ.) Trying to smile brightly and fight back tears as we said curt goodbyes and I was led down the vaulted, freezing stone passageway, all the way to adulthood.

I felt like a dead girl walking all the way to my first classroom, which was in a newer extension to the school, down yet more endless corridors, one leading off another, with fluorescent lights overhead that were bright enough to interrogate crime lords.

'Just relax, you'll be fine,' smiled the professor, pausing to knock on a random classroom door. So, as always, when told to relax, my shoulders seized and right on cue, my heart started to palpitate.

Next thing, we were standing at the top of the fifth-year classroom in Senior House, with thirty pairs of eyes focused on me and me alone, all staring at me with the same unnerving calm as the *Children of the Corn*. I was introduced blushing like a forest fire and Professor Proudfoot gave them a bit of background on me; told them I was newly arrived from Karachi, that I'd lived all over the southern hemisphere, that I hadn't been educated in Ireland since kindergarten and that they were all to make me feel very welcome. My entire life's CV to date, in other words.

I was aware of a couple of things happening simultaneously as the teacher waved me towards a vacant seat in the third row: all eyes following me with keen interest as a polite round of applause broke out and a pretty blonde girl grabbing my arm and whispering to me that she was my dorm-mate and that she really, *really* liked my suntan.

I'd later find out that this was Yolanda Jones and in time, we'd grow to become great pals. In fact by midnight that night, she and I would have bonded as soon as she discovered that she fitted into an awful lot of my summer clothes from Pakistan.

Yolanda was far more of a girlie-girl than me; in fact senior school to her was basically just a two-year slumber party. And even at the age of fifteen you could see that she had glamour genes buried somewhere deep in her. You know, the type of genetic make-up that makes a girl plump for hair extensions, acrylic nails and a soft-top sports car later on in life.

Next thing a chunky-looking fair-haired guy who looked like he'd be more at home in a rugby scrum than in a classroom wolf-whistled at me. Then, to a wave of sniggers, he cheekily asked me what I was doing later on that night – and that he'd be more than happy to show me around the place.

I wasn't to know it at the time, but this was one Mike Sherry, the class pin-up and something of a lust object among all the female seniors. One of those guys who didn't so much romance women as play roulette with their feelings. Later on that same day, he'd indicate romantic interest in me by tying my shoelaces to my desk when I wasn't looking and later that same week, he'd top that by grabbing the towel I was clinging on to to keep me as covered up as possible in the swimming pool . . . and flinging it into the deep end. Mike was one of those guys who didn't believe in acting cool or ignoring women he fancied; no, he was from the PT Barnum school of flirtation.

'That's it, Annie, the seat to your left, right by the window,' said the teacher helpfully, as I tripped over myself in full view of everyone in the classroom, still unused to the clunky, Amish-like school shoes I was wearing. More giggles and I honestly thought I'd hurl myself out the shagging window if the spotlight wasn't taken off me very soon.

Next thing I was aware of a big, beefy hand grabbing my arm to steady me, helping me up with my heavy schoolbag and putting it on the floor beside the desk. A firm grip, strong. I slipped into the empty seat and turned to whisper a heartfelt thanks to this giant, rugged-looking stranger. And honest to God, for a split second it was almost as though I was looking into my mirror image; sallow skin, dark, unruly hair and a pair of dark chocolate brown eyes stared back at me. Then a twinkling, crooked smile and a warm, friendly handshake.

'Don't pay the slightest bit of attention to Mike,' this guy said gently, in a soft-spoken voice, 'he won't bite. But if he gives you any hassle, I'd be more than happy to sort him out for you.' I smiled back gratefully.

'You're Annie. It's great to meet you. Welcome to life at Alcatraz. It sucks. You're going to love it.'

I laughed at this and then it was as if he read my thoughts.

'Oh and by the way?' he grinned. 'My name is Dan.'

Chapter Two

Thing about The Moorings is that first thing in the morning it honestly resembles the chaos of Grand Central Station at rush hour. Because the surgery is in an extension at the side of the house and is open for business from early morning, by eight am, without fail, the house is always wide awake and buzzing.

I do not befeckinglieve this. The one morning I didn't want to oversleep. My cunning plan was to get up at the crack of dawn and wake Dan before he did his usual disappearing act, so I could grab my chance to bring him up to speed on the latest development in my life. Before half the village descended on us, that is.

But by the sounds of it, I'm already too late. I'm up in our bedroom, frantically pulling on jeans and a warm woolly jumper and from downstairs I can already clearly hear Andrew Leonard stomping around, letting himself in with his own key like everyone else seems to.

Andrew is Dan's father's old veterinary partner, by the way and at seventy-five years of age, he's still going strong and working every bit as hard as he did twenty years ago. He and Dan always start the morning surgery together and so Andrew, a widower who lives alone, has got into the habit of calling here for breakfast beforehand most days. And by the sounds of it, he's with James, the practice's new intern as well.

As I hurriedly pull on a pair of boots, I can hear the two of them chatting away and clattering open the kitchen cupboards, before Andrew shouts up the stairs at me that there's no milk for the tea and would I please mind running out to get some?

Next thing I hear old Mrs Brophy. the practice's elderly and very cranky receptionist, clattering in and yelling up at me that if I'm going to the shops anyway, would I mind picking up a few sticky buns for the tea as they ran out yesterday when I wasn't there to do a run to Tesco?

Oh God, oh God, oh God. This is what happens when I'm missing for one single afternoon and when I oversleep on one single morning? Dear Jaysus . . .

'AND WILL YOU GET SOME TEA BAGS WHILE YOU'RE AT IT TOO, ANNIE?' she screeches upstairs at me and I call back down that I'm on my way. Mrs Brophy, I should tell you, has worked here since old Dan Senior's time and point blank refuses to let me help her out with the surgery's paperwork in any way whatsoever. Honest to God, even if I as much as answer the phone and take an appointment when she's in the house, she feels threatened and, I'm not kidding, will actually go into a sulk about it that can often last for days on end. I've been here ever since Heaven started, she'll snap at me, and I do NOT need your help, thank you.

Nor does she have any intention of retiring in the fore-seeable future and believe me, every carrot you can think of has been dangled at her to entice her off in that direction – a Mediterranean cruise, a week's spa break in a five-star hotel, you name it. But no, nothing doing. She gets offended if I even offer to give her a hand and there's no budging her to leave either; a classic catch twenty-two. She's also chronically hard of hearing with the result that anyone ringing up the house or surgery tends to holler down the phone at whoever answers, just in case it might be her.

A sudden, disconnected thought flashes through my mind: how weird it is that I should feel so completely isolated and lonely in this house and yet I'm constantly surrounded by other people.

Anyway, I scrape my hair back into a ponytail and race to the bathroom, where Dan's just stepping out, washed, shaved and ready for the day. Perfect chance for me to nab him, because I know only too well that once he launches into his day's work, trying to hold a one-on-one conversation with him will be pretty much like trying to nail mercury to a wall.

'Dan, before you go downstairs, I really need to . . .'

'Hey, you were out so late last night. Where were you?'

'Yeah, I know, I had to go to Dublin . . . I phoned you, didn't you get my message?'

'You left a message? No, never got it. My phone must have been out of coverage. Oh rats, that reminds me, I think I must have left my mobile in the car last night . . .'

Absolutely zero interest in *why* I had to go to town, not even a raised eyebrow, nothing. He's thundering down the main staircase now, taking two steps at a time in that long-legged way that he has and I'm racing just to keep pace with him.

'The thing is, Dan, I have to talk to you and it's really important . . .'

'Sure, sure, yeah . . . MRS BROPHY? DID PAUL

FORGARTY CALL ABOUT THE RACEHORSE WITH THE BROKEN FEMUR?'

I'm not joking, that is the actual decibel level you have to speak to Mrs Brophy at.

'You see, I got a phone call from my agent in Dublin yesterday . . .'

'MORNING, DAN,' says Mrs Brophy, sticking her head around the kitchen door. 'WHERE DID YOU DISAPPEAR OFF TO YESTERDAY, ANNIE? THERE'S A LOAD OF SHOPPING NEEDS TO BE DONE.'

'DON'T WORRY, MRS BROPHY, I'LL GET TO IT . . .' I yell back, before trying to grab Dan's arm. 'Look, something's come up that I really need to talk to you about, before you rush off to start work . . .'

'YES, PAUL FOGARTY RANG; HE SAYS WOULD YOU MIND CALLING OUT TO HIM AT SOME POINT TODAY, WHEN YOU'RE ON YOUR ROUNDS,' Mrs Brophy cuts in.

'TERRIFIC, WILL DO,' says Dan, rubbing his eyes exhaustedly and dropping his voice a bit when he sees that between Andrew, James and Mrs B, we've got a kitchen-full of guests.

'Morning all,' we both say together, as I wonder how in hell I can try collaring him again.

'Ah, there you are, Annie love. Any chance of one of your lovely juices?' Andrew grins at me over his *Irish Times* and I grin back and say, yes of course, it's on its way.

Juicing every morning is a little ritual I've had, ever since I discovered, a long time ago, that it was the only way I could make sure Dan was getting some kind of vitamins into him, given the number of mealtimes he'd end up skipping when he was out doing farm calls. Except these days, because our kitchen is like a bus station more often than not, I end up making juices for everyone else as well. So I head to the pantry, grab some apples, fresh carrot and ginger and get chopping, while Dan fills Andrew in on the difficulties he had delivering a calf late last night.

'ANNIE, DID YOU NOT HEAR ME TELLING YOU TO GET TEA BAGS?' Mrs Brophy snaps at me, on her way to open up the surgery with our new intern in tow.

'YES, ON THE WAY,' I smile back at her through gritted teeth, tempted to tell her that not only did I hear her, half of County Waterford did as well. Quick as I can, I feck the veggies into the blender as Andrew continues to quiz Dan about the intricacies of dystocia in cows.

(Loosely translated as a tough birth, for eejits like me.)

'Any superfetation during the pregnancy?' asks Andrew, peering over the top of his newspaper, with eyebrows exactly like one of the Marx Brothers.

'No symptoms. But just to be on the safe side, I did prescribe a course of . . .'

'. . . Anti-inflammatories. Good, good, that should do the trick. But no harm for you to pop out there on your rounds and check in again.'

'Yeah, of course . . . don't worry, I'll make a point of it . . .'

'And what about Fogarty's racehorse?'

'Hard to tell, I don't anticipate any long-term damage, but I doubt he'll be running again for the rest of the flat season . . .'

OK, I don't mean to be rude, but I know only too well that this conversation could go on for about half an hour. And time is of the essence here before Dan disappears for the whole day, which leaves me with no choice but to step in.

47

'Guys, I'm so sorry to interrupt, but, Dan, if it's alright, I really need to have a lightning quick word with you before you start work . . .'

'Oh yeah, you were telling me about . . . emm . . . sorry, what was it again?' says Dan distractedly and even though I don't have his full attention, I go for it. Let's face it, it's now or never. Knowing him, there's a fair chance I mightn't see him again till about two am tomorrow morning. If I'm lucky, that is.

'Yeah . . . well, the thing is, it's good news. At least it might be . . . I have an audition, you see . . .'

'Hey, good for you,' both Dan and Andrew chime disinterestedly, just as Dan's mobile rings.

'It's today, you see, the audition, that is, and it means going back to Dublin for it . . .'

'Hang on one sec, Annie, this might be Paul Fogarty. Hello?'

And just like that, I've lost him. He takes the call, of course he does; phones never, ever go ignored in this house. Turns out it's a local farmer who needs him to call out ASAP. No surprises there; just about every call we get to the practice is urgent. In fact, the day a client calls and says take your time in calling out, sure there's no rush whatsoever, is the day that hell will freeze over.

Dan immediately whips out a pen and starts scribbling down symptoms on a spare supplement to Andrew's paper that's lying on the kitchen table, still talking away on the phone and never for one second losing focus.

'OK,' he says patiently, 'just slow down, I'm on the way. Any symptoms of fever or loss of appetite? No progressive paralysis? General listlessness? OK . . . I'm on my way. Give me thirty minutes and I'll be there. And don't panic, I'm pretty certain we can sort this.'

48

I pour out two juices while Dan wraps up the call, then hand one to Andrew and try giving the other one to Dan, but he's too busy packing up his bag and pulling on his warmest coat from where it's hanging on the back of the kitchen door.

'Sounds to me it might be a straightforward case of Listeria,' he calls back to Andrew, 'but I'd better go out there and take a look to be on the safe side. Are you OK handling the surgery here on your own till I get back?'

'Of course, you head off and I'll see you later on.'

I grab the juice I made for him and follow him down the kitchen passageway, as he strides on ahead of me, huge and hulking, making the passageway seem smaller just because he's in it.

'Dan, I still haven't told you the most important part of my news . . .'

'Can this wait till I get back?' he asks, heading out the side door and over to where his jeep is parked.

'But I mightn't be here when you get back, that's what I'm trying to tell you. My audition is up in Dublin, you see, it's for a part in a new play . . .'

'Good, good, good,' he says automatically, although I know right well that he's only half-listening. 'Best of luck with it, love. You know I'll be rooting for you.'

He's already clambered up into the driver's seat by now, engine on, raring to go.

'Dan, that's not really what I wanted to tell you . . .'

'OK, gotta go. You'll do really well at your . . . emmm . . . your whatsit . . . your audition . . . I'm certain.'

'That's not actually the issue here . . .'

'. . . and I'll try my best to catch you tonight . . .'

'Dan! Don't leave just yet, I urgently have to talk to you . . .'

Suddenly one of his black-eyed glares.

'Annie, can you not just understand? I really have to go . . . so this'll just have to wait. We'll talk about whatever it is later, OK . . .?'

He's sounding irritable and narky now which I try my best not to take personally; deep exhaustion always makes him a bit snappy.

'But this will only take two minutes! I still haven't explained to you why . . .'

Jesus, by now my face must be blue from the pressure behind it of needing to talk, but he doesn't even seem to notice. And what's really stabbing me is that I remember a long-distant time when he would have actually paid attention. Would have listened.

God knows, might even have been supportive.

'See you when I see you, drive safe to Dublin.'

And just like that, he's pulled the car out of the driveway and is gone, sending gravel flying in twenty different directions in his haste to get away. Most astonishing of all though is that this is actually the longest conversation we've had in I can't remember how long. Honestly.

Which leaves me feeling yet again like I'm the lowest priority in my husband's life. Or worse, that I married a man who's just not that into me. Because everyone, absolutely everyone and everything else comes ahead of me: cats that need neutering, constipated race horses, his mum and all her neuroses, his sister Jules and her cash flow problems, Lisa shagging Ledbetter and her entire catalogue of woes . . . you name it. Show any kind of weakness or neediness and Dan's your man, whereas a strong, capable woman trying to make the best of the hand life has dealt her will always be bottom rung on the ladder as far as he's concerned.

50

Not his fault; I sometimes think that he's just not calibrated to bring happiness to one person, not when he can serve the many instead.

Funny, isn't it? How women spend the longest time trying to separate romance from friendship. And for the longest time, I thought I was the luckiest woman on earth because I had both.

And now it looks like I've neither one.

He never even touched the shagging juice.

Chapter Three

My audition is at lunchtime in Dublin, which gives me barely enough time to run to Tesco and buy everything that Mrs Brophy was whinging we didn't have in the house earlier on. Plus I also have to call Agnes at the book store to let her know that I won't be into work today. But if I was expecting her to be a bit put out at this, I was wrong; honest to God, the sheer relief in the woman's voice when she realised she wouldn't have to pay me for yet another day would have broken your heart. No problem whatsoever, Annie, she'd said, sure why not take a few extra days off too while you're at it?

Anyway, between all of that, there's barely enough time for a lightning quick shower before I have to hop into the car and start the marathon, two-and-a-half-hour drive to the city.

Right then. As I pull out onto the motorway, I make a decision. I'm going to use this incredibly rare bit of alone time to try to clear my head and concentrate on nothing but the audition ahead. So as I boot the car up into fourth gear, I start doing all the little pre-audition relaxation tricks I remember from long ago: some deep yoga breathing for starters, in for two and out for four, in for two and out

for four . . . easy does it . . . then I start to creatively visu-
alise a positive outcome . . . imagining myself bouncing
into a rehearsal room . . . being a proper, paid actor
again . . . being back in the city and far, far away from Grey
Gardens, sorry, I mean, The Moorings . . . earning money
at a career that I actually love and adore . . . after three
long years of treading water by stacking shelves in an empty
bookshop . . . oh and let's not forget sweeping dead headed
roses off the floor while doing yet another part-time job
in the local florist's . . . then I think back to that book I
read because everyone was reading it at the time . . . *The
Secret* . . . So I focus on attracting only a positive outcome
and not dwelling on forgetting my lines or blanking out
with nerves or similar . . .

Anyway, I'm just drifting into a lovely, soothing, zoned-
out happy place, when suddenly my phone rings, totally
shattering my concentration.

Audrey, surprise, surprise.

'Where *are* you, Annie?' she whimpers in the little-girl-
lost voice. 'I'm at The Moorings and Mrs Brophy tells me
you've disappeared off to Dublin for the day *yet again* . . . can
that be right? Would you really do such a selfish thing
without telling me? I worried myself sick about you
yesterday and you know how worry brings on one of my
little turns. And not a phone call from you for the whole
day, nothing.'

Do not let the guilt get to you, I tell myself sternly, *at all
costs, don't allow her to guilt trip you.*

'Because I'm still not feeling very well today, you know,
after all the worry of yesterday, and I need you to run a
few little errands for me . . .'

I hear her out as patiently as I can and explain that

everything is fine, and that I'm just going to Dublin for an unexpected audition. A pause, and I'm half-wondering if she'll bother to ask me anything at all about it. You know, stuff a normal person would ask, like what's the play, what part am I up for . . . but no, she doesn't. Of course not. There's the usual half second time delay while she filters the information I'm offering, then immediately figures out whether it'll affect her negatively in any way. And decides that yes, it does.

'But that's no use to me, Annie, I'm doing my Christmas cards today and I need you to be here. You should have been here to help me yesterday and it's not my fault that you weren't.'

I can just picture her as she says this, all swelled up like a gobbler with enough ammunition to bitch about me behind my back for weeks to come. Then I sigh so deeply it's like it's coming from my feet upwards and wonder what she wants me to do exactly? Write out all the cards for her? Wouldn't surprise me.

Anyway, at this stage I've had years of practice in dealing with her, so I draw on all my experience and do what I always do: lock my voice into its lowest register and at all costs, don't let her turn me into her emotional punchbag. I calmly tell her that although I'll be gone for most of the day, I'll be back later in the evening and will be perfectly happy to take care of whatever she needs then.

'But you're not listening to me, Annie, I have to get my Christmas cards posted *today* and I need you to get to the post office before it shuts. You know perfectly well I can't go by myself. Standing in queues brings on one of my weak spells and I've really not been myself all morning, you know. And another thing – you still don't have the Christmas tree up yet, Annie. I don't understand, what exactly have you been doing with your time?'

I let the veiled insult pass and suggest that, since it's so urgent, maybe she should just ask Jules to do the post office run for her?

'Well if I'd known you were flitting off to Dublin for the day then of course I would have, but Jules was still asleep when I left the house and I don't like to wake her.'

I can't help smiling in spite of myself; typical Jules. She's a terrible stickler for getting her twelve hours' sleep. Plus, she always says that even if she's lying wide awake in bed it's a far, far better thing to stay put, than to get up and enter Audrey-land. And, in all fairness, can you blame the girl?

'Oh and another thing, Annie, when I went upstairs to use the bathroom just now, I had a little look around and I couldn't help noticing that you still hadn't made your bed and that there were unlaundered clothes belonging to poor Dan strewn all over the floor as well. You know I hate to say it, but I really think you should think about organising your household chores a little bit better. It really upsets me when I see that the house isn't being cared for properly and no man likes to live in a messy house you know . . .'

Just then I lose the signal on my phone, so mercifully this conversation ends before the mental image of Audrey combing through our bedroom when I'm not there takes root deep in my psyche.

Note to self: if I don't get this job, then I'm asking Dan if we can buy a caravan for our back garden so we can go and live in it instead. A little mobile home that could sit in the back garden and look like it was adopted by The

Moorings out of charity. With deadbolts on every door and window, to ensure some minor degree of privacy. Or if it comes to it, then I'll just move out and live in the shagging thing on my own. Because life in a four-wheel trailer certainly couldn't be much worse than life at Grey Gardens, could it?

Anyroadup, I arrive in Dublin a good forty-five minutes before the audition starts, park the car and head back for the National theatre. It's a miserable winter's day – icy cold, with a sharp wind blowing and only a weak, watery sun desperately trying to break through the heavy overhead clouds . . . but to me, with an audition to go to and with a spring in my step, it's only bloody beautiful.

Funny, but in The Sticks I'm completely surrounded by natural beauty and probably the most stunning scenery you're ever likely to see, yet somehow, I never seem to notice it. But being here, back in the city and striding purposefully down a busy, bustling street packed with stressed-out Christmas shoppers tripping over each other to grab their last minute bargains . . . everyone laden down with bulging bags, looking frozen and panicky and with mounting hysteria practically ricocheting off them . . . and I can't help thinking that it's just the loveliest sight I've seen in I don't know how long. But then I suppose, after living in the dark for so long, a glimpse of the light can suddenly make you giddy.

Tell you one thing; even if I don't get this job, at least one good thing has already come out of it – just being back in the city and doing an audition has put the bounce back into me and aligned my spine again, as if I just got a jolt of vitamin B straight to my heart. And a flood of gorgeous, cheering memories come back too; when Dan and I first left school, we both came to Dublin to study at Trinity College, him to do veterinary medicine, me, drama studies.

We shared flat after flat in the city, gradually working our poverty-stricken, dole-poor way from renting places where the washing machine had to double up as the dining table, all the way up to the dizzy heights of actually owning our very own apartment right after we got married. Happy, happy days – by far the happiest of my life – and now it's like every street corner I turn holds a very different memory of a very different time.

Buoyed up with adrenaline, I run into a little coffee shop just across the road from the theatre to grab a bottle of water and no one knows me or any of my business and it's bloody fantastic. No one asks me about Dan or Audrey or whether Jules has any intention of getting some kind of a job any time soon. No Bridie McCoy telling us about how useless her chiropodist is, no Agnes Quinn to playfully elbow me in the ribs and remind me that I'm not getting any younger, then ask me when exactly I'm going to put that huge nursery up in The Moorings to good use? No Father O'Driscoll to gently probe me about whether he might see myself and Dan at Mass one of these fine days . . . I am utterly and totally anonymous here and it's wonderful. Feels like being able to breathe freely again after years of long, silent suffocation.

I bounce along to the stage door of the National and the receptionist is almost flight attendant friendly. Yes, they're expecting me and I'm to go ahead to the green room and wait there. She politely offers me tea or coffee while I'm waiting and I thank her but say no. Then I find my way to the green room which is directly behind the main stage, guessing that some other poor actress is out there strutting her stuff right now. I plonk down on a faded leather armchair and start thumbing through the script yet again.

Fag Ash Hil was at pains to point out that, at this stage, I wasn't expected to have actually memorised the lines, considering the short notice I'd been given to come and read for the part in the first place, but I know well enough how these things work. You're told, 'Oh, no need to be off book, darling,' but the reality is that you're expected to have studied the script the same way Egyptologists study tomb writings and it doesn't matter a shite how late in the day you got the script.

So I'm just re-reading through a pivotal scene for the character when the door opens and the stage manager comes to get me. No time to react, no time for nerves. I get up and obediently follow him.

Two minutes later, and I'm standing on stage and it's beyond weird having sat in the audience last night, now to be over on this side of the fence. The set, by the way, is a health spa in a five-star resort, with sun loungers dotted across the stage and offstage doors leading to a sauna, pool and steam room. It's dimly lit and hard to see, then suddenly a split second later, it suddenly goes Broadway bright. I'm momentarily dazzled but then a disconnected voice from the dark auditorium tells me to come on down to the front of the stage. I do as I'm told, clutching the script like a talisman.

Next thing, a striking-looking, long, lean guy is swooping down the centre audience aisle and striding towards where I'm standing centre stage, in a ball of sweaty tension.

'Well, hello there,' he calls out smoothly. 'I'm Jack Gordon.'

Not every day you come face-to-face with the David Beckham of the theatre world, so even though I'm blinded by the hot stage lights, I manage to squint through the darkness to get a half decent look at him. He's a lot taller and slimmer than I'd have thought, wearing an impeccably-cut, slate grey suit with an open-necked, crisp, white shirt underneath, which somehow makes him look older than he actually is, even though he can't be much more than early thirties. For a second, I can't actually remember the last time I saw a proper well-dressed, metrosexual guy in a proper suit, outside of the local courthouse in Stickens, that is. Blue eyes and light brown-ish hair, but with slanting eyebrows that kind of give him the look of a satyr when he frowns downwards. And self-confidence that practically bounces off the auditorium walls; not a word of a lie, if the guy had antlers, they'd probably be well past his shoulders.

In short, he looks like a Michael Bublé song.

Anyway, he marches all the way down to the apron of the stage, walking as though he's in his own spotlight and extends a smooth, lotioned hand out to me.

'You must be Annie Cole,' he smiles, flashing teeth brighter than a toxic blast from a nuclear bomb. 'So good of you to come at such short notice. It's an absolute pleasure to meet you.'

And his voice is thicker than a jar of Manuka honey. A twenty-fags a day voice, if ever I heard one. Anyway, I mumble something inane and shake his ice cold hand. He's focusing really intently on me now, keenly looking me up and down, then down and back up again and it's making me bloody nervous. And the danger with me is that when nervous, I tend to act like I've got St Vitus's dance of the mouth and start gabbling like a half-wit about complete and utter shite. Mercifully though, he doesn't initiate any more chit-chat or small talk; just directs me towards the scene that he'd like me to read, coolly telling me to start in my own time.

And for better or for worse, I'm on.

Good sign: I'm asked to play one particular scene five different times, and in about five different ways. The logical part of my brain says, would Jack bother spending so much time on me if he thought I was really shite?

Bad sign: As I leave the stage, I meet the other actress who was in before me, having a fag in the tiny yard off the green room. We both instantly cop on who the other is, the giveaway being the script we're both clutching to our chests and each of us launch into a big post-mortem. Anyway, she says she was asked to do exactly the same thing. So much for that.

Good sign: One of the pivotal scenes, feels completely fantastic. It's impossible to describe the massive adrenaline rush I get from performing it – closest thing I can imagine would be like what a fighter pilot must feel on take-off. Or a cat burglar. For the first time in years, I find myself feeding off the sheer pleasure of acting and loving every second of it, thinking feck it anyway; even if I don't get the part, I've come this far, so I may as well enjoy myself.

Jack does a kind of deep, throaty, snorting laugh at some of the gag lines I deliver and this I find hugely encouraging.

Bad sign: Then he excuses himself to answer his mobile phone and does precisely the same laugh.

Good sign: After I've been put through my paces, he politely asks me about my personal life and whether the significant commitment involved in this gig would be an issue for me.

Bad sign: When I tell him that I'm married but haven't had a chance to discuss it with my significant other yet, he just nods curtly, giving absolutely nothing away. My gut instinct is to tack on, 'But you know, everything's OK, because it's not like we have kids or anything!' but I manage to restrain myself. I mean, yes of course I'd love the job, but do I really want to come across as a complete desperado?

Shit anyway. Should have just told him the truth.

That I've a husband who I honestly doubt would even notice I'm gone.

Worst sign of all: When I'm leaving the stage, he shakes my hand quite formally and says, 'Best of luck. We'll be in touch.' Otherwise known in the acting profession as the 'don't call us, we'll call you', kiss of death.

So now there's nothing to do but wait it out.

It's only early evening but already pitch dark by the time I get back to The Sticks. Dan, not surprisingly, isn't back yet, but this would be perfectly normal. In fact it might be hours and hours before he does come home. So I decide that I'll wait up for him, even if it's two in the morning before he eventually does stagger in.

My plan is thus: I will stand right in front of him, hands on hips like something out of a Western, blocking his path so he can't dodge past me, claiming exhaustion and that all he really wants to do is go to bed. I will firmly say what I've got to say and not get fobbed off by his mobile ringing or him brushing me aside and saying, 'We'll talk later.' Flooded with determination, I make up my mind. No more repeat performances of this morning. No more being brushed off.

Enough's enough. Some discussions just can't wait.

I let myself in through the side door that leads down a long, narrow, stone passageway to the kitchen and am delighted to see Jules standing there, wearing her pyjamas with a pair of my slippers and raiding our fridge, as per usual.

'And where the feck have you been all day?' is her greeting, not even looking up from the coleslaw she's eating straight out of the tub.

'Jules, please tell me you didn't go out dressed like that? You look like the kind of woman that ends up getting escorted out of Tesco. You're like a candidate for care in the community.'

'Ahh, leave me alone, will you? I couldn't have been arsed deciding what to wear, so in the end I just didn't bother. But I did put a duffel coat and Wellingtons over my PJ's before I left the flat. Besides underwear as outerwear is a hot look right now, I'll have you know. Anyway, you're in deep shite with the Mothership, I can tell you that for nothing. We came dangerously close to having a code three on our hands today.'

This, by the way, is a system Jules and I have set up to monitor Audrey and her many and varied 'little turns'. The lowest level, code one, means she's prostrate on the sofa whinging and in need of sugary tea but if she ever makes it up to code four, the only thing to do is dial 999 toot sweet, then call the local GP and await subsequent fallout.

'So where were you, Annie? You keep disappearing and re-appearing these days. Not unlike that TV show *Scrubs*.'

'Up in Dublin doing an audition,' I beam proudly, peeling

off my coat and gloves. 'You have my permission to be impressed.'

'And you didn't take me with you, you bitch! For feck's sake, I could have done some Christmas shopping! With money you'd have had to lend me, obviously. I could have done with getting out of Dodge today; Lisa Ledbetter sat here at the kitchen table moaning for the entire afternoon. Not much point in me coming here to escape from my mother if I have to put up with The Countess Dracula instead, is there? Phrases about frying pans and fires spring to mind.'

I groan as I reach to put the kettle on.

'You have my sympathies, hon. So tell us, how was the Countess today?'

'What can I say? Like Lisa Ledbetter. If whining was an Olympic sport, we'd have the gold medallist living right here in our midst.'

Not an exaggeration, by the way. We all have a Lisa Ledbetter in our lives and the thing is, you just can't allow yourself to get sucked in or else sure as eggs is eggs they won't be happy till they drag you down with them.

'You should have heard her,' Jules goes on, wiping coleslaw off her face with the back of her hand. 'She even rang Dan on his mobile to ask him for another lend of cash to tide her over Christmas. Oh, and apparently one of her kids wants to do pony riding lessons, and she got the big soft gobshite to agree to shell out for that too. I was pretending to be watching TV but heard the whole conversation. What a shameless cow; I mean, doesn't she realise that scabbing money from Dan is my department?'

I roll my eyes to Heaven pretending to be pissed off, although I'm actually delighted that Jules is here and even more delighted that by some early miracle of Christmas, I've managed to miss both Audrey and Lisa. Because Jules is the perfect antidote to the pair of them.

Jules, I should tell you, is only nineteen but looks an awful lot younger still, particularly today when she's dressed in her favourite baby-blue fleece pyjamas with her dark, jack-in-the-box curls that normally spring past her shoulders tied back into two messy, pigtails. Honest to God, the girl looks like she should still be getting ID'ed in bars.

And I know she treats this house like she's a non-rent paying lodger, but then Jules is one of life's naturally adorable people so it's pretty much impossible to get irritated with her for very long. She's Dan's baby sister but it always feels like she's mine too – I've known her ever since she was a spoilt, over-petted four-year-old girl and what can I say? From day one, we just bonded. I'd always wanted a little sister . . . and I certainly couldn't have asked for one who made my life more entertaining.

And yes, of course it's a bit weird that a nineteen-year-old college dropout should spend her days lounging around watching afternoon TV with absolutely no inclination whatsoever towards getting an actual job and supporting herself, but that's our Jules for you. She's one of that rare and dying breed – the entitled generation. You know, young ones who grew up having everything handed to them on a plate by doting parents and who assumed that life was all about five-star hotels and three holidays a year and wearing nothing but designer labels on their well-toned backs. The generation that landed with the hardest thump when the recession hit and suddenly all the privileges they'd taken for granted during the good years were crudely revoked.

At the time Jules had started college but when she flunked her exams last autumn, she quickly realised she'd actually have to stop partying five nights a week and actually knuckle down to some hardcore work if she ever wanted to pass. And needless to say, that was the end of that. So she moved back into her mother's flat about five months ago and even though she claims it drives her nuts being nagged at morning, noon and night, she doesn't seem to have the slightest intention of ever leaving. Like she hasn't actually made the link in her own head yet between her actions and their consequences.

Don't get me wrong, I love the girl dearly, but if you were to look up '*indolence*' in the Oxford English dictionary, chances are it would say '*See Jules Ferguson*'. She's like a zenned-out, calm bubble of *Que Sera Sera* and believe it or not she's perfectly contented to crash out at Audrey's for the foreseeable future, living on cash handouts from her big brother. Oh and spending all her afternoons here, the minute Audrey's safely out of the way and the coast is clear, thereby avoiding her as much as possible. A bit like weathermen on one of those old-fashioned clocks; one goes in just as the other one is coming out.

Anyway, I pour myself out a big mug of tea and follow her into the TV room, where she's laid out a little picnic for herself consisting of last night's leftovers plus a bag of tortilla chips. She's also lit the fire, but then that's the one household chore you can actually count on her to do. I'm deeply grateful though because in this house, with the high ceilings and ancient hot water pipes, even with the heating on full-blast, it rarely gets warmer than a degree or two above freezing. Ellen DeGeneres is on TV in the background, interviewing some teen queen about her latest movie and Jules plonks down in her favourite armchair, eyes glued to the screen.

'So,' she says, taking a fistful of tortilla chips and stuffing her face with them. 'Tell me all about your audition. Is it a half decent part? And by that I mean . . . is it worth elevating my vision from the TV for?'

I bring her up to speed on all developments in my life, debating in my mind whether I should tell her the full, unexpurgated truth. Half of me thinks what the hell, she'll find out soon enough anyway, but the other more rational side of me thinks, no, this isn't fair. Not till I've spoken to Dan. If I ever get to speak to him, that is. So I skirt around the truth and just give her the bare skeletal outline of the story.

But if I thought she'd be impressed, I was wrong. All she does is flop back onto the armchair, still munching tortilla chips, and deep in thought.

'Shit on it anyway,' she eventually mutters. 'I just realised something deeply unpleasant.'

'What's wrong?'

'If you get this, and if they're only looking at three other actors, then let's face it, you've got a thirty three per cent chance . . . then . . . just think . . . you'll be gone all day when you're rehearsing and then gone all night when the show is playing, won't you? Tell me the truth, Annie, what does your gut instinct say? Do you think you'll get the gig?'

'Probably not.'

'Don't say "probably not". That worries me. What's wrong with ordinary "not"?'

I can't help smiling at her. You should see her, looking at me all worried, with the innocent expression and the big, saucer-black eyes. Honest to God, for a split second, she looks exactly like she did when she was about twelve years old.

'Because if you did feck off to Dublin,' she goes on, playing with a pig tail, 'that means I'd be stuck here on my own, without you, doesn't it? Bugger and double bugger it anyway. You've no idea what it's like here when you're not around, Annie. Between the Mothership with all her little turns and Lisa Ledbetter and her whinging, this house is like an open casting call for *One Flew Over the Cuckoo's Nest*. I'm not sure that I could handle it without you. Perish the thought, but if that were the case, then I might actually have to do the unthinkable and . . . pause for dramatic effect . . . go out and get a job myself.'

Vintage Jules. The first question she'll always ask when faced with a new set of circumstances is . . . hold on a minute, let me have a think. Now how does this directly affect me?

'Well, it may not even come to pass,' I say, taking a sip of tea and trying to plumb the fault line in my heart to gauge my own reaction if it didn't happen. Or, even more unthinkable, if it did. Oh God, just the thought of what that would involve instantly makes me break out in a cold, shivery sweat.

But Jules is already gone off on a tangent.

'Well anyway, lucky for you, though, Annie, there's no need to feel guilty, because as it happens, I do have an ace up my sleeve. You know how Dan's been on at me lately about cutting my allowance unless he sees me at least out looking for some kind of work? Well, I had a brainwave last night. While watching a repeat of *Britain's Got Talent*, when I get all my best inspiration.'

'Ehh . . . let me guess. You've decided to become a pop

star and you're going to go and audition for Simon Cowell and Amanda Holden? Isn't it a prerequisite that you have to at least be able to sing first?'

'No, I'm going to use my *own* talent, you gobshite. I'm going to become an author. I've even got the title for my first book all worked out. It's a loosely autobiographical story, based on the life of a stunningly beautiful, gifted nineteen-year-old girl, who's just dropped out of college and is forced through cruel economic circumstances into living with her nut job of a mother in a tiny little backwater, in the back arse of nowhere. It's called *I Love You, But Please Die*. So whaddya think?'

'I honestly don't know which of us is worse. You for dreaming up this crap, or me for listening to you. Although I will say this: if you did turn to writing, it would certainly put that over-active imagination of yours to good use.'

That's another thing about Jules – she's famous in the family for being the greatest exaggerator this side of Heather Mills. When she was a kid, she was forever getting into trouble for telling tall tales. Famously, on her first day in primary school she told her entire class that her parents were circus performers; that her mum was an acrobat and her dad could tame lions. When the truth came out, that her father was actually the local vet and her mum was a housewife, she never batted an eyelid, just said that her dad *used* to be a lion tamer but now looked after sick animals, while her mother was forced to abandon her acrobatic career through injury. Psychologists say that most kids tend to grow out of this carry on by the age of six, but Jules is now nineteen and still hasn't.

'Well, missy,' she says, glaring at me, 'if you're going to disappear off for . . . how long? Couple of months I'm guessing? Then the pressure will all be on me to find work. So if you think about it, it's all your fault, abe. Feck you anyway for getting a smell of a job. Now I'll have to run out and get my debut novel published or everyone will think I'm a complete and utter loser. How long will your show run for anyway?'

I don't answer. Instead, I busy myself tidying up the little picnic Jules has littered around the TV room floor and try my best to tune out her question. Like I say, until I talk to Dan, it's just not fair to confide in his family first.

But Jules smells something and is straight onto me.

'Annie? Why won't you answer me?'

Again, I ignore her and focus on picking up loose kernels of popcorn strewn all around the armchair where she's sitting.

'Are you aware that right now your face is flushing like a forest fire?' she insists tenaciously, like a dog that's just picked up the faintest scent of blood.

'You know, as a little treat for us, I went to Marks & Spencer when I was up in Dublin and bought some of the gorgeous beef in a black bean sauce they do. Do you fancy some for dinner?'

'Hello? Earth to Annie? Can we stick to the subject at hand please? Is there something you're not telling me? Something about your play?'

She even lowers down the volume on the TV, so there's no avoiding her question. Then suddenly, she clamps her hand over her mouth and gasps, horrified.

'Christ Alive, don't tell me there's full frontal nudity in the show and you're too mortified to let on!'

'No, there is absolutely, categorically no nudity what-soever. Now would you just go back to doing what you do best – watching daytime TV and let me get dinner started?'

'Annie . . .' she says threateningly.

'Or if you don't fancy the beef, I've the makings of a nice chicken casserole. What do you say? I know a day isn't over for you unless you've eaten an entire alphabet full of additives, but do you fancy eating something with an actual vitamin in it for a change? Instead of just another bag of tortilla chips, that is.'

'Piss off, I'm stress eating.'

'*You?* Stressed? You never gave a shite about anything in your life.'

'Stop changing the subject. I know right well when I'm being fobbed off . . .'

'. . . and maybe you'd like a healthy fresh salad with dinner? Maybe?'

'Bitch! You tell me the truth this minute or I'll break your nose with my bare forehead . . .'

'Lovely talk. Where'd you pick that up, living with your mother?'

'*Annie!* You know I'll wheedle it out of you sooner or later, so you may as well tell me now, while you have my undivided attention. Now, quick, before *Home and Away* starts.'

I sigh so deeply it feels like it's coming from my bone marrow, knowing right well that the game's up.

'You're just not going to let this go, are you?'

'Not a snowball's chance in hell.'

Right then. I slump back down onto the sofa beside her. I hadn't wanted to tell anyone ahead of Dan, but then I figure . . . knowing him, it could be a full twenty-four hours before I actually manage to nail him down. Plus I honestly

feel like I'm carrying around the third Secret of Fatima –
it'll be a relief to get it off my chest. Not to mention a good
dress rehearsal for what's to come.

So I tell Jules the truth. The whole truth and nothing
but.

There's silence.

I didn't expect silence.

Suddenly it's like all the life and energy has been
completely sucked out of the room. I look at her expectantly
and she looks at me and I honestly think I'll fling one of
Audrey's revolting china shepherdess figurines into the fireplace if she doesn't say something.

Eventually she speaks.

'Right. That settles it then. I'm getting wine.'

In a single hop, she's up and over to the drinks cabinet
and pouring us out two oversized glasses of Merlot. I don't
argue. I need the drink just as much as she does. If not
more.

'OK,' she says, handing me the wine and simultaneously
taking the mug of tea away from me, like it's suddenly
become poisonous. 'So I may not like what you've just told
me, but feck it, you're like the only normal person in my
daily orbit and if it's the last thing I do, I'll find some way
to help you deal with this. So, let me just tap into my
amazing powers of insight here.'

'Ehh . . . sorry, did you say your amazing powers of
insight?'

'Yeah, that's right. I'd use them on myself only it just so
happens that I don't have any problems.'

I fling a cushion at her which she neatly catches, then
uses to balance her tortilla chips on.

'Right then,' she says assertively, sounding more adult-like than I think I've ever heard her. 'Let's start by doing pros and cons, will we? OK, I just thought of one. Pro: you'll probably be dead in like, another fifty years, so chances are it won't even matter.'

'That's your idea of a pro? Jaysus, I'm really looking forward to hearing the cons.'

'Con: you have to tell Dan. And good luck with that, love.'

'I tried telling him this morning, but then you know what it's like trying to get him on his own. I might as well try to . . .'

'Nail jelly to a wall, yeah I know. Funny but I thought he was only like that with me whenever I was trying to wheedle money out of him.'

She's slumped back in the armchair now, long legs dangling over the side, frowning deeply and playing with her pigtails. All her little-girl mannerisms totally at odds with the glass of wine in her hand.

'Pro,' she goes on, taking another slug of the wine, 'you may not even get the job in the first place, so is there really any point in bothering to mention it to him at all? You might only end up worrying him over nothing.'

'No,' I say, shaking my head firmly. 'It wouldn't be fair not to tell him. Aside from the fact that I physically get heartburn when I try to keep secrets from anyone. It'll be unpleasant in the short-term, but it's got to be done. Besides, you know what he's like. The whole way back from Dublin this afternoon, all I could think was . . . if this did happen and if things actually went my way for once . . . I wonder if he'd even notice that I wasn't around any more?'

'I take your point,' says Jules, nodding sagely. 'There's

every chance you could take the job, disappear off and he'd barely even cop that you weren't here.'

I throw her a grateful smile. God, it's so lovely to talk to someone who understands exactly where I'm coming from. Really understands that is, as opposed to telling me what a lovely husband I have and how lucky I am to be married to such a hard-working man with such a strong work ethic who always puts his job first and blah-di-blah.

'Oooh, here's a thought. You could always just leave a note behind, saying that you'll explain it all to him on your deathbed.'

'Serious suggestions only, please.'

'I was being serious. You're a living saint to have put up with everything that you do round here, Annie, I really mean it. Remember the anniversary? You were so *patient* with him. I think I'd have flung my stuff into a suitcase, jumped into my car and headed straight for the nearest motorway after that episode.'

I shudder a bit just at the memory. The anniversary she's talking about wasn't our wedding anniversary by the way, but the anniversary of when we first got engaged, oooh, what feels like about two hundred years ago, when we were both just twenty-three years old. It was early December and at the time, we were in New York on holiday, in the dim and distant days when we still did romantic couple-y things together. Dan had just passed his finals in college and I'd just finished my first, proper acting gig at the National, my big breakthrough role, so this was like a double celebratory trip for us. We were young, we were in big love, in proper astonishing *movie* love and it honestly felt like the world was our oyster.

Anyroadup, one night we went ice-skating in the Rockefeller Center . . . that is to say, Dan was ice-skating while I was clinging onto him with one hand and onto a railing with the other, petrified I'd fall. And it started to snow very lightly and he turned down to kiss me and . . . well, that's when he proposed. Completely spontaneously, totally out of the blue and yet if he'd stage managed the whole thing, the moment couldn't have been one iota more flawlessly perfect. Even the snowflakes gently showered us, as though on cue. And it was just so unbearably romantic that ever since, that's the date we've always celebrated as opposed to our wedding anniversary. December the first.

So this year, given the ridiculous hours he'd been working and the fact that we'd barely spoken to each other in I don't know how long, I really made the effort and pulled out all the stops. I booked dinner for the two of us in Marlfield House, a stunning five-star country house hotel about fifty miles from here – one of those super-luxurious places where the staff all call you Madam and even the cushions have cushions. Not only that, but as an extra surprise, I even booked an overnight stay there for us too. That way neither of us would have to drive home and so it really would be like the second honeymoon the two of us so badly needed. All proudly paid for from my humble book shop earnings, so he couldn't back out of it by saying it was too expensive for us either.

Anyway come the big day, Dan was out doing TB testing, a laborious, time-consuming and ongoing part of his job, so I went ahead of him to Marlfield House in my own car so as not to waste the day, arranging to meet him there in good time for dinner. But . . . disaster: he got a last-minute

74

emergency call to deliver a foal on a farm a good forty miles away and wasn't able to make it, leaving me at the hotel all alone and all by myself. Stood up by my own husband. Not his fault of course, but then it never is, is it? And it's impossible to have a row with Dan, ever. He's just way too reasonable and always takes full blame for everything himself, in a sort of row-avoidance, pre-emptive strike.

Completely and utterly pointless my even getting upset about it – this is the life of a country vet and by extension a country vet's wife. This is what I signed up for. Of course I understood and didn't get annoyed . . . sure how could I? And what was I going to do anyway? Get snotty because Dan works hard at a job that's pretty much twenty-four-seven?

But it left its fecking sting all the same.

Suddenly I'm up on my feet, pacing. Dunno why but I can't seem to sit still any more.

'This evening,' I say firmly. 'For better or for worse, I have to tell Dan this evening. Even if I have to throw his mobile phone into the fish tank and physically grasp his head between my two hands in a vice grip to get his attention.'

'Hmmm, I know what you mean,' says Jules, wolfing back a bag of nachos now. 'Terrible pity you're not a sick animal, isn't it? You know Dan, he can't resist the scent of the wounded.'

I nod, knowing only too well what she means.

'Tell you something though, Annie.'

'What's that?'

'This could just be the fright that he needs to put manners on him. You know, when he realises that you've actually got a life and a career of your own outside of here. God knows, you've made enough sacrifices for him these past few years, and you get sweet feck all in return. If you ask me, he totally takes you for granted and never once have I heard you complain.'

She gets absolutely no argument from me on that score.

'So,' Jules goes on, stretching her long legs out towards the fire, 'maybe this'll be just the kick up the arse that he needs. I mean, when you tell him that you're not prepared to sit around and play the surrendered wife any more. Hey, I don't suppose there's any chance I can stay and watch?'

Unsurprisingly, I do NOT let her stay and watch. Come eight o'clock, there's still no sign of Dan, *quelle* surprise and it turns out Jules is meeting up with one of her pals from college, who lives in Lismore village not too far away. So I wave her off, full of promises to report back the full, unexpurgated transcript of my Big Chat with Dan later on.

It was my full intention to wait up for him, so he couldn't head straight for bed without saying two words to me, like he normally would. But by half eleven, I'm stretched out on the sofa in front of the fire with the TV still on, out for the count and utterly drained after all the hoofing up and down to Dublin earlier today.

The dogs are the first to wake me; Dan often takes them out with him on farm calls and they always go bananas whenever they get back home. So the minute I hear barking and paws scratching to get through the living room door, I'm groggily hauling myself up, all set for the almighty show-down.

'Dan?' I call out, sleepily stumbling to my feet, 'I'm in here.'

76

Our three Labradors are first into the room, jumping and slobbering all over me as I pet each one in turn. Then I look up . . . and there he is, filling the door with his huge, broad-shouldered, hulking frame, still wearing the giant, oversized wax jacket he wears out on farm calls and looking more exhausted than I've seen him in months. Honest to God, the dark circles lining his face are now exactly the same shade of black as his eyes.

'Hey, you're still up?' he says, in a voice flat with tiredness. 'I thought you'd have been in bed hours ago.'

'Emm . . . yeah, I. . . . well . . . I wanted to talk to you,' I say, with a highly inconvenient knot suddenly appearing in my stomach. 'How did you get on today?'

'Oh same old, same old,' he says, coming in towards the fire for warmth, as ever, the room suddenly seeming smaller just because he's in it. He's left his Wellingtons in the hall but even in stockinged feet, he still towers over me by about a foot and a half. He brings the cold outside air into the room with him and smells of the outdoors: horsey and leathery. Unsurprising, given that he's been on an equine farm for the past sixteen hours. Must be raining outside too because his thick, black hair looks damp as he runs his hands through it, trying to dry himself out a bit.

'I was up at Fogarty's most of the evening – Paul insisted I call over a second time, after I'd done the rest of my calls. But all is well, I think. I did another endoscopy on the filly and there's nothing sinister. He's just panicking because she won't be fit for the flat season, that's all.'

I smile up at him and change the subject.

'Hungry?' Good tactic; a full stomach will possibly make him more amenable to what I have to say.

'No thanks,' he yawns, 'I'm just so, so tired. But James

has taken the phones now, so at least I can crash out for a bit. I'll just feed the dogs then get to bed. Early start tomorrow, you know yourself.'

It flashes through my mind how polite and passionless our conversation is. More like two flatmates who hardly ever see each other than husband and wife.

'I'll look after the dogs, don't worry, but before you do go to bed, Dan, there's something we really need to talk about.'

'Could we leave it till later? I doubt I can take too much in right now.'

He's half way out the door and I know this is the only chance I'm going to get, so I go for it.

'Dan, remember I told you I was up in Dublin today for an audition?'

'An audition? Really? You never said.'

I let that go on the grounds that the guy is practically sleepwalking with sheer knackered-ness and has probably even forgotten talking to me this morning. Chances are I'm just a big, blurry shape to him now.

'Yes, I was and I don't know how it went but, well, you know how it is. I just have to wait by the phone now. Oh . . . and say a lot of novenas,' I tack on lightly, smiling nervously.

'Well . . . best of luck. I hope it all works out for you.'

Another massive yawn from him as he winds up the conversation and makes to go upstairs.

'Dan, that's not the whole story.'

'No, no, I'm sure it's not . . . but can't you tell me about it tomorrow?'

For a second my heart goes out to him; the guy is physically swaying on his feet with exhaustion right now.

'Dan, I'm sorry, but no, this won't wait any longer.'

OK, now I have his attention.

'Well, what is it? Some big movie role or something?'

He's starting to sound a bit narky now, like I'm delaying him from precious sleep time.

'It's a play, a new play that's on in the National in Dublin. One of the actresses is pregnant and has to drop out, so I'd be taking over from her. If I landed the part, that is.'

'Hey, that's terrific . . . well, let me know as soon as there's news.'

'And . . . you see . . . there's something else too. Something important.'

OK, now I'm learning a big life lesson. Namely that when on the brink of a potentially volatile conversation with one's other half, never EVER leave the TV on in the background. Because it has the power to throw the oddest curve balls into the mix. Right now, there's some late-night American soap opera on TV where a wife is having a showdown with her husband and is telling him she's leaving him.

'I am sick of this marriage and I'm sick of being taken for granted!' the wife is yelling at the top of her voice.

'So what's that then?' Dan asks politely enough, but with 'then can I please go to bed?' practically etched across his forehead.

'I've had enough of the way you ignore me!' screams the TV, as I fumble around for the right words. Shit, and I wouldn't mind, only I'd rehearsed this in my head about a dozen times this evening.

'Well, you see, if I were to get cast . . .' I start, gingerly picking my words.

'Do you understand? You are so emotionally unavailable to me and I've taken all I can of this. There's only so much

79

neglect a person can put up with!' fed-up TV wife is still yelling in the background. I rummage around the sofa for the remote control to switch the shagging thing off, but of course can't find it.

'. . . the show wouldn't actually be running at the National,' I say, gathering a bit of momentum now.

'*And, after years of putting up with the way you treat me, I've had enough of you and your white silences and it's time you heard a few home truths,*' TV wife continues to screech, as I root under the armchair cushions where Jules had been sitting earlier, still searching for the remote. No joy, so I just lunge for the telly to switch it off manually. But not before TV wife gets in the final clincher: '*Because I've sacrificed my own life and career for you and get absolutely nothing in return. I've barely had as much as a sentence out of you in months, years in fact. We're not man and wife any more – we're barely even on speaking terms. So now you leave me no choice but to walk out that door and never come back, do you hear me? Enough's enough . . . I'm leaving you and you've got no one to blame but yourself!*'

'Annie, I've just worked a fifteen-hour day, in yet another month of fifteen-hour days. I'm this close to collapsing with sheer exhaustion. Is there any chance you'll just stand still for two seconds together and tell me whatever it is that you're trying to tell me?'

Deep breath. Stay calm. And remember it's not like I even have the job yet.

'What I'm trying to tell you, Dan, what I've been trying to tell you since this morning, is that if I got the part, I would be going to Broadway. To New York.'

My mouth frames each and every word. And suddenly the fireplace is at the oddest angle.

'But hey, that would be terrific for you . . . you love New York . . .'

'You haven't heard the whole thing . . .'

'Which is . . .?'

'Which is . . . that I'd be gone for one full year.'

First sparks.

I was barely twenty-four hours at Allenwood Abbey when one accepted fact was drummed into me as received wisdom; namely that my dorm-mate and New Best Friend, Yolanda, fancied the actual knickers off Dan. It seemed that everyone knew, even, it could only be presumed, the guy himself.

As it happened, the following day he and I were sitting together for my very first class – as bad luck would have it – maths. By a mile my worst subject. Yolanda had warned me that Miss Hugenot, the teacher, had a weepingly annoying habit of picking on any poor unsuspecting moron whose concentration she suspected might have drifted out the window, then hauling them up to the whiteboard to write out trig equations. In full.

Anyway, in clattered Miss Hugenot, dumping a pile of uncorrected homework on her desk, before standing imperiously at the top of the class, surveying us all down her long, thin, aquiline nose. I later discovered that she was a perfectly humane woman, but to the terrified, fifteen-year-old me on my first, proper, full day, she might as well have been the Wicked Witch of the West minus the green face-paint, the broomstick and the dum-di-dum-di-dum-dum music in the background.

Please dear Jesus don't let her pick on me, I semaphored shyly across to Dan, who just grinned back confidently with all the calm of someone who was well able to understand the finer points of differential calculus; not least what the shagging thing actually meant.

'So, let me guess,' he whispered, registering my panic and twinkling kindly down at me. 'Either you don't know the answer or . . . could it be that you haven't done your homework?'

'Ehhh . . . both,' I hissed back. 'I meant to, it was just that last night . . .'

'Your dorm-mate kept you up chatting half the night?' he guessed knowingly, the black eyes dancing.

'Something like that, yeah.'

'Sounds like Yolanda all right,' he said, but kindly and not in any way putting her down.

Meanwhile the girl herself, seated two full rows ahead of us, had heard him utter the magic word . . . her own name . . . and turned around to beam suggestively and swish her blonde, freshly-washed locks at him. Now don't get me wrong; I liked Yolanda very much, but even at this early stage I was starting to learn that she wasn't much of a rules girl and didn't for a single second believe that if a guy liked you, he'd find some way to ask you out. No, she was of the 'take no prisoners and bludgeon a fella into submission until you eventually become his girlfriend' school of thought. She smiled when Dan smiled and her eyes barely left his, like he was her magnetic North. And I just knew from the mildly inquiring look on her face that I'd have to relay every detail of the conversation I'd had with him back to her at lunchtime, omitting no detail, however trivial.

Then . . . to the soundtrack of a drumroll in my head for dramatic effect . . . came the dreaded phrase.

'So,' said Miss Hugenot, glowering at me with beady grey eyes that spotted fresh blood. 'Let's all hear from the latest addition to our class, shall we? Miss Annie Cole? Let's see what they've been teaching you out in Karachi, then. Would you care to come to the top of the class and derive from first principles, x, x squared and x cubed, sin x, cos x and tan, from your notes? In full, if you please.'

Mike Sherry was on the opposite side of the class to me and, to a chorus of giggles immediately made this really annoying kissy-kissy noise that almost sounded like he was calling a horse, while I stumbled to my feet, trembling like jelly.

But that was all it took to distract Miss Hugenot. The full headlamps of her attention momentarily turned on Mike, to berate him for displaying such immaturity and in that split second and with sleight of hand that a professional magician would envy, Dan instantly switched copybooks with mine. So there was the answer, all perfect and neatly written and all I had to do was transcribe. Honour was saved and for the first time in my life, I was actually able to leave a maths class with my head held high.

Later on after class, as I was packing up to leave, Dan grabbed my arm and caught up with me as I stumbled off to try and find my next class.

'Hey, wait . . . where are you headed?' he asked me as I consulted an unintelligible map of the school.

'Ehhh . . . room 201?'

'Wrong way. Here, let me show you where it is.'

He took my books and strolled alongside me and to this day I can still remember the nervous, nauseous sensation of butterflies suddenly hitting my stomach. Bear in mind, I'd only ever been to all-girls schools before this and was totally unused to male attention, never mind the dense, sweaty atmosphere of sex that practically ricocheted off the walls at Allenwood. Sex and teenage pheromones that is, impervious either to open windows or deodorant. And now here was Dan, all tall and earthy and confident, utterly secure in his own popularity as only a captain of the school rugby team could be. The approximate size of a block of flats and so muscular he looked like he rowed everywhere. Handsome is such a Jane Austen-esque word, I thought, and yet it was the only possible adjective you could use to describe Dan Ferguson.

I tried to thank him for digging me out in maths class, but he just grinned and brushed it off. Then he abruptly changed the subject and asked me how I was settling in.

'Great,' I answered, trying my best to match his cool confidence. 'Everyone's being really friendly.'

That much was a polite, white lie; I was crippled with shyness back then, and the truth was that apart from him and Yolanda, I'd barely said two words to anyone else to date.

'You must really miss your family though,' he said gently, suddenly stopping in the packed corridor to look intently down at me. And I really do mean to look down at me – even at fifteen he was pushing six feet tall.

'Very much,' I nodded, 'but I'll see my mother at mid-term. And at Christmas, of course.'

'She's in . . . South America, isn't it?'

'Georgetown,' I nodded, then stupidly tacked on, 'in Guyana.' By now people were starting to bang into us in their haste to get to the next class, but still Dan didn't budge.

'And your dad?'

'Remarried. Lives in Moscow now. His new wife is Russian. I don't really . . . that is, I don't really see him all that much. In fact . . . I don't see him at all.'

I think he must have guessed this wasn't a subject I particularly wanted to be probed on, so he tactfully changed the subject back to Mum.

'Still though, South America's a helluva long way for you to travel to see your mother,' he said, worry suddenly flashing into the coal-black eyes. 'And then keeping in contact can't be easy either. All those long-distance phone calls, emailing the whole time . . .'

'Oh no, it's absolutely fine, I'm well used to it.'

I might have sounded all sure of myself and blasé, but his quick mind seemed to read me accurately and he easily sensed the insecurity that lay beneath.

'Do you have any other family here in Ireland?' he asked kindly.

'My grandmother . . . but honestly, I'm completely fine about Mum being so far away. As Yolanda pointed out to me, I've got to look on the positive side.'

'Which is?'

'She said I'm probably the only one in this school who can go home for the holidays and pick up a suntan at the same time.'

He smiled his gorgeous crooked smile at that, then changed the subject, saying that there was a big rugby match that Saturday in the school grounds against Clongowes Wood, a rival boarding school, and did I fancy coming along to watch?

'I'm playing in it,' he grinned and in that second I was utterly sucked into his easy, relaxed charm. 'And believe me, if last night's training session is anything to go by, we need all the support we can get.'

Course at lunchtime, Yolanda cornered me and didn't so much ask as demand to know the exact nature and substance of what we'd been talking about. So I told her, correctly guessing that she wouldn't like it.

'He invited *you* to watch the match?' she hissed, her blue eyes a beautiful study in wounded pride. Bless her, she'd been kind and welcoming to me; really bad idea to go pissing her off now. And given that I had a social circle that consisted of one girlfriend, the last thing I needed was to start making enemies.

'Come on, Yolanda, he meant as friends, that's all,' I stressed. 'He was asking me about my mother being so far away and just felt a bit sorry for me, that's all. For God's sake, it's only a rugby match. Won't half the school be there supporting the team?'

This mollified her a bit and by the time I reminded her that Dan was only being nice to the new girl, she'd finally started to cool down a bit. But not before impressing on me that Mike Sherry had expressed interest in me, that he was a sweetheart and that I'd be a right moron not to really, really, *really* consider giving him a whirl.

'You know you really should give Mike a chance,' Yolanda had said for about the thousandth time one evening during study time, as she stared out the window and through the lashing rain at Dan training hard on the rugby pitch, rolling around with the rest of the team and covered in shite. Incidentally, him at his happiest, I'd later discover.

'You could do a lot worse than Mike, you know. Oooh, and just think; over the Christmas holidays, you and he and me and Dan could all meet up and go out together as a foursome! Wouldn't that be, like, the coolest thing ever?'

Like I said, everyone knew that Yolanda and Dan were a couple just waiting to happen.

At Allenwood, it was accepted fact.

Chapter Four

Christmas Eve and still no word about the play. And Dan's lukewarm reaction to the whole thing? 'Look, you don't actually have the job yet, so why don't we just cross that bridge when we come to it?' Cue him collapsing with deep exhaustion into bed for the next seven hours and that to date has been pretty much his one and only comment on the subject.

But deep down I know he's right, of course. As of now I don't have the job, so nothing for me to do but try and put it right out of my head. Which of course is like trying not to breathe. A few days after my first audition, Fag Ash Hil rang saying they wanted to see me for a call-back. Good sign. So up I traipsed to the National in Dublin: same drill all over again, with Jack Gordon sitting there cool as a fish's fart and apologising for hauling me all the way from Waterford for a second time, then telling me, actually saying it to my face, that he still wasn't any closer to making a final casting decision yet. That he needed to mull it over for a while longer and 'give full thought to the chemistries between each of the characters'. So I was put through my paces all over again and now there was nothing to do but wait it out.

That aside, I've got two secret Christmas wishes in my heart: one is that I'd have news about the job . . . whether good or bad . . . by Christmas. Because nothing on this earth is worse than the not bloody knowing. Not to be though.

Lizzie rang me yesterday, hung-over as a dog after the National's Christmas party the previous night, to celebrate the show coming to an end, 'prior to Broadway transfer'.

Funny, but just hearing her stories about the mad piss-up they had, then how they'd all staggered into Lillie's Bordello and stayed there till five in the morning, made me stop in my tracks. Like I'd suddenly just got a flash of the parallel life I might have had, if I'd never married. Because you know, that might have been me . . . out on the tiles . . . celebrating a blossoming career . . . off to play Broadway for an entire year . . .

God, it might yet be me, I suddenly thought, if I get good news, that is. For a split second, I allow myself to get sucked into the fantasy, the excitement of not knowing what other wonderful work opportunities might come from playing Broadway . . . which American agents might come to see the show and maybe even take me on . . . then put me up for other big jobs . . . I mean, who could tell? Maybe even the ultimate dream might miraculously come about . . . that I'd somehow get a crack at a few movie castings too?

Then a stab of reality so sharp it almost winds me; that's Lizzie's future I'm describing, not mine. For the coming year, the world is her oyster and if I'm being honest with myself, I envy her from the very depths of my bone marrow. And right now, she's out partying and having hangovers then staying in bed till the crack of lunch, like you're supposed to when you're twenty-eight and when you've absolutely no one else to answer to but yourself.

And here's me, stuck in my mother-in-law's house, listening to all her passive-aggressive little digs for not clearing out ash from the grate properly AND for using cranberry sauce out of a jar and not making it from scratch, like all Ferguson women have done for the last two millennia.

But then I've no choice in the matter. Because I'm married, aren't I? With my husband of course, nowhere to be seen. Leaving me yet again feeling like I'm trapped in a cage of my own making, watching everyone else have fun in the outside world, through reinforced steel bars.

Lizzie, bless her, made the right noises on the phone, saying all the things you need to hear when waiting to find out about a job that could potentially change your entire life. That no news was good news for starters. Oh, and that Jack had taken himself off to London for a few days to accept some award, so chances were I wouldn't hear anything till New Year and I'd just have to put it out of my head till then.

'Though why in the name of Jaysus he bothered leaving town just to collect some award, I couldn't tell you,' she'd croaked down the phone to me in a just-out-of-bed voice, though it was well past three in the afternoon. 'The guy has so many by now, I'm surprised he doesn't have them up for sale on eBay'.

And so to my second Christmas wish: some alone time with Dan. Did you ever see a couple that needed it more? Now traditionally at the practice, we always host a little mulled wine and mince pies party on Christmas Eve, just after the surgery closes and before everyone drifts off their separate ways. We're only closed till the twenty-seventh and of course, I'm cooking Christmas dinner for Dan and his family tomorrow, but I'm still hopeful that not only will Dan and I get to spend all of Christmas night alone together, but the whole of Stephen's Day too.

I've totally spelt it out to him. I've told him that this is *our* bit of time, for us and for no one else. That this means an awful lot to me and that by God we were going to make the most of it. No work, no farm calls, no phones ringing, no half the town descending on the house, just him and me. A.L.O.N.E. That with a possible year apart hanging over us, surely he agreed that we had a lot to talk about? Course his mobile rang in the middle of my big speech, so I doubt he took in most of what I was saying, but still.

Point made. Cards laid on table.

Come Christmas Eve and I'm at The Moorings, frantically getting everything organised for said staff drinks party. I'd already decorated the house, even remembering to put up the Christmas tree in the exact spot ordained by Audrey year-in-year-out. Though why she doesn't just put masking tape on the carpet to save her all the bother of whinging at me that it's not in its precise place, I'll never know.

Anyroadup, if I say so myself, the place looks terrific: the fire in the drawing room is blazing away, cheesy, cheery Christmas songs are playing in the background and the mulled wine is mulling. I think to take my mind off the play, I've been over-compensating by acting like Nigella on speed these past few days. By some miracle, I've managed to do all the shopping for Christmas Day and not forget anything, tidied the house from top to bottom and still found time to squeeze in an appointment to get my big bushy head of hair blow-dried straight for the holidays.

Well, straight-ish, given that my hair actually grows outwards and not downwards. Not unlike Sideshow Bob's in *The Simpsons*.

Come six pm and just as the last patient leaves the surgery, suddenly the drawing room seems packed with people: Dan, Andrew, James, the intern, Mrs Brophy yelling at everyone and of course Jules who's been here all day, supposedly helping me, but who's actually spent most of the afternoon slumped on a couch with a bridge of saliva between her knees and chin, watching *It's a Wonderful Life* on TV.

The room is buzzing, everyone's laughing and enjoying themselves and just as I'm racing around in my good Karen Millen LBD, topping up glasses and making sure everyone's stuffing their faces with mince pies . . . surprise surprise . . . the phone in the hall rings.

Silence as we all look at each other and all you can hear is Shane McGowan rasping 'Fairytale of New York' in the background.

'WHAT WAS THAT?' yells poor, half-deaf Mrs Brophy.

'Phone,' says Andrew, pointedly not budging. 'Must be a patient.'

Shane McGowan and Kirstie MacColl are growling out the bit where they call each other scumbags and maggots, while tension suddenly bounces off the four walls of the drawing room.

'I'll take it,' Dan volunteers.

'No, no, stay and relax, I'm sure whoever it is will understand that it's Christmas Eve and that we've closed up for the holidays,' Andrew smiles benignly. But it's loo late – Dan's already out the door. I'm focusing on handing out mince pies and desperately trying to convince myself that this is absolutely NO indication of how things will be over the short holiday when the practice is closed and when Dan is meant to be *taking a break*.

Two minutes later, he's back in the room, rubbing his eyes with the back of his palms, the way he always does whenever he's really exhausted.

'Everything OK?' Andrew asks politely, glass in hand.

'That was Beatrice Kelly,' Dan replies and I know with absolute certainty what's coming next. Beatrice is an elderly widow who lives on her own and is passionately devoted to her horses, which she treats almost like surrogate children. In fact, it's a kind of joke around here that if there is such a thing as reincarnation, then to come back as one of Beatrice's horses would be karma of the highest order.

'It's that hunter she had trouble with last week,' Dan tells Andrew.

'Oh, the hyperperistalsis case?'

'That's the one. Now she thinks it's full blown colic and she's panicking. Right then, sorry to break up the party, but I'd better get out there.'

I get a justifiable flash of irritation when I see that neither Andrew nor James as much as offer to go with Dan, but just sit there nursing their mulled wine, nibbling on mince pies and looking at him blankly. So, silently fuming, I dump down my tray of empty glasses and follow Dan down the freezing cold kitchen passage and out the side door.

'Sorry about this,' he says, pulling on a pair of Wellingtons. 'But it's all my own fault. I told Beatrice that if she had the slightest concern about that horse to ring me immediately. And you know what she's like when it comes to her horses.'

I force my mouth into a stretched smile and utter the one phrase that pretty much summarises my life at The Moorings to date.

'It's fine, it can't be helped.'

'No, course not.'

'I'm only sorry you're missing the party, that's all.'

'I'll be well back in time for Midnight Mass, don't worry.'

I manage a genuine smile at this. Although neither Dan nor myself are the slightest bit religious, still Midnight Mass is the one time of year you can count on us heathens to cross the threshold of the local church. Useless pair of hypocrites, I know, but it's just such a lovely service, with the kids singing carols and the big tree and most of the town there, half pissed.

'I'm not a bit worried about the party,' I say calmly, even managing to make myself believe it. 'Sure we've still got all day tomorrow and the day after. Don't we?'

I reach up to gently brush a tufty bit of his thick, black hair that's standing upright on his forehead, then go to gently stroke his cheek, but he's distracted and doesn't respond.

And two seconds later he's gone out into the dark, icy cold evening.

Half eleven that night and he's still not back, so after I've tidied up the house, Jules and I walk to Midnight Mass on our own. Well, that is to say I walk and she staggers, having spent most of the evening knocking back approximately half a bucket of the mulled wine. I'm still hopeful that Dan might meet us at the church or even join us late during the service, but when we get there, there's no sign of his mud-soaked jeep anywhere.

A sudden stab of worry: he shouldn't have taken this long, should he? Maybe there'd been some kind of accident? So I call him but he doesn't answer. Which only makes worry work like yeast in my mind.

By the time the choir get to *Silent Night*, Jules has fallen asleep and actually snores for the rest of the service.

Holiday = not off to a good start.

Christmas morning and the sound of a mug being plonked down on the beside table next to me wakes me up. It's Dan, still wearing the same clothes he had on yesterday and looking more shattered than I think I've ever seen him. And older too; for the first time in the bright morning light I notice grey hair starting to sprout round his temples. All the ridiculous hours he's been working finally taking their toll.

'Hey, Happy Christmas, sleeping beauty,' he says softly, sitting down on the edge of the bed beside me and rubbing his eyes exhaustedly with the back of his hands. 'Made you some tea.'

'Dan! Where were you? I mean, what happened last night? I was so worried . . .'

'I know and I'm so sorry, love. It was all hours by the time I got back, so I just crashed out on the sofa downstairs so I wouldn't disturb you. Believe me, I couldn't get away any sooner.'

I haul myself up onto the pillows, waiting for the morning fuzziness in my brain to clear and for that two-second time-lag to pass before my thoughts come back into focus. Yeah, now I have it; he went to Beatrice Kelly's farm last night, something about a colicky hunter.

'Problem with the horse?'

'Well, no, not really,' he says, the black eyes suddenly miles away, full of concern. 'I think the main reason Beatrice called me out was that she was feeling a bit lonely. You know how tough this time of year can be for anyone living alone. I think she just wanted the company more than anything else. I tried calling you but of course, no signal on my phone up there.'

I nod and say nothing, knowing it's completely pointless to. I can see it all too clearly: Beatrice was all alone on Christmas Eve. And of course Dan with the biggest heart in the south east, stayed up with her and talked the night away. So what can I do? As usual, nothing. Neediness always gets top priority in Dan's life, always. It might as well be engraved on his forehead: 'the squeaky wheel gets the grease'.

We exchange gifts and I give him his first. A satnav, which I know he wanted and which I bought when I was up in Dublin doing my call-back audition. It cost a packet and I had to go to loads of trouble to get it, but get it I did and he's delighted with it . . . then he hands me a slim, white envelope, looking at me sheepishly.

'Merry Christmas, Annie. This is . . . well, let's just say it's my small way of trying to make things up to you. For the anniversary night, for everything.'

I open it and almost fall out of bed with shock. It's a voucher for the two of us for a weekend at Marlfield House, the posh country house hotel where our last, disastrous, aborted anniversary night was supposed to take place.

'Dan!' I manage to stammer, utterly overwhelmed at the gesture. Not just by the thoughtfulness of it, but by the fact that he actually intends to take a full weekend off just for the two of us to be together. The best Christmas present I could possibly have asked for.

'This is completely wonderful . . . thank you . . . so, so much . . .'

I smile up at him and he gently takes my hand and starts massaging it.

'Annie . . . I know things haven't been easy here for you

and you've been so amazing to put up with everything the way you do. But you do know why I'm doing all this, don't you? Why I'm working so hard and putting in all these ridiculous hours?'

'Course I do . . .'

'. . . all I'm trying to do is build up the practice . . .'

'I know . . .'

'. . . and then there's so many people relying on me to keep things going. Depending on me for a living. Mum, Jules, Andrew, James, Mrs Brophy . . . and I couldn't live with myself if I thought I was letting anyone down. You know that Dad left things in such a bad way when he died, and the only way I can haul us all out of this is just to keep on working at this pace . . . for the moment, at least.'

'Dan, shhhhhhh, it's OK and for what it's worth, I do understand . . .'

He's completely focused on my palm now, which looks tiny in his huge tanned hands, like he's some sort of giant that's played tricks with scale. But we're only inches apart and it's the closest and most intimate we've been in I can't remember how long. The most emotionally available he's been to me, literally, in years.

'Just bear with me for a bit longer, Annie, that's all I'm asking. The time will come when the practice is running smoothly and then we'll have more time for each other, I promise.'

'Hey, look, we've got the whole of today, don't we? No work, no call-outs, no interruptions . . .'

'Now that's a definite promise, no working today,' he smiles . . . the crooked smile that I love so much. Then he looks at me tenderly, in a way he hasn't done in the longest time. I slowly slide my hand up his arm, wanting nothing more than to kiss him, to feel his huge, warm arms wrapped around mine, to pull him back down into bed beside me.

'So we've got all day today then? You give me your word?'

'The whole day,' he half-whispers, moving in closer still as I lock my arms around his tanned, broad shoulders.

Next thing, from downstairs, the dogs start to go mad at the unmistakable sound of someone letting themselves in through the front door.

'DAN? ANNIE? Where are you? I thought you'd already be in the kitchen getting the turkey organised by now, what is going on? Don't tell me you're still in bed?'

Sweet baby Jesus and the orphans, I do not believe this. It's Audrey; arrived early and letting herself in with her own key, like she always does.

Mood shattered, romantic moment well and truly over.

Half an hour later and I'm up, washed, dressed and whizzing round the kitchen, full of hope for the day ahead and absolutely determined to make sure that everyone has the Best Christmas Ever. We'll be like the family in the Dolmio ad, I think, efficiently basting the turkey, checking the stuffing hasn't fallen out of it and pre-heating the oven.

Jules trails in mid-morning, yawning and demanding to know if I've got any Solpadeine lying around, that she's dying with a hangover. So I efficiently whirl round the place sorting that out for her, while getting Audrey settled with a sweet sherry in front of the fire, then getting back to the kitchen, at all times acting the part of perfect hostess-cum-dutiful daughter-in-law.

Never in my whole life have I gone to so much trouble; I have officially busted my ass for this Christmas dinner and the only thing that's getting me through is the thought that tonight, when everyone's gone, it'll finally, finally, finally just be me and Dan. A.L.O.N.E.

Next thing Jules ambles into the kitchen in her lazy way, wanting to know where the Quality Street are. I'm just about to be a total Irish Mammy and tell her she's not allowed eat them now, that it'll only ruin her dinner, when next thing a car swooshes into the driveway.

A familiar looking, bashed-up green Nissan with two child seats in the back.

'Ah, for feck's sake!' yells Jules, suddenly more animated than she's been ever since she got here. 'Hide! Quick! It's the Four Horsemen of the Apocalypse! Lisa shagging Ledbetter . . . the Countess Dracula herself!!'

I almost drop a boiling pot of carrots on the floor. 'I do not befeckinglieve this!'

'Even from here I can hear you blaspheming, Annie,' Audrey berates me from the drawing room. 'And can someone kindly bring me another sherry? In one of the good *crystal* glasses this time, please?'

'Lie down flat on the floor, quick,' says Jules, 'maybe she didn't see us. Maybe she'll think we're all out . . . visiting . . . or . . . at Mass or something.'

But it's too late. Already I can hear Dan opening the hall door to Lisa as her eldest son starts yelling the place down that he got a football from Santa and will Dan come outside to play with him? She has two kids, by the way; Harry is seven and Sue is four. Harry, I'm fond of – he's cute and easy to baby-sit and God knows I should know, having been called on to do it often enough. But Sue is a different story; moany, sulky and whingy, a kid that's never, ever in good form, no matter how many treats you throw her way. But then, as Jules is forever at pains to point out, the apple doesn't fall too far from the tree, does it?

And there's something else about Lisa that drives me mental too, something I've been at pains to keep to myself all this time. Call it what you will, women's intuition maybe, but I've always felt that Lisa has her eye on Dan and has had for a long, long time. There's just something in the way her voice changes gear whenever she talks to him that never fails to alert my suspicions and while I'm far from jealous – Dan barely even notices me half the time, never mind when someone else is flirting with him – it does get annoying after a while.

Anyroadup, Jules starts dum-dum-dumming the theme music from *The Omen* under her breath as Lisa slithers into the kitchen, full of abject apologies for disturbing me in the middle of cooking dinner, but nevertheless, still big fat doing it anyway. Vintage Lisa; at all times, just barge right on ahead and completely suit yourself regardless.

I grudgingly have to admit that she's attractive, naturally tall and skinny, the jammy cow, but most of the time she streels round the place looking care-worn, thin, pale and permanently unsmiling. Red hair, but with her natural dark roots showing; yet another source of incessant griping from her. That she can't afford to go to the hairdressers any more and has to make do with home colours instead, all while her husband Charlie still somehow has money to go down to the pub, night in and night out. And I'm sorry if this sounds a bit unsympathetic but bear in mind that when it comes to whinging, this is a woman who'd give Gillian McKeith a right run for her money.

We exchange Merry Christmas air kisses as Jules scarpers back to the safety of the TV.

'You see Charlie bloody well buggered off to have drinks with some boozing buddy in Lismore this morning,' Lisa moans, making it sound like he did this with the sole intention of getting at her, 'leaving me all on my own with the kids. And of course my sister in Dublin is having my parents over to her this year and never even bothered to invite us, can you believe it? Which means I have to cook a dinner myself. And I haven't even started it yet so my turkey probably won't be done for about another seventeen hours. Anyway, I thought I might as well pop in and wish you all a happy Christmas. Everything looks lovely, Annie,' she sighs enviously. 'I wish I had enough money to go all out, like you always do.'

I usher her into the drawing room to say hello to Audrey and then offer her a drink. She notices Jules drinking champagne and asks for the same.

Immediate burning sensation, exactly like heartburn. She's drinking. This means that not only will she end up leaving her car here and have to come back to collect it during my precious time out with Dan, but worse, far worse . . . Jaysus knows when she intends to leave. Not being inhospitable or anything, but if the measure of a good guest is someone who knows when to go, then the Countess Dracula is most definitely NOT one of them. It wouldn't be uncommon for her to pop in for a coffee in the afternoon and still be here with her kids asleep upstairs in one of the spare rooms well past midnight. With absolutely no intention of going home either, even at that hour.

'So what did Santa Claus bring this morning?' Dan asks little Sue, who's plonked herself on the sofa beside Audrey, pulling a doll along by its hair. Dan, by the way, is normally great with children and for their part, kids of all ages love him . . . with the sole exception of this little madam.

'That,' she says disgustedly. 'I didn't want a stupid doll. I hate dolls. I wanted a bike.'

'Couldn't afford it,' says Lisa focusing solely on Dan and only Dan, completely indifferent to the fact that the child isn't deaf and can clearly hear her. 'Although her father still manages to have enough money to keep up his sixty fags a day habit, doesn't he?'

No one says anything to that. Then Harry starts noisily kicking his soccer ball around the drawing room, and Audrey presses her hands to the onion-thin skin on her temples, in a gesture I know the meaning of all too well. Meanwhile Lisa flops down on the sofa, telling the room about how exhausted she is and how no one ever appreciates the sheer amount of work she does at this time of year, to much behind-her-back-eye-rolling from Jules. I excuse myself and get back to the kitchen to start getting the vegetables on.

A sharp stab of worry; what do I do if Lisa invites herself and her kids to stay for dinner? But I let it go. Her husband, Charlie, is presumably only out visiting for the morning and will be back later, so she won't have any choice but to leave. Because surely not even the Countess Dracula would gatecrash our Christmas dinner? Would she?

The phone rings out in the hallway, but I let Dan get it. I check the clock on the kitchen wall, not yet midday. Only seven am in Washington where my mother is, way too early for her to call yet. Next thing, just as I'm up to my elbows in Brussels sprouts, Dan strides into the kitchen, kicking off his shoes and pulling on the pair of Wellingtons he'd left by the side door last night.

Very bad sign.

103

Burning feeling like indigestion returns with a vengeance.

'You going out to play soccer with Harry?' I look up and ask him deliberately, already dreading the answer.

Because he couldn't, could he? Take a work call? Not today of all days, not after he specifically promised he wouldn't.

'Ehh . . . no, not exactly.'

A cold fear clutches at me and suddenly the air between us starts to throb.

No more information forthcoming. Which is what Dan does whenever he senses that I'll be annoyed about something. Proffers absolutely nothing and leaves it to me to ask all the questions.

Bad burning feeling suddenly gets about a hundred times worse.

'Because dinner will be ready pretty soon, you know,' I say and somehow my tone of voice manages to make even that innocuous sentence sound like a vague threat.

'Annie, look, I know this is inconvenient, but that was Mike Nolan on the phone . . .'

I swear to God, at this my knees actually loosen, like they might buckle from under me at any second. Mike Nolan is a regular client here and lives on a massive farm a good two-hour drive away. He's also a well-known worrier, famous for calling anyone at the practice out for very little reason whatsoever.

'. . . and he's very anxious about some of his cattle.'

'Dan, for the love of God, please tell me you're not heading out to do a farm call. Not right now, not today of all days.'

'You see, he thinks it might be ringworm and God love the guy, he's in a blind panic.'

Dan doesn't even make eye contact with me at this, like he knows I'll flip and is just doing his best to get out of here before all hell breaks loose.

'He thinks it might be *ringworm!*' Now I'm raising my voice, something I don't think I've ever done in this house. I know they can all hear me in the drawing room and I don't care.

'But ringworm isn't even remotely serious!' I splutter at him, absolutely stunned that he's even considering heading all the way out to Mike Nolan's. 'There's no possible way that this can be classified as an emergency! For God's sake, it's Christmas Day and I'm about to serve dinner. Surely, this can wait till tomorrow? Or, if you really feel you have to go, can't you at least hold off till after we've eaten?'

'Mike's a good customer and he practically begged me to drive over there just to take a quick look. That's all.'

'That's *all?* It's at least a two-hour drive there and back! Plus the last time he hauled you out there, you didn't get back till the following day!'

'Look, I've told him I'd go – I gave him my word and I can't go back on it. He needs my help and it would be wrong to let him down.'

'You gave me your word this morning that there'd be no call-outs today!'

But his feet are well and truly dug in now and I know of old that whenever that happens, I'm on a loser.

'Can I ask you one simple question, Dan? Does all the trouble I've gone to mean absolutely nothing to you? Only this morning you told me we'd have the whole day to ourselves. You promised.'

A low card I know, but feck it anyway. His promises are

clearly worth about as much as the Zimbabwean dollar and I want him to know it.

'Annie, please, can you please stop making me feel worse than I already do about this? I'll do my best to be back as soon as possible. But . . . it might be a while. I won't really know till I get out there.'

A slash of sudden pain shoots through me and suddenly . . . that's it. Break point. The straw has finally broken the camel's back. A rumble of fury starts to bubble up from deep within me. In my liver it gathers bile and becomes toxic, in my stomach it gathers acid and in my blood . . . heat.

No room in my hot little heart now for anything but the furies of hell.

'Dan,' I say, trembling, with days, weeks, months and years of suppressed anger finally breaking through the surface. 'I. Have. Had. Enough. I can't live like this and I won't. Do you even know the trouble I've taken to have everything perfect for this dinner? If you take this call you know right well that you won't be back till God knows when . . .'

He looks at me, genuinely puzzled and a bit irritated that now, on top of everything else, he has to deal with a domestic scene.

'Why are you behaving like this, Annie? I know you're angry but like I say, it's a once-off emergency . . .'

'It is NOT a bloody emergency. If it was, I wouldn't mind. If it was a calving or a foaling and if an animal might die, then I mightn't appreciate the timing, but I'd still let you take the call. But it isn't. This is just Mike Nolan selfishly taking advantage of you because he knows right well that you're the only vet within a hundred mile radius who'd even think of abandoning their family on Christmas Day . . . you're the only one who's soft enough . . . you're the only one whose wife clearly means nothing to you . . .'

Oh God, right now, more than anything, I need to be articulate. I want to remind him . . . yet again . . . that with a possible year apart hanging over us, how much this pathetically short little break means to me.

But the rage that was in me a moment ago has now subsided and turned to a hard tough little lump deep in my gut. Then it travels up to my throat where it quickly turns to tears. Bucketloads of them. Messy, uncontrollable weeping that I never allow myself. Instead of an inner core of steel to draw on, I only have access to vowels and tears and snot.

And it's not pretty.

'Annie, come on, love, you're blowing this completely out of proportion. You know I've got to take the call,' he says, seeing the state I'm in and instinctively moving into hug me. But I'm in no mood for yet more of his everlasting apologies and roughly shove him away.

'Right then,' he says, stepping back and looking wounded. 'In that case, I'll see you when I see you.'

And that's all folks. His final, parting shot before he's out the door and gone.

It takes a long, long time for me to collect my thoughts and for coolness to come over me, but eventually I somehow manage to compose myself and head back into the drawing room. As evenly as I can, I tell the others that Dan won't be joining us for dinner after all, and their reactions still say it all.

Even Audrey, Dan's champion and number one fan, looks back at me with her pale fishy eyes, a polite, frozen smile camouflaging the shock beneath, when she realises that it's not an emergency call-out at all and that he mightn't be back for hours.

If at all, this evening.

Jules is the only one who asks me if I'm OK. I can't answer, so I just shrug. But you can always rely on the Countess Dracula to get her oar in.

'Well, you know if you've got extra food going abegging, Annie, we'd love to stay and have a bite to eat with you. The kids are starving and the smell of food from the kitchen is starting to drive them mad. Don't worry a bit about setting the extra places, I'll take care of that for you.'

In my dull-witted state and before I even have time to register what she's saying, as usual, she's gone and steam-rolled right over me. A second later, she's thrown open the drawing room door and shouted at the children who are running riot up and down the stairs, 'So who's hungry? Who'd like to stay and have dinner here at Auntie Annie's?'

And I swear to God, the meal lasts longer than your average Wimbledon men's singles final. Between Lisa's moans about how Charlie would stagger home half-pissed later on and still expect there to be dinner for him and Audrey's veiled whimpers every time the kids start screaming at each other, which is like a constant background noise . . . I'm not certain how much more I can take.

Audrey by the way, who normally has the appetite of a hump-back whale, only picks at her dinner, mainly because the kids are making such a God-awful racket involving a fork, a fistful of carrots and the last of the Brussels sprouts. Eventually she just shoves a half-eaten plate away from her, pleading a headache and warning us all that she feels one of her 'little turns' coming on.

Even Jules, my dependable ally, lets me down too. Normally, the girl is so laid-back, you could dot deck chairs around her and sail her through the Caribbean, but not today. She has a tendency to regress a bit when Audrey is around and throughout the whole miserable meal, what little energy she has is taken up with being irritated by her mother. She just sits there, chin cupped in her hand, occasionally mouthing at me whenever she catches my eye, 'I'm a celebrity, get me out of here.'

And so the white hot tension round the table is broken only by Lisa harping on . . . I'm not joking, for a full *hour* . . . about how her wealthy sister is heading off skiing for New Year with her family, while she's stuck at home with absolutely nothing to brighten up her entire Christmas holiday.

Meanwhile I just stare ahead, picking at dinner and only answering direct questions on automatic pilot, as she bleats on and on and on. Then ages later, I notice that Jules has finally started to wake up a bit and now looks like she's only one vodka shot away from sniping across the table at Lisa, 'Well, how about the obvious remedy? If money is such an issue for you, then go out and get a job locally, like Annie does and shut up your bloody whinging!'

And of course, Lisa won't leave. Not when Audrey heads home to her TV movies and Jules scarpers off to her pal's drink party. Not even when I pointedly tell her that I'm expecting a call from my mother in the States and that I'll probably be on the phone for ages. Fine, she tells me. I'll just sit by the fire with the kids and watch *Toy Story* on telly.

Worse, when Charlie calls her to see where she is, she just invites him over without even asking me if it's OK.

Then, to add insult to injury, she throws in, 'And I'm sure you won't mind if he has some of the Christmas dinner, will you, Annie? It's such a shame to let all those leftovers go to waste and it would save me all the bother of having to cook when I get home.'

I just nod dully, with all the life and energy of a used tea bag, feeling utterly drained as I always do after more than a few hours of Lisa's company. And, of course I let her have her own way. What the hell, my Christmas is ruined anyway, how much worse can it get with Charlie barging in on top of me as well?

One ray of light: Mum Skypes me, as she always does, on the dot of five pm, right after she's come home from church, six thousand miles away. Curse Skype anyway – of course she can clearly see my blotchy eyes and hear the wobble in my voice. The giveaway is that my eyes keep wandering down to the bottom left-hand corner of the screen to check just how bad I look and of course, she's straight onto me.

'Are you sure you're alright, Annie dear?'

'I'm fine, fine. Really fine.'

'One more "fine" and I won't believe you.'

She has to ask me a couple of times before I eventually tell her what's wrong, but then it all comes tumbling out. The full, unexpurgated story about the whole rotten, miserable day. The fact that I'm one plum pudding away from a Yuletide breakdown.

Even on the grainy computer screen I can see her reaction when I tell her about how Dan disappeared off on Christmas Day and never came back.

Her face doesn't change, but her lips actually go white.

Ever the diplomat though, Mum doesn't carp or criticise.

In fact, never in my entire life do I think I've as much as heard her raise her hushed, soft spoken voice. And she doesn't now either; just twirls the pearls around her elegant, willowy neck and says over and over again how surprised she is at Dan. And Mum, by the way likes him. The same way everyone does. But then not liking Dan is a bit like not liking The Beatles; completely impossible to imagine.

I tell her everything, no holds barred. That I feel and have felt for the longest time, that I'm the human solvent that's holding my shaky marriage together and that I'm not sure how much more of it I can take. I'm little more than UHU glue and who wants that carved on their headstone anyway? My patience has been ground down to nothing and now I'm thinking the thought that dare not speak its name.

Does even the most impossible love come with a sell-by date?

Come to Washington, Mum says crisply and decisively. Book a flight and come over for New Year. Money's no object, I'll pay. You need the break and we can talk more freely here about what's to be done.'

This instantly brightens me up a bit because what I want now more than anything is to get away, to see her, to be with her, to listen to her sage wisdom and calm, soothing words of advice. I agree and tell her I'll call back in a day or two to arrange the details.

But by then the goalposts of my life have shifted irrevocably.

Because bright and early on the morning of the twenty seventh, I get a hysterical call from none other than Fag Ash Hil.

'You better be sitting down for this!' she screeches,

coughing and spluttering with excitement. 'Because guess what?'

My heart swells up at this, till it feels too big for my chest and starts beating in odd, jagged little jerks.

Then come the words that will change the whole course of my entire life.

'You got the part!'

I feel a million things all at once . . . but the first thing is this.

Finally, finally, finally, I'm free.

Everyone's reactions to my brand new job

Jules (Looking as pale as someone bleeding from an internal wound.)

'So how exactly did you expect me to react to this news anyway, Annie? Did you think I was going to turn the oven on and stick my head into it? Well you're quite wrong because as it happens, here's my reaction to your selfishness in just fecking off on me. It's not so much that I'm losing my sister-in-law, as gaining a pad in New York to crash out in. For a full year. And don't for one second think that I won't turn up on your doorstep, 'cos you know me, babe, I will. If I can cajole Dan into forking out for the flights, that is. And what's more it'll serve you right for being such a bad bloody bitch, deserting me and leaving me to put up with the Mothership and the Countess Dracula all on my own.'

Then, swishing one of her curly pigtails in my direction, she stomped upstairs to my home office-cum-skip and told me she was going to 'Facebook her angst'.

Phew. One down, four to go.

Audrey (With a polite smile masking the frozen look of horror in her eyes.)

'I can't quite believe what I'm hearing, Annie. New York? For a year? Is it possible that you're being serious? Do I have to remind you that you're a married woman with responsibilities? And quite apart from that, who's going to do all my little jobs for me when you're gone? You know, come to think of it, I'm not feeling so well at the shock of this, I think I may have to have a lie down . . .'

Typical Audrey; she may not have said much more to my face, but by God, she really went to town on me behind my back. Neighbours in Stickens who she'd hardly spoken two words to since her husband died, were suddenly accosted in the street and asked if they'd heard the news? That I was abandoning poor hard-working Dan, for a full year no less? To go off and do a play! When at my age the only thing I should be thinking of producing was grand-children! Utterly shameful, she sniffed in her frail, wispy little voice to anyone who would listen and imparted with all the shock and condemnation of the small town.

Like marriage is something that you can just take a gap year from as and when it suits you......etc, etc, repeat ad nauseam.

Liz (After all her screams of excitement had finally died down. Which, by the way, took a good twenty minutes.)
'Oh Christ, Annie, this is the best news in the whole worldwide history of news! Do you realise the fun and the craic we're going to have? Because by Jaysus, your Auntie Liz is going to show her secluded little countrified housewife pal the absolute time of her life in the Big Apple! I'm talking about you and me going out drinking and clubbing every night and I will NOT take no for an answer. I've even done my research, you know. Apparently there's this really hip late night bar where all the Broadway actors go after shows, called *Don't Tell Mama* and all the singers from the big musicals perform live, night after night, and it serves booze till well after dawn . . . it's meant to be amazing! Oh, we are SO there . . . and best of all, you'll be able to party all night long and not worry about running home to the back arse of Stickens . . .'

She chatted on about all the heavy-duty socialising she was planning for us and I laughed along with her, still on a high from my un-befecking-lievable news.

'So have you told Dan yet?' she asked me, before she hung up.

'No, he's at work. Tonight, when he gets back. Though God knows when that will be. And God knows how he'll take this.'

'Oh, he'll be fine. For Feck's sake, the guy worships the ground you walk on, Annie, and he wants you to be happy, doesn't he?'

I said nothing to this.

'Just tell him that a year is absolutely nothing and that it'll go quicker than a Katie Price marriage.'

My mother

'Oh darling, it'll be so wonderful to have you so close to me after all this time! You know Washington is only a three-hour train ride from New York City? But I must say, I am a little worried. What does Dan think of all this? You could be gone for a full year, after all. If you really want to get back into acting work again, wouldn't you be far better off waiting for a job to come along in Ireland?'

Entirely my own fault and it serves me right for confiding in her on Christmas Day and pouring out all my woes to her. Now that I've effectively been handed a 'get out of love free' card, I reckon poor Mum thinks I'll end up in the divorce courts. And like I said, she likes Dan and always did.

No, for all that she'd be delighted to have me on the same continent as her, I can't allow myself for a second to think that she's dancing round the place at the news. Long-distance relationships are a nightmare, she reminded me, quoting a cautionary tale from decades ago. This was when she was still married to Dad and was suddenly posted out to Botswana, taking the five-year-old me with her. Dad stayed behind in Ireland, as he'd just started a new job here working for some IT firm and was either unable or unwilling to join her.

Worst time of her life, Mum said. The strain of being apart, plus the constant worrying about him eventually took its toll on the marriage and ultimately brought about their eventual break-up. Well, that and the fact that while she was abroad, Dad went and met someone else, now his new wife. Are you really sure, Mum gently probed, that this is absolutely the best thing for you both right now? Honest to God, even over the transatlantic phone line, I could clearly hear the sound of her worriedly twisting her pearls round and round again.

And so for the first time in I can't remember how long I found myself disagreeing with my mother. Yes, I told her firmly, this is absolutely the right thing, not a doubt in my mind.

Because to me, after three long years of slow, silent suffocation, this is the Universe finally paying up. This is it. I feel like I've just pulled three lemons on the one-arm-bandit of life, and no power on earth is going to drag me from my winnings. Not after everything I've been through. Of course, a moralist like Mum disagrees and thinks everything in life, even a year on Broadway, comes with the most massive price tag attached, but I'm part-pagan and disagree.

I now fully believe in breakthrough bursts of astrological beneficence.

Sure, after this spectacular piece of good fortune, how could I not?

Dan

I told him as soon as he got home late that night; me, edgily sitting up on the bed in my nightie and him fresh

116

out of a hot shower, having been out in sub-zero tempera-
tures all night. I'd been dress-rehearsing this talk the whole
day and by the time I finally nailed him down face-to-face,
my nerves were raw and jangling with worry.

But if I thought he was going to asphyxiate at the news,
I was quite wrong. He didn't even look surprised when I
told him, more resigned, like he knew this was coming all
along. As if he suspected as much and had just been quietly
expecting confirmation. He sat down on the bed beside
me, huge and hulking, towelling off his wet hair and
smelling of musky cedarwood shower gel. His taut, muscled
body, still tanned, even in the depths of midwinter.

'So you'd be in New York. For a full year?' he asked me,
but gently, his whole heart suddenly in his soft, black eyes.

'Dan,' I said, my tone pleading, 'I know a year away sounds
like a long time, but you have to understand . . . if I don't
go, I'll always regret it. Opportunities like this *never* come
along and I just feel that, what with you so busy all the
time . . . what I'm trying to say is, you're so rarely around
these days. Is it so terrible of me to want to go so badly?
Because when you think about it, twelve months isn't really
all that long, you know . . . and also, even though the show
is slated in for a year, it might get ripped apart by the critics
and close early, because that's been known to happen too,
in which case I'd be back a lot earlier, but then . . . it has
had rave reviews here, all the American producers love it
and they're really confident that it'll last the course . . .'

Here I go, I thought, vintage Annie. Whenever I've something important to say, an attack of Saint Vitus's dance of
the mouth inevitably strikes.

'I know, I know all that,' he nodded, staring ahead of
him, miles away.

There was a silence but not an easy, comfortable one and I could feel an unwelcome knot of tension beginning to form in the pit of my stomach.

Bad burning feeling like indigestion returned with a vengeance and perspiration slowly started to seep its way from my armpits to my ribs. We'd barely seen each other or even spoken since the Christmas Day row and now I landed this on him?

He broke the silence first.

'Look, I can see that things aren't easy for you . . .'

I didn't give him any argument there. Utterly pointless being polite and plastering over cracks now.

'. . . and I sometimes think that you're unhappy here.'

Then he looked directly at me, his black eyes scanning mine, trying to get a read. .

'Annie, tell me the truth. Are you unhappy?'

And if ever there was a time for heartfelt, gut-wrenching openness, this was it.

'I've been doing my best, I really have . . . but it can be hard going.'

'I can see that . . . and you know how sorry I am for letting you down on Christmas Day . . .'

'It's not just that, Dan, it's . . . out of the blue, this big chance comes along and it's like . . . I can't *not* take this job. I just can't. I know it's selfish, I know I'm putting a job ahead of us and that there's all kinds of rules about that kind of thing if you're married, but . . . if I don't do this, I'll spend the rest of my life wondering what might have happened if I had gone . . . and you know, if we had kids, I wouldn't even be able to consider doing this, so when you think about it, this is probably the last chance I'll ever get to grab an opportunity like this . . .'

118

Suddenly my thoughts became clear and detached. I had to be brutally honest here. After all, Dan put work ahead of me all the time, didn't he?

In the long run, I knew it would be for the best.

'It's for my sanity, as much as anything else.'

There was a long pause, a tense one, like when the jury head out to consider their verdict.

'I see,' was all he said before getting up and going over to the armoire to find a clean T-shirt. He pulled it over his head and slumped into bed, rubbing his eyes with the palms of his hands, always a sign he's genuinely exhausted.

'And for what it's worth,' he said, not able to help himself yawning as the tiredness finally caught up with him, 'I can see where you're coming from. Of course you have to go.'

I sat on the duvet beside him, scarcely able to believe how unbelievably easy that had been. How well he'd taken it.

Scarily well.

'We'll phone each other every day,' I said, slowly beginning to allow myself to get excited now that I had his tacit approval. 'And we'll Skype. And maybe you'll come over for a holiday, when you can get the time?'

'Eh . . . yeah. Sure. That would be great.'

OK, so maybe we both knew that was a polite lie; Dan hasn't taken a holiday or even a night off in three years, but I did appreciate him playing along. The mood between us had shifted a bit too; before it was tense, whereas now it was tender and more mellow. So much so that you'd nearly swear the two of us had knocked back a glass of wine each.

'To be perfectly honest,' he said gently, interrupting my thoughts, 'I think a year away from here will do you the power of good.'

And of course, he's absolutely right. It's not just that I want this job so desperately; it's that I *need* to get away. From Stickens, from The Moorings, from Audrey, from Lisa, from everyone and everything. From the whole lot of them.

Not forever. I just need a sabbatical, that's all.

'I haven't seen you smile in the longest time, Annie Cole,' he said quietly. 'Go, find your smile again.'

And in that second I absolutely knew that everything would be OK. I got into bed beside him, leaned over him to switch off the bedside light and my hand brushed lightly over his chest as I did so. I half wondered if he'd reach out to hold me that night, maybe even if we'd make love, but no.

Two minutes later he was sound asleep and snoring.

I didn't mind though, because somehow I'd found my smile again.

In, of all places, the National theatre.

Always the last place you look.

Chapter Five

Can't remember the last new year that got off to such an amazing start! For the first time in I don't know how long, I'm bouncing around the place, busy and buzzing, full of excitement about getting back into a rehearsal room again. It's like I can see the world in colour again, having lived my life in black and white for so long. In fact, I feel a bit like Dorothy in the *Wizard of Oz*, when the screen suddenly goes from dull monochrome to glorious technicolour.

Don't get me wrong though, it isn't all fun and games. In fact, if anything, it's massive pressure; we only have two weeks to rehearse up in Dublin, then we travel to New York for a week's 'get in' where the set and lighting will have to be rigged at the Shubert Theatre on Broadway. After that, we've a full week of technical rehearsals and that's followed by more than a full, exhaustive month of previews before we open on, of all the red-letter days, Paddy's Day, March the seventeenth.

Rehearsals start at ten am sharp, so I've been on the motorway from Waterford since seven, but I'm feeling more full of energy than I have done in years and absolutely raring to go. In spite of all the passive-aggressive wailing phone calls I've had from Audrey since last night, bemoaning the fact that today is her grocery day and who's going to do all her fetching and carrying for her, with me up in Dublin all week? That of course, led to a follow-on row involving Jules, who now has no choice but to start pulling her weight a bit around the place. The end result of which is that back at The Moorings, I'm about as popular as yesterday's vindaloo. But am I bothered? For once in my life, no.

I've both apologised and explained to everyone that I'm not going to be around as much and shrugged my shoulders in response to all the cries of, 'Oh, but, *Annie!*' Sorry to have to be firm with everyone, but let's face it, it's a pretty good dress rehearsal for when I'm really, properly gone. Which unbelievably, is a mere two weeks away. So close, I think I'm developing yet another duodenal stress ulcer every time I think about it.

Anyway, for my part, I've pretty much spent the entire Christmas holiday reading the script frontways and backways till it's worn, battered and ragged and now, it's time to 'get it on the floor', as actors say. It's early January, but bright and crisp as I arrive into Dublin, all set for day one. Town is just as packed as it was before Christmas, but this time with all the sales shoppers going demented at the sight of red 'reduced to clear' stickers in the windows. I smile to myself, loving the atmosphere and the people-watching and the buzz that's like a stun gun to my soul and think: if this is how exhilarating it is here . . . wait till I get to New York!

I find parking in a car park close to the National and, as I've got time to spare, nip to the little coffee shop across the road to grab a herb tea to go. Anything to try and calm my jittery nerves a bit. Then onto the theatre and . . . it's just extraordinary. Like I'm already part of the team. The lovely receptionist at the stage door greets me with the brightest smile and a big, 'Hey, Annie, Happy New Year! You got the part, congratulations!' I thank her warmly and tell her that I feel like I've just cashed in on the Euromillions Lottery of Life. We're not rehearsing on the stage, she patiently explains to me, as it's getting rigged for the next production; instead we'll be working upstairs in the rehearsal room, at the very top of the building.

So up I troop, all five floors of the way and arrive panting and sweating and needing pints of water and several Kit Kats to recover. And sitting there, all alone and cool as a fish's fart is none other than Jack Gordon. It's just him and me alone in the rehearsal room, no one else has arrived yet and it comes back to me in a sudden blood rush just how elegantly cool and utterly laid-back he is.

He's in a dark navy suit today, with an open-necked shirt on underneath it and is looking so dapper and well put together that you'd nearly swear he was gay, or at the very least metrosexual. Groomed like James Bond, as played by Daniel Craig, if you're with me. Anyway, as soon as I puff and wheeze my way into the room, he's on his feet and strolling lazily over to me to plant light air kisses on each of my cheeks. He smells of expensive cologne and with his smooth, perfectly moisturised skin, it flashes through my mind that he probably has more expensive products and takes better care of his face than I do with my own.

(Simple soap and Nivea are my preferred products of choice due to severe budgetary restrictions in the Ferguson-Cole household.)

'Annie!' he says smoothly, in his deep, twenty fags a day voice as he looks me up and down. 'Welcome aboard. Good to have you here. Broadway, here we come, eh?'

Yet another attack of Saint Vitus's dance of the mouth

as I gush on about how happy I am to be here and how much this job means to me, blah-di-blah-di-blah, but he waves me silent.

'The pleasure, I can assure you, is all mine,' he grins, this time giving me a full panoramic view of his perfect, nuclear-white teeth. No messing, he has one of those smiles that should nearly come with a ping! sound effect.

'From the minute you walked through the door at your first audition,' he says, sitting back down again and casually folding one leg over the other, 'I knew I wanted you. I knew you were just perfect for this part. Apologies for the call-back and for the inordinate delay in getting back to you, but I just had to be certain. You see, I'm a firm believer that shows stand or fall on casting alone.'

Next thing, the most senior cast member comes in, one Blythe Arnold, a sixty-something, silver-haired legend of the theatre and TV scene around here and overall national treasure. In short, our country's answer to Judi Dench. I've seen her in dozens of shows over the years but have never actually met her properly and as we shake hands, I'm struck by the twin illusion of familiarity and strangeness. One of the hardest-working actors in the business, Blythe also appears in a Dublin-based soap opera, playing a wise but loveable granny who's also the local cornershop keeper and who doles out salt of the earth advice to all the younger characters from beneath the rollers she permanently wears. Honest to God, you never heard so much life-wisdom come out from under the same hairnet. Her character is called Nana Hughes and the temptation for me to call her that is just so huge, I have to keep biting my tongue. But she's absolutely lovely, warm and welcoming and says that she's really looking forward to working with me.

124

Next to drift in is Alex O'Hara, who's playing the spa therapist and who's about twenty-two in real life but looks even younger still, almost child-like because of the oversized tracksuit she's wearing which her tiny, wiry body is just lost in. Short, spiky, low-maintenance red hair and not a scrap of make-up, like her DNA is approximately twenty per cent male. With a sinewy, gym-starved look about her too. We both have the same agent and have met each other socially, so meeting her isn't quite as scary as meeting Blythe. She gives me a shy hug, welcomes me on board and says nice complimentary things about a show she remembered seeing me in, oooh, about a hundred years ago.

I like her already.

Then last of all, there's Chris Gardiner, who's playing my older sister and who's probably in her late thirties in real life, with alabaster white skin and long Indian-straight black hair all the way down to her bum. I later discover that apart from myself, she's the only other married woman in the cast – Blythe has long since separated from her husband and Alex and Liz are both single.

Chris and I bond a bit chatting about this, swapping stories about how stressful it was to tell our husbands that we'd be gone for a full year. Turns out her position is far more enviable than mine though; her fella's also an actor who's not working right now, so he's going to come to New York with her and hang out there for as long as his visitor's visa will let him. She's got a little boy too, who's just turned four and he'll stay with his dad while she's working.

'And will your husband come over to the States to see you in action?' she asks me politely. And of course I lie and say that although he's really busy, yes, I'm sure he'll try to find the time, etc. etc.

125

God, if only it were true. But if I'm being honest, I envy Chris and if it doesn't sound awful, I'm starting to half-wish that I was married to someone unemployed too.

Finally Liz bounces in with bed hair, in her leather and lace, early Madonna gear in spite of the fact that it's freezing outside and apologises for being late. 'Overslept!' she laughs at the room, all attitude and laddered tights and I catch the slightest hint of an eye roll from Jack, which makes me think that this might be a fairly regular occurrence. Later on, while we're all standing round looking at a model of the slightly expanded set we're using for the Shubert Theatre, Liz whispers to me that she intended getting an early night last night, but then she got a phone call at the last minute and ended up hitting the town for a few drinks instead.

'Never thought vodka and beer would be such happy bedfellows,' she hisses in my ear, 'but I was happy to be there at their birth. Please say that you've got Solpadeine in your bag, Annie? Dear Jaysus, my head's in agony. I swear, there isn't this much pain in the burns unit of an A and E.'

Anyroadup, Jack settles us all down and we sit around a table to do a full read-through of the play. Which is mostly for my benefit and must surely be a massive bore for everyone else here, given that it's only Christmas week since they finished performing it, but Jack is insistent. Then he talks through a few of the plot points and scenes that he feels could benefit from some extra work and everyone throws in their tuppence worth. I'm the new girl, so I just sit quietly, eyes wide open, mouth shut tight.

Interesting though, being a relative outsider and observing the group dynamic. With Blythe, everyone is respectful and courteous; with Alex, they all seem to josh and slag her off the whole time, which she takes good-naturedly enough. Chris is one of those women who demand respect and tend to get it from all around her, while the entire room just laughs at Liz, like she's the company's very own Tina Fey. The only person who treats everyone exactly the same is Jack. And as for me? Well, my role appears to be as the straight man to all of these fascinating, scintillating objects whirling around me.

After the read-through, we're straight up onto the rehearsal room floor, which has practice chairs and sun loungers dotted all around it for us to rehearse on, exactly like the set proper. And so we start 'blocking', which basically involves being told where I come in, where I stand and when I sit, etc. Tedious as arse for everyone else, all of whom can recite the play inside out, but in fairness, not one of them makes me feel like I'm stuck back in remedial acting class. I frantically scribble down all my moves and try to get it right and not bump into the furniture . . . easier said than done with my nose shoved into a script, which I'm frankly clinging onto for dear life.

However, if the others thought they were in for a dossy, jammy day while the new girl got broken in this morning, they had another think coming. Jack goes through the opening scene with a fine toothcomb, honing it down finely and coming back to parts of it that he wants to try differently. Over and over again we play just that one opening scene, till by lunchtime, not only have I got all the moves down pat, but I'm pretty much off the script as well.

Interesting, watching the mighty Jack Gordon at work too – he may give the surface impression of being laid-back and cool, but he's actually an obsessive, ferocious perfectionist; trying things this way and that, ruthlessly throwing out anything that doesn't work even if some of the cast protest that they've 'always done it that way before and it's never been a problem'.

I can detect elements of a bully in him too, but unlike most bullies, it's not rooted in malice or in sheer bloody mindedness, it's because he just cares so passionately about the show and desperately wants it to be as good as it can be. Chris in particular tries it on with him a number of times, constantly standing up to him, challenging him and bossily demanding to know why he's changing things that are working perfectly fine as they are.

'I don't get it, Jack,' she says to him loudly and sternly, arms folded, 'if it ain't broke, don't fix it.'

Silence around the rehearsal room and although Jack doesn't actually lose his temper with her, the eyebrows knit downwards, giving him that slightly dangerous, satyr look. And a mightily pissed off satyr at that too.

'Except that it didn't quite work, did it, darling?' he flung back at her, the eyes cold and mocking. God, he can even caress the word 'darling' and still manage to make it sound like a veiled insult.

No, Jack Gordon is not someone you cross. The only person in the room he leaves alone is me. For the moment.

Come lunchtime and everyone drifts off their separate ways for the hour-long break. It was my intention to run out, grab a sandwich, then come back here while the rehearsal room was quiet and get stuck into some more line-learning on my own, but Liz stays glued to my side. So the pair of us stroll to the deli across the road, grab some take-out grub, then head back to the rehearsal room; Liz tucking into her bacon sarnie hungrily, as only someone with a crucifying hangover can.

God, I miss being young and carefree like her, when all it took to put the world to rights was an all-day breakfast roll, a packet of crisps and a cappuccino.

'So what do you make of our Jack, then?' she probes me between stuffing her face with mouthfuls of the bacon and cheese sarnie.

'Jack? Well . . . I've a feeling that he's just going easy on me for the minute,' I half-grin back at her, 'but I'm pretty confident my turn in front of the firing squad will surely come.'

'No, you're getting me wrong,' she says, gulping the cappuccino. 'I meant did you think he was attractive or not.'

There is just no right answer to that question, so I say nothing, just munch innocuously away on a ham sandwich. She's looking at me expectantly though, so with my mouth full and making um-nom-nom-nom noises I rummage round for the right thing to say, then eventually mumble, 'Seems very charming.'

'Runs in the family. His grandfather was a snake.'

'Stop taking the piss.'

'Reason I ask is because I always think he's one of those fundamentally unlikeable guys that women always seem to end up falling for,' she goes on. 'It's hard not to, he's just so completely sexy. Even I can see it, and I've just about zero interest in the guy.'

I don't answer her, just wipe away a blob of mustard from my chin.

'Personally though,' she goes on, 'I think he has nothing but disdain for all women. He excels at saying things that he doesn't mean. Like, "I'll call you." Tell you something, if I could have a proper chat with that little one from the box office he's supposedly going out with, I'd tell her that the surest way to get the Jack Gordons of this world eating out of your hand is to treat them like shite under your feet. That's the only proven way to guarantee that they'll come running back for more. Which is why men like Jack always end up with such complete bitches.'

'Listen to you, the dating oracle.'

'Jack, let me tell you,' she says, burping out loud then laughing, 'is on my top ten list of guys that I categorically don't fancy, who don't fancy me back and yet I can see, clear as day, why they're attractive as hell to other women. Oh, here's a good one for you, name this one if you dare: "the first time you view a house, you see how pretty the paint is and buy it. The second time you look to see if the basement has termites. It's the same with men."'

'Ahh, Lizzie, not the quotation game . . . not today! My nerves are shot, I can barely think straight!'

'You're only chickening out because you don't know the right answer. Lupe Velez, FYI. I thought it was an apt quote because it kind of puts you in mind of our Jack, doesn't it?'

The afternoon session is even more intense, as we block the second scene of the show, going through it over and over again exhaustively. Come half five, when we finish up, I'm bone tired, but ecstatic at how well my first proper day went. In fact, during the whole long drive back to The Sticks, all I can think is that I've got the luckiest, jammiest job on the face of the earth. No wonder they call actors players. Because that's what it feels like: grown ups at play-time.

Anyroadup, come Friday evening, and the rest of the cast are all off to the local pub for a well-earned drink, to celebrate the end of a long week. We're all standing out on the pitch dark, icy cold street outside the National and I'm saying my goodbyes to everyone, to cries of, 'Ah, no don't go home yet, Annie! Come for just the one!'

I'm just in the middle of protesting that I've still got the marathon drive back to Waterford ahead of me and that I'd better get a move on if I want to get home sometime before dawn, when next thing, Jack grabs my elbow and steers me across the road and right into the pub, brooking no disagreement.

'Come on, one soft drink won't kill you,' he grins, flashing the megawatt smile at me. 'Besides, I want to talk to you.'

So I shrug and laugh and head into the pub with everyone else, under director's orders it seems. Jack politely asks everyone what they're having as Liz, Blythe, Alex and Chris pile into a quiet little booth and start peeling off layers of coats, hats and jackets, all giggling and laughing, all in great form and happy to be celebrating the end of a long, tough week.

'Annie, give me a hand with the drinks, will you?' Jack calls after me, so I obediently head back to the bar to wait with him there. The place is packed with Friday night boozers, students mostly, all in jeans, woolly hats and layers of scraggy jumpers. For a second it strikes me just how much Jack stands out against them, in his elegant tailored suit and pale blue shirt that somehow still manages to look as crisp and fresh as it did at ten o'clock this morning.

'I didn't want to say this in front of the others,' he begins, not looking at me, intent on grabbing the busy barman's attention, 'but you really did a great week's work, you know.

You're bringing a whole plethora of new layers to the character that I think will work out beautifully. So I just wanted to say well done and keep it up.'

'Wow . . . emmm . . . thanks so much,' I manage to stammer, totally unused to positive reinforcement. And this from the impossible-to-please Jack Gordon of all people?!

'I mean it,' he goes on, waving impatiently at the barman now. 'And believe me, I'm not a man who gives praise lightly. I think you're bringing a whole fresh new dynamic to the show and I'm very happy I cast you.'

I'm stunned into silence at this. I glance over to where Liz is sitting and she throws me an are-you-OK-do-you-need-rescuing-type glance, so I quickly grin back to reassure her that all's fine.

'But let me assure you, my dear,' he grins cheekily, 'that's probably the last civil thing you'll hear from me till opening night.'

I smile back thinking that this sounds more like the Jack Gordon I know, but it's almost a full month before I realise he's actually telling the God's honest truth. Anyway, the barman comes and he orders, then as we're waiting, he turns to face me full on, propping himself up against the bar with one elbow and completely changing the subject.

'So you really live all the way down in *Waterford*?'

He couldn't have sounded more disbelieving if I'd said I happened to live on a halting site somewhere outside Pluto. I tell him yes and he interrupts me immediately.

'And do you mean to tell me that you've been commuting up and down from there all week?'

'Well . . . yeah, but it's nothing really, I'm well used to it by now. Motorway for most of it, you know . . .'

'I don't particularly care if it's a Grand Prix track for

132

most of it, I won't have you tiring yourself out like that. That's what, five hours a day you've been spending behind the wheel of a car? On top of working like a dog for me at the National all day? Not on.'

'Jack, it's fine, really . . .'

'It most certainly is not fine. And next week is going to be even harder, because I want to start running each act as a whole. Can't you stay with some friend in Dublin? How about Liz? She's a mate of yours, isn't she?'

I don't actually say anything, just smile weakly at this. Mainly because if I were to stay with Liz for the week, chances are I'd end up crashing out on the passenger seat of my car, on the grounds that I'd probably get far more peace and quiet there.

He's looking at me directly now, his sharp blue eyes expecting an answer.

'You see, I'm afraid I can't just stay up in Dublin, Jack,' I eventually say. 'It's . . . well, let's just say, it's complicated.'

'I'm reasonably confident that I can keep up with you. Go on, explain why.'

'Well, you see . . . it's our last week before we go away for so long and, emmmm . . . I'm anxious to spend as much time as I possibly can with my husband.'

'Oh, your husband. Yeah. I keep forgetting you're married. You don't act married.'

I'm tempted to ask how exactly married women act anyway? Do they go around in a housecoat, a hairnet and rollers, phoning and texting their husbands forty times a day, whenever they're not worrying about the gas bill? But I keep my mouth shut and unconsciously start playing with my wedding ring.

'OK, well at least I see where you're coming from. And

no doubt your husband will want you around as much as possible next week.'

'Yeah, yes, he will. I mean, yes, he does, of *course* he does,' I smile brightly.

Funny how easy the lie just tripped off the tongue.

Then my mind wanders back to all the Post-it notes that have been waiting for me on the fridge for the past few days and I half wonder if next week will be any different. This morning's was a particular beaut: as I left the house at dawn, Dan had left a note for me that read, 'Think the cat might be constipated. Can you monitor her litter tray and let me know?'

'How long have you been married for, then?'

'Almost five years.'

'You must have been very young when you took the plunge.'

'We were both twenty-four. But we'd been together ever since we were fifteen. I was his first girlfriend and he was my first boyfriend. And until this job came along, we've basically never been apart, in all that time.'

TMI as Jules would say about people who tweet too much. Too much information. Don't even know why I bothered telling Jack all that, he doesn't even seem to be listening to me, he's just staring into the middle distance, miles away. All I know is that he's making me nervous and I don't know why. For some reason, I don't act like myself when it's just him and me, alone.

'So you were childhood sweethearts,' he eventually says.

'Yeah, we were. I mean, yeah, we are.'

'Very romantic.'

'Yeah, it was. I mean . . . of course it is.'

'Never had the urge to tie any knots and get married

myself, you know. Just couldn't see the bloody point. All that stuff about till death do us part? In this day and age? Marry in your early twenties and I can guarantee that by your mid-thirties you're two completely different people. Because people change over time. We all do.'

'When you meet your one true soul mate, it's different,' I say, flushing and getting a bit defensive now.

'How quick married people are to justify the ties that bind them.'

'It's not like that, Dan and I aren't in any way . . . *manacled* to each other . . .'

'So he's called Dan then?'

'Yes, he is.'

'And you seriously expect me to believe that you and Dan are both exactly the same people you were at aged fifteen? That neither of you has changed one single iota in all this time?'

'It hardly matters whether you believe it or not, the fact is that it's true,' I smile back at him. 'Just because you don't happen to believe in marriage doesn't mean that it's a useless institution.'

'Marriage is punishment for shoplifting in some countries, you know.'

'Tell me you don't really believe that?'

'Oh please. So you believe in marriage? And tell me, do you still believe in the tooth fairy as well?'

'We're talking about love, not Santa Claus or the tooth fairy, of course I believe in it.'

He's teasing me now, I know right well he is, and I also know I'm flushing to my roots. I just don't get it; why is this guy turning a perfectly ordinary conversation into a duel of wits?

'Look, it's like this,' he says, scrutinising me carefully, the satyr eyebrows knitted sharply together. 'Getting married is a bit like saying, I know exactly what I'm going to be wearing in twenty-five years' time. But you can't possibly know that, no one can. To torture the metaphor, it means that flares would still be in fashion. Not a life for me, I can tell you.'

'Jack, let me just get this straight. You're honestly comparing marriage to flares?'

'No, I'm just saying, commitment isn't for everyone. Particularly a long-distance one. Then you're really asking for it.'

'When you really love someone, you'll move heaven and earth to make it work,' I say primly.

'Glad you seem to think so, my dear,' he replies smoothly. 'And I'll be watching your progress throughout the coming year with the greatest of interest.'

Chapter Six

And now, somehow, it's the night before I'm leaving and I can't quite believe it. My very last evening. Two suitcases are all packed and neatly lined up in the hall and I'm wondering if it's stabbing Dan as much as it is me, just seeing them sitting there. Looking like two twin accusations.

You turned out not to be such a great husband after all and now look what's happened. You see? This is the price you pay for neglecting your wife. You may have thought this whole going to New York thing was no more than an idle threat but look . . . HA! Here we are, proof that it wasn't. So now the laugh's on you, mate, isn't it? . . . they almost scream in my head every single time I walk past them, driving me so out of my mind with guilt that I end up shoving them into the boot of the car, just so I don't have to look at the shagging things any more.

I have a totally irrational Pavlovian response to packed suitcases, you see; they never fail to give me an instant memory flashback to when I was five years old, freshly back from an overseas posting with Mum when out of the blue, my dad casually informed us that he was about to move out.

Course I was too young to take it all in; how could this

137

be happening? Me and Mum and Dad were the three Musketeers, why would Dad want to leave us? D'Artagnan and Aramis wouldn't be any use without Porthos, would they? Vivid memory to this day; the enormity of the whole thing not even hitting me until I saw his packed suitcases waiting by the hall door. Then I came crawling back upstairs and cried myself to sleep, knowing then that my dad was really, really going for good.

And I know it's ridiculous, but this feels exactly the same; like I'm leaving Dan, even though of course we both know that I'm not. This is just temporary time apart, that's what I keep telling myself, over and over again. It's all transitory and I'll probably be back before it really hits him that I've even left.

I have to say though, in his own way, Dan has really surprised me and come up trumps, promising me that not only has he cleared his schedule so we can have this last, precious night together, but that he'll also drive me all the way to Dublin airport tomorrow too. Equally important to me, as I've spent so much time talking about him to the others in the cast that I really want them all to meet him properly before we leave. He knows Liz, of course, but not the others, and it means an awful lot to me that they'll at least be able to put a face to his name.

Anyroadup, it's a Sunday evening, the surgery is closed, so the only thing that might possibly keep us apart tonight is some last-minute emergency farm call. But James, our intern, has very kindly offered to take the phones this one night, so unbelievably, it is actually . . . for once . . . looking like Dan and I will have . . . pause for dramatic effect . . . this last, precious night alone together.

You just wouldn't believe the bother I've gone to. I've

decided not to cook for once, but instead to order some take-away grub from the Chinese restaurant in the village that Dan loves so much. (I'm not joking, the food there is so delicious that you just want to drool over it saying, '*hellooooooo, Clarice*,') I've even splashed out on a bottle of really pricey Chateau Margaux because it's what we drank at our wedding reception and we loved it and I want tonight to be another blissfully happy memory, just like the wedding was.

Because I've planned this evening with military precision – this is to be a night of sex and seduction like we haven't had in years. I've dotted placed flickering candles all over the drawing room, not only because it makes the place look so romantic, but dim lighting also helps to minimise the full glaring horror of Audrey's grotesque wallpaper and plaid carpet. Plus I look better in flickering light and this is how I want Dan to remember me; a sex kitten wife, and not this pale, exhausted wreck, nervous as a turkey at Christmas about what lies ahead. For the first time in years, I'm even wearing stockings. And OK, so I might look a bit like a bad Christmas, but what the hell; we need this last night and by God, if it's the last thing we do, I'm determined that we're both going to enjoy it. Just the two of us.

Earlier in the day, I made a point of calling round to Audrey's apartment in the village, to say goodbye to her properly.

Now if there's one thing I've learned about my esteemed mother-in-law ever since I got this job, it's this: in order to really rub in her utter disapproval of my taking off, sulking has become her preferred form of attrition. My phone has totally stopped ringing, almost deafening me with its silence and if I happened to give her a duty phone call from rehearsals to see if she needed anything dropped into her on my way home from work, she'd just sniff that she was perfectly fine, then hang up on me, making full sure that she really, *really* laid the guilt trip on with a trowel.

So I steeled myself to make the farewell courtesy call just to show that there were no hard feelings on my side, although why I bothered, I don't know. She didn't even bother to lower the volume on the TV and when I tried to give her a peck on her papery thin cheek to say goodbye, she pointedly turned the other way, nose parallel to the ceiling.

But when I got back to The Moorings Jules was there, thank God, sitting at the kitchen table eating the remains of last night's chicken curry . . . the perfect antidote. She was an absolute doll and told me not to pay the slightest bit of attention to the old gizzard, that it would all blow over soon enough. Then, bless her, when she copped on that I'd a whole romantic night of passion planned, she tactfully offered to make herself scarce and, for once, I didn't argue.

We hugged in the hallway and because we both hate and despise the finality of goodbyes, Jules promised to call over to The Moorings the next morning before we left for Dublin airport, so we could say a last final farewell. But we both knew that this was just a polite, face-saving lie; the airport check-in time was one pm latest, which meant leaving The Sticks at around ten am, and bar her house was on fire, there's just no way on earth she'd ever be able to haul herself out of bed at that ungodly hour.

I squeezed her, tearing up a bit and told her that I'd see her in New York.

'You better believe it, bitch!' she laughed, but I knew

right well she was getting a bit wobbly too. Jules doesn't often have adult emotions but I think she had one this afternoon, knowing I really was going and that she'd really be left totally alone, with only Audrey for company.

I felt a massive pang of sympathy for the poor girl and there and then resolved to pay for her flight to New York myself, as soon as I'd saved up enough, then give her the time of her life when she got there.

Least I could do for my old ally.

It's now just past seven and Dan is only out at Paddy Jackson's farm, which isn't far away, only about five miles or so. It's not an emergency call either, so I'm confident he'll be home any minute now. In the meantime, I'm running demented around the house, frantically ticking off a last-minute checklist in my head.

Fire blazing cosily away? Check. Scented candles tastefully dotted around the drawing room? Check. Me scrubbed, exfoliated, waxed and polished to within an inch of my life? Check. Wearing my one and only sexy 'serial result' black lace nightie with matching flouncy dressing gown, courtesy of Marks & Spencer? Check. Half a can of serum in my bushy, wild hair in an effort to get it to sit flat? Check. Chinese take-away on speed dial? Check.

I'm just up in the bedroom squirting a bottle of Jo Malone Fresh Lime Blossom perfume into a haze, then walking through it, when I hear a car scrunch up on the gravel drive outside.

Showtime.

I race down the stairs, yelling out, 'On the way, love! I'm coming . . .' trip over to the front door and just as I'm stretching up to the ancient overhead bolt to yank it back, one of those random, worrying thoughts suddenly flashes through my mind . . . why don't I hear the dogs barking? Dan took them out with him this afternoon and they always go mental whenever they get home . . . odd.

Quick as I can, I push the heavy oak door open . . . and standing there, looking as pale and pinched as ever is none other than Lisa Ledbetter. The Countess Dracula herself.

'Look at the state of you, Annie,' is her snide little opener when she sees how I'm dressed. 'Don't you know that it's below freezing outside? Put on something warm or you'll get pneumonia.'

She tries to push past me but for once I don't let her. I block her way, with my arms folded and my face I'm sure looking like thunder at this intrusion. Rude, I know. Unwelcoming, I know, but just this once I don't happen to care. This is my last precious night with Dan for God knows how long and she is NOT going to hijack it on me. Over my dead body. So I just stand in front of her, pointedly not inviting her in and I'm sure, given the way I'm dressed, looking a bit like the madam of a brothel in an amateur production of *The Best Little Whorehouse in Texas*.

'Lisa,' I manage to say as evenly as I can, 'I didn't expect to see you . . .'

'Don't be so ridiculous, Annie, it's your last night! Did you honestly think that I was going to let you disappear off to the States without at least giving you an American wake?'

Shit, she intends staying then. Oh who am I kidding? This is the Countess Dracula, of course she intended to stay all along. I hold firm though and for once don't let her bulldoze over me.

She looks at me, irritated.

'So are you going to let me in or what, Annie? In case you hadn't noticed, it's bloody freezing out here.'

''Fraid not, Lisa. Really, really bad time. Couldn't be worse. I'm expecting Dan home any minute now and I've sort of planned a dinner for the two for us. *Just* for the two of us, unfortunately. But it's sweet of you to call and I'll tell you what, why don't I ring you before I leave in the morning . . .'

'Oh for God's sake, will you kindly let me in and stop being so bloody dismissive? Don't worry, I'll leave as soon as Dan gets home . . .'

I take this with the massive pinch of salt it deserves; the Countess Dracula has never once in her entire life under-stayed her welcome. One good thing though, if I'm not going to see Dan again in so long, I certainly won't have to look at this one either, so does it really matter if I'm discourtesy itself right now?

'Lisa,' I say, trying my best to stand tall in my ridiculous little fluffy slippers, 'ordinarily, you'd be more than welcome, but not this evening. Sorry, but it's my last night and I really had plans to spend it with my husband. Alone. Anyway, I'd really better get going . . .'

She looks at me a bit winded, totally unused to my standing up to her and for one brief, shining moment I think I've actually won the day when next thing, the hall phone starts ringing.

'Probably him,' I say curtly, glaring at her with what I can only hope is a look of chilled steel. 'So if you don't mind, Lisa, I'd better get going, but thanks so much for thinking of mc . . .'

'Oh, don't be so ridiculous, do you know all the trouble I went to to get out this evening? I had to practically strong-arm Charlie into babysitting the kids for the night so if you think I'm letting this free pass go to waste, then you've another think coming. Now, for the last time, will you kindly let me in before I catch my death standing out here? One quick little glass of wine, and then I'll go.'

I'm glaring at her now, white anger bubbling up inside me, fighting the impulse to tell her a few home truths. I want to yell at her that she annoys me more than a little . . . oh and by 'more than a little', I actually mean more than any person I ever met in my life, ever.

I want to tell her that I'm calling an end to this pretence of a friendship because she's not a friend at all and never has been, she's a frenemy of the worst kind. And most of all . . .

Shit and double shit. Just as I'm mentally tearing strips off her, the answering machine in the hallway clicks in.

It's Dan.

But even though I race to pick up the phone, I don't get to the shagging thing in time, and his voice starts to reverberate around the massive stone hallway, echoing so loudly that Lisa hears him too, loud and clear.

'Hi Annie? It's me. Are you there? Look, I was on my way home when James rang to say that he'd had an emergency call-out to Paul Fogarty's . . . he thinks one of his fillies is suffering from early parturition . . .'

My heart sinks. Even I know what that means. A miscarriage. Which means Dan could be out for hours more, at the very least.

'. . . James can't possibly handle this on his own, so it's going to be a while longer before I get back . . .'

I manage to snatch the phone up before he says more and we talk a bit more privately. Well, as privately as I can given that the Countess Dracula has now jubilantly let herself in, whammed the hall door shut behind her and is now standing right beside me, peeling off layers of jumpers and scarves.

'I'm so sorry about this,' Dan says to me, 'I really wanted to be there for you tonight, you know that . . .'

'I know that,' I say, trying to mask my disappointment. 'Don't worry, it can't be helped. I understand.'

'It's just that James is way too inexperienced to deal with this, and Paul is terrified he'll end up losing the mare . . .'

'It's fine. Just do what you can and I'll be here when you get home, OK?'

He's driving as he's talking and we lose the signal then. Just as I'm thinking, OK, for this last night, I'll still be here when you get home, but . . . well . . . after tonight . . . then that'll be all, folks, won't it?

'You see?' says Lisa triumphantly. 'He's held up at work, so now aren't you delighted that I stopped by? I couldn't in all conscience let you spend your last evening sitting here all on your own, now could I?'

With that, she's flung open the drawing room door, taking the whole room in at a glance.

'Oh look! Lovely roaring fire and what's this? A bottle of Chateau Margaux? Only my very favourite wine ever! How did you know? Run and get us two glasses, will you, Annie? My tongue's hanging out for a glass of vino.'

Sure, Lisa, no problem, Lisa. Any other orders, Mussolini?

The shrillness of my mobile phone alarm wakes me up the next morning and I spring up, coming to with a heart-stopping jerk. Dan is beside me, completely out for the count, sleeping in the shape of someone who's been crucified. Swear to God, I was so wiped out going to bed that I never even heard him come in last night.

The Countess Dracula of course, stayed till well past midnight, ignoring my yawns, knocking back most of the fancy wine and bitching about everyone she'd ever met in her entire life ever. And after she'd finally gone, somehow I crawled to bed, feeling like I'd been run over by a steamroller, drained and wrecked as I always am after prolonged exposure to her company.

No, not the final night I had planned at all. Half of me wonders if I should wake Dan up for a last final seduction scene, but given that he probably didn't get home till all hours, it just seems like meanness of the highest order to even think about taking advantage of him so shamelessly. He's hardly my sexual bon voyage card, now is he? Plus, he's probably so wrecked, it would be a bit like doing it with a corpse.

So, shivering with cold and still wearing my un-ripped off sexy nightie, I head for the bathroom and hop into the shower. Anyway, by the time I'm scrubbed clean with my hair washed, he's up and dressed, still in our room and looking at me with a funny combination of deep exhaustion and . . . something else. An expression I haven't seen on his face in so long that I barely recognise it. Takes me a minute or two to cop onto what it is.

It's guilt. Pure and simple.

'Annie . . . I can't apologise to you enough about last night,' he says gently, moving towards me. 'I know you had plans for us, but . . . you see, there's just no way I could have left James to handle the filly on his own . . .'

'I know and it's fine, really . . .'

'You must hate me, and if you don't . . . then what's wrong with you?'

I smile, unable to remember the last time he even attempted to crack a joke with me.

'So what happened to Paul's horse in the end?'

'We lost her.'

'Oh . . . I'm so sorry.'

'At least it was for the best that I was there; poor old James has never had to put an animal to sleep before and your first time is always tough as hell. Anyway I took care of it for him, then ended up staying with Paul for a long time afterwards to calm him down. He's devastated, but then you know what he's like over his horses. Like surrogate kids.'

I nod silently, completely understanding where he's coming from. It doesn't seem like all that long ago when Dan himself had to put his first animal to sleep and I'm not messing, he grieved for days, torturing himself over and over again by asking the one question all vets have to deal with sooner or later – 'could I have done more?'

He's standing right beside me now, towering over me as always, and next thing, he's slipped his arms round my waist. Instinctively I lean into him, snuggling into the deep, comforting, pulsating warmth of him, and we stay like that, peacefully and in silence. It's tiny, it's nothing, but it's the closest and most tender we've been in weeks, ever since Christmas morning.

I think, OK, so if we can't part as lovers, then let's at least part as friends. There are yards of things that I want to say to him but this is the first soft, intimate moment we've had in an age and I don't want to cast a ripple over it. Plenty of time on the long drive to Dublin for us to talk.

To say what needs to be said, to say goodbye properly. For now, I just want to hold him, to hoard him, to memorise him.

Next thing, he's running his fingers through my hair and I'm stretching up to kiss him.

'Oh Annie, my little Annie. What in the hell am I supposed to do without you?'

For all of about three seconds I contemplate not going at all.

I think about staying here with Dan instead. My mainspring. I think about trying harder to make things work . . . making more of an effort . . .

'DAN? ANNIE? ARE YOU BOTH STILL UPSTAIRS? I JUST WONDERED IF YOU BOTH WANTED TEA BEFORE YOU LEFT FOR THE AIRPORT?'

Mrs Brophy and just like that . . . mood instantly shattered. Hot on her heels, we both hear James and Andrew clattering in through the front door, demanding tea/juices/breakfast/whatever's going. All the normal Monday morning chaos.

'There's our cue,' he sighs and I can feel him lightly kissing my hair. Next thing, we've broken apart as he goes downstairs to them, while I do a last-minute check of the bedroom and bathroom, making sure I've left nothing behind.

The goodbyes downstairs are brief and to the point, like I'm just heading off for a long weekend and will be back before anyone even notices I'm gone. No rudeness intended, it's just that as per usual, the phones have started hopping and everyone is suddenly swept up in the usual pandemonium that's all part of life at The Moorings.

Virtually unnoticed, Dan and I walk side by side to the

car, him carrying my heavy carry-on luggage for me and easily swinging it up into the boot. Car door clunks and we're off. Our last and final two hours together for a full year. I have it all planned out; that he'll walk me right up to the boarding gates . . . I'll finally get to introduce him to Blythe and Chris and Alex, to prove to them that I actually really do have a husband and that he really does exist, thanks very much. That we'll have coffee and hold hands and kiss passionately at the point of no return, when they're calling my flight. We'll be like a couple in a nineteen forties black-and-white movie, I think romantically, like *Brief Encounter*, with him starring as Trevor Howard and me as Celia Johnson.

But surprise surprise, it's not to be. Practically the minute we get onto the motorway, his mobile rings. Paul Fogarty, from last night, asking Dan if he and James can bury the mare that had to be put to sleep last night, that between the three of them they should be about able to manage it. Course, Dan says obligingly, except I'm on my way to Dublin airport now and won't get back to Stickens till lunchtime at the earliest, blah-di-blah-di-blah. I hear the whole conversation playing out like a radio play on Dan's hands-free phone. But burying the mare will take hours and will have to be done before nightfall, insists Paul, the subtext being that Dan better dump me at the drop-off bit of the airport, then race back.

Ooo-kaaay then, I think numbly. So no coming inside the terminal to meet all the others, then. No romantic farewell at the boarding gate. Jeez, it's a minor miracle I even got him to drive me to Dublin in the first place.

Then other clients start calling him, non-stop, one after the other, it seems every single one of them yet another emergency: more and more people demanding a piece of him. And it's the same, old same old. By now, we're almost halfway there and we've barely said two words to each other.

'Sorry about this,' he keeps saying to me over and over, and I nod and manage a watery smile as I stare dully out the window.

'By the way, Annie, when we get there, is it OK if I just drop you at the terminal door? Paul really needs me ASAP and that'll be another two hours' drive back.'

'Fine. Whatever.'

I even throw in a shoulder shrug to convey complete flippancy. Because if saying goodbye means so little to him, then why should it mean so much to me? What did I expect anyway? I think, suddenly, irrationally furious. That Dan might . . . perish the thought . . . switch off his mobile so we could have this last, precious time together? And of course, the usual thing, not his fault . . . can't be helped . . . all beyond his control . . . yadda, yadda, yadda. I rummage round for a feeling but can't find a single one. Nothing but the same dull acceptance of everything I've been putting up with, year in, year out. Of all the disappointments and let-downs he's put me through lately, this is a relatively minor one, so why, I wonder, am I even bothered?

Worst of all though, for the brief spells when he's not on the phone, we've got nothing to say to each other. Me because I can't seem to properly articulate everything that's going through my head right now, while he just stares tensely at the road ahead, occasionally filling awkward, dead air by commenting on the traffic. No mention of the fact that I'm going away for so long, no promises to call me when I arrive, no talk of him coming to New York to see me, nothing.

150

Then disaster; when we finally arrive at the turn-off for the airport, there's been an accident on a roundabout, and the traffic is backed up for what looks like half a mile. It's not budging either and now it's getting scarily close to check-in time.

Next thing an empty taxi pulls up beside us which Dan spots immediately.

'Annie, I could be stuck here for another hour at least and you're going to be late . . . what if you grabbed that cab and let it take you the rest of the way? At least the driver could use the bus lanes so you'd get to the airport on time. Then I could turn the car round here and make it back to help out Paul that bit faster.'

Seems I've no choice if I want to make the flight so I say yes, fine.

And so this is how I end up saying goodbye to Dan. On a busy motorway in the middle of a traffic jam, with car horns blaring all round us.

The airport scene is even worse. I've often thought that airports are like giant amphitheatres of emotion, with security lines and check-in desks designed to interrupt the sheer awfulness of being wrenched apart from loved ones. Designed to muffle the pain of separation.

As soon as I get to the terminal building, I can see Chris hugging her husband and little boy, all three of them in tears and I feel a quick stab of jealousy. Because they'll all be reunited again in a few weeks for the opening night. Whereas God only knows when I'll see my significant other again.

Blythe is here too, wearing a coat that looks like it was made out of cut-up bus seats and sniffling away as she bids her thirty-something son/pride and joy goodbye. But then she brightens a bit when she realises she still has duty-free ahead of her to bargain hunt in.

No sign of Liz, so I figure she's either gone on through to clear security or else knowing her, she's already holed up in the airside bar, doubtless with an eye-opener on one side of her and a single man on the other. Then I spot Alex in the distance heading for a bookshop, with a giant oversized backpack strapped to her and looking to all intents and purposes like she's going off InterRailing for her gap year.

'Hubby not here to see you off, then?' says a voice at my ear, nearly making me leap with fright.

Jack.

Looking as effortlessly cool and unruffled as ever, in a bespoke suit, carrying an ipad in one hand and a latte in the other.

'He was . . . that is to say . . . emm . . . we got stuck in traffic outside the airport, so I jumped in a cab to take me the rest of the way,' I manage to say evenly enough and without any tell-tale cracks in my voice.

'Good last weekend together though?' he asks politely, keeping pace with me as I make my way through the crowds to the Aer Lingus check-in desk.

'Wonderful,' I lie stoutly, wondering why I'm even bothering. What does it matter now? Who even cares?

'And I'll finally get to meet him on opening night, of course?'

'Of course you will.'

Which sounds false, even to me.

'Well, I'll see you on board then. God, don't you just hate airline travel? God's way of making you look like your passport photo.'

I force a wry half smile at this, but luckily there's no further awkward chit-chat though, as Jack is flying Premier class and so after a few more wisecracks about having to practically get half undressed at airport security, he nods goodbye, then makes for the posh check-in desk – the one with no queue, where you just sail through.

I queue up at economy, collect my boarding pass and head for the security gates.

And then, totally alone, I head through the gate of no return.

SPRING

Chapter Seven

Stop the world, I want to get on! It's unbelievable. It's extraordinary. I'm in love. Head over heels in love. But not with a bloke, with New York City. And just like any first love, it's the most massive and overwhelming head rush. It's completely swept me up in its wake and I cannot remember the last time in my life that I was this ridiculously, insanely bird-happy. I actually wake up singing, like some demented cartoon heroine; in fact, all I'm short of is a little Disney robin landing on my shoulder and helping me do the laundry, *à la Snow White.*

Something tells me that New York and I are going to be a lifelong affair. It's not just the vibrant energy of the place I love, the exuberance, the way that everyone is in such a mad, tearing haste twenty-four-seven, it's so, so much more.

Now bear in mind that I've just spent the last three years of my life in a remote country village where the giddy height of excitement might either be Bridie McCoy getting her bunions lanced or else Fagan's pub being raided after hours yet again, ho hum. And to come from all of that to all of this? It's just so breathtaking and exhilarating and though I'm practically sleepwalking with exhaustion from jetlag, not to mention all the technical rehearsals we've been having, I swear there are nights when I can't bring myself to conk out; I'm just too buzzed up on the sheer adrenaline rush of actually being here.

Funny, but even though I had one flying trip here years and years ago with Dan, another lifetime ago when we first got engaged, this still feels like my first proper visit. Probably because he and I barely left our hotel room on that holiday – we were so revoltingly, toe-curlingly loved-up that we existed only in a little cocoon of our own making, completely oblivious to our surroundings. In fact, we could have been on Mars and frankly neither one of us would have noticed.

But now that I'm actually spending a decent amount of time here and really seeing New York without the love goggles . . . oh my God, it's even more than I could have ever possibly imagined it to be. Weird, but in many ways, it already seems so familiar to me from watching a thousand movies shot here, not to mention the entire box set of *Sex and the City*. Like every time I turn a corner, I nearly expect to trip over a camera crew shooting an episode of *Gossip Girl*.

If every city has its own unique smell, then New York's has to be strong coffee and pretzels and the sweet fresh smell of challah bread from the thousands of delis you pass on each and every street corner, all somehow mixed in with the stale smell of sweaty, hassled pedestrians who power walk up and down the city's streets and avenues, twenty-four-seven. And it's fab and I love it and somehow all the problems of home just seem to be a million miles away.

If all that wasn't amazing enough, you want to see the apartments where we've all been billeted for the duration of the show! They're right beside each other in a stunning, art deco, nineteen twenties building on Madison Avenue at East Forty-Fifth Street, only a stone's throw from Fifth Avenue and a short hop to the theatre. Sorry, ahem, I mean *theater.*

The even-more-phenomenal news is that unlike most rentals in the city, they're not studio apartments the approximate size of a child's play tent; no, they're all one-bedroomed and unbelievably spacious which effectively means that we're living the life of luxury, like Russian oligarchs. Or one of the Hilton sisters, dependent on taste.

Another thing, at the grand old age of twenty-eight, I have a confession to make – never once, in my whole life have I lived alone and I've taken to it shamelessly. I love and adore my gorgeous apartment, which is big and bright by the way, with massive windows in the living room that overlook Forty-Fifth Street, a staggering twenty-five floors below me. It's beautifully decorated too: everything is in delicate shades of white, cream and magnolia and all the furniture is blonde – the sofa, the armchairs, the floorboards, everything. Kind of makes you feel like you're in Heaven's departure lounge.

But it's more than having this gorgeous space all to myself; I love it because it's mine, all mine and no one else's. It's the pure fact of being on my own and actually being independent for the first time in my life that I'm getting such a kick out of. I'm someone who went straight from living with my mother to boarding school, then straight onto living with Dan so I've never only had myself to think about and I can tell you, it's addictive.

For the first time in my life, I never have to tell anyone where I'm going or when I'll be back. I don't have to worry that there's no food in the fridge in case Dan or Jules stagger in late and starving and wanting cold pizza. I can leave the living room like a tip if I feel like it and there's no Audrey to lecture me the next day. I don't have to cook at all if it doesn't happen to suit me, and half the time here I never bother; none of us do. Eating out is just way too easy. I can leave the place exactly as it pleases me, with knickers strewn all over the floor if I couldn't be arsed picking them up. I can walk round stark naked should the mood take me. And when the show opens and we're finished doing technical rehearsals during the day, I can stay in bed all day every day if I want, eating noodles straight out of the box, then flinging it on the floor beside me. And if it felt weird at first having a whole bed to myself and not being woken up by a stray arm or elbow or knee digging into me, (when overtired, Dan tends to thrash around in bed, like someone running), I astonished myself at how quickly I adapted.

Unparalleled luxury beyond compare. The whole set up here is bliss. Sheer, unimaginable bliss. I'm really, truly free and I'm loving every blessed second of it.

'I've found *myself* in New York City!' I gush to Liz one morning while we're strolling down Madison Avenue, drinking it all in, gazing upwards at all the skyscrapers, then walking slam bang into lampposts and parking meters. Basically looking like a right pair of tourist gobshites.

'You found *yourself*? Didn't realise you were missing.'

We don't have to be at the theatre till this afternoon, which gives us the luxury of a whole morning off to shop or sight see or else just bounce around the place; still on an absolute high just from being here. So Liz and I head out for brunch to this fabulous little deli we've discovered on Forty-Fifth Street called Dishes, just a few blocks from the apartment building. And just as an aside . . . brunch!

Don't cha just love it? When I used to watch *Sex and the City*, I never envied the central quartet all their freedom or independence or money or shoes or the fact that each of them had a different and yet more gorgeous fella on her arm in every second scene . . . no. What I used to be mad jealous of was that four girlfriends could meet for regular long, leisurely brunches, take the world apart then put it all back together again. That they had the time for that, not to mention that they had each other.

Far cry from life in Stickens, where the only person I had to chat to was Jules, provided I could manage to drag her away from the TV for long enough. And even at that, all we had to talk about was which one of us the Countess Dracula was annoying the most. A whole other planet away now.

Anyroadup, back to Dishes and the food is astonishing; like nothing I've ever tasted before. We grab a table, serve ourselves and I immediately get stuck into the most divine smoked salmon bagel smothered in fresh herb cream cheese . . . too mouth-watering for words. But Liz, I've discovered, is one of those vampire-like people who don't actually need to eat and on the rare occasions when she does, her dietary requirements from food are a) that it can be microwaved in under ten seconds, b) contain as much monosodium glutamate as possible and c) be eaten straight out of a container which can subsequently be re-used as an ashtray.

In short, a girl with a very casual approach to trans-fats. Who even more annoyingly still manages to stay a size eight, ho hum.

'So listen to me, hon, because I've made a decision,' she says, sipping on an Americano and playing with a box of Camel Lights while I stuff my face like a mucksavage.

161

'After the tech rehearsal finishes up tonight, you and me are hitting the town and I'm not taking no for an answer. I know we've got work tomorrow but what the hell. Just for the one.'

'Yeah right. Just for the one, as everyone knows, is the world's greatest lie. With you, it's more like just the one bottle.'

Only the truth. In all my born days I've never witnessed anything like Liz's capacity for alcohol; honest to God, the girl can slosh them back like a camel fuelling up before a Saharan crossing.

'Oh come on, what's the point of coming to the city that never sleeps if all you want to do is sleep?'

'But, Liz, we've a theatre call tomorrow afternoon and if we stay out till all hours . . .'

And then comes the one phrase Liz will throw at me if she wants to get under my skin and really persuade me to throw caution to the wind.

'Listen to you,' she says sarcastically, shaking her head, 'I don't know what marriage and living in the wilderness has done to you, but you never used to be this boring and over-cautious and . . . middle-aged.'

'Am not!' I protest, rising to the bait. 'The official first sign of middle age is when you find yourself wandering round the clothes department in Marks & Spencer's saying, "Ooh those slacks with the elasticated waist look really comfortable," and I'm a long way off that, thanks very much.'

'Now you're starting to make some sense, babe. You do realise that this whole NYC sabbatical for you is compensation for the marginal little life you've been leading for so long? Trouble with Annie Cole, is that you've never really had the time of your life and I'm telling you here and now, that's all going to change. Come on, admit it, aren't you sick of being such a good girl all the time? It's such a disgusting curse.'

And so later on that night when rehearsals have finally finished up, Liz and I stay back for a bit longer in the dressing room, filching each other's clothes and make-up, laughing and giggling, wearing age-inappropriate clothes that I know I'd be arrested in back home, getting all dolled up for our night on the town. (Liz in a sexy leather dress and me in a super-tight mini she lent me, that a seventeen year old would have difficulty pulling off.)

And I'm having the best laugh I've had in I don't know how long. Because this feels like the single life that I never really had; you know, having the freedom to head out for the night, then crawl in at all hours, being able to stay in bed till noon tomorrow if I feel like it, giggling the night away with Liz and loving every second of it. Laughter lines are even beginning to appear on my face in the most unexpected places.

Psychiatrists say that if you skip out on a part of your life, then you'll find some way to go back and reclaim it and that feels exactly like what I'm doing now. Reclaiming the single years I never had, the girl-about-town years, the mortgage-free, husband-free, fun-soaked years.

And loving every precious second.

Anyway, all glammed up and ready to go, the pair of us slip out the stage door of the theatre, miraculously find a cab, then Liz takes me to a new place she's discovered called the Vander Bar on Forty-Fifth Street, close to the apartments where we're staying. When we get there the place is still sardine-packed with after-work boozers and just as I'm ordering a vodka for Liz and a Pinot Grigio for myself, next thing, two guys slowly saunter over to us and strike up a conversation.

Now bear in mind that the last time I was chatted up by any man not my husband was back in the mid-nineties and you'll understand just how understandably naïve I am in these matters. One of them, who has a shaved head, not unlike a statue on Easter Island, corners Liz and immediately starts flirting with her, asking her to describe herself in three words.

'Stylish, insane, high-maintenance,' she shrugs carelessly, giving him the get-lost-mate-fish-eye. But somehow she's captured his attention, because then he starts buying her drink after drink, telling her all about his last tour of duty in Afghanistan and I'm not messing, boasting about how he'd actually once been tear gassed. Like this is something calculated to impress.

A couple of vodkas later and Liz begins to flirt back with him a bit, all nicotined-up by now and not adverse to a bit of action. And believe me, she truly is a sight to behold when she's got sex on the brain; after a few drinks, I notice, she's actually looking at his big Easter Island head like she's the spoon, and he's a tub of Häagen-Dazs.

'Afghanistan?' she starts to purr, swishing her hair extensions and beginning to feign interest now. 'So what was that like, then?'

'Tell you one thing I learned out there. Never invade Russia.'

Meanwhile his friend, who's about as tanned and lacquered as a life-size Ken doll, zones in on me and in my gobshite innocence, I'm standing there thinking we're having a perfectly inane chat about how he's one-quarter Irish on his maternal granny's side and how he's never actually visited the country but plans to very soon, blah-di-blah. All completely innocuous, until I slip off to the bathroom and by the time I get back, Liz has disappeared off with Easter Island-head guy. Completely vanished. Never even told me she was leaving, never said a word, just took off.

Bad, burning sensation just like heartburn immediately starts to flare up; my own personal ulcerous early warning system on high alert.

Realising that just leaves me and lacquer-head-Ken-doll uncomfortably standing together on our own, I make an excuse about how I have to leave; saying I want to go home and call my husband back in Ireland. What with the time difference I stammer, getting increasingly flustered, this is actually a really good time to catch him, blah-di-blah-di-blah.

Your husband, he asks disinterestedly? Yes, I answer prudishly, deliberately twiddling with my wedding ring. No problem he says smoothly, in that case, you must allow me to walk you home. Absolutely no need, I say with a slight panic beginning to rise, I only live a stone's throw away. But he absolutely insists, and I start to feel gradually more and more nervous as we walk the two blocks home, not helped by the fact that he keeps slipping a sweaty arm around my waist and I keep pulling away on the pretext of skipping off to admire stuff in shop windows. Shop windows with metal grilles pulled down in front of them.

Then, as soon as we get to the door of my building, I rummage around the bottom of my handbag for my key but next thing, before I even know what's going on, lacquer-head has pressed me roughly up against the wall, and is forcing his tongue into my mouth. The smell of his aftershave nearly chokes me and I try hard to pull away from him but he's so much stronger than me.

'Hurry up and open the door,' he says thickly, 'I'm coming upstairs with you.'

'Stop it,' I yell, really panicking now and desperately trying to shove him off, 'I'm married!'

'Yeah, sure, baby, with a husband five thousand miles away. What he doesn't know won't hurt him, now will it?'

Somehow, I manage to give him an almighty dig right in the solar plexus and by some miracle of synchronicity, a neighbour happens to come out of the building at the exact same time, so I'm able to slip inside without having to grope around for my key. Trembling and shaking, I stumble upstairs and try calling Liz, but she isn't answering either her door or her phone. And of course, I can't exactly call Dan because what in the name of Jaysus would I say to him?

Anyway, late the following morning, Liz texts me to arrange to meet for brunch in Dishes and in she swans, a good half-hour late and still in the same clothes she had on last night, except now with laddered tights, very sexy scraggly blonde bed hair and an unmistakable love bite on her neck, that she's wearing like some kind of badge of honour.

'Christ Alive, Liz, where in the name of arse did you disappear off to last night? I was worried sick about you!'

'Oh relax . . . and grab me a coffee while you're at it, will you?'

'Just for the record, you left me alone with a complete sex pest . . .'

'Take it easy . . .'

'. . . and you didn't even tell me where you were going . . .'

'. . . honey, it's waaaaay too early in the morning for me to listen to this . . .'

'. . . so I've spent the whole night worrying about you . . .'

'. . . I need an Americano and a fag in that order before I can even begin to take in what you're saying . . .'

'. . . there I was, wondering if we'd end up on page three of the *Daily Star* in a homicide case, with everyone saying, "Wouldn't you think her pal would have raised the alarm when the poor murdered girl disappeared off?"'

But I'd forgotten one thing about Liz; she doesn't do contrition. Instead she just cackles her smoky, hung-over laugh at me, teases me for being so parochial and tells me I've a lot to learn about single life.

'But when you disappeared, I was nearly about to call the police!'

'And thank Christ you didn't. Last thing I'd want is my photo appearing on the six o'clock news. Recent pictures of me are very jowly.'

'Liz, you got plastered and went home with a total stranger! Jesus, you'll end up with an electronic bracelet around your ankle one of these days.'

'Oh for feck's sake, can't you just get past this? My head hurts. Need caffeine. Now.'

'No, you're still in the penalty box with me. Suppose I hadn't been able to get rid of hair lacquer guy?' I insist, still vividly remembering the stench of his aftershave overpowering me and the horrible feeling of his darty, rough tongue in my mouth. Jesus, I thought he was having an epileptic fit.

Gak, gak and gak again.

'But you *were* able to get rid of him, weren't you? You're a big girl and you're well able to take care of yourself. Now loosen up a bit and stop acting like such a prematurely middle-aged aul one, or else I'll be forced to go out and buy you a cat, to really complete the image. So a guy walked you home and then tried it on with you. Big deal, happens all the time. Welcome to my world. And just remember, you're a long way from The Sticks now, babe. Like I say, you've never had the time of your life and now you're having it.'

I'm about to primly tell her that fencing off some lecherous git isn't exactly what I'd call having the time of my life, but I let it pass and just put the whole thing down to gobshite stupidity on my part for even getting myself into that situation in the first place. Because deep down I know Liz is right; there *are* things missing from my life.

Like, a life for starters. And this is all part of its rich tapestry, isn't it?

Anyway, the whole thing blows over quickly enough and of course I forgive Liz, it's impossible to stay mad at her for long, but boy have I vowed to be a bit less of a trusting moron from now on. Nor will I ever set foot back in the Vander Bar as long as I'm alive, which is a pity because I really did like the place.

A few days later and now we're in the throes of our second full week's work: dress rehearsals night after night, leading right up to the first preview, next week. Which, because I'm the only cast member who's never actually performed the show in front of a live audience, kind of feels like my own personal and deeply terrifying opening night.

The Shubert Theatre, where we're playing is stunning by the way, an old Victorian playhouse on West Forty-Fourth Street and Seventh Avenue, just a handy, ten-minute walk from the apartment building. It's been recently renovated to the nth degree and has amazing backstage facilities as well, like ensuite bathrooms off each dressing room . . . pure unadulterated luxury. And when I think of some of the dumps that Liz and I played when we were both young and struggling and desperately trying to get our Equity Cards I'm reminded of just how far we've both come. Because believe me, compared with them, this is sheer bloody Heaven.

It's not only the plushest theatre I've ever played in my life, it's also by a mile the largest. My stomach still does flip-flops every time I walk out onto the stage in front of the empty auditorium, feeling like Alice in Wonderland, shrunk small with everything around me magnified. Christ Alive, I can only imagine what it'll be like to have two thousand pairs of eyes looking back at me, assessing me, weighing me up, wondering if I'm good enough to even be here in the first place. In fact, just the thought of it makes me wonder if I've even got room for another ulcer.

We didn't see all that much of Jack last week, he was too absorbed with getting the technical end of the show honed down to perfection. Plus he's not staying in the apartment block with the rest of us; he's . . . get this . . . staying alone in his friend's apartment at The Plaza hotel.

'Who's the friend, I'd love to know,' Chris mused dryly when she heard this. 'Donald Trump, perhaps?'

But from here on in, right up till opening night, we're all his and boy is he working us like dray horses. To a high achieving perfectionist like Jack, his natural default setting is 'genius', and it's like nothing is going to come between him and a five-star review in the *New York Times*, a standing ovation on opening night and a Tony award nomination for best director. Not if it kills him and all around him in the process. There's a lot of talk about Tony awards being bandied around these days; mind you, most of the talk is coming from Jack himself, but still.

He's a man possessed, his eye is on the golden prize and he's got that tunnel vision that you only really see in people of greatness. Every single day this week he calls us to the theatre in the early afternoon, then painstakingly rehearses the show in the most minute detail over and over again, driving us on and on, well into the night, till every nerve ending in my body feels stretched to breaking point, like taut elastic bands.

Jack can be terrifying and these days I'm seeing a merciless side to him that I'd heard about but never actually witnessed before this. For instance, the hair and make-up assistant did something different to Blythe's hair the other night before a dress rehearsal and when he came backstage for a note session afterwards, he raised one of his satanic eyebrows and cuttingly asked who exactly had done her hair? The council? Lucky it was Blythe he said it to, as she's well able to stand up to him and regularly puts him in his place, like an adoring Mammy ticking off a favourite son. Had it been shy little Alex, I think the poor kid would have burst into tears.

Then he turned on Chris about a particular scene she's in, which he's forever harping on that he's never been fully happy with.

'I am trying my best in that scene, I'll have you know,' she snapped back at him, standing tall and thin, swishing her Indian-straight black hair imperiously over her shoulders and matching his satanic glare with a ferocious look of her own. You should have seen the pair of them squaring up to each other, like an episode of Jeremy Kyle waiting to be Sky-plussed.

'Yes, I'm well aware that you're doing your best,' was Jack's cool answer. 'Which is why I know you won't get any better. For fuck's sake, Chris, I've seen toll booth attendants show more emotion at the shrugged acceptance of a two Euro coin.'

'And what makes you think you have the right to speak to me like that?' she demanded, steam practically coming out her ears.

'Habit.'

'What is it about cruel men who have power that makes them weirdly attractive?' Liz asked me later on when the two of us were back in the privacy of our shared dressing room. 'And the mental thing is, I don't even particularly like Jack. Half the time he's a pain in the arse. In fact scratch that; if I just isolate the pain to *just* my arse, I'd be delighted. But he's just got that thing going on, you know, where men want to be him and women want to change him.'

'Biggest mistake any woman could ever make,' I said firmly into the dressing room mirror, lasing make-up remover onto my face to take off the heavy stage make-up, which is not unlike Polybond. 'It's impossible to change any man. Cruel men stay cruel and the women who stay with them end up having a shit life.'

'That's rich, coming from you,' she snorted. 'You're married to the nicest man on earth. What in the name of God, pray tell, would you know about men treating women badly?'

I let it pass.

Anyway, our routine now pretty much revolves round living in the theatre, or else crashing out back at the apartment, surviving the nightly dress rehearsals and counting down the days till first preview. No time for anything else, not right now. In fact the short walk to and from work is the only bit of fresh air and exercise any of us are getting these days and the only one of us who hasn't actually tested this out is Liz. Not in her shoes, not on your life

All of us, again barring Liz, have temporarily put the brakes on our social lives, at least till the show has opened, and we've got some measure of our lives back again. But in spite of the intensity of all this hard slog, somehow I'm still dancing round the place like Annie in Wonderland, loving being here, and still unable to get my head around the fact that I'm really, actually about to open on a Broadway stage!

I've already met the senior producer, one Harvey Shapiro, who tends to wear white suits a lot, has matching white hair and a white goatee beard and who looks exactly like Colonel Sanders on the side of a bucket of Kentucky Fried Chicken.

'What else does Harvey produce?' I innocently asked Liz one night.

'Everything. You name it. Films, treaties, rabbits out of hats. The whole works. Even just his name being attached to this means we're already big news.'

Bless him, he was good enough to be complimentary about all of us after the first dress rehearsal he sat through. As was his wife, whose name is either Sherry or Terry, I can't for the life of me remember which. When we were introduced, I was way too distracted by her size zero 'look no carbs!' frame with fake boobs that looked like they'd been stuck onto her bony little ribcage. All I know is that her name sounds a bit like a country and western singer's.

Even more unbelievably, Jack is giving me a fairly easy ride too; in our lengthy and exhaustive notes sessions his constant refrain to me is, 'Just do what you're doing. And for Christ sakes, try and have a bit more confidence in yourself!'

In fact, everything is going so swimmingly, unbelievably well here that there's only one fly in the ointment to report.

Who happens to be called Dan Ferguson.

Hard as it is to believe, I've been here for almost three weeks now and in all that time, he and I have had exactly two conversations. TWO. And one hardly even counts, as it was four in the morning my time, but nine in the morning his time, so I hardly even got a chance to say hi before Mrs Brophy started bellowing at him that there was a client waiting for him in the surgery with a cat that had already vomited all over the waiting room.

I'll ring you back, he'd promised, but when he eventually did, of course I'd conked out, it being well past five am over here.

Then another time, I actually managed to get him on the phone while we were taking a break from rehearsals, at about seven in the evening Irish time. He answered, but ended up having to hang up on me, as right then, he was trying to stay upright in slithery, knee-deep muck while attempting to get a look at the undercarriage of a maddened, manure-spurting bullock.

Don't get me wrong, I've left countless messages for him, both at The Moorings and on his mobile, but most of those go unanswered. And it's hard, bloody hard and getting harder. Now I'm actually starting to get a sneaking feeling that I'm actually pestering him if I leave messages. Dear God, if I thought it was tough to deal with his being distant and remote when we were living under the same roof, try factoring in having the Atlantic ocean between us.

Nor is any of this helped by Chris either. It's not her fault at all, it's just that every time we're chatting at the theatre, she's all full of news from her husband Josh, counting the days down till he's over for the opening night with her little boy.

'He and I have a rota worked out to combat the time difference,' she announces to me one day, as we walk to work together. We're just on the busy corner of Fifth Avenue and East Forty-Fourth Street, waiting to cross the road, and she practically has to yell at me, the noise from the traffic is so deafening.

'Anyway, I Skype Josh every single morning at nine my time, so he can tell me all about his day, then he stays up and sets the alarm so he can Skype me at ten at night my time, so I can tell him all about mine. That way we never miss out on each other's news. Because I really feel that to sustain a successful long-distance relationship, it's absolutely vital for two people to share all the trivial minutiae of their day with each other, when you're so far apart. Don't you agree?'

I'm not messing, by the way, this is actually the way she talks. Like a kind of human self-help book.

'So what about you, Annie? How often do you get to talk to your Dan? How do you two work at keeping your relationship alive and flourishing?'

I mutter something about how busy he always is, how hard I'm finding it to keep things going, what with the time difference, and how difficult it is with the hours he works, etc, etc.

Chris, of course, being Chris, gives me one of her horrified head-girl glares, then takes full charge of the situation in her well-meaning but slightly domineering way. As it happens we're just passing a large branch of the Barnes and Noble bookstore on Fifth, so she immediately steers me inside and marches straight to the non-fiction section, scanning through all the shelves till she finds a self-help book called, I'm not joking, *The Long-Distance Relationship Bible; Keeping Your Relationship Alive From Afar.*

'Brilliant, this is exactly what I wanted. You'll find all the answers are in here,' she says briskly. 'Just read this and you'll be fine. I guarantee it.'

So that night in bed, I flip through it. A lot of practical stuff mixed in with an equal load of self-help-y shite, pretty much as you'd expect. Such as *'laying down the communication boundaries and rules: how much contact do you need to feel comfortable and connected with your partner when you're apart?'*

Jaysus, if I got five minutes of quality time with Dan, I'd count myself lucky. And that, by the way, was when we were living under the same roof. Then there's another bit about *'vowing to stay tuned in at all times.'*

'To avoid making your partner feel taken for granted, try to make far more effort and pose more questions about significant things that are going on in his or her life. Phone far more often than you normally would if your parner has a big event coming up. Be supportive and let them know you care, even if you can't physically be there.'

I actually snort laughing at this and am almost tempted to fling the book across the room, as far away from me as possible at this. Here's me, about to open in a Broadway show, the single biggest thing that's ever happened to me in the whole course of my career and not once, not a single time has my significant other even asked how it's all going for me.

Then, just before I went to sleep, my eyes chanced to fall on a single paragraph which read, 'Know Your Shelf Life. Many good long-distance relationships just don't work out, even with the best of intentions, both parties having tried their best. Consider agreeing on an expiration date, at which point you both acknowledge your relationship is no longer working and don't be afraid to communicate this to your partner. If one of you reaches a point where you can take no more, then you have a duty to let the other know and as quickly as possible. Many long distance relationships fail and remember, there's no shame in this.'

Makes for lovely bedtime reading, I can tell you.

First preview night and I'm almost ready to vomit with nerves. The others are bad, but not quite as overwrought as me, given that this is my very first outing in the play in front of a live audience. We've spent an exhausting day in the Shubert with Jack drilling us over and over again like army recruits and now we're on a short meal break before showtime.

I'm actually shaking, physically trembling like I'm about to face a firing squad, so Chris takes charge of me, whisking me out of the theatre and across the road to the Edison hotel on West Forty-Seventh Street, one of our little finds since we got here. It's got a real New York diner on the ground floor that serves the most amazing matzo ball soup, which Chris reckons is the one-size-fits-all cure for just about everything; loneliness, stage fright, nerves, homesickness, the whole lot. Mind you, the state I'm in, I reckon that all food will only end up tasting like barf now.

It's just her and me in the Edison – Liz opted for a snooze in the dressing room before the show, the only one of us sufficiently chilled out enough to actually be able to sleep at a time like this. Gym-starved little Alex strapped her iPod on and, as it's one of those New York glass-clear days, said she was going for a brisk walk as far as Central Park to clear her head. Meanwhile the ever budget conscious Blythe always reckons eating out is an extravagance right up there with *not* shopping in discount stores, so she just brought in food from a local deli to eat in the theatre instead. But then that's Blythe for you; three words you never hear slipping her lips are, 'that's reasonably priced', while she maintains her favourite sentence in the whole of the English language is 'reduced to clear.'

As usual with Chris, the chat inevitably turns to her husband and son and how she has the days counted till they're both over for the big opening night, just three weeks away now. She politely asks me if Dan has booked his flight to come over yet . . . and that's the only catalyst I need to start me off.

I don't know if it's just pre-show jitters, but for absolutely no reason that I can think of, I open up to her. Really open up, I mean, as opposed to smiling and obfuscating and changing the subject whenever Dan's name is mentioned, like I normally would. Without my even knowing why, it all comes spilling out: the growing distance between us, how stifled I perpetually felt back in Stickens with him hardly ever around, the disaster that was Christmas, the bigger disaster that was our final weekend before we left . . . the whole shooting match.

Slowly I watched Chris's face change from interest, to

177

concern, to . . . her favourite emotion of all . . . white hot fury.

'But this is outrageous!' she says way too loudly, thumping her fist off the diner table. 'How can you stand for this? You have GOT to do something, Annie!'

'Ehh . . . I think there's a guy on Fifty-Third Street who may not have heard you. Any chance you'd lower your voice?'

No, of course not – I've inadvertently handed Chris her daily jihad now and there's no shutting her up.

'Did he call you to wish you luck in your first preview?'

'Well . . . not exactly . . .'

'Did he or didn't he? Answer me!'

'No, but you don't understand, the hours he works are mental; every time I phone him he's either dealing with a bullock that's got a bad case of diarrhoea, a vomiting cat, a racehorse with a gammy knee . . . I could go on and on but we'd only miss the curtain call.'

'Totally unacceptable behaviour,' she splutters indignantly, 'and you know what the absolute worst thing about this is? He's got you thinking that this is the norm. That being ignored and brushed-over is all that you deserve.'

'No, hang on a minute there . . .'

'Stop defending his behaviour. You sound like a victim of domestic abuse, standing there with two black eyes and still saying, oh but I love him!'

Shit. She's gone off on one of her rants now and there's no stopping her. I try my best to explain that I'm not actually married to Robert Mugabe and that Dan is actually The Nicest Man on the Planet. I mean, everyone says so. Or at least, they certainly used to. And yes, of course I'm frustrated and exasperated at how he treats me, but when it boils down to it, the only charges I can really lay at his door are thoughtlessness and being a workaholic. Aren't they? I mean, it's not like he cheats on me and beats me up, now is it?

'Now you just listen to me, Annie Cole,' Chris goes on, picking up her soup spoon and brandishing it at me, like it's a weapon. 'First thing tomorrow, you have GOT to call him and tell Dan that's he's coming over to the opening night and that's all there is to it. Book the ticket for him if you have to, then it's a *fait accompli* and he can't wriggle out of it. All marriages need work and it's up to him to put in a bit of effort here. For feck's sake, Annie, does the guy have a brain tumour or something? Doesn't he know that he's in real danger of losing you?'

Two hours later, all my nerve ends jangling and feeling white hot terror like I've never known before in my life, I step out under the dazzlingly bright stage lights with closely husbanded courage and make my Broadway debut.

It's well past three in the morning before I get back to the apartment, completely buzzed up and totally ecstatic about how the night went! I've never in my life known an adrenaline rush like it; like something fighter pilots must feel. Or burglars maybe. The show went astonishingly, beyond-our-wildest-expectations well and the word from the producers is that we'll easily pack out the theatre for the full year and very possibly even longer.

Even impossible-to-please Jack actually looked reasonably satisfied afterwards and although we're all in for another one of his long and exhaustive note sessions before tomorrow night's show, he at least had the good grace to say 'well done' to each of us in turn. Praise from Caesar indeed.

Then Harvey Shapiro very kindly insisted on taking the whole cast to this fabulous, glass-walled, glass-ceilinged restaurant on Broadway called The Blue Fin, where we all partied like life offenders who'd just been handed eleventh-hour reprieves from death row.

'Still a few creases to be ironed out, but overall . . . not bad. Not at all bad,' Jack said to me, leaning against the bar, looking cool and unruffled in one of his Hugo Boss suits and sipping some kind of fancy looking pink cocktail that only a man deeply comfortable in his own sexuality could pull off.

'So how does it feel to have played Broadway? Not too many actresses can boast of that, you know.'

'*Ohmygodohmygodohmygod*,' I gushed, still having to be scraped off the ceiling from the whole experience, 'it was just the most unbelievable experience! There were laughs where I never expected them to be, and rounds of applause that I never saw coming . . . and when they gave us a standing ovation at the end . . .'

'You better get used to it. Because I can tell you right now Annie Cole, that this show could change the course of your career. Possibly even your whole life.'

He looked at me hard, in that intense, focused way he has and I didn't have time to even ask him what he meant before Chris commandeered the conversation, the way she somehow manages to commandeer all conversations, demanding to know exactly what he'd thought of her performance in an apart-from-that-Mrs-Lincoln-did-you-enjoy-the-play type manner.

It was well late by then and a lot of our gang had drifted off, so I made my excuses and went to grab my bag and coat.

Just as I was outside, hailing a taxi, Jack came out for a cigarette.

'Home to ring the hubby?' he asked, lighting up a Marlboro and casually studying me with interest.

'As a matter of fact, yes I am.'

'Do tell him I'm looking forward to meeting him. The elusive Mr Annie Cole.'

'Don't worry, you will.'

Anyroadup, it's well past three in the morning and I'm back in the apartment now, way too hyped up to sleep and just about to call Dan. Eight in the morning his time, perfect. I dial the house number and Mrs Brophy answers, yelling even louder than usual, as if to compensate for her voice travelling across the Atlantic.

No, she screeches so loudly I have to hold the phone away from my ear, Dan left the house early for a call out to Lismore, but she'll pass on the message. Will you tell him I need to talk to him urgently, I say, unapologetic about the theatrics. Best way to get his attention, I figure. I go back to bed and snooze for a bit, then try his mobile later on in the morning. Still no answer, but I'm determined to talk to him at all costs. As ever, it takes five goes to actually get hold of him, but eventually I do, at two in the afternoon my time, just as I'm heading out to the theatre for yet another notes session.

'Dan? Is that really you?'

Jaysus, it feels like I've just got through to the White House.

'Annie, I'm sorry for not getting back to you, it's just been . . . well, you know what it's like here. Same old, same old.'

Then a few stilted half questions from me and a few

mumbled answers from him. I tell him how brilliantly last night went and he apologises for not calling to wish me luck but he'd no signal on his phone all day . . . then he breaks off to tell me he's got a call coming through and is afraid it's a client ringing about a constipated goat, or similar.

I couldn't quite tell because he hung up so fast.

And so the pattern repeats itself over and over again; I leave countless messages in tones ranging from exasperated to desperate to angry, via nagging. A good three days later, he calls back at seven in the evening my time, just as I'm getting ready for the show and of course I can't talk, so I just get snappy with him for ringing at what he must know is the worst possible time for me and he gets defensive, saying that all he's doing is returning my fifteenth message. Then I get irritated and of course, it all ends in a bloody, blistering row.

Unfair, I know, because it's classic misdirected anger; what's really annoying me is that I know it'll be yet another three days of missed calls and unreturned messages before we actually do get to speak again. And even at that, I can already tell you exactly how that call will go: I'll be tense and fraught, he'll be busy, busy always busy.

Funny to think, but at one time, my proudest boast was that it was impossible to have a row with Dan, ever. Now it's a complete doddle. All we have to do is speak to each other. And I'm surprising myself at how bitter I'm sounding. How ground down I am by the pointlessness of it all. Even our measly little half-slivers of conversations only leave me feeling more frustrated and confused and a whole pile of other emotions that are alien to me.

Also, a worrying number of times when I've rung home,

Lisa Ledbetter has answered the phone, making me highly suspicious that she's physically gone the whole hog and moved herself and her kids in, all the better to sponge off Dan. At least, I can only hope that's the only bleeding reason she's been hanging around the house so much.

In fact these days, the only person I have any kind of regular contact with from home is Jules via Facebook, who's basically been giving me a run down of all the bitching Audrey's been doing about me behind my back since I deserted. 'She's off in New York, taking a marriage sabbatical,' is apparently her killer phrase to anyone who'll listen.

And you know something? Frankly, from where I'm sitting, it's not starting to look like a bad idea. I strongly suspect that Chris has been doing her fair share of blabbing about my private life too; ever since I opened up to her that night in the Edison hotel, everyone else in the cast and even some of the crew too have been gently asking me how I'm coping and if everything is OK at home.

I'm well beyond putting on a brave face at this point, so when questioned, my policy now is just to roll my eyes heavenwards and make some smart arse comment about long-distance relationships being such a bloody nightmare. Nearly always works, bar when Chris is around, in which case I get a lecture right in the ear about how she's in a LDR too and yet she's able to make it work, isn't she?

And I'll bite my tongue and remind myself that she doesn't mean to be smug; she's actually trying to help, in her own ham-fisted way. Blythe chips in her two cents' worth too, telling me that I'm not to worry. 'Sure all marriages go through bumps in the road, love,' she gently assures me. 'Did you really think you were going to dodge that bullet?'

Blythe, I've noticed, is beginning to talk in Americanisms now.

Even Liz, who was dying with a hangover said to me in the dressing room the other night, 'You don't need to worry about Dan being so distant from you, hon. Everything will work itself out. You two were made for each other.'

'Does absolutely everyone here know about my private life now?' I asked her frustratedly. 'What is this, published somewhere?'

'Oh relax. We're actors, we like following real-life soaps, that's all. And remember, this is Dan we're talking about, for feck's sake. Mr Perfect Husband.'

Sad to think that there once was a time when she was right. But most definitely not now. Now it's like Mr Perfect Husband has long since left the building and there's some distant, remote stranger standing in his place.

With less than a week to go to opening night, finally, finally, I get to say what's on my mind to Dan. As usual, it takes approximately two dozen attempts to get a hold of him, but when I do, I tell him straight. I'd like him to come over for the opening night.

But I've got to work, can't possibly take the time off, no one can cover for me etc, etc, etc, he predictably says. But my antennae are on high alert, I'm fully ready for him and have my reply all rehearsed. It's on St Patrick's Day, I retaliate, it's a bank holiday at home, surely to God you could take two days off? That's all I'm asking for, I tell him, two lousy days, purposely keeping the stakes low. It's Paddy's Day, I insist, even the twenty-four hour Asian store in Stickens closes on Paddy's Day, for feck's sake.

He ifs and buts and pretty soon tempers begin to get strained, with me realising that here I am, actually pleading with him to come over and how wrong that seems. How un-be-fecking-lievable, in fact. I mean, shouldn't he actually *want* to come over to see his wife without my having to resort to begging?

The conversation rapidly disintegrates fast, as they always seem to do these days, but by the end of it, I feel a sliver of hope that he might come round. Between them, Andrew and James could easily cover for you, I tell him firmly. You need the break, we need to spend time together and it means a huge amount to me that you'd be here for what's probably the biggest career night of my life.

And so he eventually agrees to ask them and I leave it at that, promising to look at flights for him first thing in the morning. Next day I text him, asking if I can go ahead and make the bookings and late that night when I still haven't heard back from him, I call again.

Miraculously, unbelievable, I actually get him on my first try. Do you think you'll be able to make it over, I ask him straight out, utterly dog-tired and shattered with it all by now. But there's just one condition I forgot to mention. What's that, he says, sounding like he hasn't slept in a week. If you do say you'll come, then I need your absolute guarantee, your solemn word that you *will not* let me down.

Because it's like this; I cannot handle being let down one more time, I tell him, inwardly marvelling at how firm and resolute living alone in New York has made me. So if it's no, it's no, I say. But if it's yes, then I need you to tell me that no power on earth will prevent you from being here for me. I need your word. I need that from you now.

Feck's sake, is it that much to ask for?

OK then, yes, he eventually says. Go ahead and book the

flights. I'll make it, I'll find the time somehow and I'll get there.

Well whatdyya know, I think exhaustedly, slumping down onto a chair, utterly ground down by all the plea-bargaining and begging.

Finally, finally, finally. A breakthrough.

Chapter Eight

March already and the previews are racing in, each one getting incrementally better and better and I'm reasonably confident of this, mainly because our notes sessions with Jack are becoming proportionately shorter and shorter, always a good barometer. Now opening night nerves have eclipsed all else, heightened by the fact that between the rest of the cast, we have almost a planeload of people coming over from Ireland for the big night. A bit like a big gang of soccer supporters, minus the green face paint and vuvuzelas.

Except for me, that is. I just have Dan, but that's enough. Frankly I don't know what I'm more stunned about, that he's actually agreed to take time off work to be here for me, or that I'm going to be seeing him in no time at all. And that it'll be real, proper quality time too.

Yet more good news: my mother is travelling down from Washington for the big night too – the first time I'll have seen her in over a year! Ever the diplomat, once she found out that Dan was coming to stay with me, she tactfully booked herself into the nearby New York Palace Hotel, so as to give us some privacy. Bless.

Anyway, come the big day and I take one final, last look

around my shining, sparkling, blonde apartment. I've been cleaning and tidying it like a lunatic all week, dotting candles around the place and stocking up the fridge with champagne and a load of extravagant little nibbles. I even went out to Filene's Basement (a discount store much favoured by Blythe) and treated myself to brand new high count Egyptian cotton bed linen. Not only that – I figured, feck it anyway, not every night you open on Broadway, so I splashed out and really spoilt myself with a brand new Donna Karen dress for tonight. Cherry red, Dan's all-time favourite colour on me. All ready for his arrival . . . unbelievably in just a few hours' time!

Dan's travelling on the afternoon flight which gets in at four pm, by which time I'll have to be in the theatre, so I've asked him to come straight to the apartment. I've left a spare key for him with Stan, our gorgeous doorman, so he can let himself in and freshen up for the big night ahead.

It's bizarre, almost like I've torn right down the middle into two different Annies. One is nearly paralysed with nerves over all the critics being out there this evening, while the other one is practically dancing round the place with excitement because in just a few short hours, it'll almost be like a second honeymoon for me and Dan. And everyone will finally get to meet him too, at the after show party in . . . where else? Sardi's the famous restaurant, which has become a bit like our canteen by now.

Plus on top of all this, we've got the whole day tomorrow to look forward to as well! His time here is unbelievably tight, so I've got his whole trip worked out a bit like a military operation. Because let's face it, everything works better with a plan. Weddings, murders, everything.

Brekkie tomorrow in the Carnegie deli which I know

he'll adore, then a stroll through Central Park; lunch in Tao, this really cool Asian restaurant, then back to the apartment so I can get organised for work. Plus I've got him a ticket to see the show again in the evening, and last but not least . . . the pièce de résistance . . . I've booked dinner for the two of us after work at the Rockefeller Café which overlooks the ice skating rink, where we first got engaged all those years ago. So the two of us will be enveloped in happy memories for forty-eight blissful hours. Everything is planned right down to the last detail and right now, I'm starting to feel a bit like a character in a soap opera who says, 'But what can possibly go wrong?'

Time passes so extra-slowly that I nearly want to tear my hair out with nerves, so unable to take it any more I finally leave the gleaming, spotless apartment at noon. Even though it's a drizzling, grey day, I decide to take a calming stroll to the Shubert. Fifth Avenue is all sealed off for the Saint Patrick's Day parade and although I wish Dan was here to see it, I'm consoled by the fact that he'll be here in the blink of an eye.

My mind quickly does some calculations: he must be heading to Shannon airport by now his time, probably even checking in. I try calling his mobile, but it's switched off, which I take to mean that he's possibly already on board the flight and on his way.

When I get to the theatre, it's like Kensington Palace the week Diana died – nothing but a sea of bouquets waiting for all of us, filling every available nook and cranny.

'Hi, Annie!' says Hayley, the gorgeous front of house manager, 'good to see you! So, how are those nerves then, huh?' Hayley, by the way, is one of those fabulously positive people who make you want to spend the whole day basking

189

in their magnificent good cheer. She's always in good form, always laughing and messing around. I manage a weak, watery smile and she tells me she's already put my flowers up in the dressing room I'm sharing with Liz.

'Now don't you go getting stagefright on me, honey,' she says cheerily, clocking the rabbit-in-the-headlamps terror in my eyes. 'You're gonna be just fine! Just get out there and kick the living hell outta the show, babe!'

'I'll do my best!' I grin back at her and race up the stairs, my heart thumping, wondering who the hell would be sending me flowers anyway? Dan? Would he have had time before he left Ireland?

Three magnificent bouquets worthy of the Chelsea Flower Show are waiting on my dressing table: one from Jack to say good luck, one from my mother to say she's looking forward to seeing me after the show, and the third and most impressive one . . . impatiently I tear the card open. It has to be from Dan, I think, just *has* to be. He wouldn't forget to send flowers on such a big, important night, would he?

But they're from Harvey Shapiro.

You're doing great, kid. Keep up the good work, I'm real proud of you!

Seven thirty and I must be driving poor Liz nuts with my non-stop pacing up and down the dressing room floor. Once I get out on stage I'll be grand, it's just all the shagging hanging around that's a killer. We're both in our costumes, hair done and fully made up, all we need is for eight o'clock to come.

Jack comes in, looking like a pagan prince in a suit so sharp you'd nearly get a paper cut off it. He hugs both Liz and me in turn, his touch both ice cold and rock hard, the only one in the building who's not betraying the tiniest scrap of nerves. It flashes through my mind; how exactly does he do it anyway? Stay so calm at a time like this? Sedatives strong enough to knock out a rhinoceros, perhaps?

'Just do what you're doing, Annie Cole,' he says, looking me straight in the eye. 'And you'll knock 'em dead.'

A quarter to eight and I'm just about to head backstage for the act one beginner's call when my mobile rings. It's been beep beeping for the past hour, but I've just been ignoring it. I know it's nothing urgent, just good luck messages coming through and that there'll be plenty of time later on to read them all. But as it happens, I'm waiting on Liz who's still messing around with her eye make-up, so I answer.

A crackling tone, like it's coming long distance.

Then I hear Dan's voice.

Immediately my entire digestive system clenches with foreboding. Suddenly I have to remind myself to breathe.

'Annie? I'm so glad I caught you . . .'

'Where are you?' I ask stupidly, in a rare moment of prescience knowing the answer before I'm even told.

'I'm still in Stickens.'

Silence.

Static over the phone.

And all of a sudden . . . I don't know how to feel. There's been an emergency, he tells me, an outbreak of foot-and-mouth disease in a local Waterford farm and there was just no way he could travel. He's so sorry to let me down, but he wants me to know that it couldn't be helped . . . he'd been texting earlier but I never answered . . . he wants me to understand that him leaving was out of the question . . . all the same excuses that I've been listening to for years are trotted out.

Meanwhile I just stand there.

I probably blink.

I'm utterly mute and there's a time-delay while pain finds its way to my brain and eventually I do feel something. The exact same sensation you'd get if a knife was plunged directly into your heart. Deep shock on a cellular level.

Because *of course* he still could have come. He could have made it if he'd wanted to.

He could have taken two days off. Andrew and James could easily have coped without him for two lousy days. They'd have managed, of course they would. That was all I was asking for, forty-eight hours of his poxy time. After all my meticulous planning, after looking forward to seeing him for so long. After spelling it out to him that I couldn't stand being let down again.

And now this.

'Miss Cole, Miss Shields, this is your five minute call,' the tannoy crackles above us.

'I have to go,' is all I can say into the phone, before heat rushes to my face and a sudden wave of nausea sweeps over me. I race into the tiny ensuite bathroom and barely make it in time before I'm violently sick.

Liz is amazing, but then as she says herself, she's got a lot of experience in dealing with vomit.

'Oh come on, honey, you're just nervous, that's all,' she says firmly, splashing cold water on my temples, 'you'll be grand once you get out there. Opening night jitters is all that's wrong with you. I've a small emergency bottle of brandy in my bag – do you fancy a little slug? For medicinal purposes?'

'No, Liz. And this isn't nerves.'

'Course it is. It's adrenaline, the poor person's cocaine. That's all that's wrong with you.'

'You don't understand. He's not coming. Dan's not coming.'

She looks momentarily as stunned as I feel, but just then the tannoy crackles to life again – the stage director, sounding distinctly panicky now.

'Miss Cole, Miss Shields, will you standby *please*.'

'Come on, babe,' she says, gently getting me to my feet. 'I know it's hard, but this will just have to wait till afterwards. We've a show to do.'

One good thing has come out of all this: the sheer terror I was feeling all day has completely vanished. An icy calm has taken over me and I actually wonder if I'll ever be able to feel anything again. I'm like someone on mute autopilot as I walk down the stairs and patiently wait backstage. To look at me from the outside, you'd even think I was calm. And as I step out onstage, I hear my own voice, so surprisingly cool and detached, so completely unemotional.

Dan doesn't love me anymore, is the thought that keeps playing like a loop in my head.

What? Says my logical mind. What was that treacherous thought you just had? It's true, says my subconscious. And once the thought gets its feet under the table, there's no budging it to leave. He doesn't love me any more and what's more, I think the final, last vestige of any sliver of affection I felt for him has now well and truly been stomped underfoot.

But this is Dan we're talking about, insists my logical mind, he's the hook on which everything else in my life hangs, isn't he?

But in my heart, I know my subconscious is on the money.

My marriage, long sickening, has just died.

R.I.P.

The after show party is held in Sardi's Restaurant right across the road from the theatre, which would comfortably sit three hundred, uncomfortably sit four hundred but tonight there must be at least five hundred people here; the place is packed to the rafters and it's pure, organised PR hell. Not so much a guest list as a small town.

And the atmosphere is dense with the sweet smell of success. I've never actually smelled success before, but not even someone as punch-drunk from the body blow I've just taken could possibly mistake it. It's actually not unlike sweat, only stronger. Anyway, we took a total of seven curtain calls and the standing ovation at the end of the show lasted for a good five minutes, so everyone seems to be walking on air.

Except me, that is.

Liz is terrific and doesn't so much link as solder my arm to hers all the way from the theatre to the restaurant, as if I might stumble over or else run away given half the chance. But as soon as she shoves and elbows her way through the packed doorway, she immediately makes for the bar jubilantly yelling out that she smells free wine. I lose sight not only of her but of the rest of the cast in the throng as well.

The only time I crack a smile is when I spot my mother, with her neat, dark bobbed hair, hair that behaves itself and lies flat for her, unlike my side-show-Bob-from-the-Simpsons effort. Mum, of course, like a good little diplomat, is wearing green for Paddy's Day this evening – a beautiful pale olive Louise Kennedy trouser suit, but then that's my mother for you: patriotic and supportive of all things Irish to the bitter end.

The minute she sets eyes on me, her impeccably made-up

face creases with worry as she instantly cops that something is wrong. Flatly, I blurt out that Dan never came and still she doesn't betray the slightest scrap of emotion, but then she never does.

'Smile graciously, dear, and we'll discuss this tomorrow,' she says, pencil-lipped. From the corner of my eye, I can see Chris hugging her husband, Josh, who then snogs her right in the middle of the bar, in full view of everyone.

So that's what true love looks like, is all I can think, dully. Glad I saw it before I died.

Then I spot Blythe, sitting in prime position at the head of a table, basking in compliments and graciously waving over to me like a duchess. Her son/pride and joy/reason for living is beside her, waiting on her hand and foot, leaping up to the bar whenever her drink needs refilling. For her part, every time she as much as looks in his direction it's like she's going to physically burst with pride.

His name is Sean and he just flew in this afternoon on the flight Dan was supposed to be on, which makes me, quite irrationally, dislike him. Ridiculous, isn't it? Even though I've never actually met the guy, already I want to smack him round the head.

Someone shoves a weird looking green cocktail for Paddy's Day in my hand and next thing Jack is striding towards me and actually managing to displace air; his usually high confidence levels now rocketed somewhere up around the stratosphere.

'Well twinkle, twinkle little star,' he says, kissing me lightly on each cheek, smelling sharp and citrusy, his touch still icy cold even though it's like a bleeding furnace in here. I'm just wondering how the hell he does it . . . vampire blood perhaps? Then he gives me one of his up and down,

down and up glances, taking everything in, not missing a trick.

'I couldn't be prouder of you, by the way. That was a magnificent performance and you rightfully belong on cloud nine. Nice dress, by the way, red really is your colour.'

As calmly as I can, I introduce him to Mum who of course, can always be relied on to say the right thing. She congratulates him warmly and makes a few intelligent and insightful comments about the show, lamenting the fact that there's not much by way of decent theatre in DC; that you've got to travel all the way to New York for that.

Jack chats to her about Washington for a bit, unleashing the full force of his kilowatt smile on her, then after a polite bit of conversation he turns to me and completely changes the subject.

'So now do I finally get to meet the elusive Mr Annie Cole? Where is he, anyway? Up at the bar?'

I can't answer him, so instead I just stand there, feeling like I just took a bullet.

Mum, ever reliable, smoothly steps in on my behalf.

'So tell me, Jack, now that the show has opened, how long do you intend to stay in the city? Do you have another production to direct lined up already? Or perhaps you're travelling back to work in Europe?'

It's an adroit subject-change for which I'm deeply grateful, but just then another tidal wave of nausea comes over me and I know I just can't do this. Stand here and make small talk and chit-chat about complete shite like Mum can. Act like everything's normal, when my whole life has just gone into freefall.

'Would you excuse me?' I manage to stammer. 'It's so hot and crowded in here, I just need a bit of air.'

'Annie? Are you OK? Here wait, I'll come with you,' says Jack, suddenly looking concerned, but Mum manages to collar him by asking yet another question about the show and I make my escape through the dense throng of people.

As I somehow push and elbow my way through the mêlée, random snippets of conversation waft over me.

'And you're really a lesbian? Full time?' I overhear an elderly woman, the living image of Joan Rivers, say as I try to wriggle past her, with the door finally in my sights. Honest to God, her face is so pulled back, it almost looks like she could be skydiving.

I pause, momentarily in shock at what I've just heard and when I look to see who's she's talking to, I realise that she's got poor little Alex wedged up against the bar, unable to escape from this awful woman and her incredible rudeness. Alex is actually wearing a dress tonight, unheard of for her, with the ginger hair twice as spiky as it normally is, which somehow makes her look even more fragile and child-like than ever.

For a second, our eyes lock.

I fucking hate this, she seems to be signalling over to me.

I fucking hate this too.

We'll get through it though, won't we? her big blue saucer eyes seem to ask.

I don't know.

Next thing, I'm out into the ice cold of Forty-Fourth Street. Free.

Typical Paddy's Day weather: the light drizzle of earlier has now broken into a fully-fledged storm and it's lashing rain. Thunderbolts and lightning, very, very frightening. But I don't care. The earth has spun round more than once for me today and somehow, I need to bring it to a pause.

The street keeps tilting, then righting itself and I just keep on walking. I don't care that my new dress is ruined or my shoes and hair and make-up.

I just need to pound the pavement.

Which I do. All the way down as far as Times Square, then, as it starts getting really torrential, I stop under an obliging canopy outside a bistro to shelter for a bit.

Try to breathe, try to breathe, just keep breathing . . .

A couple of smokers standing outside courteously ignore me and look the other way, for which I'm deeply grateful.

How much despair has been absorbed by these very streets, I absent-mindedly find myself wondering, staring down at the rain-splashed sidewalk. How much pain and hopelessness? How many broken hearts just like the one I'm hauling about have walked this way before me?

In my deadened, numbed state, I still can't fully accept that it's come to this. Because there's no turning back now. Dan coming over for my opening night was my white flag in the sand and he just walked . . . no . . . wrong word, *bolted* in the opposite direction away from it.

As personalities go, I'm an accommodator, a pleaser, a hand-wringer. But tonight I've reached my cut off point and there's just no going back. I can't live like this and what's more, I won't. Always making allowances for him, always accepting my lowly position at the very bottom of his list of priorities in life.

The thought of one whole year of a long distance relationship at one time seemed like a challenge that we could both possibly rise to, now it's a case of . . . why in the name of arse am I even bothering? If he won't even meet me halfway, then it's about time I faced up to this one insoluble truth – I'm on a loser from the get go. The pillars supporting our whole relationship just crumbled to dust before my very eyes, the moment weight was applied.

And now the pain really begins to hit; the kind of pain you experience from a body blow, or when you lose something essential.

Next thing I hear sobs, big ugly hopeless sobs and realise that they're coming from me. The two smokers glance over at me, standing there in my party dress, soaking wet, then look away uncomfortably, unsure of what to do. I even catch them semaphoring to each other that I'm like someone clearly out on day release, whose temporarily escaped from the clutches of my carer.

And I keep on sobbing, on and on, getting more and more pathetic by the second, indicating to them that they should just take a step away from me, but on absolutely no account get involved. Finally, they stub out their cigarettes, head back inside to the warmth of the restaurant and on I sob, in peace this time.

I'm not sure how much time passes, but after a while, from some distance behind me, I hear the neat click-clack of expensive high heels. I know without even turning around that it's my mother, come to find me. Come to take me back.

'Annie, there you are,' she says calmly, like me whinging on a street corner in the middle of a thunderstorm is a perfectly normal occurrence. 'I've been looking up and down the whole of Forty-Fourth Street for you.' She shelters me with her umbrella, then produces a bunch of tissues from out of nowhere and hands them over.

'I know that you're upset, dear, but remember, all your colleagues are back at Sardi's looking for you and your duty is to be there with them. We can discuss everything else tomorrow, at a more appropriate time.'

God, I'm inclined to forget that about my mother. She'd nearly give the Queen a run for her money in the 'duty first, raw emotion second' stakes.

'Mum, you don't understand . . .' I sniffle into the hanky.

'I understand perfectly, but come on, darling, there's a time and a place to discuss the matter and this is neither. Now, dry your eyes and link my arm, please. I'm taking you back to the party. And you will put on a brave face and you will smile and you'll never betray that there's the slightest thing amiss and we'll get you out of there as quickly as possible.' She's taking over but I know I need her to. The state I'm in, it's kind of comforting to have someone make my decisions for me, so I obediently do as she says. Taxis splash past us as we walk back to Sardi's in the driving rain and I squeeze her arm, so glad that she's here. So glad that to someone like my mother, my having a crying jag in the middle of the street is simply a matter of faulty plumbing.

'I can't do it anymore, Mum,' I say, falling into step with her as the cold air dries my tears, sticky and cool against my face.'

'I know, dear. And I did warn you that it wouldn't be easy.'

Another good thing about my mother – somehow her thoughts always manage to keep pace with mine. She always seems to know what I'm thinking without the necessity of a preamble.

'I'd ask for a separation, only what's the point? I already have one.'

'Tomorrow, dear. We'll talk about what's to be done in the morning.'

'What's to be done? For God's sake, Mum, if my marriage was an animal, you'd have put it to sleep a long time ago.'

'I said, this will wait till tomorrow.'

'If we were a computer program, you'd reboot us.'

'Annie, how many more analogies have you got?'

'As many as it takes to convince myself that it really is over.'

It's still so jam-packed in Sardi's that by the luck of God, no one bar Jack seems to have even noticed that we'd disappeared for a bit. Harvey Shapiro is standing in the middle of the bar, puffed up and swollen with brandy and success in his trademark white suit, looking like a man who owns the civilised world. He's reading out the reviews from a stack of newspapers beside him which, unbelievably, all seem to be raves. One brilliant review miraculously after the other, like ducks in a row.

I stay discreetly at the back with Mum's overcoat draped over my shoulders, so no one clocks how soaked to the skin I am, while raucous cheers go up time and again for each five-star review. In fact, review is the wrong word: dear Jaysus, these notices are more like love letters. Jack is likened to a young Sam Mendes and hailed as the brightest new talent on the Great White Way. I spot him out of the corner of my eye, at least having the good grace to look faintly embarrassed about all the fuss. Like someone who's just won the Lotto, but who doesn't like to brag about it.

All of the cast are showered with praise too, even me. But the most glowing tributes of all are reserved for Liz, whose performance is lauded time and again, confirming what we'd all long suspected – that she's the true star of the show. 'The kind of presence that can elevate sports stadiums into Nuremberg rallies,' as the *New York Times* has it. Bloody hell.

I look around to give her a congratulatory hug, but there's no sign of Liz anywhere, so now that the duty part of the night is over, I whisper to Mum that I'm going to slip away quietly.

'Good idea, dear. I'll get your coat for you and I'll meet you outside.'

Getting to the door is a lot easier said than done though because well-wishers keep pulling me this way and that. Then I see Chris imperiously wave me over from the other side of the bar and I know right well this'll lead to twenty questions about Dan's whereabouts. Which I'm hopeful I may be able to fend off sometime in the distant future, but I certainly can't, not right now.

Just get me out of here, I'm silently praying, *just get me out the shagging door and home to safety and I'll deal with everything tomorrow . . .*

'Surely not leaving already?'

Fuck.

It's Jack, doing his quizzical raised eyebrow thing and eyeing me up and down, as usual, missing nothing.

'Emm . . . yeah . . . I'm just . . . not feeling the best . . . it's been an exhausting night . . .'

'You're missing a great party.'

'I know, but I really need to go . . .'

'I so enjoyed chatting to your mother, by the way. An amazing lady, a real trailblazer. I can see where you get it from.'

'Emm . . . yes . . . she's wonderful . . .'

'Annie, I don't mean to pry but . . . you'd tell me if there was anything wrong, wouldn't you?'

'Course I would.'

Another unexpected thing about marriage breakdown; turns you into the most shameless liar. The fib sounds lame, even in my own head.

'Sure you won't stay to enjoy the celebrations? You deserve it. We can now officially say the show is a smash hit, and you're a considerable part of the reason for its success.'

'I really have to go,' is all I can say, unable to listen to another sentence from him, physically starting to feel my knees buckle.

'You're not well, come on, let me at least take you home,' he says, gently steering me out the door. Just then Mum appears with my coat and our bags and politely says that she'll take it from here.

Jack just nods wordlessly, hails a cab for us, sees us both into it and politely waves us goodbye.

Then he goes back to the opening night celebrations and I go home to face up to the shards of my broken marriage.

'You were way too young getting married, I distinctly remember saying so at the time,' Mum says to me the next morning over breakfast in my little apartment, all Hermès and pearls and serene, calm efficiency.

I'd spent so much money buying in gorgeous food for Dan and me, it seemed a crying shame to let it all go to waste, so I invited Mum over for cream cheese bagels and coffee. Well actually that's a lie; it would be more correct to say she's eating them, I just rearrange mine on a plate then shove it away, my appetite long gone. I couldn't bear to think of all the other plans I'd made for Dan and me today; it still hurt too bloody badly.

203

'What's more, Dan's family agreed with me too,' Mum goes on, as calmly as ever.

'See more of the world, I said to you both. Why rush into this? If you both still feel the same in a few years, then let's talk about marriage. I did advise you at the time, dear. You must remember.'

'I know,' is all I can automatically reply, plonking two Tylenol into a glass of water, then staring at them while they dissolve. Funny thing; I feel like I've a thumping hangover even though I hardly drank at all last night the headache from all the crying is that bad.

'But then, you've always been an old head on young shoulders and for that matter, so has Dan. And you were both just so in love with each other back then, it seemed futile to come between you both.'

If I had the energy to lift my eyes from the glass and give her the evil eye, I would. She's only trying to help, I have to remind myself. She's come all the way from Washington to be with me and now here I am, being rude to her. But then, that's the thing about this depression business.

You're too miserable to give a shit

'But having said that, I still feel that marriage is not something you run away from lightly, you know. After all, it's not like there's any third party involved . . .'

I wince a bit at the ghost she's just invoked. This would be Mum's elegant and slightly oblique way of referring to Dad, who cheated on her all those years ago while she was busy working abroad, thus hammering the final death nail into their marriage. She looks at me expecting an answer and I know I won't get away with just grunting back at her; gotta somehow find the energy to string a coherent sentence together.

'It's no use, Mum,' I somehow manage to sigh. 'You see, this isn't just a one-off case of Dan letting me down, this is the culmination of three long years of constantly being let down and put last and glossed over, time and again. And I've reached break point. Long distant relationships are bloody hard enough when you've got two people who are prepared to work at it, but he just won't. And I can't go on like this anymore. As we say in showbiz, there's no fool like an about-the-title fool.'

Then comes the unspoken thought that's been playing like a loop in my head over and over again, all night, all morning, non-stop. I've spent the entire night tortured by malign, ghostly whispers, all saying one thing:

Yes, Dan was once my magnetic north, yes he was my mainspring, yes once our hearts used to beat only for each other . . . but that was then and this is now . . . because he doesn't love me anymore. The fact is, our marriage has come to an end with barely a shrug on his side and it took some-thing as momentous as this to happen, for me to finally open my eyes and see the truth clearly.

'So what do you plan on saying to him, dear?'

Bloody good question. What do you say in these situations? He was my first boyfriend, I've never even been with anyone else, let alone broken up with anyone before. I'm told 'it's not you, it's me' is customary, but that's hardly the case here though, is it?

'I don't know, Mum. Maybe, the truth. Maybe – it's not me, it's you.'

For once in my life, I don't accurately predict what Dan will say or do, but then maybe all this geographic distance is making me lose my touch. When we do eventually get to talk, properly talk that is, as opposed to leaving approximately fifteen messages for each other or else him having to run off to vaccinate a cow against foot-and-mouth disease . . . there's a resignation and acceptance in his voice. Like someone who knew exactly what was coming and who had the foresight to go ahead and build their own emotional, lead-lined, air raid shelter before the inevitable fallout.

He's measured and understanding, compassionate even.

'I know this is hard on you and I won't even bother trying to make excuses,' is all he says to me, simply. 'You know how it is here, you know better than anyone what my life is like.'

'Yes, I do. And I need you to understand that I can't do this anymore. If you're not prepared to make the effort, why should I?'

Then, the single sentence I never in an aeon thought I'd ever find myself saying to him.

'I've had enough . . . I think I want out.'

A long pause and I can hear the crackle of the wind down the phone from whatever field he's standing in. I know I've hurt him, I know I've drawn blood.

And a small, petulant, childish part of me is glad. He hurt me, now we're quits.

See how he fecking likes it.

Then Dan plucks out a quote from, of all people, Audrey.

'My mother keeps saying over and over again that a marriage is something you can't just take a gap year from . . . but Annie . . . do you think there's any chance that you and I could try?'

'I . . . I . . . don't know what you mean.'

I'm wrong footed now. What's he on about?

Silence, then more static over the phone.

'What I mean is that yes, this is a strain on both of us and you're right, it clearly isn't working out. But seeing as how you're away for a year anyway, then . . . well, what I'm suggesting is . . . let's call this our gap year.'

'Meaning what exactly?'

'That we take a break from each other, a break from being married. That we have a marriage sabbatical, if you will. One full year of not being married. No obligation whatsoever on your part to feel the need to call or check in or try and keep us alive. No pressure, no long-distance relationship, no stress.'

A pause while I try to digest what he's saying.

'I'm saying that I'm prepared to let you go, Annie, for one full year.'

For once, I'm lost for words. *He had this all worked out,* I think, blood suddenly rushing to my head. He knew what was coming and was armed and ready with a counter-proposal.

'But, Dan, then . . . what happens when the year is up?'

'I wish I knew but I don't. I suppose we just cross that bridge when we come to it, don't we?'

In the last weeks, I've made a miserable discovery: that there's a very unfair dichotomy at work in the Universe. The intensity and depth of misery is not at all matched by the intensity and duration of joy. Not by bleeding half. I'm someone who used to believe in a fair and balanced Universe and now my whole belief system has crashed spectacularly. Turns out life isn't like a stage play with clear directions for everybody; it's a mess. It's chaos.

Everyone around me is being amazing though, even on the days when, apart from going to work, basically you couldn't blast me out of the apartment. Mum is back in DC, but the frequency of her phone calls is in direct proportion to how cheery or down I sounded the previous time we talked. But I've come to depend on her and need to hear her drip-feeds of wisdom as often as I possibly can.

Garbo-esque, most of the time I just vant to be alone, revisiting places where Dan and I were once happy, like the Rockefeller Center. Wandering around like love's handicapped, minus the parking space. Wondering if I'll ever be really happy and in love again. But then love is a bit like lightning, it doesn't tend to strike twice, so things aren't exactly looking rosy for me in that department.

Churchill once said when you're going through hell, keep going and that's exactly what I'm trying to do. At the theatre, I keep my head down and get on with the gig as best I can while everyone around me keeps a respectful distance.

Especially Chris, who tried to give me a well-meaning but ultimately misguided dose of tough love by telling me to snap out of this and to remember how lucky I was to have such a wonderful job.

Tough love? Yeah, right. Soft hate, more like.

I suspect Liz told her to back off though, because since then she's kept her distance and now we just exchange curt pleasantries backstage, that's when we have to talk at all. Liz is being terrific though, it's as if she knows all I need is time and space and she's giving it to me in droves.

This evening, she even manages to get me to come out for a quick drink with her after a Saturday night show, when all I want to do is crawl home, eat Ben and Jerry's straight from the tub and watch Letterman. But she's insistent and drags me off to The View, an amazing, revolving cocktail buffet-bar on the eightieth floor of the Marriot Marquis hotel on Times Square, with panoramic views right over the city, all the way out to the Hudson.

As she knocks back one vodka after another, I sip on a glass of white wine while she cracks jokes and reminds me that we all have a duty to strive for happiness, no matter how impossible a goal that may seem.

I know in my heart that she's right, of course. After all, I was happy in New York when we first came here all those weeks ago and I know I will be again. I'll gain on happiness yet. Some of us just need to work a bit harder on it than others, that's all. For now though, my only intent is to feel better and by that I mean to feel nothing at all.

Soon I'm tired though, and I hug Liz before I wearily haul myself out of the bar, leaving her to a bus boy who works there that she's been having an on-off fling with this last while. It's a mild, pleasant night so I walk home, the stroll to and from the theatre so completely familiar to me now I could almost do it blindfolded. Liz is right. It's time for me to let go and move on. Dan clearly has, so why shouldn't I?

I'm at Times Square now, heading east, as ever almost blinded by the glare of the neon lights, so bright it could almost be twelve in the day and not midnight. The crossroads of the world they call it and it's easy to see why. Right now, there's a typical Saturday night buzz about the place, one I've come to know and love so well – taxis are blaring their horns as hordes of people head out to party into the wee small hours, girls dressed in skimpy evening dresses and ridiculous heels are staggering through the traffic, all desperately trying to hail down free cabs, rare as hen's teeth on a Saturday night in Manhattan. The usual pandemonium and chaos you'd expect in the heart of the city that never sleeps.

And it's funny, but in a weird way, some of the exhilaration and sheer joyousness of the city is slowly, very slowly starting to filter through my pores, perking me up again and filling me with an utterly unfamiliar sensation . . . hope. Something I never would have thought possible.

I cross at Broadway, head down West Forty-Fourth Street and stop by a street vendor who I now know by name. I root around for a five-dollar bill and buy Sunday's papers; typical New York, already-printed and available to buy the night before.

'Hey there, Irish,' he greets me cheerily, his nickname for me. 'How was the show tonight?'

'Great thanks, Fred.'

As I hand over the bill and wait for change, I even manage a slight smile.

Slowly the past is beginning to dissipate and now, I force myself to think, it's all about the future.

I'll get through this, I know I can.

After all, this is America, a country where happy endings are a religion.

Maybe my happy ending will be that somehow Dan and I end up as friends.

It's just a question of saying . . . and somehow meaning, this one simple thing.

Goodbye old life. And hello new.

Chapter Nine

Already Easter Sunday. It's a stunningly warm and sunny April day, one of those days that make people roll their eyes at each other and say 'uh-oh, global warming.' Anyroadup, by now myself and the rest of the cast have already settled into a sort of pattern come the weekends: we do a matinee performance at three o'clock on a Sunday afternoon, then we're free till the following Tuesday's show, as on Mondays, Broadway traditionally 'goes dark' for the night. So, in other words, we have the sheer, unadulterated luxury of two blissful nights off, back to back. Believe me, after a long, hard week of eight shows plus two matinees and in the state of mind I've been in of late, two whole nights to myself is pure ecstasy.

Given the day that's in it, we all decided to book a cast meal after the Easter Sunday matinee at Cipriani's restaurant on Forty-Second Street. My first proper night out with the rest of the gang since the horrors of opening night, so this is something of a minor breakthrough for me.

Cipriani's, by the way, is the sort of place you'd only ever go to for a rare treat – the entrées alone cost as much as it would take to clothe a small child and when you factor in bottles of wine on top of that, it's makes for a fairly pricey night out. But it's Easter Sunday and we're all in a Broadway smash hit; a double celebration, so Liz books a table for the lot of us and off we trot after work.

The restaurant is completely stunning, and as we arrive and are whisked off to our table by the maître d', I'm glad we decided to push the boat out this evening for my own little private re-induction back into society. Cipriani's is inspired by the Italian Renaissance; all towering marble columns and soaring ceilings with Chihuly chandeliers gracefully catching and reflecting light in twinkling prisms around us. Everyone is in great form too and some of that seems to rub off on me as if by osmosis; we've had a long, hard week, we're all longing for the two-night break ahead, but most of all, our tongues are collectively hanging out for a decent glass of wine after the sheer slog of today's matinee performance.

There are seven of us in total for dinner and once we're seated, my eye unconsciously wanders around the table resting on each face in turn, pondering on how, in our own way, each of us has come so far since we first arrived in New York.

Funny, but as the weeks have worn on, somehow we've really copper-fastened into a proper little family unit, however dysfunctional. Like all families, at times we're all getting along and at times there are daft, silly rows that flare up out of nowhere, last for a day or two, then blow over like a tropical storm. Usually involving Chris, it has to be said, who's just one of those people who has to be permanently at the dead nucleus of everything, arguments included; like her whole life is one big clenched fist. But that aside, for better or for worse, somehow an incredible bond has been forged between the lot of us, something which in my drifting, aimless state, I for one am particularly grateful for.

And so, in our little family, Blythe has definitely morphed into the Mammy figure; always worrying about the rest of us, fretting and lecturing, but never nagging; her concern for all of us manifests in a more warm-hearted way, worrying whether we're all eating enough green veggies or getting enough vitamin D, that kind of thing. Just like a slightly dotty favourite aunt, but one that you could confide absolutely anything to. For instance, that your husband wants a gap year off from being married to you, that sort of thing.

She and I have grown close in the past few, Godawful weeks and I know she was deeply worried when the news first broke about me and Dan. Often she'd phone me in my blond apartment during the long, lonely afternoons before we were due at the theatre and invite me upstairs to her own apartment for tea, buns and a nice soothing chat. I'd always accept, mainly because spending so much time alone was frankly starting to wreck my head. My apartment, I was beginning to think, meant nothing just that . . . a place to be apart.

Blythe would listen to me sympathetically and when I thanked her for being so understanding, she told me why. It seems she'd been through the whole thing herself and this to her, was little more than history repeating itself.

The theatre is a cruel mistress that effectively broke up her marriage too, she calmly told me, doling out yet more English breakfast tea. (Vile over here; what is it about tea at home that's so much nicer?) She was about my age at the time too, touring with a play out in Sydney for a full twelve months and . . . and same thing really. The long distance relationship thing was way too much for her husband to handle, so by the time she came home, it was all over bar the shouting.

I baulked a bit at this and insisted that my marriage hadn't really broken up as such, we were just having a little gap year off. Nothing more. Blythe said nothing though; just looked at me with understanding and pity in her little sultana eyes. As much as to say, window dress it all you like, love, but I know a broken marriage when I see one.

Anyway, if Blythe is the heart of our family, then Chris is definitely the head. She's sitting opposite me in Cipriani's now, giving out at the top of her voice about how ridiculously expensive everything is here and demanding to know why Liz didn't book Sardi's, like we always do, which is so much more child friendly. Owning the table, her voice dominating, as always. Like she's permanently chairing a meeting. Her husband Josh sits obediently beside her, while her adorable little four-year-old, Oscar, runs around to each of us in turn asking us if we have any colours in our handbags that he can play with.

Oscar and I have become great buddies of late and I've even babysat the odd afternoon for him, to give Chris and her fella a bit of time together. I figure, since I'm home alone most afternoons, then why not make myself useful while I'm at it?

Chris, by the way, is still keeping the kid gloves on around me, although she did come into my dressing room one night and leave a little gift for me. A book from Barnes and Noble in the recovery classic series called- and I really wish I were joking – *Healing the Shame that Binds You*. I thanked her politely, then Liz and I had a good giggle about it the minute she left the room. Not a whole lot else we could do when faced with a book with a title like that, now was there?

'There's a sequel to that self-help book I gave you, you know,' she hissed at me backstage another night. 'It's called *Losing Love: The Next Great Stage of Growth*. Say the word and I'll get it for you, Annie, it's absolutely no trouble.'

She didn't mean any harm I reminded myself, so I let it pass.

Then, sitting beside her, there's little Alex, the baby of the cast and by far the quietest and most unassuming. In fact, after the intensity of the past few months, I know less about her than I do about anyone else here. Except that she's gay, single and actively looking for someone. An intensely private person, she's also one of the most enigmatic people I've ever met. In fact, if you told me she was in the CIA, I wouldn't be a bit surprised. Keeps herself to herself and rarely gets drawn into conversations, but whenever she does join in as she's doing now, it's obvious that for all her youth, she has far older, all-seeing eyes than you'd think. Misses absolutely nothing and the more I get to know her, the more I think that she's the single coolest, calmest and most mature member of the cast.

By far.

Which brings me to Liz – the wild child of our little family unit. And growing wilder by the day it would seem. Time was when she was actively looking for love, but something's shifted since we got here, and now she seems contented with a string of one-night stands, one after the other. Not one of these guys seems to survive her little acid test of lasting longer than a set of her acrylic nails either, and it's such an impossible task to keep pace with all the men who constantly come in and out through the revolving door of her sex life, that I've effectively given up.

Turns out her man of the moment is called Seth; an out-of-work actor that she met one night in Don't Tell Mama, her favourite late-night haunt. She's sitting right beside me at the table, filling me in, all delighted with herself.

'I've been seeing him for almost three whole days now, you know,' she says in her husky, smoky voice, pretending to eat but really just playing with a goat's cheese salad, while I horse into the most sublime roasted spring lamb I've ever tasted in my life.

'Come on, Liz, three days is an antibiotic cycle, not a relationship. Relax, hon, give it time. Get to know each other a bit better.'

'Oh for God's sake, I pretty much know all I want to about him. You know me, I'm not looking for anything serious, I just want a bit of action, that's all.'

'Well . . . what does he do for a living?' I ask, mouth full of delicious pommes frites.

'Trained at the Jacques Lecoq school in Paris, then spent the last eighteen months working on a character called Zebedee for a show he's threatening to write . . . oh, any year now.'

'But if he's not working, then how does he manage to support himself?' I limit myself to asking, knowing that none of us would need to trouble to remember his name for too long. There'll surely be someone new along in a week or so. Always is.

'He pretends that people have backed their cars into him, then sues them into the poorhouse. Very lucrative, it would seem. Anyway, listen to you, the dating I Ching. If you'd any sense you'd be out there, doing exactly what I am.'

'Liz! If you mean that I start dating . . .'

I can't even bring myself to finish the sentence. I've spent so long being a smug married that the very idea of even dipping a toe into the same dating whirlpool that Liz spends her whole existence wallowing in, is way beyond me.

Such a bizarre thought. I was always a carrier for the loyalty gene and now here I am with a husband thousands of miles away, doubtless with his arm up a cow's uterus, actually *craving* a year's break from me, actually being the one to suggest it . . . and still the very idea of infidelity would never even enter my mind.

'No, dope-head,' she laughs throatily. 'Grab this year off with both hands and make the most of it. For feck's sake, Annie, you've just been handed a "get out of jail free card" and yet you've spent the past few weeks moping around the place like someone in self-imposed solitary confinement. You've been given a chance to make relationship history here, so why not go for it? You're always saying that you were a bit like a Victorian bride getting married because you'd never led the life of a single girl, so here's your chance to do exactly that. You missed out on the fun years first time round, so why not reclaim them now, when you've been handed such a golden opportunity?'

Why not indeed.

Anyway, just after Easter Sunday dinner has been wolfed down and as we're all having the great will-we-won't-we dessert debate, a surprise guest lands in. Jack, fresh off a flight from LA and obviously at something of a loose end for the evening. Wearing one of his razor sharp suits and frankly looking more like he just stepped off a catwalk during fashion week in Milan, and not a sweaty five-hour airbus flight from LAX. He works his way around the table, lightly kissing all of us on the cheek, smelling of expensive sandalwood and bringing a brace of ice-cold air into the room with him, as always.

'They told me at the theatre that you guys were all here,' he grins disarmingly, with the megawatt smile set to dazzle. 'Mind if I gatecrash?'

A not-entirely convincing chorus of 'of course not' and 'sure, you're more than welcome!' from everyone as another chair is found and a glass of Veuve Clicquot plonked in front of him. But the atmosphere has shifted down a gear – like the headmaster just landed in on us and will start doling out performance notes any minute now.

Truth be told, I've barely seen Jack since the opening night; yes, he's been in and out of the theatre to monitor the show the odd night, sticking his head into our dressing rooms to give us yet more notes and keep us on our collective toes. And I'm told he's been going to Sardi's after the show on occasion with the others as well. But because I've been in such self-imposed isolation, I've been well out of the loop. So anything could be going on in his life and I'd be the last to know.

Although I did hear from Liz that he's been spending a lot of time out on the West coast, being feted, wined and dined by a string of movie producers, all no doubt flinging film scripts and mega budgets at him, begging him to direct. Kind of the next logical career move for him, when you think about it. According to Liz at least; he's conquered the theatre world, so an Oscar on his sideboard would doubt-less be next on his to-do list.

Predictably, our little Easter dinner breaks up pretty soon after Jack arrives, with Chris anxious to get Oscar home to bed and Blythe asking if she can share a cab with them so as to save on taxi fare. As we all stand round on the pavement outside saying our goodbyes, little Alex quietly says she's off to a downtown place below Tenth Street she likes hanging out in, called *The Celebrity Club.*

'Sounds good to me, let's all go,' says Jack, but stops himself short when he picks up on a momentary flash of annoyance in Liz's expressive eyes.

As Alex power walks off for the subway with her backpack strapped to her, Jack turns to Liz and asks, 'What was all that about?'

'Just giving the kid a bit of privacy,' shrugs Liz, lighting up a fag. 'Besides, I hardly thought gay bars were your thing, darling.'

A taxi with its light on passes and I'm just about to flag it down and say my good nights, when next thing I know, I'm physically being strong-armed away from it by both Liz and Jack. One on each side of me, like a pair of bouncers.

'What the . . .? What do the pair of you think you're doing? What is this?' I almost yell, struggling to shake them off.

'Oh for feck's sake, come on,' says Liz, fag teetering on the edge of her lip. 'I'm taking you to Don't Tell Mama. You think you're getting home this early when it's taken me weeks just to get you to stay out beyond eleven o'clock at night?'

'I'll second that,' laughs Jack, his hand icy cold against mine. 'Besides, I haven't seen you for ages and I want to talk to you.'

I'd shrug if I could, but each of them has one of my arms in a vice-like grip as if I might bolt at any second, so like a hostage, off I'm dragged and before I know where I am, I'm sitting between the two of them in the back of a taxi. Doors locked, windows locked, no escape.

Turns out Don't Tell Mama is actually a late night cabaret bar in a converted cellar on West Forty-Sixth Street, and clearly Liz is a regular as we've no bother whatsoever getting in, despite a long, snaking queue outside the door. Two seconds later, we're being ushered to a prime table right in front of a tiny, makeshift stage with a piano centre stage and footlights dotted in front of it, a bit like an old Edwardian vaudevillian hall.

'This place is legend!' Liz tells us, excitedly scanning down the drinks menu. 'Anyone is welcome to get up and bash out an old show tune and believe me they do. It's kind of like it's a magnet for everyone who got rejected by Simon Cowell on *American Idol.*'

'Come to think of it, I've actually heard of Don't Tell Mama,' says Jack, taking it all in, his sharp eyes as usual missing nothing. 'I believe you get singers from the back-row chorus of the Broadway musicals coming here to belt out the big show stopping numbers, in the hopes of impressing any stray producers who may be passing through. Or indeed,' he adds cheekily, 'directors, for that matter.'

'It's brilliant, you'll both love it,' says Liz, getting up to go to the bathroom. 'Will someone order me a glass of champagne? Back in a sec.'

A short, tense silence after she's gone. I can feel Jack's icy, intense eyes on me and as ever, I'm at a complete loss as to what to say to him whenever it's just the two of us on our own and it's not show-related. Not helped by the fact that the place is loud and buzzy, with skimpily dressed girls who look like models wafting about the place serving drinks, while an invisible DJ plays 'Poker Face' by Lady Gaga.

So to fill dead air, I politely ask him about his trip to LA and this takes up a good five minutes, with me silently willing Liz to hurry the feck up and get back to the table the whole time he's talking.

What in the name of Jaysus is keeping her anyway?

'So have you ever been out to LA on your travels?' asks Jack politely.

'No, never,' I smile, grateful to him for keeping the conversation going.

'Disneyland for grown-ups. Two things you always need to remember about the place: one, everyone, absolutely everyone is mental. Completely and utterly off their heads. All terrified of losing their coveted place by the fire and seeing as how most of them have no idea how they got there in the first place, that obviously makes for sheer lunacy. And two, no one is prepared to make a decision because they're all so afraid of failure. Believe me, I've had meeting after meeting in these massive sky-rise offices, stuffed with movie executives, with titles like Vice President in charge of this and CEO in charge of that – all salad. Because each studio has one and only one green-lighter at the apex who actually has the go-ahead to make a decision. Beats me how anyone gets anything made at all.'

I laugh at this, relaxing a little and he chats on pleasantly enough. You won't believe this, he tells me, but he's actually gone and got himself an agent now. He challenges me to name any movie superstar who flits into my head then laughs and says, yup, that his agent handles them too. He's been inundated with scripts over the past few weeks, but the vast majority are complete shite. A load of sequels that they might just be prepared to try an untested novice film director on, or else pictures with titles like *Jessie James Meets Frankenstein's Daughter*.

'You have got to be making that one up,' I laugh, feeling

my guard coming down for the first time and pleasantly surprised at just how easy he is to chat to.

'Not a word of a lie. It's comparatively easy to get a crap script to direct. But what I'm really looking for is a low-budget indie flick, where I wouldn't have a studio breathing down my neck and where I'd be able to have some degree of artistic control.'

I nod and smile, unable to imagine a control-freak like Jack being dictated to by any studio head and feeling sorry for any poor misguided eejit who'd dare try.

'Like *American Beauty*, that's the kind of project I'm looking for,' he goes on. 'You know, a small film, but with a cracking screenplay and terrific roles for the cast. And where I'd get to rehearse with them for months in advance of shooting.'

'Spoken like the true successor to Ken Loach.'

'Well, now you're just flattering me, Miss Cole.'

Don't quite know what to say to that, but just then Liz finally, finally, finally gets back from the bathroom, dragging a gorgeous looking black guy in her wake.

'Everybody, this is George, George, meet everybody. We just met outside the loo. Isn't he a fine bit of stuff, as we say back in Ireland? Georgie, turn around so everyone can see your tight little bod.'

George looks faintly embarrassed at this and in fairness, would you blame him? But Liz insists on twirling him around, then pinches him playfully on the bum, all the while looking adoringly up at him. Then, in a flash, she notices the empty table and her whole expression suddenly becomes thunderous.

'Hey . . . where's the champagne?' she demands, thudding her bag down. 'Didn't I ask you to order me champagne

222

when I was gone? I want champagne and I want it now! Jack darling, can you make that happen?' Another instantaneous gear-shift in her mood and now she's looking at him flirtatiously and almost purring, 'You're so good at making things happen.'

A waiter passes and Jack takes his time ordering; a guy who sure as hell knows his way around a wine list. A second later, Liz disappears off to the still-empty dance floor with George in tow, then about two minutes into Eminem and Rihanna singing 'Love The Way You Lie', she starts to flagrantly kiss him, all tongues and hands disappearing down the back and pretty soon the front of his jeans, not giving a shite that we're all staring at her, aghast.

Hard not to, the girl's a complete sideshow.

'Emmm . . . you know, I've never seen her like this before,' I tell Jack, feeling that I should say something, that somehow not acknowledging her carry-on is somehow only making it worse.

'Oh really? Because I've *only* ever seen her like this.'

Suddenly he turns away from the floorshow she's laying on, then swivels back to me, the satyr eyebrows slanting dangerously downwards. 'So tell me something and I'd like the truth, please. How long has Liz been doing lines of coke for?'

'*What* did you say?'

'Oh, you heard me.'

'She's not . . . I mean, she isn't . . . come on, Liz is clean, she doesn't do drugs!'

'Really, my dear? And since when?'

'Since . . . well I don't know, since forever. Yeah she likes a drink, but then don't we all?'

'You haven't exactly been hanging around with her that much lately though, have you? Or with anyone else for that matter. So tell me this. How exactly would you know what she's shoving up her nostrils in her spare time?'

'No,' I say firmly, shaking my head. 'She wouldn't do drugs, I know she wouldn't.'

'Open your eyes, my deluded little innocent and take a look. The wildly dilated pupils, the voracious behaviour, not caring that she's making a complete exhibition of herself, strutting round the place looking like she belongs on a truck mudflap . . . she's coked off her head. Believe me, I've seen enough snow in my time to know.'

I stare back at Liz, which is actually hard not to, half the club is as well. Now she's temporarily abandoned George and is gyrating like a pole dancer up against a short, wiry guy, letting him run his hands all over her arse and boobs while she throws her head back and laughs lustily, blonde hair extensions swishing enticingly, knowing she's the centre of attention and lapping it all up. And now George is at her back, grabbing the G-string from behind her jeans and roughly kissing her neck . . . Honest to God, it's like watching a soft porn threesome in the making.

Christ Alive, I think, Jack's right. This isn't just Liz being wild and carefree and abandoned like she normally is on a night out. It's coke. Has to be. Suddenly I realise that what he's saying makes perfect sense.

'I'm sorry if I've shocked you,' he says, leaning into me closer still, 'but believe me, I know high when I see it. The question is, what do we do? What the girl does in her own free time is, after all, her own business and thankfully no concern of mine. But if her personal habits ever start to affect the show, then that's when I'll be forced to step in. If her behaviour, even for one minute, threatens to jeopardise things . . .'

There was no need for him to even finish the sentence. Because we both knew exactly what would happen next. She'd be on the next plane home and an understudy would take over, rave reviews or no rave reviews. Jack's not someone you mess with. What he says, he means.

'I'll talk to her tomorrow,' I say, already dreading it. Wondering how in hell I'll even bring up the subject and already half-knowing what her response would surely be. To laugh at me first, then accuse me of being a prematurely middle-aged aul frump. But I'll still try talking to her anyway, I silently vow. Maybe this is just a one-off thing, maybe she's only tried it because she's got a few nights off from work . . . maybe it's all perfectly OK and I don't even need to worry.

Jack expertly cracks open the bottle of champagne and pours each of us a glass.

'But of course, Liz is far from being my only concern among the cast.'

'What do you mean?'

'Annie, I know it's absolutely none of my business, but the trouble is that I'm neither blind nor stupid. I hear things. And I want you to tell me honestly if everything is alright with you. In your private life, I mean.'

'Who said anything to you about . . .?'

Then I break off, thinking, oh holy shite. I don't even need to finish the question. Could have been Liz or Chris or any of them, on one of those long boozy nights in Sardi's when I was home with a tub of Ben and Jerry's and the TV. No secrets in showbiz, none. And if it's one thing I've learned of late, it's this: in the Shubert Theatre, there seems to be more leaks than a winter vegetable medley.

'I'm sorry,' he says, looking keenly at me. 'I didn't mean to pry. Just checking that you were OK, that's all.'

'I'm fine. Absolutely fine.'

Probably no need for the absolutely, makes me sound so *not* fine.

'I felt such anger on your behalf on the opening night, I really did . . .'

'You know something? Bad old subject.'

I hard-wire my mouth into a smile and half raise my glass of champagne, as if to say, let's find something else to talk about. Anything. Because frankly, this feels like he's probing at scar tissue that hasn't yet had a chance to heal.

But Jack's looking for answers and isn't letting go till he's got some.

'I did try to warn you, remember? Back in Dublin, at the end of our first week's rehearsals. Long-distance relationships are a disaster. I did tell you. I've been there myself and I can tell you from bitter experience that after a while, it's pretty much akin to banging your head off a granite wall. Would you agree, my dear?'

I give a rueful shrug, thinking . . . he's right. Banging my head off a granite wall was almost exactly what it felt like.

'Which is precisely why I don't do relationships,' he goes on smoothly, topping up our champagne glasses. 'But then I've always found the whole business of Eros to be such a bloody nuisance.'

I take a sip and cast around for something else to talk about. But Jack's on a roll now and there's no deflecting him.

'You see, I'm not the marrying kind,' he goes on, 'but believe me if I were, there's no way on earth I'd let any wife of mine take off on her own for a full year. At least not without either coming with her or else doing everything in my power to try and stop her. Otherwise, what's the point of even being married in the first place? What I'd very much like to know is this: what was that Dan guy even *thinking?*'

Dan. Usually I've got lightning quick at booting him out of my thoughts or affections on the rare occasions when he creeps in, but . . . maybe I've drunk too much, maybe it's the way Jack is questioning me so keenly, so interested in everything that's going on, that slowly makes me want to open up just a bit.

'If I hadn't taken this job,' I tell him slowly, trying to articulate thoughts I haven't allowed to bubble up to my conscious mind in a long, long time, 'then . . . then, I'd have felt like a shipwrecked passenger who let the only rescue boat sail by. If that makes any sense.'

'Things really all that bad at home?' he asks, his voice full of genuine concern now.

Which is touching and sensitive of him, but still I don't answer. It's not rudeness, I just can't bring myself to.

'I'm sorry,' he says simply, squeezing my bare arm with his ice cold hand.

'I fully apologise and withdraw that last sentence. It was ungentlemanly. Never quite know when to pull back, do I? I just wanted to make sure that you were OK, that's all.'

A conciliatory statement, so I meet him half-way.

'It's not that things were that bad at home,' I tell him, glugging back a mouthful of champagne for Dutch courage, 'not at all. But at the time, before this job came along and rescued me that is, it really did seem that way. I used to wake up every single morning knowing exactly how the day ahead would pan out and feel like I was suffocating. As surely as if someone had tied a plastic bag over my head. In fact, there were times . . . I mean . . . I often used to think . . .' and that's when I break off.

Too hard to put into words. Not something I can articulate, and certainly not right now.

'It's no use, Jack. I don't think you'd understand.'

'Try me. I've been told I'm a good listener.'

'Well . . . let's just say . . . I often thought that because I'd married so ridiculously young, that I'd missed out on a huge chunk of my life, the best years in fact, the fun, single years and somehow, this job seemed like the best possible way to somehow reclaim all that missing time. If that makes any sense to you.'

He's looking at me so intensely that I find myself trailing off a bit.

'Never mind, it's impossible to explain. Maybe I'll try and explain it to you someday, but not here and not now.'

'I might just hold you to that.'

'Oh, but just for the record, in spite of what you may have heard, here's the truth straight from the horse's mouth. Dan and I haven't broken up, we're just taking a bit of time out, that's all.'

'Time out?'

'That's right. A marriage sabbatical, if you like.'

He whistles. 'New one on me.'

'A bit like a gap year.'

There's a long silence now, one I make absolutely no attempt to fill and eventually Jack cops on that this really isn't something I particularly want to discuss in a Forty-Sixth Street dive bar with a relative stranger. He leans in and takes my hand, but tenderly.

'You know, I think I owe you an apology, Annie,' he says more softly. 'It's your first night out in a long time and the last thing I wanted to do was to upset you in any way. And I faithfully promise not to mention your private life again, unless expressly given permission by you. Am I forgiven?'

Funny thing: I've known Jack to be tough, acerbic, brilliant, sarky and passionate, but he sure as hell keeps this side under wraps. The kinder, gentler, more concerned side, that is, that I'm only really seeing for the first time tonight. A man with leagues and fathoms of depths to him, I decide there and then. A guy who really takes some getting to know, if women ever really do get to know the real Jack Gordon.

I say yes of course he's forgiven and thankfully, he changes the subject.

'So how are you liking New York then?'

The satyr eyes slant downwards as his expression relaxes and he winks at me. 'That a safe enough subject for you?'

I smile a bit.

'Yes, good and safe. And I love New York, at least the little bit of it that I've seen.'

'Have you done the Empire State yet?'

'Nope.'

'The helicopter tour at sunset?'

'Never even knew there was one.'

'Strawberry Fields at Central Park?'

'Ehh . . . 'fraid not, sorry.'

'The Hudson River in the moonlight?'

'The river? Oh come on, do I look like Mark Twain?'

He laughs at this, but keeps on questioning me.

'Ellis Island and the Statue of Liberty?'

'Emmm . . . no. Though according to Blythe, there's a great discount store near it called Century Twenty One.'

'Annie, what in God's name have you been doing with your free time here?'

Watching telly, I want to say. Moping. Trying to do anything other than think about Dan. I'm too ashamed to tell him that, like a guinea pig trapped in a wheel, the only bits of the city I'm familiar with are all within a tiny three-street radius of the theatre.

'Right then,' he says firmly. 'That settles it.'

'Settles what?'

'Well, you're at a loose end during the day and I've got all this free time until the right movie project comes along. So, in the meantime, why don't you and I become tourists?'

Much, much later, Liz and I are in the ladies loos together.

'I need to talk to you,' I hiss at her into the mirror as she piles lip gloss on top of yet more lip gloss.

'Shit, what is it with this fucking mirror?' she says, ignoring me and squinting at her reflection up close and personal. 'Some mirrors are our friends, but not this one, sadly. All I see looking back at me is a big pile of O.L.D.'

'Liz, will you please listen to me?'

'I am, I am. As it happens, I need to talk to you too, babe. So what's the story with you and Jack?'

'No story, we're just talking,' I say defensively, then drop my voice so as not to be overheard. 'Now what I want to ask you is . . . are you by any chance doing lines of coke tonight?'

'Oh shit, sorry,' she says lightly. 'Did you want some? It's right here, in my bag. Should be enough for a couple more lines, at least.'

'Liz!'

'What's your problem? Everyone does it, for feck's sake.'

'Everyone does not do it and I'm concerned about you. What's more, Jack's noticed and now he's up the walls worried as well.'

'Relax, grandma, I've been doing it for a long time and trust me, you'd like it. Makes you feel like the whole world is in love with you. Aaaa-mazing. I feel phee-nomenal.'

'Liz, you're doing coke on top of all the booze you've drunk? Christ Alive, what is with you? You won't be happy till you've partied yourself into an ICU and end up being fed through a shagging straw!'

'Oh please, I've hardly drunk anything. Few cocktails, some champagne, nothing more. I may be American drunk, but I'm Irish sober. Besides, who gave you the right to start acting like my conscience? For Christ's sake, Annie, look at you, perched on my shoulder, judging me. Well you can piss off with yourself; I don't want to be judged, I just want to have a good time. And by the way, you really shouldn't pull that disapproving face, you know. Makes me see what you'll look like when you're older.'

Bugger it anyway, I think. Pointless talking to her when she's this high, so I decide to wait till tomorrow, when she's come down a bit.

'Besides, you never answered my question about Jack,' she says, turning back to the mirror and lashing on more bronzer than you'd normally see on the whole of Girls Aloud. 'Mightn't be my type, but I can see that some sex-starved women might find him completely fuck-able. Like you, for instance. Don't you just want to drag him home

231

and do it with him once . . . just to get it out of your system? So come on, tell me. What's going on with you and him anyway?'

'It's called having a conversation with a man without sticking your tongue down his gob or letting him paw you up in front of two hundred people. You should try it sometime.'

Her reply could strip metal.

'Still so bloody middle-aged,' she sighs into the mirror. 'Little countrified wifey let loose on the big city and all you can do is wag your parochial finger in my face because I'm having a fabulous time and you're not. All I'm suggesting is that Jack could be like your own personal sexual nicotine patch, that's all. To help wean you off Dan. You need to get laid, honey, and badly. It would help remove that stick you've got lodged up your arse. Make you far more fun to be around as well, which would be no bad thing.'

'Right that's it, I'm going,' I say, picking up my bag. 'See you outside.'

'Oh, I've pissed you off, have I?' she says, her voice dripping with sarcasm. 'Dear oh dear, how WILL I sleep at night? Oh yeah, I just remembered. I've got pills for that too.'

Seems I'm learning another lesson about Liz when she's coked up. It turns her into a very dislikeable version of herself. The very worst version of herself, in fact.

The Princess of bleeding Darkness.

'Oh did I hit a nerve?' she asks dryly. 'Are you having a little anxiety stroke because I dared to tell you the truth? Or maybe you're just cranky because it's well past your bedtime. Must be . . . ohh . . . what . . . almost midnight by now? Time for your warm milk and Ovaltine in front of your new best friend, the TV, surely?'

232

'Goodnight, Liz.'

My hand is on the exit handle with one foot outside the door, when suddenly she calls me back.

'You know what Jack told me a while ago?' She's eyeballing me in the mirror now, while readjusting her boobs so they jut out provocatively over her top.

'I couldn't give a shite what he told you. See you later.'

'Chris and I were in Sardi's with him a few weeks back,' she continues, ignoring me, 'and one of the hostesses was practically flinging herself at him. So we were teasing him and probing him about whether he was single or not . . .'

'For God's sake . . .'

'And you know what he told us?'

'I don't know and I don't care and what's more I really am leaving now.'

Don't know why I even bother entertaining her when she's high like this. Completely futile exercise.

'That there was only one woman he really wanted, but he couldn't get her. Know why?'

'Course I don't.'

'Because she's already married.'

And then she turns to stare pointedly at me.

That night, the dreams started

It was New Year's Eve after my first term at Allenwood and Dan had invited me down to Waterford to stay with his family. But as it happened, that night his parents had taken the seven-year-old Jules to visit cousins a good forty mile drive away, when after dire weather warnings, the worst snowstorm in twenty years enveloped the whole of the south east. Which meant that the roads were utterly treacherous and his family had no choice but to stay put.

Which meant that Dan and I were left together at The Moorings. All alone for the whole night.

I'll never forget it – the house was so icy cold that we pretty much camped out by the fire in the drawing room, the only room in the whole place where the temperature was fluctuating somewhere above zero. I had just spent Christmas with Mum in hot, humid South America so as far as I was concerned, this, by contrast, was like something out of Charles Dickens. The snow was beating down outside and the fire crackling away while he and I toasted marshmallows and sipped hot chocolate, side by side on the sofa, with a giant fleecy rug tucked over me for extra warmth and snugness. We'd chatted and laughed and watched *The Truman Show* on DVD and warbled our way through every Christmas-y song we knew.

But now that it was close on midnight, the mood between us had shifted and become more mellow. I'd only arrived back in Ireland the previous day and was trying my best to stifle yawns as the jet lag finally hit me.

Meanwhile Dan was stretched out beside me, hands behind his head, staring into the fire and lost in thought.

'So,' he eventually said after a long, easy silence. 'You and Mike Sherry.'

'Oh don't,' I shuddered. 'He annoys me.'

'Good. I'm glad, he annoys me too.'

'Dan?' I had to ask the question. Opportunities rarely came as golden as this one.

'Yup?'

'You and Yolanda?'

He turned on his side to face me and even in the dim firelight, I could see him grinning.

'Yolanda who?'

For a delicious moment, neither of us spoke, we just looked at each other, exchanging souls. I smiled, afraid to say any more in case I broke the spell. Then, I started to shiver involuntarily as the fire began to die down.

'Hey,' he said, 'you're frozen. Slide over here. Allow me to be your personal electric blanket for the night.'

Well, I couldn't resist him for another second. Gently, he pulled me towards him, wrapping his strong, chunky arms tight around me, instantly warming me up. He smelt musky and as my head lay in the crook of his arm, all I wanted was for him to bend down and kiss me. If I was frozen a minute ago, suddenly not only was I hot, but it was making me hotter just to look at him.

Then, a mile away from Stickens village, we heard the church ring out the bells for New Year.

'Happy New Year, Annie,' he murmured gently, so close to me that I could feel his lips gently graze my ear.

'Happy New Year, Dan.'

Bliss, I thought. A rare and perfect moment. Lying here in his arms is sheer ecstasy and nothing, absolutely nothing could possibly improve this magical night.

'Any new year's resolutions?' I whispered through the silence.

'Just one.'

'Which is . . .?'

'Never, ever to let you go.' And I swear, his voice was as soft as breath.

If that's true, I thought, then before it's barely started, my life just got made.

I looked up at him. Slowly, barely perceptibly, he moved his head down towards me and a second later, his soft lips were on mine. We kissed slowly at first, gently, tenderly. And then it began to grow more and more passionate and intense as all the months of waiting for him, longing for him, finally paid off.

Next thing I knew, my fingers were running through his thick, black hair while his hands were running down my waist and up my thighs, pulling me even closer to him, kissing me far, far harder now, far more intensely, his tongue in my mouth and mine in his.

I was wrong it seemed. The night could and just did improve dramatically.

I can pinpoint the exact moment that I fell in love with Dan and this was it.

On the stroke of New Year, nineteen ninety-nine.

With a heart-stopping jolt, I suddenly wake up in my apartment in New York City. It's past four am but I don't care. I just have an overriding need to talk to Dan. With absolutely no idea what I'd say to him even if I actually got him on the phone, which doubtless, I wouldn't.

I just want to talk to him, that's all.

Just to hear his voice.

I even get as far as dialling the first three digits of his mobile number.

Then I remember and hang up the phone.

SUMMER

Chapter Ten

June already. New York is getting hotter and more humid by the day. The streets are packed with tourists now and at this stage I can nearly spot them a mile away, with their *I Heart NY* novelty T-shirts and baseball caps, queuing up day and night at the half-price ticket booth at Times Square, all looking for discounted tickets to get into *The Lion King*.

The native New Yorkers are easy enough to spot too: they're the slightly terrifying army of professionals that you see striding in and out of buildings like the MetLife, who wear black all winter long, then abruptly switch to white around now and keep on wearing it till Labor Day. Like it's some kind of uniform. I see them everywhere I go, strutting down Madison and Fifth, rushing, rushing, always rushing, talking into cellphones, gulping back their travelling soya lattes from Starbucks; some of the women cleverly producing fans from their Hermès Kelly bags, then wafting them in front of their slightly too-immobile faces, trying to stave off at least some of the hot, dead air that's smothering the city like a blanket.

Never in my life did I think I'd be so grateful for air-con at the theatre and in the apartment: I've known humidity in my time, but nothing compares to the clammy dryness of a New York summer. Small wonder rich people vacate the city in droves around now, to party at elegant summer-shares in the Hamptons, then return when the city cools down a bit, come the fall. (American for autumn.)

The good news is that the show is continuing to pack them in night after night and although I should be on cloud nine about this, I've got one constant nagging worry that just won't go away: namely, Liz. Because if her behaviour was a mild worry a few weeks ago, now it's escalated into a full-blown, major cause for concern. Which for the moment at least, I'm desperately trying to keep to myself, lest it leak out among the cast that her general carry-on is growing more and more unstable with every passing day. Containment, I figure at least gives Liz a chance to get her act together in private, without the white-hot glare of scrutiny from all sides, which would only escalate things out of all control. The principal worry being that if Chris hears about it, it'll be all over the theatre in the blink of an eye and then of course the minute it filters back to Jack, the game's up. Liz could very well find herself out of a job and frankly, I think work is the only thing that's even remotely keeping her on the straight and narrow right now.

Ever since that awful night at Easter in Don't Tell Mama, I've noticed that there are good days and bad days with her, except that now, the bad days are well and truly starting to outnumber the good ones. Example? A few weeks back, one morning at about eleven-ish, I got a call from her on my mobile, sounding completely out of her head. She was so panicky and paranoid it took me an age to get the full story out of her, but apparently, she'd gone home with some guy the previous night and had now woken up in his apartment, totally alone, not knowing where she was or who she'd been with and without any money, not even for the taxi fare home.

Root around the place, I told her firmly, look for mail or even a household bill with the owner's address on it. If he has a desk, try there. If necessary, go through drawers. After much coaxing and encouraging, I eventually got her to do it and as luck would have it, she discovered a phone bill stuck to his fridge.

With a Brooklyn address.

'Stay where you are, honey, I'm on the way. And try to stay calm!'

Took me a good half hour just to find a cab that would drive me all the way out to Brooklyn, but eventually I did and when I went to buzz the intercom for Liz to let me in, I saw she was already downstairs waiting for me, trembling and terrified, a million miles from her usual swaggering, overt, sexy confident self. I got the shock of my life seeing her: she was a complete mess, her clothes were torn and manky and her eyes bloated and raw red from crying. Most frightening of all though, her nose was battered and bloody, like she'd been punched square in the face.

'Jesus, Liz, what happened?'

'He didn't mean to do it,' she sobbed, 'we were just fooling around, we'd each done a few lines and . . . it was an accident. Honestly.'

I cradled her into the cab, made her lie back to try and arrest the bleeding and asked the driver to stop off at the nearest A&E. But Liz, so weak and helpless a minute ago, suddenly kicked up. No, she insisted, I'm fine. I can't face hospital, she said, that would mean blood and urine tests and all sorts of questions being asked.

But she and I both knew what was really worrying her.

Given what was probably floating around in her bloodstream right now, who knew what hospital tests might lead to? Drug offences? Maybe even charges? In a blink, she could find herself on a flight back home, out of a job.

Next thing, she was pleading with me.

'Please, Annie, I need you to be a pal and say nothing about this. Not to anyone. I'll be fine for tonight, I swear. Just help me clean up my nose and no one will suspect a thing. And I'll stop doing the stuff, I swear I will. No more lines, ever. This'll be the last time. I promise.'

Well what could I say? I had that awful feeling you get when your back's completely to the wall and you're faced with no other choice.

'Right then, this time, I promise,' I eventually sighed. 'On condition that it never happens again. You have got to stop doing coke, Liz, or it's going to kill you.'

'It'll never happen again. Never. I give you my word.'

And I desperately wanted to believe her, so of course, I did.

But now, every time my phone rings, my heart stops in my mouth just in case it's her, lost somewhere, beaten up maybe, needing help. Worse still; she's not hanging around with the rest of us nearly as much as she used to. Instead she seems to have fallen in with a shadowy new group of friends, who we're never introduced to or even invited to meet. She just disappears off after each show saying she's 'got people to see' and that's as much as you'll get out of her. Like this is a whole side of her life she wants to keep separate from us.

And every night when I walk to the theatre, I don't really relax until she saunters into the dressing room. Even if she's not in great shape, I feel nothing but deep relief. Because at least if she's showed up for work, then that's something, isn't it?

In fact, the only bright light on the horizon for me on these long, hot, sultry days are the little touristy excursions I've been having with Jack. Nothing extravagant, nothing flashy, but by now, we've covered a fair amount of the city and I'm amazed at how familiar it's all becoming to me. Funny, but under his guiding hand, I'm slowly turning into a real-live native New Yorker.

Ever since Easter we've been meeting up in the afternoons, maybe a couple of times a week, to see the sights. He's become like a kind of indispensable Sherpa to me, filling my head full of facts and tales about the city I never knew. We take turns, so one day he'll pick a particular excursion for us to do and the next time I'll decide where to go. Whenever it's Jack's call though, he'll invariably go for an art gallery and I swear to God, at this stage, I don't think there's a single square foot of the Guggenheim or The Met that we haven't nearly worn the floor down on.

His knowledge of art is exhaustive and his frame of reference is unlimited; he knows everything there is to know whereas I know feck all, so effectively he's been coaching me. I've come to enjoy these lazy, cool afternoons strolling through room after room in MOMA and The Met as he explains to me the intricacies of neo-classicism and how after the First World War, there was a move away from Cubism and Expressionism and more towards the work of modern classical artists like Jean Cocteau and de Chirico.

Strange to think that I was terrified of Jack when I first met him: now that I've really got to know him, I look back on that petrified girl who first stumbled out onto the National theatre stage to audition for him, ooohh, what feels like about a hundred years ago . . . and I smile. Because now, not only am I'm starting to look forward to our little touristy jaunts together, I'm actually having a laugh with him. Yes, he can be tough and work-obsessed and a total perfectionist, but at least now I understand why. There's a deep passion behind his drive, an overwhelming need for excellence and flawlessness in everything he does. But behind that, he's smart, sharp, terrific company, always attentive and witty and best of all . . . he's the only person in my life who never asks me questions about my private life.

Nothing. Nada. And nor do I quiz him about his personal stuff either. Like a kind of unspoken pact between us.

Which right now, is something I'm deeply appreciative of.

Anyroadup, one baking hot, clammy afternoon, he asks me to meet him at Barneys on Madison and Sixtieth Street, an uber-posh designer store, where unless you sweep into it looking rich, rich, rich, then the doorman looks at you a bit like a head butler showing in a chimney sweep. Which is why I've avoided it till now. But Jack insists we go there and as ever, point blank refuses to take no for an answer.

'I've got a bachelor party to go to tonight and I need to get a tuxedo for it,' he explains, flashing his toothy smile at me as we head through the revolving doors and into the ultra-chic surroundings. 'Mind helping me pick one out?'

'Of course not,' I smile, actually delighted to be in out of the heat and wafting around a crisp, cool air-conditioned store. 'Just don't expect me to buy anything, that's all.'

Jack looks so at home here, I think, strolling beside him towards the elevators, so elegant and cool in his chinos and a loose white linen shirt. In fact you'd nearly swear he'd just been styled by *GQ* magazine for a photoshoot.

'Oh now come on, who knows?' he teases, glancing at me suggestively as we wait for the elevator, 'you might just see something for yourself here that you have to have. You know, I think you'd look absolutely fantastic in a Diane von Furstenberg wraparound dress . . .'

'At the prices they charge in here, are you kidding me?'

'Just try one on. It'll be fun. Trust me.'

And so I do and I have to admit, this is the best fun I've had in I don't know how long. I don't have any shopping buddies here in New York: barring Blythe, none of the others have the slightest interest in clothes and Blythe herself limits her shopping to all the midtown bargain basement discount stores. And of course back home Dan's such a man's man, he'd have to either be chloroformed or else be physically dragged, kicking and screaming, to even get him within a ten foot radius of the nearest department store. But here in Barneys, it's like I'm really seeing Jack in his natural element – when he's surrounded by exclusive, expensive goodies, all with designer labels hanging off them.

Most fellas would be bored stupid and stand yawning or else looking at their watches in a women's fashion department, but not Jack. He spends ages wandering around the Diane von Furstenberg section, holding dress after dress up against me, eventually settling on a scarlet wraparound one. He insists I try it on and patiently waits for me outside the changing room, stretching his long legs out on a pale mink sofa, the picture of laid-back cool. When I do emerge, he gives me one of his keen, appraising up-and-down-looks, then wolf-whistles.

'Stunning! You're an absolute knockout in that dress. Why don't you wear red more often? It really is your colour, you know. And you should put your hair up too. Suits you off your face.'

'Spoken like Gok Wan himself.'

'Guilty as charged,' he laughs playfully, 'I'll freely admit it – there's nothing I enjoy more than being surrounded by beauty. And you, my dear, happen to be a very beautiful woman. Trouble is that no one's ever really told you. You're completely starved of personal compliments. You're a bit like parched earth in need of watering.'

'Come off it, will you?'

I'm blushing like a forest fire now and it's embarrassing me.

'Only the truth.'

'I am a married woman, I'll have you know.'

But he says nothing more, just raises one of his eyebrows and gives me a half-smile.

I head back to the sanctuary of the fitting room, brushing all this mildly flirtatious carry-on aside, but the truth is that every now and then I remember what Liz flung at me that night back in Don't Tell Mama. About Jack wanting some woman he couldn't get because she was married. And just as quickly, I dismiss it out of hand. Besides, I remind myself, unwrapping the dress off me and nearly passing out when I see the price tag (seven *hundred* dollars? Are they kidding me?), Jack tells me all the time, day and night, that he doesn't do relationships – ever.

Which is absolutely fine by me. In fact, thank Christ for that, because frankly if any guy hit on me right now, chances are I'd just look at them blankly, not having the first clue what to do.

246

Like that part of my life has just irretrievably shut down.

Not long after, one hot, sunny morning – the kind that hits eighty degrees even though it's barely eleven am – out of the blue, Jack calls me at the flat. We've arranged to go sightseeing today, except last time, at my behest, we did the Empire State, so this time it's his turn to choose. There's an art gallery he really wants to check out called the Ronald Feldman on Mercer Street in SoHo, he tells me, so he suggests meeting there in about half an hour. Great, I tell him, see you there. Then I fling on the coolest, most summery dress I own – a long, floaty white number I bought in Anthropologie in the Rockefeller Center and I'm just on my way out the door when my phone rings.

Liz, in a blind temper.

'What's wrong, hon?' I ask, my heart already beginning to palpitate.

'I need to talk to you,' she practically spits down the phone. 'Now. And no, before you ask, it won't wait.'

'Liz, deep breaths, calm down. Where are you now?'

'Upstairs, in my apartment.'

'Stay right there, I'm on my way.'

Two minutes later, I'm at her door and she's already standing there waiting for me, looking like death on a plate. I never see her without make-up and now that I do, it's actually a massive shock. Her face is drawn, ghostly white, with black bags you could put luggage in and cheekbones you could grate cheese on. But not in good RPattz way, more in a concentration camp victim way.

'What's the matter, hon?' I ask, my stomach cramping with anxiety.

'That insidious, nosy, bossy bitch Chris is inside my

apartment right now, making all kinds of ludicrous allega-tions against me and I swear to God, if she doesn't apologise to me, I'm not working with her tonight. Do I need to spell it out any further? I refuse to walk out on stage tonight unless I get a full apology. OK? You with me? No apology, no show tonight!'

She's talking nineteen to the dozen, really spitting fire, repeating herself over and over and it's only now that I notice the wildly dilated pupils, the trembling hands, the extreme agitation. All the signs, present and correct.

She's off her head on coke again, I know it. Just know it.

I grip her firmly by her rail-thin little arm and steer her back into the tiny hallway of her apartment, where Chris is still in her dressing gown, standing tall and firm, swishing back her long, Indian straight black hair, maybe not gunning for a fight, but still, fully prepared for one. The place is a complete mess too, I can't help noticing: empty bottles and overflowing ashtrays are lying all over the place and it stinks like Satan's gym bag in here.

'Morning, Annie,' Chris says evenly, on seeing me come in. 'I'm so sorry that you've been dragged into all this unpleasantness, but Liz insisted.'

'Fucking right I insisted!' Liz practically screeches into her face. 'I want a witness for this!'

'Can someone please tell me what's going on?' I ask, completely at a loss.

Chris, in fairness to her, remains utterly resolute and fully in control.

'To bring you up to speed, Annie, money has mysteri-ously been disappearing from our dressing rooms during the show. Between myself, Blythe and Alex, there's over fifteen hundred dollars gone to date.'

248

Suddenly, I feel a sharp shock to my gut like I've just been electrocuted. No. Not possible. Is it? Would Liz really have . . .? My head spins and my mind starts to race.

She's borrowed money from me before, worryingly large amounts of money, well over five hundred bucks, but when I asked her why, seeing as how we're all so well paid in the show, she just floundered around and never gave me a straight answer. Needed to pay off some dealer, I figured, so then I just cut her off and stopped lending it to her. And lately, whenever she touches me for cash, I don't even bother making stupid, transparent excuses about not having any on me, I just tell her straight out. If this is for coke, then no, you're not getting a red cent from me. Caused untold tension between us, but I've managed to stay firm.

And now this?

'The problem,' Chris continues crisply, 'is that, as we all know, the cast are the only ones who have access to the dressing rooms during the show, and out of the cast . . .'

'You devious bloody cow!' Liz practically spits into her face and for a split second I really do think I'll have to physically restrain her from punching Chris smack in the face. 'So you've got it all worked out, do you?' she fumes, pacing up and down now. 'I'm the only one offstage for long enough to sneak around the place stealing cash from other people's handbags, is what you're trying to say, isn't it? So why don't you just have the guts to come right out and say it?'

My mind is up to fifth gear now. Because that much is actually true – of the whole lot of us, Liz is the only one with a good twenty minutes offstage on her own while the rest of us are still out there. By a process of elimination, she's the only one who has the time to do it.

And, though it kills me to say it, but the motive too.

Somehow, Chris manages to keep her head in the face of a spewing Liz which, given that the girl is fit to be tied, is a lot easier said than done.

'I'm not here to make idle accusations,' Chris says crisply, totally in command of the situation. 'Money going missing is regrettable, but it happens once and you learn from it and make bloody sure not to bring cash into work with you again. The most you'll find in any of our dressing rooms from here on in is loose change and nothing more. What I've come here about is something far, far more serious . . .'

'Chris, what is it?' I ask, feeling my heart twist and almost dreading the answer.

'Last night, when I came offstage, my engagement ring was missing. I can't wear it onstage as you know, so I always leave it in a drawer in my dressing table. You went home early last night, Annie,' she nods to me, then slowly she pivots round to face Liz, who's red-faced and sweating now, actually sweating.

'. . . whereas you'd scarpered off with God knows who.'

'Oh, so now I've suddenly morphed into a jewel thief, have I?' Liz screams at her so loudly that I think the superintendent might be up in a minute with complaints from the neighbours about the din.

'How dare you?' she yells, right into Chris's face. 'How bloody dare you burst in here and start flinging all these ridiculous accusations at me? *You* lose your engagement ring, suddenly put two and two together and now you have me marked down as the Artful fecking Dodger?'

'You would be well advised to just cool the head and listen to me,' says Chris curtly, arms folded, eyes slitted. 'I couldn't particularly give a shite about what you choose to shove up your nose in your spare time, it's absolutely no concern of mine and believe me, I'm extremely grateful for that. But we all know that you've been on the scab for money lately; you've already asked Blythe and myself as well as Alex, not to mention some of the box office staff too. Word has gone round.'

'You get the hell out of here right now, do you hear me? I could sue you for this! Do you realise I could have you up for slander and defamation of character?'

'I wasn't finished,' Chris snaps back, standing her ground, not for one single second threatened. 'Now you just listen to me, missy. My engagement ring is the single most precious thing I own; it's of massive sentimental value to me. So if you have it, I strongly suggest you hand it back to me right now. I'm offering you this one last chance. And in return, I won't take this any further.'

'Fuck off out of my apartment and never speak to me again, you stuck-up bitch!'

In her hyped-up, fuming, strung-out state though, Liz is absolutely no match for Chris's well-thought-out cool.

'Well if you *don't* have it,' says Chris, changing tack, 'then I assume you'll have no problem if I just do this?'

With that, she strides over to the hall table, where Liz's big, oversized, overstuffed handbag is lying, a massive, glittery, gold thing, the approximate size of a small child that goes absolutely everywhere with her.

'You put that down this instant . . .' shrieks Liz, but it's too late. In a flash, Chris has upended it and emptied the contents out onto the floor. Everything comes tumbling down in one massive thud and for a split second Chris and I just stand there, utterly stunned.

Suddenly we both find ourselves looking at several tiny, white, see-through plastic sachets containing what looks like baking soda, but clearly isn't. Three baby bottles of vodka tumble out and crash to the floor too, all empty. The size that you only ever see winos on street corners drinking out of brown paper bags.

In an instant Liz is on her hands and knees scooping everything up, but it's too late; we've all seen what's there and what's more, she knows it.

There's a horrible silence while she fumbles round the floor, then with a face like a hatchet, she looks up and almost hisses at Chris.

'I cannot believe you just did that, you thundering bitch!'

Chris, who still has the bag in her hand, completely ignores her and is now rooting around in one of the side pockets.

'All this stuff isn't even mine you know,' Liz says to me, like I'm going to believe her.

'I'm just holding onto it for a friend as a matter of fact, that's all . . .'

'Is that so? And were you just holding onto *this* for the same friend too?' demands Chris, triumphantly whipping out her engagement ring from a tiny inside zip pocket.

It's definitely her ring alright; the same little red ruby stone that I've seen her wearing a thousand times. Chris slips it back on her finger and stands glaring at Liz, face exultant, waiting for an answer.

For a second I think I might be sick. I slump against the hall table with my head pounding, unable to take it all in.

'Oh yeah,' Liz mutters, unconvincingly, '*that* ring. Yeah . . . I meant to tell you, but it slipped my mind . . .'

'You meant to tell me what, exactly?' demands Chris.

'I . . . ehh . . . found it on the stairwell at the theatre and meant to give it to you, but I never got a chance to . . .'

'Don't Liz, just don't. You're only making it worse,' I say, wanting desperately to wake up from this horrible nightmare.

'Well, in that case I think there's nothing further to be said,' says Chris, making for the door. 'I told you that provided I got my ring back, I wouldn't take this any further. This time. For the sake of the show and nothing else. But let this be a warning to you, Liz. If you ever even attempt to pull anything like this again, I'm going straight to Jack to tell all, and what he decides to do with you is entirely up to him. No second chances. Do you understand?'

Liz just nods, then slumps down onto the floor, her back to the wall, staring ahead blankly. With a curt nod in my direction, Chris is gone, slamming the door behind her with an authoritative thud.

I hunker down beside Liz and gently take her hand, which is trembling and clammy.

'You OK?' I ask.

'What do you think?' She flings me a sideways look that would freeze mercury.

Fair enough, it was a dopey fecking question.

Then she's up on her feet again, pacing the floor, all her manic energy suddenly flooding back to her.

'It was a stupid thing to do, OK? I know that, I realise that. But you have to understand, I didn't know what I was doing at the time, I needed cash fast and I just wasn't thinking straight . . . there's some people that I owe money to, you've no idea what they're like . . .'

'Liz,' I gently interrupt, trying to reel her in slowly. 'If I asked you to go and see someone, would you? We could go to a doctor . . . right now . . . and maybe get a referral to someone who works in drug rehab. I'll go with you, I'll be with you every step of the way . . .'

Now she turns on me.

'You think I need help? You stand there, smug as you like and have the barefaced cheek to tell me I need help?'

'For God's sake, of course you need help! Surely you see that this is not normal behaviour? Chris could have easily pressed charges back there you know and you're bloody lucky that she didn't!'

'How DARE you! How fucking dare you suggest that I've got a problem! This, from the girl who can't even hold on to her own husband? Go on, feck off out of here! Get out of my apartment!'

'Liz, just cool down, OK? I came here in good faith to help you,' I manage to say, my head swimming at the suddenness and severity of her mood swing.

'And no doubt you'll go blabbering to everyone at the theatre that the rest of the cast now have me down as a thief! I'll tell you something, Annie Cole, you can get the hell out of my sight and don't you dare speak to me again, unless it's to crawl on your hands and knees and beg for forgiveness!'

There's nothing more to say. Impossible to even reach her right now. So I say nothing, just leave as quickly as I can. Liz follows me and does a door slam worthy of a daytime soap opera, leaving me standing outside in the corridor.

Alone and utterly shattered.

I'm now seriously late to meet Jack and by the time I get to the SoHo gallery, he's already there, waiting outside for me, as ever looking like the master of elegant cool, in aviator shades, tailored denim jeans and a grey Gap sweater, with freshly washed hair flopping lightly over his forehead. He's lounging up against the wall of the gallery, long and lean, but as soon as he sees me he immediately stubs out his cigarette and straightens up.

In an instant, his sharp blue eyes are all over mine, scanning my face, instantly sensing that something is up. I give him a wobbly smile and try to act normal but he's too good a director not to be able to spot a hammy performance when he sees one. Now I'm one of life's conflict-avoiders, I'll run a mile rather than have it out with someone I care about, and so events of this morning have left me rattled and on edge and so worried about Liz that it's nearly making me sick.

'You OK?' he asks me, concerned, the eyebrows knitted downwards.

'Long, long story,' I say, doing my best to brush the whole thing aside. 'Sorry for the delay, it was . . . let's just say it was beyond my control. So, will we go inside?'

It'll be cool and quiet inside the gallery, is my reasoning. I won't have to talk and I'll be able to think clearly in there. But Jack's having none of it.

'Sod the sodding gallery. Let's skip it and go and have a talk instead. I know the perfect place too. Come with me.'

Fifteen minutes later we're sitting at an outside table in the Magnolia Bakery on Bleecker Street in SoHo.

'This place is famous for its cupcakes,' he tells me, passing me a menu. 'I absolutely insist that you try one. Take a look

255

for yourself if you don't believe me; these are miniature works of art.'

I give him a watery smile, even though the very thought of food is enough to make my stomach heave. But we scan through the menu, which I have to admit, is stunningly impressive. Just about every confection known to man is here: coconut, lemon, carrot, banana, you name it, and the counter top displays would make your jaw drop at the artistic heights it's possible to scale with just the humble cupcake. We order a chocolate devil's cake for him, an Americano for me and just then his iPhone rings. He whips it out, checks the number, then mouths at me that it's his agent from LA so I wave at him to go right ahead and take the call. All the more time for me to try and clear my head, which frankly is starting to pound right now.

Jack chats away easily on the phone while I run a mental check list in my head.

Liz has turned to larceny. And she was most definitely using this morning, clear as day. On the plus side, Chris has promised not to take the matter any further, so at least Liz's job isn't at stake. For the moment.

Soon, too soon, our Americano and cupcake arrive, just as Jack winds up his call. Which means I'm going to actually have to make conversation and try to sound normal.

'Emm . . . so has your agent come up with any . . . ehh . . . interesting screenplays for you to have a look at?'

Boring as arse, I know, but it's the best I can do under pressure.

'Annie, stop it. Stop trying to gloss over whatever's really going on with you,' he says, taking his sunglasses off and looking directly at me in that really intense way that he has. Like it's just him and me alone here and I'm the sole focus of his attention. Which, for some inconvenient reason, is starting to make me jelly-legged. And very glad that I'm sitting down.

'Now suppose you tell me the facts and let me help.'

'Suppose I can't.'

'Is it your husband? Are you having trouble at home?'

He's leaning right into me now, his face inches from mine.

'What? Ehh . . . no, no, not at all . . .' I stammer, confused and at the same time relieved that he hasn't guessed the truth.

'Because if you are, I want you to know that I'm here for you.'

'Well . . . thanks for that, but . . .'

'You and I never talk about personal stuff, about our private lives, that is. And there are very good reasons for that, I know. But if you ever wanted to, you know I'm a sympathetic listener'

'I know. And thank you.'

'Maybe one day, you'll trust me enough to open up to me and if you ever do, just know that I'll be waiting for you. You will remember that, my dear, won't you?'

Liz is behaving like a sulky child at the theatre this evening, but frankly I'm just so relieved that a) she turned up for work and b) that she's come down from her high, that her moodiness is the least of my worries.

Word has rippled through the cast about what happened earlier today though and now there's almost an invisible Berlin Wall that's suddenly sprung up, with Liz on one side and myself, Chris, Alex and Blythe on the other. Chris in particular, is acting with cold disdain towards Liz, like she's in some way holding power over her. I could have reported you today, her body language seems to scream, but I didn't, so therefore I'm the bigger person and don't ever forget that you owe me. Liz, for her part, just blanks out the whole lot of us, only making eye contact when absolutely necessary, i.e., onstage.

But somehow we get through the show and Liz is as mesmerising onstage as ever, leaving me in awe of just how capable she is of pulling it out of the bag when she really needs to.

Understandably, no one is on form for going out tonight and I for one am back in my little blonde apartment early-ish, by about eleven pm. It's a miserable, God-awful night; an almost tropical summer rainstorm hit the city earlier and there wasn't a taxi to be had on the whole of Broadway, so I had to walk home through the monsoon and am now freezing, starving and drenched right through to my knickers.

It's pitch dark when I let myself into the apartment and I'm just about to start peeling off my soaking wet gear when something on the doormat stops me in my tracks.

Total surprise: a letter waiting for me from home. Waterford postmark. Which is weird. Jules never writes, she either emails or sends messages to me via Facebook and it's highly unlikely that Audrey would ever put pen to paper and write to me, bar it was to give out.

I rip it open and my eye scrolls hungrily down the page.
Darling Annie,
I know you needed space, a year off, time out from your life here . . . I know all that and I understand.
But that doesn't mean that you're not missed, every single hour of every single day.

Just thought you should know.
With love always, come what may,
Dan.

Try as I might, I can't sleep. Well past one in the morning and I'm still tossing and turning, unable to believe that Dan actually wrote. Knowing him as I do, for him to actually find the time to write a letter, however brief, then find a stamp and then a post box in that order . . . absolutely unheard of!

Feck it. Sleep won't come, but an idea slowly does. I could call him, couldn't I? I mean, I know we're on our marriage sabbatical and all that, but it doesn't mean that I couldn't pick up the phone and talk to my erstwhile best friend, does it?

So I chance it. I pick up the phone beside me and call his mobile. Past six in the morning his time, maybe just maybe, he'll answer . . .

It's months since we've spoken, not since that awful phone call where we both agreed to take a year off from each other and my heart's walloping off my ribcage as I dial his mobile number with shaky fingers.

But I'm in luck. Bingo, he answers on the fifth ring, sounding groggy, like I've just woken him up from the deepest sleep

'Hello?'

'Hi.'

'I'm sorry . . . who's this?'

'Dan . . . it's me.'

'Annie? Oh my God, it that really you?' he says, sounding . . . dare I say it . . . really pleased to hear from me.'

'Were you sleeping?' I ask tentatively.

'Trying to, but . . . oh Annie, it's so good just to hear your voice,' he says and even from the far side of the Atlantic, I can still hear the smile in his voice.

'I got your note,' I say simply.

'Oh yeah . . . well I just wanted you to know that you're much missed, even if you don't think that you are.'

My throat catches a bit.

'Oh and by the way, there's a surprise on its way to you,' he says, sounding a bit more awake now.

'Oh my God, what is it?'

'Now if I told you, it wouldn't be a surprise, would it? You'll just have to wait till next week. But I think you'll like it. At least, I hope you will.'

A silence, but an easy comfortable one.

'Tell me what you're doing right now,' he says.

'Looking out the window. It was lashing rain here earlier, but now it's cleared and there's the most incredible full moon out.'

'Hang on, I'll take a look,' he says. Then I hear him walking to the window and the sound of curtains being pulled back. 'Yup, I can see it from here too.'

Amazing. Here we are three thousand miles apart and yet we're both looking at the same moon. So somehow, it doesn't really seem like we're all that far apart.

'Meet me at the moon, Annie Cole,' he says softly. 'And tell me all about your life.'

And so I do, everything. Even about Liz and what an agonising worry her behaviour has become. He listens patiently and it's bizarre because I can't remember the last time that he really listened to me. God, now I know how the radio must feel. He advises me to immediately get help if she ever breaks out again. To frogmarch her to the nearest

A&E if I have to, and not to take no for an answer. And for his part, he tells me the news from home, how busy he is, all the usual stuff. But I listen attentively too and it's wonderful and somehow I get a warm, comfortable feeling deep down. He sounds so different to the Dan of the past few years, far more like the Dan of old. The one I first fell in love with all those years ago. And suddenly, out of nowhere, I want to tell him to jump on a plane right now and to come over, not to even think about it, just to do it. But I know it would be futile and pointless and would only lead to yet more disappointments. So instead, I settle for a perfectly civilised chat about our respective lives. Like friends. Like good friends who aren't making any demands on each other. Who are well past all that.

Who just care deeply about each other and want to catch up with each other, nothing more.

But I can tell you, it's the single nicest thing that's happened to me in a long, long time.

Meeting Dan at the moon.

Chapter Eleven

Late one lazy day the following week, I find out exactly what the surprise was that Dan mentioned. It's boiling hot, well over ninety degrees and I've just spent a deeply relaxing afternoon up in Blythe's apartment drinking iced tea and lolling around in her little balcony, just the two of us, me in a pair of swimming togs, flip-flops and an oversized T-shirt; her in a wafting kaftan so huge and billowing, it could nearly double up as a cover for a Hummer.

'I know I look a bit like Dame Edna,' she sniggered, 'but it was such a bargain, Annie love, it would have been a sin to leave it there. Only fifteen dollars in the reduced to clear bin at Filene's Basement! Can you believe it? I'm on an economy drive at the moment, you know, because poor Sean needs me to send him home some money this month, to help out with all his car repayments. That Lexus is just cleaning the poor boy out. Shocking.'

I bite my lip, change the subject and the pair of us idle away yet another hour looking down onto Forty-Fifth street shimmering in the baking heat below us, inventing back stories for all the people swarming around, each and every one of them sweltering. And oh my God, is it hot! So hot that even the glasses of water beside us are sweating.

Anyroadup, it gets close to four in the afternoon, when I know Blythe always likes to take a little nap before the show: time for me to skedaddle back downstairs to my own apartment and leave her to it. And so I'm just flip-flopping out of the elevator on my own floor and into the cool of the marble hallway, head shoved into my handbag as I rummage around for my door keys, when suddenly I spot a lone figure slumped up against my door. Standing beside two stuffed suitcases and looking like a delivery that's been waiting for me for hours.

Takes a split second for my eyes to adjust to the dark hallway, but when I realise who it is, I nearly fall over in shock.

'*Jules Ferguson!* Am I seeing things? Is it really you?'

'Surprise!' she yells so loudly that I think half the building might hear and next thing we're hugging each other for all we're worth. I'm overwhelmed to see her; she's like a breath of air. A breath of air from three thousand miles away. From home.

'I can't believe I'm really, finally here!' she squeals at me, as I open up the door to let her in. 'Dan paid for my flight over, but on the strict condition that I wasn't to breathe a word about it in any of my Facebook messages to you. Said he wanted it to be a complete surprise. But my God, I've been just bursting to tell you, Annie; these last few weeks I've felt like I was carrying round the third secret of Fatima. You know me, I'm no good at secrets – keeping anything to myself always makes me constipated.'

I snort laughing, having completely edited out Jules's lunatic sense of humour and keep hugging the girl over and over, absolutely thrilled that she's here and flooded with determination to give her the single best holiday she's ever had in her whole life. I let both of us in and Jules nearly passes out when she sees just how gorgeous the apartment is in the late afternoon sunshine, when it always looks its best.

I proudly show her around, but what impresses her most of all is the stunning view from the long, blonde, floor-length windows down onto Madison Avenue, hundreds of feet below us. She wolf-whistles at the very sight of it, then skittishly dances around the place like a character straight out of *Glee,* high just on being here.

'This is just unbelievable!' she roars, laughing at me. 'I mean, come on, Annie, you do realise what a rare treat it is for me to actually be staying somewhere that doesn't smell of Yardley Lily of the Valley talcum powder and dentures and old skin? With pension books and blister packs of tablets lying on every surface?'

I smile fondly at her, remembering only too clearly how exhilarated I felt when I first came here, five full months ago now, but frankly it seems like it was back in another lifetime. When I too felt so full of promise and fun and hope. When I couldn't get my head around the contrast with life in Stickens, where an eventful day might include Biddy at the post office closing early on account of her sciatica being at her, or else Sergeant Flynn busting a local farmer for a tax disc that's three months out of date. And to come from all of that to all of this? Wouldn't be in the least surprised if Jules never goes home again.

The girl is starving, but then Jules is always starving, so I rustle up a chicken and pesto salad for her, which she wolfs into at the living room table, all while filling me in on the latest news from home.

'So anyway, the Mothership has gone from bad to worse, if it's even possible to believe that,' she says, mouth stuffed.

'Spends most of her time stretched on the chaise longue up at The Moorings telling mad Mrs Brophy or the Countess Dracula that she's not much longer for this world. She's developed this death wish you see, even though Doc Martin says there's absolutely nothing wrong with the old bat – more's the pity.'

'Jules!'

'Come off it, Annie, you know as well as I do she's as healthy as a horse. All you need to do is watch the old battleaxe eating to know that. Like watching a vulture feed off a corpse.'

I snort a bit at this, can't help myself.

'Anyway she's on some pills now because she says she can't sleep properly any more, that it feels too much like death,' she happily chats on, helping herself to more salad. 'Spends half the morning going through the death notices in the paper, checking she's not in them, more than likely. And whenever someone rings her, she answers the phone by saying, "Who's dead?" God Almighty, Annie, coming from that gene pool, isn't it a miracle that I'm normal?'

I smile, only too well able to imagine what the poor kid has been through since I left.

'There's more though: she has a major fatwa out on you, hon. Still harps on in her feathery little voice to anyone who'll listen about how you'll rue the day you upped and left your husband, repeat ad nauseam. That we don't just dispose of things we love and that marriage isn't something you can just walk away from, blah-di-blah-di-blah. Honest to God, between her and the Countess Dracula, then factor in Mrs Brophy screeching at everyone . . . and I'm telling you, these days The Moorings is more like a mental home where every-one's streeling around on the wrong medication.'

'So how did you manage to get away in the first place?'

'Dan had to hire a nurse for her. She arrived the day before yesterday and it's only hilarious; she's a big beefy one called Noreen and she's mad into physical therapy and keeps forcing the Mothership to take long walks and to exercise for at least an hour a day. Says that fresh air will help her to sleep better than any bottle of pills. So there's a right battle of wills going on at the moment as to who'll break who first. Mind you, my money is on the Mothership.'

Next thing, the mobile phone in her jeans pocket beep beeps as a text comes through.

'Speak of the devil,' says Jules, rolling her eyes when she reads who it's from. She carelessly tosses the phone over to me and I quickly scan the message. From Audrey.

AM WORRIED SICK ABOUT YOU, BUT TRY NOT TO STRESS ABOUT ME TOO MUCH, IF I TAKE A TURN FOR THE WORST, DAN WILL LET YOU KNOW. HAVING A BAD DAY TODAY AND NOREEN DOESN'T BELIEVE ME WHEN I SAY I URGENTLY NEED TO SEE THE DOCTOR. BUT TRY TO ENJOY YOUR HOLIDAY, IF YOU POSSIBLY CAN, MOTHER XXXX

'Oh dear,' I say, handing her back the phone. 'I see what you mean.'

'Amazing, isn't it? That the Mothership can emotionally blackmail me even through the medium of a simple text message. Quite a gift, when you come to think about it.'

'I wouldn't worry about it, hon. You'll be fine after a few years of expensive therapy.'

Jules snorts laughing, then with a belch worthy of a builder on a halting site, she shoves the empty plate away from her, rips the tab off a can of beer that I plonked in front of her then slouches back onto the sofa. The picture of chilled-out relaxation. You'd swear she'd been living here for a full month instead of barely an hour.

A good moment for me to ask the one question that's burning me up.

'And . . . emm . . . how's Dan?'

Weird: after all her chatter and gossip, now there's a silence. Jules stares off into space before she answers, playing with her Jack-in-the-box springy black curls and looking no older than about thirteen, max.

'Well, if you ask me,' she says slowly, so slowly that I want to scream impatiently, what? What? If I ask you *WHAT*?

'I think he's totally lost without you, Annie,' she says, putting on a funereal voice. 'Completely and utterly devastated. Looks like shite, hasn't slept properly since you left, goes round the place crying like a baby for no apparent reason, is neglecting his work, in fact the whole practice is falling apart because he just can't hack it anymore. And sometimes when I'm up at The Moorings, I can hear the sound of him sobbing to himself behind the surgery door, when everyone's gone home and when he thinks no one's there . . .'

I throw an impatient cushion across the coffee table at her, which she deftly catches.

'I'd forgotten about Jules Ferguson and her rightly-famed overactive imagination,' I tell her. 'Now supposing you take your foot off the exaggerator and tell me the truth?'

'But the truth is so boring.'

'Jules!'

'Right, right, keep your knickers on. Well, you know Dan – he's out of the house from dawn till dusk, running round after every farmer in the greater Waterford area . . . sure I hardly ever see him at all. So nothing new there. But I will say this though, I think you taking off for a year has been the best thing that you could have ever done. Talk about giving him the kick up the arse that he needed! You know how you never realise how good you had something till it's gone? Same thing with you and him, I bet. Not that he's actually *said* anything to me, but then he doesn't need to; I just *know*. I feel it and you know how accurate my intuition always is. Money on it that he's slowly coming to his senses and copping onto the fact that your life was unbearable . . . and an awful lot of that was down to him.'

I give her a frustrated smile, remembering that you've always got to prune back at least sixty per cent of anything Jules comes out with, to allow for, shall we say, her casual over-embellishments.

'Have you not heard from him yourself?' she asks me frowning, can of beer clamped to her hand.

And so I bring her up to speed. Editing out the worst of our rows when I first came over here, but still telling her the truth and nothing but; that the hard, cold fact was that neither one of us was able to make the whole long-distance relationship thing work. No one's fault, no one's to blame, it was just one of those things that was doomed from the get-go. So like two mature adults, we therefore decided the best thing was to take the pressure off and give ourselves some time out from each other, for the rest of the year. At *his* behest, I add, not mine. But being brutally honest and now that so much time has passed, I do finally see the wisdom behind it. It was the only way forward for both of us and certainly the only way for me to stay even remotely sane.

Jules does a wolf-whistle loud enough to hail a taxi, then slumps back onto the sofa.

'Wow,' she eventually says. 'A year off for bad behaviour, I love it. He never breathed a word of this to anyone at home, but then, you know what those strong, silent types are like. There are times you'd need a head shrink to make Dan out.'

Anyroadup, I think Jules senses that this may not be the most comfortable topic of conversation for me because suddenly, with a jolt like she's just been electrocuted, she jumps up off the sofa, hand cupped over her mouth in shock and starts pacing up and down the room.

'Jesus, Annie, I am such an idiot, albeit a stunningly beautiful one!!'

'What, what's up?'

'I totally forgot to tell you what should have been item number one of scandal on the agenda.'

'Which is . . .?' I brace myself to allow for the usual amount of over-egging she does.

'You will NOT believe this, but it seems after all this time that not only is there a Law of Karma in action but it even works in a kiphole like Stickens too . . .'

'Jules, would you ever tell me!'

'Lisa Ledbetter, the Countess Dracula herself, is now officially separated from her husband, Charlie.'

'You're kidding me! Since when?'

'She announced it a few weeks ago. Apparently he landed some job in London not long after Christmas, so he just upped and left. Course her story is that the long-distance commute over and back is what killed the relationship, but I reckon he just realised how much pleasanter life was with an ocean between them. And in all fairness, would you really blame the guy? So now the Countess Dracula is up at The Moorings day and night with her kids, moaning about being a deserted wife, all while freeloading off Dan . . .'

It takes a few goes for Jules to convince me that she's not exaggerating; for once, the girl is actually telling the truth. And for some reason, an alarm bell goes off in my head and my stomach ulcer suddenly starts to burn me up. A second later, my whole digestive system clenches up with worry.

Does this mean that her kids will start referring to Dan as 'New Dad'?

And even if that were to happen, what exactly could I do about it from three thousand miles away? When, at his behest, we're having a gap year off from being married to each other?

Absolutely nothing, except to try and put the whole thing out of my head. But try as I might, I still can't shake off the feeling that this is bad news.

Very, very bad news indeed.

Jules takes a nap to help her get over the jet lag while I shower and get organised for work this evening. Then I walk with her to the theatre, getting as much of a kick out of her reactions to the sights and sounds of Fifth Avenue as she is herself. Honest to God, it's like dragging a small toddler through Toys R Us; every two seconds something bright and shiny and new will catch her eye and she keeps on running into shop after shop until eventually I laughingly have to haul her out of Sephora on Fifth and remind her that I have a show to do. And that if I don't get to work soon, my understudy will be shoved on at short notice.

'Sorry, Annie, I just want to skip around the place,

drinking it all in!' she chirps. Then she spots the Empire State shimmering away in the distance, the observatory at the top, crystal-clear even from street level on a cloudless day like this. Two seconds later, Jules has whipped out her camera phone and is snapping away.

'What are you giggling at?' she asks, all innocent saucer eyes. 'What's so funny?'

'You. You remind me of me, that's all.'

When I eventually manage to drag her to the theatre, absolutely everyone on the box office staff is warm and welcoming and lovely to Jules. The show is sold out, but I still manage to wheedle a house seat for her, which she's thrilled about. All thanks to Hayley, or as we all now refer to her, The Queen of The Box Office. She lights up when I introduce Jules, then waddles her huge frame out from behind the box office to hug her, warning me that I'm to give her the time of her life in the Big Apple.

Then just as she's handing over Jules's ticket, she drops her voice a bit and asks, 'Have you heard the good news yet, honey?'

'No,' I answer, 'What news?'

'Oh darn it,' she almost gulps back the words. 'Me and my big mouth! I'll let them tell you when you get upstairs. But I think you'll be real pleased, sweetheart.'

Not having the first clue what's going on, I lead Jules round to the stage door and the first person I bump into is Chris, half made-up with her hair in rollers, wearing just her dressing gown and hyped up to the ceiling. I don't even get the chance to introduce Jules to her; Chris just jubilantly hugs me, then excitedly tells me that Jack is waiting for all of us in the green room, that he has an urgent announcement to make and wants us all present and correct. So I usher Jules in with me and sure enough everyone's there ahead of us, cast, backstage crew, the whole lot of us.

And the atmosphere in the room is electric There's a massive buzz in the air and for the life of me I can't figure out why. We stand at the back of the tiny room, now packed to the rafters, eyes open and mouths shut, as Jack's already in mid-patter.

'Sorry to drag you all in here when you're busy getting ready for the show,' he's saying calmly, dressed head to toe in a sharp black suit and looking like he should be starring in a Wim Wenders movie. 'But the fact is that I've just received some exciting news, which I thought you'd all like to hear. As you are no doubt aware, the Tony awards will take place in three weeks' time . . .'

'What are the Tony awards?' Jules hisses at me, looking completely blank.

'Theatre of New York,' I whisper back. 'It's a really big noise over here. Like the theatre world's very own Oscars.'

'. . . to be held at Radio City Music Hall,' Jack continues as an excited murmur ripples round the room.

Next thing, with a theatrical flourish, he elegantly whips out a fax from his shirt pocket and teasingly waves it at us, looking just like Chamberlain about to declare 'Peace in Our Time'.

'And now . . . the moment you've all been waiting for . . . this has just arrived and an announcement to the press is being made concurrently . . .'

'Get on with it, will you? I've still got to do my hair before the show!' Chris yells at him impatiently.

'The Tony award nominations are . . . for best new play, Wedding Belles!'

A raucous cheer goes up, there's whooping and hugging

and it takes Jack ages to shush everyone down before he can continue.

'The nominations for best featured actress in a play are . . .' He reads out the names of four other big, marquee Broadway names, all appearing in plays that are competing alongside us. Then, to the sound effect of a drumroll in my head, he announces, 'and finally . . . for *Wedding Belles* . . . none other than . . . Miss Blythe Arnold!'

Screeches of joy nearly bring the roof down and suddenly everyone's on top of Blythe like a rugby scrum, congratulating her and hugging her to ribbons.

'Jesus, Mary and Joseph,' she calls out in shock over the din, her voice sounding smothered because we're all trying to hug her at once. 'Are you absolutely sure, Jack love? You didn't make a mistake? Check that bit of paper again, will you?'

'Definitely no mistake,' he grins back at her, 'now calm down everyone, I'm not even close to being finished yet!'

At this stage he actually has to shout over the excited babble to try and get us all to quieten down. Blythe looks pink with pleasure and has to be ushered to a chair, she's that shocked. It takes another few goes on Jack's part before it's quiet enough for him to read on, but once he gets going again, he's on a roll and there's absolutely no stopping him.

The nominations keep coming thick and fast. Best lighting design . . . *Wedding Belles*. Best sound . . . *Wedding Belles*. Best costume design . . . *Wedding Belles*. Best set design . . . you've guessed it. Jack then takes a modest pause before announcing the nominations for best director and the room goes stony silent till he reads out, 'And, for *Wedding Belles*, ahem, ahem . . . Jack Gordon.'

An eruption of cheers and now it's almost like there's an

impromptu party starting to break out, minus the booze. My head is swimming, unable to take in all this miraculous news. So far, we've a grand total of *seven* nominations; unheard of for such a low-budget show with a largely unknown cast. Unbelievable. Astonishing.

'And now . . . if you'll all just keep it down to a dull roar for one last and final nomination,' Jack pleads with the room, 'then I'll let you all go, on the condition that you all join me in Sardi's after the show. Let's show these New Yorkers how we Irish like to celebrate in style!'

Massive enthusiastic applause and one of the assistant stage managers yells out, 'Fine by me, Jack, but just remember, you're paying!'

More shushing before it's quiet enough for him to continue.

'For best actress in a leading role, the nominations are . . .' He reads out four names, again, all scarily, intimidatingly big names. The tension ratchets up a fair few notches and Jack is milking it for all it's worth, like the sublime showman that he is. You could almost hear a pin drop as he says, 'Stay with me here, people, still one more name to go!'

I feel Jules's hand, small and hot, squeezing mine as Jack eventually reads out, 'and finally . . . for *Wedding Belles* . . . Miss Liz Shields!'

We all turn to look for her in the throng . . . but she's not here.

Bad, burning feeling like indigestion flares up inside me. My own personal ulcerous early warning system gone into overdrive.

When we all disperse to the four winds, I find Liz already upstairs in our dressing room, putting on her make-up. Seemingly oblivious to what's just happened. And what's worse, looking like she doesn't particularly give a shite either way.

'Liz, you missed it . . . where were you?' I ask her all excited. 'We've been nominated for a barrow load of Tony awards, and guess what? You're up for best actress!'

I make the mistake of going to give her a spontaneous hug and I'm not joking, the girl almost jumps away from me, like she's just been physically repelled by a strong magnetic force field.

I lock eyes with her in the mirror as much as to say, *what in the name of God just happened there?* She says nothing though, just throws me an irritated glare. You'd nearly swear I'd just told her that the show was about to fold, that we were all out of a job and heading back to Ireland, barefoot, broke and having to pay our own airfares home.

Sweet Jesus, it's like sharing a dressing room with Joan Crawford. With a bad dose of PMT.

For a split second I stare helplessly back at her reflection, genuinely shocked by her non-reaction.

'Aren't you even pleased?' I eventually ask.

'Whatever,' she sighs, then gets up to use the bathroom, slamming the door firmly shut behind her.

She doesn't come to the after-show celebrations either. Just disappears off into the night, saying absolutely nothing to a single soul.

It promises to be a terrific night at Sardi's, all benevolently hosted by Jack. But Liz's absence is a bit like Banquo's ghost hovering over the proceedings. Harvey Shapiro, our white-goateed producer asks if there's something wrong with her? Is she ill? And when Jack notices that she hasn't bothered to turn up, I can practically see his antennae ratchet up to high alert.

The restaurant's hostess, a tall leggy, swishy-haired, model-y looking one called Isabella has obviously heard the news about our clean sweep of the Tony nominations, because as she's escorting us to our table, she doesn't just massage our egos, she leaves the lot of us with chakras nearly humming like xylophones.

'Such wonderful news, you guys!' she gushes. 'You're all SO amazing, everyone of you deserves to win . . . you know I just loved, loved, your show so much!'

Then she throws Jack an overtly sexy stare, full eye contact, Bambi eyelashes fluttering like twin butterflies, the whole works. 'And if any of you guys need a date to the Tony awards, you sure as hell know where to find me!'

For Jack's part though, he just smiles politely and asks to see the drinks menu, like he's used to being bombarded by part-time models who look like Bond girls on a daily basis. Which in fairness, he probably is. He expertly scans down through the wine list and without as much as raising an eyebrow, lowers his voice and says to me, 'So, where has she disappeared off to then?'

'I don't know,' I answer truthfully. No need for him to even mention her by name, we both know only too well who he's talking about.

'She should be here. Looks bad that she's not. Looks very bad. If this is what I think it is . . .'

'It's not,' I interrupt him. Only hoping to Jaysus that I'm right.

Because I'm ninety per cent certain that Liz has been staying off coke for the last while. Yes, she's been rude and moody and non-communicative, but her work is as stellar as always, which can only be a good sign. Can't it? Course it is, I think, brushing that particular worry to one side.

I slip off to the bathroom with Jules and meet Chris there, who's gaping at herself in the mirror and lashing on the Touche Éclat like it's foundation. As soon as Jules disappears off to the loo, she fires off exactly the same set of questions about Liz. Do I know where she's gone, who she's with and most importantly, why she isn't here with the rest of us, where she should be?

I can't tell you, I answer truthfully.

An impatient eye-roll from Chris.

'But then,' I go on, deliberately keeping my voice low so no one in the stalls will overhear, 'she's most likely still mortified after the whole engagement ring debacle and being around you and me can only be a constant reminder of that. So who can blame her if she fancies socialising elsewhere? She's got to be eaten up with guilt after what happened . . .'

'Good,' Chris snaps, expertly patting the concealer all round her eye sockets. 'In that case, I hope she eats her guilt and gains fifteen pounds. God knows, the girl could do with a bit more weight on her.'

Then she swishes back her poker-straight hair and throws me a look as if to say, subject closed, now can we just enjoy our night please?

As we all troop back from the bathroom, I steer Jules to the seat I've kept for her beside me and introduce her to Jack. I'm not kidding, his eyebrows nearly slant all the way up into his hairline with surprise when he realises that this is in fact, Dan's little sister.

'Well, well, well, the elusive Dan,' he teases, sitting back in his chair, and slowly taking her in from head to toe. 'I was beginning to doubt his very existence.'

'Oh he exists alright,' Jules beams cheekily back at him, playing with her springy curls and with two bright pink triangles appearing, one on each of her cheeks. 'Paid for my airfare over here, you know.'

I should almost have it tattooed behind my eyeballs by now, I should have seen this coming a mile off. The funny thing about Jack, you see, is that he's always eager for any little titbits of autobiography about my private life that drop, particularly in relation to Dan.

A bit too bloody interested, in fact.

'So tell me all about your big brother, then,' Jack says, looking intently at Jules with unflinching, cloud-blue eyes. 'And I won't settle for any less than the full story.'

And now, suddenly, I'm uncomfortable.

'No, no, don't bother,' I say, flinging Jack a loaded glare that I hope reads, *there are perfectly valid reasons why you and I never discuss our private lives with each other . . . can't we just leave it that way and talk about something . . . anything . . . else?*

'Annie, what is up with you?' says Jules, all innocence. 'You look like a bulldog that just swallowed a wasp.'

Right. So much for me and my meaningful glares.

'OK, then,' says Jack smoothly, unleashing the full brilliance of his teeth on Jules and almost blinding her in the process. 'In that case, just give me three facts about him that I don't already know. Then I promise to be a good little boy and to drop the subject.'

Jules exhales deeply, puffing out her cheeks as she racks her brains.

'OK, well you asked for it so here goes. For starters, he'd never in a million years go around dressed in a suit like yours,' she says, as usual, opening her mouth without stopping to think first. 'Says wearing suits only makes him look like a funeral director.'

278

Shut up, shut up, just please for the love of God, shut up now . . .

'I see,' says Jack with a sardonic smile twitching at the corner of his mouth. 'Do go on, this is fascinating.'

'Oh and he's ridiculously generous too; he really would give you the shirt off his back. Wouldn't he, Annie? In fact back home, he's considered to be a bit of a one-man welfare state.'

'Anyone else ready to order?' I ask the table at large, desperate for a subject change.

'But then, he's total crap at remembering things like . . . anniversaries for instance, isn't he, Annie?'

Enough already!

'You know, I think I might go for the chicken dish for two. Will you share with me, Jules?'

'Yeah . . . and he's a total workaholic too. Dan's the type who'd get out of bed at three in the morning to drive thirty miles to sort out a budgie with diarrhoea. Am I right, Annie?'

Thank God the waiter appears just then, and like all waiters in this town, he doesn't just tell you the day's specials as much as recite a five-minute monologue about how his name is Laurent, how he'll be serving us this evening and how the sea bass is miles better than the duck confit tonight.

I, for one though, am grateful for the diversion and breathe a huge sigh of relief.

As the night wears on and the champagne is flowing, a bit of an impromptu sing-song starts at the table, led by Blythe in her trilling, wobbly soprano. Now I love the woman dearly, but her singing voice will never cost Barbra Streisand a night's sleep; put it this way, it's like the note hears her voice coming, then shies away from it. People are starting to drift off to different seats around the table or else scarper off to the loo, at least till she's finished murdering 'Queen Bee'. Perfect excuse for anyone to slip outside for a cigarette . . . even, I notice several non-smokers.

Now for someone like Jack, half an hour without dashing out for a fag is an anomaly, yet every time he comes back inside, no matter how much table hopping has gone on in the interim, he still manages to find his way to my side. I'm not imagining it and what's more, I think by the time dinner is served and cleared, other people are starting to notice too. Chris, for one, keeps throwing loaded 'we are women of the world, so just have your fling and be done with it' type glances at me and frankly, it's starting to get on my nerves.

About the fifth time this has happened, when Jules is deep in conversation at the other end of the table, Jack turns to me, swirling brandy round the bottom of a balloon glass and says, 'So that's your sister-in-law, then.'

'Yes. And I'm mad about her. She's like a little sister to me too.'

'Ah, the unalloyed joy of a whimsical teen. I love it. Also, I find it a fascinating study in human behaviour to watch your reactions whenever your husband's name is mentioned. Or to be more specific, when his name is mentioned in front of me. Care to comment on this intriguing paradox, Ms Cole?'

'You know, it's really late,' I smile in what I hope is an enigmatic and not a serial-killer-ish way, then I pick up my purse and start getting organised to leave. 'And Jules is still jet lagged . . . I really think I should get her home to bed now, don't you?'

'Go if you must, my dear,' he grins confidently, 'but don't for a moment make the mistake of thinking that this conversation is closed.'

For Jules's part, she can't stop raving about how smooth and charming and lounge-lizard-y Jack is, the whole way home in the back of our taxi. God love the innocence of the girl; she spent the whole ride back berating herself for blushing furiously whenever he as much as looked at her, but then as she says in her defence, she's just completely and utterly unused to attractive men.

I don't argue with her there; in Stickens, the most eligible bachelor in town is thirty-seven-year-old Liam Quigley, who lives with his mammy, drives a vegetable van, has about three teeth in his head and perpetually smells of cabbage.

'So how come you never told me that your director isn't just hot, he's stupid hot?' she yawns at me, the jet lag hitting her now like a tonne of lead. 'If you'd warned me, I'd at least have had a shower before I went out tonight.'

We arrive home, and just as I'm yawning and making up the sofa bed in the living room for Jules, my phone beep beeps as a text comes through. I fish round the bottom of my bag for the mobile, and read it.

It's Dan. One simple sentence.

MEET ME AT THE MOON.

I beam, suddenly all energised again as butterflies start to dance in my stomach. This has been happening pretty regularly these past few nights, meeting Dan at the moon. Fast turning into the brightest part of my evenings, in fact. Ten minutes later, when I've put an exhausted and wall-falling Jules to bed, I slip into the privacy of my own room and call him.

He answers instantly.

'So, how did you like your little surprise, then?' he asks, and I get an instant mental picture of him smiling crookedly at me down the phone.

'Best surprise ever,' I laugh, 'and I'm determined to give her the time of her life while she's here. The shops, the shows, the touristy stuff . . . the works.'

'That's my girl. I knew you'd take good care of her. By the way, you won't believe my news bulletin tonight,' he says and I swear, his voice is like balm to my ears.

'Sounds exciting, tell me all.'

'I've only been asked to make a keynote speech at the annual vets' conference in Dublin this December, you know, the one on equestrian practices.'

'Hey, that's wonderful, congratulations!' I say, knowing that this is a massively big deal for him.

'Downside is I have to make a speech, and you know how much I hate any kind of public speaking.'

'Oh come on, it'll be a walk in the park. Nothing to stress about. Call me when you have it written and I'll go through it with you if you like.'

'Would you?'

'You know I would.'

'Angel.'

In turn, I tell him all about the Tony nominations and Liz's complete and utter indifference to the whole thing, to the whole cast, to everything.

'Dan, it's a disaster; she just turns up for work, does the gig, then scarpers off as far as humanly possible from the rest of us, till the following night. Things are almost at break point and I just don't know how much longer we can all continue going on in this faux-polite vein.'

'That bad, huh?'

'I'm not kidding, it's written all over the girl's face that she'd infinitely prefer to be looking at the rest of us from the far end of an Uzi shotgun. She doesn't talk to me any more. Doesn't even trust me.'

Dan listens attentively and advises his usual creed of kindness and patience at all times. Vintage Dan of course, I think, smiling to myself. Tolerance and understanding will eventually win the day in his book, whatever the problem.

'In time she may snap out of all this moodiness,' he says gently, 'may even revert back to her old self, but in the meantime, just give her space and let her know that you're there for her. But if she ever breaks out again, remember, it's your duty to make sure she gets help.'

'I've tried, believe me, but when I even suggested we go and see a doctor together, she practically flung me out of her apartment.'

'Next time, don't take no for an answer. If there is a next time.'

And then onto the next ulcer-inducing worry that's been nagging away at the back of my mind since this afternoon. Lisa and her marriage break-up. It's exactly as I suspected; yes, Dan tells me, she's up at The Moorings most of the time now, with the kids more often than not.

Fuck, fuck and fuck again.

'She's going through a really rough time at the moment,' he says softly, 'and I'm her oldest friend and neighbour, so I've told her to consider this her home for as long as she needs. She's in a bad way, Annie, money-wise as well. She's got two kids on their summer holidays and not a bean to spend on either of them, the poor things. Your heart would go out to them. I've been taking the little fella Harry out with me on a few farm calls to give Lisa a bit of a break and he seems to enjoy it, which at least is something. He's a great little guy; we've grown to be good buddies. Now says he wants to be a vet when he grows up.'

'Wonderful. That's wonderful,' I chime automatically while thinking to myself . . . I was right. Her kids *will* end up calling Dan 'New Dad'.

Christ Alive, what am I going to do?

'Plus,' he chats on, 'at least when she's up here at The Moorings, Lisa's not running up household bills, which takes the pressure off her a bit. You know, the poor girl's been through the mill, Annie. She says that the maintenance payments she gets from Charlie are barely enough to cover her weekly grocery bills.'

But she's been bitching and moaning about never having enough for her grocery bills for years, I think, silently furious.

None of this is anything new, not a shagging line of it. Lisa is just playing Dan like she's always done and of course he can't see it because Dan is one of those rare people who only ever sees the good in others.

Weird, but over time my memories of home have gradually eroded and softened and yet one jagged bit still sticks out. The Countess fecking Dracula and how she's not happy till she's living in one of your ears and has the other one rented out in flats. And now here's Dan, all alone, all by himself at The Moorings . . . and Lisa's always had more than an eye in his direction, I've suspected that for I don't know how long . . .

Suddenly the burning feeling in my gut is like a furnace. Knowing the Countess Dracula, and unfortunately I do, this will escalate. In fact, she won't be satisfied till she's sold her own house and physically moved lock, stock and barrel into The Moorings . . . and who knows what else she's plotting besides? Now that she's newly separated from her husband?

Worry kicks my mind into overdrive. If I were home, this would never have happened, I think ruefully. But what the hell am I supposed to do from this side of the Atlantic? When we're supposed to be on a marriage sabbatical?

Bite my tongue, say and do nothing, absolutely nothing.

There's a pause while I try to gather my thoughts and then Dan, forthright and straight to the point as ever asks me how I'm enjoying my 'gap year'?

'You know how you always used to say that you felt you missed out on your clubbing, pubbing, partying years on account of me sweeping you off your feet so young?' he smiles, as a totally disconnected thought suddenly strikes me. How funny it is that you can hear a smile over the phone, even when you're thousands of miles apart.

'Well I only hope you're reliving and reclaiming every one of those years now and having the time of your life while you're at it. You deserve it, Annie, having spent so long stuck here with me, in Stickens.'

No point in the polite lie here. It's not that kind of conversation.

'Dan, it wasn't being in Stickens that bothered me, it was never seeing you from one end of the week to the other that I found rough going.'

'And you think I don't know that? You think I haven't been beating myself up about that?'

There's a long silence.

'Because I have, more and more lately; a lot more than you could ever imagine. It's lonely here without you. I never thought I could be lonely here but I am and I'm not liking it. Not one bit. I'm not cut out to live my life alone.'

But you're not on your own now, are you? At least not with Lisa fecking Ledbetter hanging around the house day and bleeding night . . .

I say nothing though, just deliberate for a second. But he's quick to pick up on my silence.

'Annie? You still there?'

'Ehh, yeah . . . I was going to say . . . *oh sod it anyway, might as well get this lead weight off my chest . . .* well . . . you've got Lisa in the house now, don't you? For company, I mean.'

'Not the same as having you here,' he says simply. 'Not the same thing at all. Don't get me wrong, Lisa's a good friend but she's hardly you.'

Oh thank you, thank you, thank you, thank you, thank you for saying that, even if you're just being polite . . . thank you God, Hari Krishna, Buddha, Santa . . . anyone who's listening . . .

I allow myself a small smile now as a wave of relief floods through me.

'Such a sweet thing to say . . .'

'Only the truth.'

'But . . . there's something else . . . something that's been on my mind . . .'

'I'm here, I'm listening.'

Go for it. God knows when I'll get an opportunity like this again . . .

Takes me a moment to cast around for the right words.

'Thing is, Dan . . . you say you're lonely, but . . . when I was around, we hardly ever spoke to each other, I mean . . . surely you remember all the Post-it notes stuck to the fridge door? I sometimes felt I was having more of a relationship with a Samsung fridge freezer than with you.'

'I know, I know,' he sighs deeply, so deeply it's like it's coming from his feet upwards. 'Believe me, I've spent a lot of time replaying the past few years in my head and asking myself what I would have done differently.'

'Oh, come on. It's not that you didn't want to do things differently, it's that you couldn't. And that's a vet's life and we both know that will never change.'

Another silence.

'Annie?'

'I'm still here.'

'You know I want you to go out and enjoy yourself this year?'

'Course.'

'Good, it's important to me that you know that. I want you to have all the freedom that you felt you never had here.'

Half of me is beginning to wonder what he's getting at, but as it's a generous sentiment, I reciprocate and say the same thing back to him.

'Same to you too,' I tell him. 'This is your gap year too, you know. Time for you to do some reclaiming of your youth yourself.'

Except please don't let's cheat on each other. Ever. I think it would destroy me. Let's have our freedom, but with full and total fidelity on each side. Surely not too much to ask for, now is it?

'Well, you see,' he says so softly I almost have to strain to hear him. 'I think there lies the fundamental difference between us.'

'What do you mean?'

'I never felt like I'd missed out on anything. Once I had you by my side, I had everything. Never once did I ever feel like I was missing out. When you were here. But I mightn't have showed it like I should have and that's . . . well, that's something I'm having to live with now.'

Another question that's burning me up.

'Dan?'

'Still here.'

'I need to ask you something that we've never talked about before.'

'Anything.'

'At the end of this year . . . when the show comes to an end, I mean . . .'

'Yeah?'

'Well . . . have you ever wondered what will happen? To us, I mean.'

It's the thought that dare not speak its name, but I'm certain he's guessed what it is that I'm obliquely referring to. This job has been the single most magical experience of my life but when it comes to an end, what then? Do I just go back to Stickens and do we both just pick up where we left off? Because seeing as how we're being brutally honest with each other tonight, we might as well continue.

Trouble is, this year out is changing both of us and what's more, we both know it. What we once wanted at the start of the year may not be what either of us wants come December.

'Tell you what, I'll make a deal with you,' he says.

'Go ahead.'

'Come this December, why don't I come to New York? I could even come over for our anniversary, on December the first . . .'

I hardly hear what he says next. I'm too stunned by the fact that he actually remembered our anniversary.

'. . . we could even meet up by the Rockefeller skating rink,' he's saying, 'where I first proposed to you, all that time ago. Remember?'

'You're kidding me! You would actually take time off from work? Oh shit . . . what was that? Sorry, Dan, I got distracted by the large pig that just flew past my bedroom window.'

'Laugh all you like, missy, but for something as important as this, yes, yes, I think I would. Course if you didn't want me to come, then that would be different.'

Of course I'd want you to come, I'm thinking . . . what kind of a get-out clause is that?

'But if you did . . .' he continues on.

'Then . . . then what exactly?'

'Then, I suppose we could just take things from there.'

It's well past three in the morning when we eventually hang up the phone, but I'm not in the least bit tired.

I feel a deep calmness, a lifting of worrying.

In fact, I feel light, light as air.

Chapter Twelve

I have to hand it to Jack; he's making a serious effort to pull out all the stops to entertain Jules while she's here, something I'm deeply grateful for. It's not that she's a difficult house guest, far from it, it's just that museums and art galleries aren't really her thing. I discovered this one hot, sultry afternoon when I took her to MOMA and, when I came back from the bathroom, found the girl half asleep and yawning, slumped up in a disabled access seat, barely interested enough to even throw the paintings a glance. When I asked her what she thought of a wall-length Jackson Pollock, her response was to stifle a yawn and say, 'For feck's sake, hand me three aerosol cans and a paintbrush and I'd do a better job myself.'

But Jack's come to the rescue and I have to hand it to him, he's been little short of extraordinary in trumping himself, time and again. There was one night after the show when he took Jules and me to see the observatory on what felt like the two-thousandth floor of the Rockefeller Center, Top of the Rock: utterly breathtaking at night-time, with all the lights of the city twinkling like the celestial heavens beneath you.

Not only that, but then he produced a bottle of champagne

and as he expertly cracked it open, I was vaguely wondering how we'd all drink it . . . maybe take turns slugging from the bottle, like teenagers with filched bottles of vodka? Not a bit of it; Jack had that covered too and astonished me by producing three long-stemmed crystal flutes from his briefcase and elegantly serving us in those. Honest to God, if he could have had a waiter floating around topping up our glasses and passing round the canapés, he would have.

I'm learning more and more about him as the summer wears on; no trouble is too much for him and few doors are unopened to him. For instance, Central Park closes to the public late in the evenings, but you can always trust Jack to know someone who knows someone and sure enough, one night the three of us were allowed a sneaky private tour of the zoo followed by a moonlit boat ride out on the lake. Unbelievable. Just magical.

Then, like he's on a permanent quest to outdo himself, the following day he arranged to meet Jules and I at the South Street Seaport, where a helicopter belonging to one of his millionaire buddies was waiting to whisk the three of us on a tour of the five islands that make up Manhattan, with Jack acting as our guide. And boy does he know his stuff. It's a bit like being out with Alan Whicker, minus having a camera crew in tow.

Flying over the skyline, with Jules and I clinging to each other and squealing like two schoolkids on an excursion, not only was he able to tell us exactly which skyscraper was which, but the whole history behind each one too. For instance he told us how the Empire State was built during the famous nineteen thirties 'race to the sky' and that the famous lightning tower was added on just so that it could be taller than the Chrysler Building, which was at the time, threatening to rival it height-wise.

Most amazing holiday she's ever had in her entire life, Jules reckons. Then, best of all, to celebrate the end of her second week here, Jack pulls yet another rabbit out of the hat. Turns out he's got a pal who has a summer share in the Hamptons and he calls one afternoon to ask if Jules and I would care to join him there for the weekend? He even has it all worked out: we'll leave right after the Sunday matinee and stay till the following Tuesday afternoon, getting me back to the Shubert in plenty of time for the curtain.

Jules is beside herself and I'm quite looking forward to the trip as well, until the Sunday morning that we're due to leave, when she and I are up in my apartment packing all our beach clothes, getting ready to go.

Next thing, she pads barefoot into my room, collapses onto the bed and then hugs her knees to her chest, staring worriedly at the ceiling, exactly like a ten-year-old would.

'What's up, hon?' I ask her. 'Why aren't you packing?'

'Because I had a deep and disturbing thought. A rarity for me, you'll agree, so I figured I'd better share it with you. Now, before I forget.'

'Shoot.'

'Well . . . it's you. More specifically, you and Jack.'

'Oh for feck's sake, Jules,' I answer back, flinging a pair of socks at her. 'Don't you know better than to listen to backstage gossip?'

'I'm serious, Annie. Why do you think he's doing all this for us? It's hardly for my benefit, now is it? I've seen the way he looks at you when you don't notice. If you ask my professional opinion as a serially single girl, I really think he has it bad for you.'

'I'm not even entertaining this,' I find myself snapping at her, without meaning to.

'Can't a woman just be good friends with a guy without it giving rise to all this shite-ology?'

'Not when one of them has the serious hots for the other. You mark my words, Annie Cole, I foresee trouble ahead and as we all know, I'm never wrong.'

'You were wrong about who'd win *X Factor* last year.'

'Stop messing. I've given this a great deal of thought,' she says primly, sitting up now and dangling her long, thin legs off the edge of the bed. 'If you ask me, Jack is the kind of guy who's used to having women queuing up for him . . . and yet here he is, blatantly single, blatantly not seeing anyone.'

I'm in the middle of packing cleanser and toner into a wash bag, but stop for a split second. Because that much *is* true and I've often wondered about it myself. In fact, I've pretty much spent the whole summer witnessing women fling themselves like blow-dried missiles in slingbacks at Jack. Happens all the time, in fact. Waitresses, hostesses, the entire female phalanx of the Shubert theatre box office, and never once does he as much as bat an eyelid.

'So ask yourself this, Annie. Does he ever act on this and go out with any of them, like a normal guy would? Or even just drag them home for quickie one-night stands?' she goes on, correctly reading my thoughts. 'No, not once. Now ordinarily, I'd write him off as gay, because let's face it, the guy does know how to dress and he always smells better than you or I, but that's clearly not the case either.'

'You've forgotten something,' I interrupt her. 'Jack doesn't do relationships. If I've heard him saying that once, I've heard him saying it a hundred times. I think his exact phrase is that he finds "the whole business of Eros so boring".'

'Excuse me, did I say I was finished? Which leads me to the logical conclusion that you have inadvertently become his ultimate challenge. Because you're not encouraging him and you're actively *not* looking for love, it's like the biggest turn-on in the world for him. Your unattainability is bringing out obsession in him and I for one know trouble when I see it coming. You mark my words.'

'Jules, I've done nothing, absolutely nothing to encourage any of this. Besides . . . he's never tried it on with me. Never once. And I see him all the time.'

'Just wait. He will. He's a director for feck's sake, he knows how to pick his moment. Trust me, Annie, it's a question of when, not if.'

By five that evening, the show is well over and the only instruction Jack has given Jules and me is to wait for him at the theatre; that he'll pick us up there. I'm innocently assuming in a cab, so we can get to Port Authority Midtown and take the Jitney bus on from there. Although somehow, the idea of Jack doing something as mundane as taking public transport doesn't quite seem to sit right in my brain.

The rest of the cast have scattered off to the four winds after the show and Jules and I are just waiting outside the box office, basking in the late afternoon sunshine, when next thing a long, black stretch limo glides elegantly round the corner, driven by a chauffeur wearing an actual uniform. Two seconds later, Jack bounds out of the back seat, looking effortlessly casual in jeans and a Gap T-shirt, then throws his head back to guffaw when he clocks our stunned expressions.

'Jump in, ladies, we've a barbeque to get to this evening!'

he grins delightedly, helping us both into the limo with our overnight bags, then slamming the door shut with an expensive clunk.

'Mother of God, where are you getting all your money from?' Jules blurts out. 'Are you secretly a rapper or something?'

'Glass of champagne?' he asks smoothly, producing a bottle of Bollinger, an ice bucket and three long-stemmed glasses from a concealed mini-bar along one of the car's side panels.

Jules shoots me a significant *all-this-is-for-your-benefit-not-mine* look which I do my level best to ignore.

'So would you ladies care to hear what I've got planned for your evening's entertainment?' he asks, handing round a china plate with olives and antipasti immaculately laid out on a linen napkin. Fecking hell, it's like the Four Seasons on wheels in here.

Jules stuffs a fistful of olives into her mouth then spits out the stones, as Jack tells us that some other friends of his who live close to the beach house we're staying at are having a barbeque this evening and we're all invited along.

'And there's someone coming who I'd particularly like you to meet,' he grins at Jules, the white teeth gleaming. 'An old pal of mine and a great investor in the theatre. Newly single, attractive, successful and dying to meet someone new.'

'Jesus! Are you setting me up on a blind date?' she squeals excitedly. 'For real?'

'Well yeah, if you want to call it that. You don't mind, do you?'

'Are you kidding me? Once he's straight, single and not recently paroled, then he passes the Jules test.'

'How come you're single anyway? Surely you must have

boyfriends back home in . . . what's the name of that place you're from again . . . Stickens, isn't it?'

She sips on her champagne, starts playing with one of her jet black, springy curls, then launches off on her favourite rant – the complete and utter lack of eligible guys aged between eighteen and thirty in the greater Waterford area. Sparing time to elaborate on her pet theory that local girls like her are a bit like the women left behind during World War One, when a whole generation of young men were wiped out in the trenches and so there was no one left for them to marry.

I can see Jack smiling at all her youthful high spirits and harmlessly insane chatter and he roars laughing when he offers her the plate of olives again and she waves them away saying, 'Are you kidding me? If I'm being matched up on a date tonight, then that's the last thing I'm eating.'

The drive takes the guts of two hours, so it's close to eight in the evening by the time we finally do arrive. Already twilight and beautifully cool . . . perfect weather for a barbeque. Truth be told, I'm a bit tipsy from all the champagne and I think Jules must be too because when we do finally arrive at the beach house, she starts guffawing and asks Jack which friend of his exactly owns the place? Simon Cowell, perhaps?

As we stagger out of the limo, the sheer size of the place takes my breath away. Because this is not just a beach house, this is the Elton John of beach houses; neo-colonial, with white Doric columns dotted all around it and a flight of granite stairs that lead up to a deluxe-sized front door. Honest to God, it's as though the owner saw *Gone with the Wind* once too often and decided to just copy the architectural design for Tara, lock, stock and barrel.

The house has seven bedrooms; 'cosy' according to Jack, who's stayed here many times before and who gives us a quick guided tour of the place. Then he finds his way to a giant double fridge in the kitchen and produces yet another bottle of champagne. 'A little something to get us into the party mood,' as he says.

Meanwhile Jules and I gape around the place with me thinking . . . you call this a kitchen? Yeah, right. Kitchen-cum-ballroom, more like. I'm not messing, there are actual chandeliers hanging over the breakfast bar. Chandeliers. In a shagging *beach* house.

With an expert crack, Jack opens the bottle, pours us yet more glasses of fizz, then tells us that the barbeque at his friend's house is probably in full swing by now and we really should get changed and make a move. So we bring our drinks upstairs with us as he guides us to our bedrooms.

My room, by the way, would comfortably sleep about seventeen, no problem. The ensuite bathroom alone is larger than my entire little blonde apartment back in Manhattan. It's breathtaking though, with long French windows and a tiny little balcony that overlooks the sea and the velvety blue sky. And it's been so long since I've heard the sound of waves, that it instantly relaxes and soothes me, half-drunk and all as I am.

I have a lightning quick shower in the mistaken belief that it'll sober me up a bit, then change into a little red and black summer dress and a matching pair of pumps that I got on sale in Filene's Basement, guided there by who else but Blythe, the Discount Queen. The usual half can of serum I need to get my hair to behave itself won't work, so I just tie it up and lash on a bit of lipstick, thinking, ah sure I'll fecking well do. In low light, I'll pass. Who's looking at me anyway? And who cares?

I bump into Jack on the staircase, looking as elegantly cool as he always does, in jeans and a long white linen shirt and he kisses me lightly on the forehead. An intimate gesture but I'm drunk enough to let it pass. Then he grabs me by both hands and twirls me round, checking out the red and black strappy sundress.

'Love it,' he grins, 'like I always say, red really is your colour.'

'You don't think I look a bit like a blood clot?'

Shit. I think I'm starting to slur my words a bit now. And him twirling me around just gave me a dose of the helicopters.

'You're beautiful,' is all he says, still holding onto both my hands, not letting go.

'Truly beautiful. And so blissfully unaware of it.'

And still his cold hand is gripping mine.

Oh bollocks, I think, pulling away from him. I wonder if Jules could be right after all.

And if I'm in real trouble here.

Anyroadup, Jules finally emerges from her bedroom all set for her blind date and I have to say, looking gorgeous in a little baby-doll yellow spotty dress that she bought in Gap; very sexy and so short that only a nineteen-year-old could properly carry it off. On me, it would look like I'd left the house in my nightie.

And so the three of us stroll across the beach to the barbeque, which is about ten houses down from us, but you'd know the party house a mile off from the dozens of coloured lanterns that are blazing away on the porch and the thumpy music that's pumping away. It's a complete throng when we get there and there's even an impromptu dance floor right on the beach in front of the house.

Next thing, I feel Jack gripping my bare arm with his ice cold hand and steering me inside the house, in the general direction of the bar. Jules is in tow, giving him instructions on what he's to say and more importantly, what he's not to say when he introduces her to her blind date. More champagne arrives, and I'm seriously starting to feel light-headed and woozy now; I'm unconsciously swaying to the music and only dying to kick off my shoes and dance out on the beach, where it seems like the real party is in full swing.

Jules's blind date appears, one Freddy Masterson, who seems like a perfect gentleman, says all the right things, makes all the right moves, but there's just one tiny hitch. At a rough estimate, he's probably pushing mid-forties, but not in a sexy older guy with salt-and-pepper-hair like Richard Gere way. No, I think drunkenly to myself, Freddy would be more in the Ed Harris, sweaty, baldy mould . . . and even he lets it slip that he's got a teenage daughter barely two years younger than Jules. A half hint of a bored eye-roll from her tells me all I need to know about where this is about to go.

Anyway, after a bit of polite chit-chat about how she's been enjoying Manhattan, I can actually see her eyes begin-ning to glaze over a bit, so I suggest we go outside into the cool air to dance. She jumps at the chance to escape and as we wend our way through the mill and back outside to the beach she hisses in my ear, 'I just had a great idea for my first book. A non-fiction called *The Official Jules Ferguson Guide to Non-Age Compatible Couples*. Whaddya think?'

'You didn't think he looked . . . I dunno . . . distinguished?'

'Oh please. Everyone knows distinguished just means ugly with money.'

It's loud and noisy out here and everyone's dancing with wild abandonment, barefoot on the beach. We join in and it's only magical; I can't remember the last time I actually danced. The music runs through me, my hips, arms, legs waist, my whole body without bothering to consult my brain and I'm just at that wonderful membrane between drunkenness and right before the hangover hits you . . . and it's only aaaaa-mazing.

Poor sweaty Freddy comes out to check up on Jules, dabbing his forehead with a hanky and all arms and legs as he dances with her, like a vaguely embarrassing uncle at a family wedding trying to act twenty-five years younger than he is. And I'm running my fingers through my hair and moving and swaying to the beat, having the time of my life, when next thing, I feel an ice cold arm slip around my waist.

I know it's Jack without even turning round. I know by the coldness of his touch. There couldn't possibly be two people on earth that bloody freezing.

'Let's go for a stroll,' he has to mouth at me above the thumpy music. 'There's something I want to show you.'

I'm not sober enough to argue so I do as he says and he steers me a good distance further down the beach, where it's far quieter . . . and before I know where I am, it's just the two of us, alone. It's much darker here too and the further along the beach we walk, the more I begin to stumble drunkenly; the only light now is the dim red dot of the cigarette he's smoking, exactly parallel to his lips.

He slips an obliging arm around me, steadying me and on we stroll towards a jetty where there's a yacht moored. I have to squint a bit through the inky blackness to see it up close and that's when I spot its name painted on the side: *The Idle Rich*. I laugh at its appropriateness and next thing, Jack's taken my hand, lacing his thin, bony fingers through mine.

'I've chartered it to take you out sailing tomorrow,' he grins, 'if you trust me to behave like a gentleman with you, that is, all alone out in the middle of the Atlantic.'

'Won't Jules be with us?'

'Aren't you tired of being chaperoned all the time, my dear? I'm desperately fond of the girl, but teenage high spirits can be a tad wearisome after a time. Besides, Freddy wants to take her off to the Lobster Bar for lunch tomorrow, so I've effectively commandeered you for myself. For a full afternoon. What luck, I hope you'll agree?'

Suddenly it's as though all the champagne finally hits me in one big whoosh, and I know I have to sit down or else I'll pass out.

'Here,' he says, quickly stubbing out his cigarette, grabbing me by the waist and in one expert movement, stretching me down onto the sand. 'Just sit here for a bit, you'll be fine. You haven't eaten anything all evening, that's all that's wrong with you.'

He sits down right beside me as my head begins to swim. The whole beach tilts, then rights itself and I want to lie back till the dizziness passes but next thing Jack's leaning over me, gently laying me down flat on the sand. And he's close now, so close that I can feel his ice cold breath in my ear, a strange mixture of mints and fags.

'Annie,' he murmurs slowly, over and over, 'Are you OK? Annie . . .?'

I want to say I'm fine really but before I know what's going on, before I've even got time to react, he's lying down beside me and suddenly his whispers in my ear have turned into gentle caresses, light as air. He expertly kisses my ears, cheeks and neck over and over, his skin so soft and tender and now his lean, cold body is stretching out on top of mine . . . stop, I want to say, stop this now, I'm married, I can't . . . then a wave of guilt comes crashing down on me when I even invoke Dan's memory . . . but what I haven't accounted for, what's completely knocked me for six is the huge swell of desire that's sweeping over me. Next thing, I can feel his bony ribcage taut against me, as his hands run through my hair, down my neck, and then slowly, teasingly onto my breasts, as he cups them in his icy cold, rock hard grip.

It's as though he's tantalising me like a maestro now and without wanting to, without even meaning to, I find myself responding, craving for nothing more than his lips on mine, wanting him to press me even closer to him. He's playing with my hair now, lightly flicking my earlobe with his tongue and beginning to moan softly.

'You know I want you, Annie . . .' he murmurs and I swear his voice is like toffee. 'And fuck knows I've waited long enough for you . . .'

The tiny part of my brain that's remotely sober wants to yell at him to let go, but somehow I've lost all control over myself. I can barely remember the last time I was touched like this, it was so, so long ago . . . now it's like every fibre of my nerve endings are thrilling to his light, delicate, cool touch . . . and I'm completely powerless.

He must hear the sound of my heart walloping off my ribcage, I think, he must.

His smooth cheek is rubbing against mine now; his long, thin, wiry body stretched out on top of mine and before I know it, my arms are slowly slipping around his neck, locking him to me, my hands running through his fine, silky hair, and I'm moaning with the pure pleasure of it all.

Then a moment later, just when I feel like I'm starting to burn up, his lips are on mine, lightly at first, almost teasingly, then slowly growing sexier and more and more intense, his tongue in my mouth and mine in his, hungrily, greedily kissing each other, neither of us wanting it to stop.

I never saw this coming, never guessed for a second that he could turn me on like this, making me blank out everything except his long, lean body hardening against mine. That sheer chemistry could do this to me. That the attraction between us could be so combustibly dangerous.

Christ, I didn't even realise I found him this sexy in the first place . . . I've never even kissed anyone except Dan before in my whole life . . . but all I can think about now is the warm, hot mouth roughly biting my neck, whispering my name over and the cool hands that are expertly unzipping the back of my dress, unhooking my bra as he slowly, tantalisingly moves down to kiss my boobs.

'You want this too, don't you?' he groans thickly and before I know it, he's spun me over so that now I'm lying on top of him. His hands are rougher now, more urgent, gripping me all over my bare back, my bum, my legs, feeling their way up my thighs, thrilling me with the coolness of his touch. I can't stop myself from moaning and so is he and it's hot and getting hotter and heavier and I know I should stop this and yet I can't and then out of all this madness I hear someone calling out my name.

Clear as a bell.

We break off and look up.

It's Jules, standing about ten feet away from us, having taken in the whole scene.

On her face is the exact same fight-or-flight expression that you see on startled deer on the Nature Channel.

Jack sits up, for once in his life completely nonplussed. I look over at him, as one of those bizarre, disconnected thoughts strike me: I wish I had a camera.

Jules turns her back on us, strides up the beach and is gone.

Oh Christ, what have I done?

Chapter Thirteen

It's late the following afternoon when Jules and I get to talk. Really talk, that is. Back home in my apartment, having understandably cut the Hamptons trip short. We're both unpacking and I'm in the middle of loading the washing machine when she turns to me with eyes that seem to see right through to the back of my brain.

'I know it's none of my business, Annie,' is her opener. 'You're on your marriage sabbatical so technically there was no cheating involved. And I don't even blame you; no one knows better than me that Dan didn't exactly behave like husband of the year when you were home. But that's not what's worrying me.'

'Hon, I've told you over and over how mortified I am about what happened,' I say, still riddled with guilt and hating every miserable bloody second of it.

Jesus, if Dan ever did that to me . . . I don't know what I'd think. Hard to believe that not so long ago, there I was eaten up with worry over the Countess Dracula making moves on him . . . and look what I went and got up to myself two bottles of champagne later? Worse still is the conversation I know I'm going to have to have with Dan at some point during one of our 'meet me at the moon' chats. Because if it's one thing I know about myself it's this: the awful, crucifying remorse won't go away until I brace myself and come clean to him.

Simple as that.

'I was tipsy and it shouldn't have happened and I'm sorry that it did. But I can tell you one thing: it most definitely will *not* happen again.'

'Oh yes it will,' she shakes her dark curls gravely.

'I already told you, hon, I had way too much to drink and . . .'

'You only ever do things you want to do when you're drunk.'

'Jules, please . . .'

'No, you *have* to listen to me. If I know the Jack Gordons of this world, and I think I've seen a fair few in my time . . .'

'You have?'

'Oh shut up, you're in no position to get smart-alecky with me. Men like Jack are the type who'll basically drill through concrete to get what they want. And he wants you, no two ways about that. Which is what's making me sick with worry. All weekend, I could see clear as day this whole other parallel life that you could be leading here, with him. Instead of back home with us. And it's not just frightening me, Annie, it's bloody terrifying me. You're like my sister and I love you and suppose, just suppose that by the end of this year, you decide that you don't want to come home? No one could blame you for making that decision either, because what's waiting for you at home? The Mothership whinging at you? The Countess Dracula bitching at you? And then Dan, gone, gone all the time, making you one promise after another and always letting you down. Supposing you say to hell with that, you want to stay here and lead a whole new life with someone else? Then what? You'd be gone out of our lives and I'd never see you again and as for Dan . . .'

I take my head out of the laundry basket and am about to tell Jules that she's taken up the tiniest germ of an idea and run wild with it, as per usual.

It's only when I turn to look up at her, that I realise she's got tears in her eyes.

Jules's last weekend in New York and after the disaster of our aborted trip to the Hamptons, this promises to be a good 'un. It's the Tony awards, broadcast live from Radio City Music Hall and the whole lot of us are like basket cases with the nerves. Barring Liz, that is, who apart from occasionally grunting at me in work, has yet to pass as much as a civil sentence to any one of us.

Because the awards are held on a Sunday night, we're all in a mad rush after our matinee show to get home and shoehorn ourselves into evening dresses suitable for the poshest black-tie bash any of us have ever been to in our entire lives. And knowing right well that she'd refuse point blank to spend money on herself, we all clubbed together and hired a professional make-up artist to call to Blythe's apartment, to help get her all dolled up for her big night. But when I say 'we all' I mean myself, Alex and Chris. I offered Liz the chance to have her make-up done professionally for the night too, stressing that this was a treat from the rest of us but all I got in return was a) a filthy glare and b) the dressing room door slammed in my face.

Christ Alive, you'd actually swear that I'd doused her in petrol, set fire to her hair, then run away cackling like Peter

Lorre, the way she's carrying on these days. And I've been actively tuning it out for so long that I don't know how much longer I can go on for.

Anyroadup, the matinee is long over, we're all back at the ranch and it's like an episode of *America's Top Model*; all of us charging in and out of each other's apartments filching bits of make-up, handbags, shoes, the works. Messing and laughing and then excitedly squealing over each other's outfits, even though we all went shopping for them together to Loehmann's designer store earlier this week, so what we're all wearing is no big surprise really.

Blythe is looking gorgeous in a stunningly elegant pale green dress and long shawl, with pearls borrowed from Chris. Meanwhile Alex looks cool and funky in a YSL black trouser suit she found on sale in Century 21 and with her red hair tightly slicked back, the whole look is very *le smoking* altogether. A slash of bright blue lipstick is her only Alex-like little rebellion. Chris, of course, looks like a model: groomed and sleek with her long, straight, dark hair up in a neat chignon and wearing a deep purple crushed velvet dress that only someone as tall and pale and skinny as her could really carry off.

As a special treat and also as a farewell pressie, I bought Jules a stunning long, black Calvin Klein fishtail evening dress, which just looked so breathtaking on her when she tried it on that I knew she had to have it. She's wearing her hair down and loose for the night, springy curls wild and abandoned, but still looks all sophisticated and grown-up, a million miles from the sloppy, oversized T-shirts she's usually happy to stomp around the apartment in all day.

'You sure I look OK?' she asks me, twirling around my bedroom while I'm blow-drying my soaking wet hair, running late and well behind schedule. 'I feel weird with my knees covered.'

'Stunning,' I assure her.

'And it's so low in front. Promise me I don't look like I'm dressed for an operation?'

I laugh back at her. 'Not a bit of it, you look so elegant and chic! I'm dead proud of you, babe. We'll have to take a load of photos to prove to Audrey how well you scrub up.'

'Yeah,' she grins at me, tossing the curls off her face, 'you're right, even if I do say so myself. I look really hot in black, don't I? Jeez, it's a wonder I don't get hit on at funerals more often.'

All our invites bossily say that we're to be in Radio City and seated by nine pm sharp, but we've all been invited to The Plaza hotel for cocktails beforehand, by Jack, who by the way continues to act like a perfect gentleman towards me. As much as to say, 'I wouldn't dream of being crass enough to embarrass you by even referring to how we leaped on each other's bones like a pair of sex-starved animals only a week ago . . . so let's just act completely normal, like nothing happened.'

Complete and utter denial that anything ever happened or that there's any kind of problem between us? Absolutely fine by me. I've had years of practice at this. I'm a bleeding maestro.

Anyroadup, just as we're all assembling in the hallway, getting ready to take cabs up to The Plaza, on an impulse, I call up to Liz's apartment. To make her feel included, to at least let her know where we'll all be and that of course, she's welcome to come with. She did her usual disappearing trick after this afternoon's show and there's been no sighting of her since. And now there's no answer to her door.

Worrying. To say the least.

But everyone else is in high good humour, giggling and messing as we all pile into the Champagne Bar of The Plaza hotel, tripping over long dresses we're not quite used to and high heels we're all stumbling around in. Five of us in total – Jules and me, followed by Alex, Chris and Blythe. Chris is on her own tonight because her husband Josh and little Oscar flew back to Ireland over a week ago, so tonight is the perfect distraction for her.

Harvey Shapiro is already here ahead of us with his wife Sherri or Terri, can never remember which, and he immediately starts handing us glasses of champagne. I look around at everyone, so proud and happy and rightly enjoying a night of celebration . . . and somehow, my thoughts keep wandering back to Liz. And how she should be here with us too. Because we're a company and we're incomplete without her. Before it's barely begun, it's like there's a pallor cast over the night and I don't know why. At least, not yet I don't.

Jack skips in from his upstairs apartment, looking carelessly elegant in an evening suit, like he was born wearing a bow tie. I've hardly seen him since the Hamptons and he makes a point of kissing and greeting everyone else ahead of me, making charming comments about how fab all the girls are looking, particularly Blythe, whose professional make-up is practically soldered onto her.

'Oh go on out of that, you old charmer!' she laughs playfully, beaming and pink with pleasure. 'At least I'm fairly sure that I won't have to make a speech tonight, I haven't a prayer of winning . . . but I've been rehearsing my "good loser" face in the mirror all week. You know, to convey just the right blend of disappointment that I lost,

310

tinged with genuine delight for whoever does win. But now you, on the other hand, Jack . . .'

'Let's just wait and see, why don't we?' he nods politely, brushing the suggestion aside.

He greets me last and lingers for just half a second longer than he probably should, giving me one of his trademark up and down looks, taking in every little detail of the dress I'm wearing. Which by the way is floor length, backless, bare-armed and white, with a skirt big enough to fit three midgets underneath it, cheekily borrowed from Chris in return for a pair of Swarovski earrings I lent her. Then he leans in and kisses me lightly on the cheek. Almost chastely. The usual tang of citrus from him, mixed with cigarettes.

'Well hello there,' he says in a deep, low voice, the eyebrows slanting sexily downwards at me.

'Hi.'

'You're ravishing.'

OK, you need to stop this, stop this right now.

'Every stitch borrowed.'

Very discreetly, so none of the others can see, I feel his hand move slowly round my waist then slowly, teasingly down my thighs, bottom, then resting momentarily on my bare back, lightly drumming his cold fingers up and down my spine . . . and suddenly, without warning my knees turn watery and begin to loosen.

Shit, shit, shit . . . no.

He's very close to me now and I know I'm blushing like a wino, feeling embarrassed and awkward, fully aware that we're in public, so I force myself to take a step back, further away from him. He raises his eyebrows quizzically, but is too polite to say any more.

And neither do I.

311

It takes two taxis to convey the whole gang of us to Radio City, and when we get there, it's the closest thing I've ever seen to Oscar night. Red carpet, TV cameras looking for soundbites, cameras flashing in our faces, yes even for us, the unknowns. And when I think of some of the big marquee names that have trod this very path before us? All of my great heroines in fact – Maggie Smith, Audrey Hepburn, Barbra Streisand . . . enough to make me feel deeply humbled and yet exhilarated at the same time.

Blythe grabs my hand nervously and I try my best to steer her inside, but it's like every two seconds, she's stopped by someone shoving a microphone into her face and asking her, as a nominee, the same dopey, inane questions over and over again, like how is she feeling? Is she happy to be here? She even gets a laugh when some reporter who I vaguely recognise from the Broadway Channel demands to know who her dress is by.

'What do you mean, who is it by?' asks Blythe, stopping in her tracks, genuinely puzzled. 'I got this in Loehmann's, love, have you ever come across it? It's a great little find of a discount store and, best of all I had change out of a hundred and fifty dollars too. You really should try it, you wouldn't believe some of the bargains. The shoes were only twenty-five dollars too and they're so comfortable, I'd swear I could nearly do Loch Derg in them.'

Roars of laughter from the crowd of onlookers that have gathered behind her as I gently but firmly lead her away, slowly working our way further on towards the entrance. She clings to my hand in a vice-like grip, shaking like she's in her own personal little earthquake and answers the rest of the questions she's bombarded with as coherently as she can. I'm not kidding, at this rate, it'll take us the guts of an hour just to work our way inside to the auditorium.

Nine pm on the dot and it's showtime. Our host is a TV comedian and chat show pundit, who launches into a little parody skit on all the big nominated shows, ours included. His Irish accent is dire, and we roar laughing, breaking the tension a bit. All of us are spread out over two rows and I'm roughly in the centre, with Jules on my right. Somehow, Jack has managed to sit on my left, with an empty seat right in front of him, where Liz should be.

Immediate bad, blazing feeling as my ulcer kicks into overdrive. She wouldn't . . . would she? Just not turn up? I throw Jack a look of pure panic, which he interprets correctly because then he leans into me and whispers, 'It's OK, don't worry, she's here. I caught a glimpse of her being interviewed outside. Shhh, relax.'

A light graze of his icy fingers against mine and I swear, it's like an electric current goes through me.

Dangerous. Very dangerous.

'Aren't you even nervous?' I whisper back. 'Supposing you win and have to make a speech?'

'If I win, the first person I'll turn to kiss will be you. In front of everyone, in front of all the cameras. And I don't care and there's not a damn thing you'll be able to do to stop me, my dear.'

He leans in closer still and brushes a stray curl off the back of my neck, then I get a quick flash of his teeth shining through the darkness. But I don't get a chance to respond because just then Liz arrives very late, slipping into the seat in front of Jack and studiously ignoring the lot of us. I stretch forward in my seat to try and catch her eye but she's staring straight ahead, like she'd rather be sitting anywhere, absolutely anywhere other than within spitting distance of us.

Christ Alive, it's as if, for tonight, she's turned down the thermostat on her relations with her fellow cast members from glacial to cryogenically frozen. She hasn't even bothered to dress up either; she's just thrown on all her early Madonna gear of torn tights, a lace see-through knee-length dress, which clearly shows her bony little shoulder blades jutting out like butterfly wings, all worn with bovver boots and the kind of earrings that dolphins jump through to please their trainers. Honest to God, I've seen her wearing this kind of stuff during the day.

After a high-octane musical interlude courtesy of the cast of *Rent*, our host kicks off the awards proper. Blythe's category is up first, best supporting actress. We're all leaning over to squeeze her supportively, but she loses out to an actress from *The Merchant of Venice* and as the applause rings out, she says to us all, 'I'm not a bit bothered at all, you know, my lovelies. I had bet a few quid on your woman to win, as it happens. Easy come, easy go.'

The pace picks up and our luck changes. By the second ad break, we've won best lighting and costume design, to much whooping from the lot of us. So much so that our host makes some wisecrack along the lines of, 'You'd certainly know the Irish are in the room, so can someone kindly close off the bar at the interval? Cut off their supplies quick, guys, or they'll drink the place dry!'

A short commercial break where we all dash to the loo and then on with the show. Liz continues to ignore us all, just sits in her seat ahead of us, staring blankly ahead, not clapping, visibly unsmiling. Most worrying of all though, her head's now starting to loll a bit from side to side. I lean forward in my seat and ask her if she's OK, but surprise surprise, she totally ignores me. So what's new?

We lose out on best new play, but before I have time to catch my breath, it's the award for best director. You should hear our host gravely announcing the nominees; it flashes through my mind that he sounds exactly like Charlton Heston reading out the Ten Commandments.

'And the Tony goes to . . .'

My whole digestive system seizes up . . . but astonishingly, the winner isn't Jack. He doesn't seem remotely bothered about this though, in fact, he barely breaks a sweat, just sits back as relaxed as you like and claps heartily, genuinely, for the winner.

'You don't mind?' I turn to smile at him.

'Oh please, gong shows. I've got a barrow full of the things at home and frankly, they're all just dust gatherers.'

'Really? You're not even a little bit disappointed?'

Somehow, it doesn't quite ring true for someone with Jack's type-A personality not to be insanely competitive about awards.

'The night is very young,' he whispers back, evenly holding my gaze. 'And I love that sexy outfit on you, by the way. Very va va voom. OK, so I've just lost a Tony award, but all I can think about is how deliciously easy it would be to slip you out of that dress, so I could get a good look at you in whatever you're wearing underneath . . .'

'Shhhhh!' I mouth silently.

'Don't be so prudish, it doesn't suit you. So what *are* you wearing underneath?'

His arms are folded, but he looks like he's enjoying himself.

'Will you stop it?'

'Do you want me to?'

'You know I do,' I hiss, but unconvincingly.

A lightning quick flash. Last week, when Jules said she could see a whole other parallel life stretching out for me . . . funny, but for the first time now, I get a quick, sudden glance of that parallel life too. And I don't know what to think about it. I rummage around my feelings, trying to identify them, and the best description I can come up with is that it's fear, plain and simple.

But then I let it go. For fuck's sake I think, suddenly incensed at myself. You are pathetic. Living with Jules has made me every bit as bad as her, it seems. I've completely picked up on her habit of taking up ideas and then running wild with them.

Just. Let. It. Go.

I tell myself that over and over and eventually it seems to work.

The night whizzes by and before I know where we all are, it's time for the award for best actress. Jack leans forward and pats Liz encouragingly on the back, saying something about how she's got a terrific chance. And I'm not joking, the girl reacts as though she's just been electrocuted.

Our host introduces a presenter who gravely reads out the nominations, each one greeted with thunderous applause. Liz's name is last and a camera shot of her appears on the big screen ahead of us, showing her scowling, sulky and with a 'Can we please just get this over with?' expression etched on her face.

'And the Tony goes to. . . .'

Drumroll for dramatic effect.

'For *Wedding Belles* . . . Liz Shields!'

We all look at each other in shock and surprise, before the clapping and cheering breaks out; by far the most boisterous we've been all night. Liz just won a Tony! I look at Jack in stunned amazement and part of me wonders if maybe this is just the miracle we need to reboot her back into being the old Liz.

She takes the stage and it's only when she stumbles slightly on her way to the podium that I really start to get concerned. And realise the reason why she arrived late and wouldn't say two words to any of us earlier.

'Ladies and gentlemen,' she begins, muttering into the microphone and slurring her words, always a disastrous sign with her. Jesus, don't tell me she's been drinking on top of whatever else she's been doing?

'You know, I've sat here all night, mostly bored out of my head . . .'

Worried looks fly amongst the rest of us. Because this isn't exactly sounding like your typical thank you speech. Not one bit. Nervous titters from the rest of the audience, wondering where this could possibly be going.

'. . . and I've listened to speech after speech from the other winners, all thanking their fellow cast members, directors, producers, ASMs who make the tea, the stage hands who sweep the stage . . . you name it. And I really do wish that I could stand here and say the same thing, I really do.'

A murmur sweeps through the packed auditorium, and suddenly it's like looking at someone who's brandishing a hand grenade over the lot of us; a grenade with the pin taken out. She's out of control and dangerous and by now my palms have actually started to sweat, terrified at what's going to come out of her next.

'Jesus,' Jack groans, 'I don't believe this. She's off her head drunk.'

'I, on the other hand, am grateful to the American Theatre for giving me this award, but I give no thanks to any of my fellow cast members. None. Nothing. Nada. You want to know why? Because I get no support from them whatsoever. Instead, all I get are accusations and threats and people daring to tell me how to live my life. Now, I notice that some of my fellow winners here tonight have thanked their directors too. Well, unfortunately I can't do that either. I'm sure a lot of you may be familiar with Jack Gordon's work, the man with the messiah complex; or as I like to call him, Mr Rarely Takes Any Less Than All the Credit He Can Get, but I can tell you right now, he did not in any way contribute to my performance . . .'

I look over to Jack and he's seething. Mind you, you'd never know it if you didn't know Jack, he's very still. Scarily still. Our host is starting to look panicky now, realising that this is not your typical, gushing acceptance speech, not by the longest of long shots.

I can see him making frantic off-camera gestures to the floor manager who makes a wind it up signal to the orchestra. But they're not off the mark quite fast enough.

The TV monitors lined throughout the auditorium are showing Liz in glorious close-up and it's glaringly obvious to anyone watching that she's completely stocious and most likely high as well.

'So to everyone here involved with *Wedding Belles*,' she's drunkenly ranting, 'I'd like to tell the lot of you to go and fuck yourselves! Every single, rotting one of you! You're all jealous of me and have been since day one . . . so fuck you and fuck off!'

The orchestra drowns her out, we cut to an unexpected ad break and the rest of us all look mutely at each other, utterly horrified by what we've just seen.

It's a disaster. What should have been a night of celebration has now turned into a nightmare that I, for one, feel I'll be recounting on some psychiatrist's couch for years to come in all its gory detail. There's an after show party organised in a private function room above Radio City, but understandably, not one of us is in the mood to go. Then Harvey Shapiro, ever the showman, points out to us that it would only look worse if we *didn't*, so reluctantly, we all troop up escalators to a private art deco bar, trying not to look like we've collectively been punched in the solar plexus.

I haven't seen Jack; he stormed out after the ceremony and Liz has taken off too, unsurprisingly. But then Blythe comes in, white-faced and stoic and tells us all that the two of them are both outside in a private corner, where I can only guess Jack is tearing strips off her. Next thing, Liz bursts into the bar, screaming, actually yelling drunkenly at the top of her voice.

Jaysus, just what we all needed, another sideshow. Just when you think the night can't possibly get worse.

'You think you can threaten to fire me? Well you can fuck right off! I just won a Tony, no one can touch me!'

Of course, everyone turns around to stare and it's a minor mercy that there aren't any TV cameras or photographers up here. A small blessing, that at least this isn't a public hanging.

Jack grips her roughly by the arm and tries to steer her back outside, keeping his voice deliberately low. I don't hear what he says to her, all I hear is her answer, which is downright unprintable. Then she swoops up to the bar, orders a double vodka martini, but he follows fast on her heels, barking at the barman to cancel the order.

'I want to see you tomorrow morning at nine o'clock sharp,' I can hear him snapping at her, his voice low, menacing, frustrated. It's that cruel, scary side of him that I haven't seen in months, not since we were all back in rehearsal.

'And I mean it, Liz,' he goes on, icy cold now. 'If you don't get help, you're out of the show, gone. And don't you dare make the mistake of thinking that you can push me on this. Do you understand? Now apologise to the rest of the cast for insulting them like this, then get the fuck out of my sight.'

With that, Jack stomps out of sight and Liz, now looking more frail and vulnerable than I think I've ever seen her, slumps down to the floor.

Chapter Fourteen

It becomes a hot story in no time. Headlines the next day, the talk of all the breakfast TV shows and worst of all, apparently Liz's outburst at the Tony's is now well on its way to garnering a million plus hits on YouTube. Christ Almighty, more than Susan Boyle on *Britain's Got Talent*. I'm in my apartment the following morning, frantically trying to get Jules organised for the airport, while fending off phone calls at the same time.

The phone's practically been hopping off the receiver since first light; it seems the news has even reached as far as Dublin, because Fag Ash Hil, my agent, calls too. In her growly croak says she has five Irish journalists all wanting to talk to me and what's more, she excitedly stresses, not only would I be able to put across the truth about Liz, but they're willing to pay me for my story too, like this is something I should be grateful for. Hil, it seems, utterly blinded by the commission she'd make blissfully unaware that this is something I'd never in a million years contemplate.

I say no to each and every one of them. Fecking vultures.

The number one priority in all this is Liz and only Liz and for all of us somehow to get her the help she so desperately needs. Because the more I think about it, the more I think that's what last night was for her; a big, deafening cry for help, so loud that the whole of America seems to have heard her.

I get a brisk, business-like phone call from Jack early in the morning to let me know that he and Harvey are personally taking Liz to one of the top drink and drug rehabilitation clinics in the city today, with the added threat that if she refuses to go, she's out of the show he tells me. Simple as that.

I offer to go along with them . . . best not, he says. Because she may try to act out on you. But she's more likely to do as she's told if her director and producer are strong-arming her there. Let me know how it goes, I say and he promises to call later on in the day with an update.

'Who was that?' asks Jules, dragging her second over-stuffed suitcase out into the hall, ready to load up the taxi for the trip to the airport.

'Jack.'

She goes back into the bedroom, singing the words to 'Torn Between Two Lovers', on purpose, just to annoy me.

Then about an hour later, just as I'm about to leave for the airport with Jules, I get a call from the stage director at the Shubert. Liz has been hospitalised and for the fore-seeable future, her understudy will take over her role. Starting tomorrow night, Tuesday, as the theatre tradition-ally goes dark on a Monday night. But we're all to be at the theatre later on this afternoon for a full rehearsal with Liz's understudy, followed by a dress rehearsal tonight.

Just hearing the word hospitalised sends me into a blind panic, so I ring Chris to let her know. In the meantime, it seems that somehow she'd managed to get a hold of Harvey, who gave her the latest news bulletin: Liz has been admitted under the care of a Dr Goldman to the Eleanor Young drug rehabilitation clinic in Albany, upstate from here. I immediately chime in that I want to go and see her right away, but Chris bossily shuts me up. Apparently the first step in her recovery is for her to get clean and part of that involves not having visitors until the medical team there are satisfied that she's in a place where she can handle it. They're very strict about that, apparently.

It's like I feel torn in two. Half of me is devastated for Liz; bright, fun, wild, exuberant, mega-talented Liz being in hospital. The other half thinks . . . well, at least she's getting help now, which can only be a good thing.

An urgent tug at my arm from Jules reminds me that we're already running late, so I give her a hand lugging the suitcases downstairs and outside to a waiting taxi.

Jules sniffs and stares morosely out the window the whole way to JFK.

'Come on, don't worry about Liz, she'll pull through.'

'I know, that's not what's upsetting me.'

'What is it then, love?' I say, taking her hand.

'Suppose you never come home? Suppose you choose your parallel life instead? Suppose the only way I ever get to see you in future is by coming over here? To see you living here, with Jack?'

'Jules,' I sigh in exasperation. Because frankly this feels like about the fortieth time we've had this conversation. 'You have got to let this go. What have I told you?'

'I know he was really amazing when I was here, with all the trips and treats and everything, but still. . . . Annie, I wouldn't be a proper pal to you if I didn't tell you the truth. Thing is . . . there's just something about him that I can't warm to. Behind all his smoothness and flashiness and the fecking teeth that would nearly blind you, take it from me – that guy is one ruthless git. Didn't you notice it after the show last night?'

'Yes,' I say, but more to myself than to Jules. 'Yes, I did.'

Liz's understudy is an Irish-American actress called Rachel Ivors, who I've met several times before, but never actually worked with. She even looks like a scrubbed up version of Liz; the same wild blond hair and sky-blue eyes, but given that Liz is such a hard act to follow, I figure it must be a tall order for the poor girl to step into such big shoes.

I take a taxi straight from JFK to the theatre, and am amazed to see a couple of hardened reporters with cameras waiting outside, already door-stepping the place. A few dopey questions are hurled at me as I try to inch my way through them to the safety of the stage door, such as, 'Hey Annie? Aren't you Annie Cole? Over here, Annie! Will you tell us just one thing? As part of the *Wedding Belles* cast, how did you feel watching your colleague berate you from the podium on live TV last night?'

I manage to keep my cool and say nothing, although the temptation to yell out, 'How in the name of arse did you think I felt?' is overwhelming.

I get to the stage and everyone is already here ahead of me, all set for an afternoon's rehearsals with Rachel. Jack bounds in, taking the auditorium steps two at a time and launches straight into an intense rehearsal session. Not a word about Liz, not a single syllable passes about what's happened or what brought us to this pass or even how she's getting on at hospital, nothing. It's like his sole focus now is the sacred cow that is the show, so that's what he works on, with all the concentration of a bomb squad.

Rachel, for her part, seems well up for it, the only one of us not remotely rattled after yesterday's events. And if I'd thought she'd be nervous, I was way wide of the mark; in fact, I hate to say it, but it's almost like there's a touch of the *All About Eve*'s about her. It's as though she's mildly sorry about the circumstances that brought her here, but at the end of the day, this is her moment in the sun and nothing, absolutely nothing is going to stop her from grabbing it with greedy, grasping hands.

Jack spends the whole afternoon pushing us, really working us like slaves, just as he used to back in the early days, going over all of Rachel's scenes exhaustively and grilling the girl time and again. That cruel side of him keeps rearing its ugly head; the side that places human beings as absolutely secondary to a successful show. He's in thunderous form, snapping at everyone for giving the wrong cues, barking at the stage manager and even losing it a bit when Harvey comes into the theatre, and interrupts practice briefly.

God almighty, it feels like we're all spending the entire afternoon navigating his mood and then tip-toeing around it.

Bloody exhausting, on top of everything else.

But never once does Rachel crack, or betray anything other than excitement at getting to step out on a Broadway stage, to play in a Tony award winning show. She even whispers to me backstage while we're both waiting to make an entrance, that her agent is bringing in not one but three casting directors to see her during the week. I say nothing, mainly because it's not like she was a friend of Liz's or anything, so why should she be concerned about her? The girl is just doing what any actor handed a golden opportunity like this would do.

I only think she's gone a bit far when she turns to me with shining, hopeful eyes and says, 'Annie, do you have any idea how long Liz will be in hospital for? It's just that, if she were kept in till the end of the week, then I could get a few movie casting people to come and see me too. Any clue? Do you think it'll be a week? Maybe longer? I only ask because you know how those drug addiction programmes can sometimes go on for ever.'

'Liz is a friend of mine,' I answer as haughtily as I can. 'A very good friend. And I, for one, am just hoping and praying that she's back to work, where she belongs, ASAP.' This shuts her up as we both step out onto the warmth of the stage, her to do one of Liz's big soapbox speeches, me thinking sweet baby Jesus and the orphans. Talk about blonde ambition.

We've got a short break before a full dress rehearsal tonight, and just as I'm about to head up to my dressing room to get organised, Jack catches up with me.

'Hey, there you are,' he says, lightly touching my shoulder.

I automatically move a step back.

'I was looking for you,' he says, staring at me intently.

'Emm . . . well, I was just about to get into costume.'

'Yes, yes, of course. Some good news to report from the box office though.'

'What's that?'

'Well, it seems that on the strength of all this press attention, whether it was wanted or otherwise, we're now looking at a sell-out show, right through to the end of fall.'

'Right. Well, that's terrific, I suppose,' I answer flatly.

I'm making all the right noises, but all I can think is . . . fat lot of good that'll do Liz, lying on some hospital bed, attached to a drip and a monitor, going through cold turkey.

I make to head back upstairs, when he grabs me by the arm, his touch ice cold, as usual.

'Look, Annie, it's been a crazy twenty-four hours, how about dinner after tonight's run-through? Just you and I, I mean? We could talk.'

I bite my lip, wondering how I can politely get out of this. No rudeness intended, it's just that it's been an emotional rollercoaster of a day, and frankly all I want to do after the show is crawl home and sleep for about four days straight.

'Would you mind if I bowed out?' I eventually say. 'I just . . . well, I really just feel like being alone this evening. I hope you understand.'

He says nothing, just eyes me up and down, then gives my hand a quick squeeze. His hand feels cool and lotioned and smooth.

And then he's gone.

Somehow we all stumble through the dress rehearsal and Rachel acquits herself competently enough, but I have to say this though – she's no Liz Shields. Liz had a raw, powerful, magnetic danger to her in the role: an irresistible magnet to the eye who commanded your attention and try as she might, Rachel just doesn't even come close to her. But we all somehow stagger through and given what's happened, that's pretty much all any of us would have asked for.

I get home early, about eleven, try to sleep and can't,

even though I'm utterly exhausted and tired to the bone marrow. The apartment just seems so empty without Jules. I never would have thought it, but I'm missing her chatter, her high spirits and all her messing so much . . . by comparison, this feels like coming home to a mausoleum. God, the irony; me that once used to love and adore being alone here and it's driving me mental.

I'm lying in bed and the sheet that's covering me is practically knotted, I'm tossing around that much. Thinking about Liz over and over again, eaten up with guilt. About how I let her down. How she was a friend to me when I needed one and how I didn't do the same for her, plain and simple. I should have seen the signs, I should have tried harder to find a way to be there for her, even if she pushed me away.

I am a horrible, horrible person and the worst friend imaginable.

It's past one in the morning, when I finally give in to insomnia. I switch on the light and am just rummaging around for the TV remote control, when suddenly my mobile beeps.

ARE YOU STILL AWAKE? MEET ME AT THE MOON.

Dan. And suddenly I'm wide awake.

We haven't been in touch with each other for a while, well over a week. Not since that disastrous weekend at the Hamptons, in fact. Guilt kept me from contacting him; or to be more accurate, a combination of guilt and cowardice, that is. Because I know I'm going to have to come clean, fess up and tell him straight out what happened and already my whole stomach is clenched with worry, just at the very thought. Every night this past week, I've secretly dreaded him calling, knowing the awkward, awful conversation we'd have to have. But he didn't get in touch or even text me once, not all week, which given the pattern we've now established is a bit unusual. No idea why, but then I figure he's busy, I suppose. Sure what else could it be with Dan?

I take a deep, nerve-calming breath and call him. It's ridiculously early his time, past six am. and sure enough, he sounds like a man talking from the bottom of the sea, completely wrecked. Weird, I have a sense of inner pandemonium, as I outwardly try to act the way I always do with him.

He couldn't sleep either, he tells me, so we chat for a bit about Jules, who, if her flight is on time, should be landing in Shannon in a few more hours. She'll be home by nine-ish I tell him and he seems pleased to hear it.

I'm inclined to forget just how well Dan knows me though, because next thing, it's as if he senses there's something up with me.

Here it comes. Just tell the truth and get it over with . . . who knows? He may even understand. After all, it's not like I slept with Jack or anything, is it?

In a gentle gear shift, he asks me what's wrong.

Tell him! Tell him now . . .

But I can't bring myself to. At least, not yet, I can't. I'm still working out how to phrase it in my head. So instead I bring him up to speed about Liz. He hasn't heard the news, but then that's Dan for you; even if it were all over the media in Ireland today, he'd never in a million years get time to read a paper or sit down to watch the TV.

'Go and see her as soon as you can,' he says softly. 'No matter how badly she acted towards you all, remember she wasn't in her right mind. That wasn't the real her. But she'll need you in the next few weeks and months and you have to be there for her. It's the right thing to do, Annie.'

329

I nod and thank him and he chats on about the general news from Stickens and how Lisa and the kids are spending more and more time up at The Moorings. Reading between the lines, it seems that the Countess Dracula is now busy inveigling herself into Audrey's good books, running round after her, doing all her little jobs, being at her permanent beck and call.

Just like I used to do, back in the days.

Immediate burning sensation flares up in my gullet. Because I can picture the scene all too clearly. Lisa playing up to Dan, feeding him all her bullshit and wheedling cash out of him, like she somehow always does. And he doesn't see it, but then he never does; Dan only sees the good in people, never the bad. It's on the tip of my tongue to say something, but I can't seem to find the right words.

Suddenly all my old worries resurrect themselves. Because who knows what machinations are running through the Countess Dracula's head right now? There's Dan, all alone in that big house, on a marital gap year with a wife three thousand miles away . . . then I remember my own carry-on with Jack and my thoughts are silenced.

I'm not exactly in any position to start laying down any extra-marital rules and regulations, now am I?

'Course when the kids are running and screaming round the place, it's a bit of a trial for Mum,' Dan smiles, 'but I think she's getting used to it. At least, she's not complaining as much as she used to, so that's always a good sign.'

'And how are Harry and Sue?' I force myself to ask. If they're already calling Dan 'New Dad' I bloody well want to know about it.

'Dotes, the two of them. I've got very fond of them over

the past while, they're great company. Lisa wants to take them to Euro Disney before they go back to school in September but of course, she doesn't have the money, so I might just give her a dig out and pay for the trip myself. She's been through so much, the poor woman could really do with a break.'

Of course you'll end up paying for it, I think, silently furious. *You were manipulated into coughing up all along, only you're too nice a guy to ever see it . . .*

Dan chats on about Lisa and her litany of woes and I haven't realised it, but I've been completely mute for a good while now, completely wrapped up in my own thoughts.

'Annie?' he says. 'Are you still there?'

'Hmmm? Oh, yeah. Still here.'

'Is there something else on your mind? You've gone very quiet. Not like you.'

Right then, here's your moment, the little voice in my head says. *Just come clean. You'll feel better in the long run. All you did was kiss Jack, no more. He'll understand and what's more, he might even appreciate your honesty.*

'Emm . . . well . . .'

'Oh, I knew there was something I forgot to tell you. I had to vaccinate all of Seamus Hogan's swine herd last week.'

I kissed someone else, Dan.

'We found pork tapeworm in about half a dozen of them . . .'

And it was sexy and it was passionate and I'm doing my best to make sure that it doesn't happen again, but my worry is that it so easily could . . .

'James had to take faeces samples and rush them off to the lab . . .'

I've never in my life kissed anyone other than you, but it's just been so, so long since you even touched me that I just couldn't stop myself. And I know that's no excuse . . .

'And it turned out to be tapeworm all right . . .'

Should I tell you or not? What's the best thing here? If you told me something like this, I think it would destroy me, even though I've absolutely no right to feel that way or make that kind of demand on you . . .

'So anyway, we treated it with Mebedaloze, a new drug that's just come on the market . . .'

Dan, what will I do? I'm lonely and I'm confused and I'm lost and none of this feels right to me.

'And the pigs seem to be responding well. No more traces in their faeces.'

It's comical – I'm trying to pour out my heart's innermost secrets to him and he's talking to me about pig dung.

'Annie? Are you still there? I'm sorry, I've been rattling on. Was there something you wanted to say to me?'

And like the moral coward that I am, I back down.

'No. No, there isn't.'

A long pause and then his voice becomes softer.

'You're much missed around here, I hope you know that.'

Please, Dan, don't. The guilt is already choking me enough without this . . .

'In fact, I constantly keep thinking back to old times, when you and I were in New York together . . . I can't stop myself thinking about it . . . when we first got engaged . . . God, it seems like decades ago now, doesn't it?'

'Dan . . .'

A half pause and I know, just know that he senses something's up.

'What is it, love? If something's wrong, then please tell me.'

332

Please, please stop being so nice to me. I feel bad enough as it is . . .

'Nothing. Nothing at all. Just that it's late, it's been a long day and I'd better try and get some sleep now.'

'Right so. Sleep well and I'll meet you at the moon very soon.'

Hard to believe, but this is actually the last normal conversation I'm to have with him.

The next morning, Blythe, Chris, Alex and I all meet up for a desultory brunch. We're all sitting round a booth in one of those diners that's like nineteen fifties sensory overload. You know, waitresses in fire hazard skirts, there's that much netting under them, waiters dressed like they've just stepped out of the chorus line in *Grease* and Eddie Cochran playing away on the jukebox.

None of us is in good form and no one's even eating. Not even little Alex who normally eats like an athlete and never fails to say that she'll turn to cannibalism if her food doesn't arrive approximately four minutes after she orders it.

'God, I miss home,' Chris eventually says, banging a spoon off her coffee cup. 'I miss Josh and Oscar so much it hurts.'

'Oh I know just how you feel, love,' Blythe chimes in. 'I can't tell you how much I miss my Sean. And money is so tight for him right now, he needs me with him back home, although he'd never say it. I know he does.'

'I miss Dublin,' says Alex. 'I miss my family and all my pals and the fact that no matter where you go at home, you'll always meet up with someone you know. It's so anonymous and impersonal here.'

'. . . I'm sick of the constant noise, the traffic, the car

horns blaring; the way that bloody twenty-four hour background racket is always there, all the time, round the clock, even if you wake up at three am. . . .'

'The heat is what's driving me mental, I can't take much more . . . I miss rain . . .'

'I miss greenery . . .'

'I miss Barry's tea, and Tayto crisps and proper butter . . .'

'. . . I'm fed up of having long distance conversations with Josh the whole time, I want to be with him . . .'

'I miss the people from home . . . I'm sick of everyone's fake bonhomie here . . .'

'Oh God, if one more sales assistant tells me to have a nice day, with one of those cheesy, fake, all-American smiles . . .'

Suddenly, I'm aware that they're all looking at me, because I'm the only one who hasn't chimed in yet. And in a million years, I never thought I'd find myself saying this, but yes, I miss home too, I tell them. I miss green grass and mountains and all the beautiful scenery that I completely took for granted for so long. I miss proper, fresh country air, so different to the layers of smog and grit that pass for clean air in New York . . . I miss having space to myself and nights that are so quiet, if you happen to hear three cars going past, it's like rush hour. I miss looking out the window at night and seeing tens of thousands of stars twinkling above me. Here, I have to squint up at the night sky and imagine that somewhere behind the sodium vapour and NYC glare, that there even are stars there at all.

I miss Jules. I miss the staff from the surgery at home. I even miss having neighbours who care about you and ask after you all the time.

But most of all I miss Dan.

Two days later, after I don't know how many frantic calls from me, I finally get a message from Dr Goldman's assistant at the Albany clinic to say that it's now OK for me to go and see Liz. Just me, alone, apparently one visitor at a time is all she's able for right now. It's early morning, so I don't even think about it, just run out of the apartment, grab a cab to Penn station and forty minutes later, am on a train to Albany, upstate New York. The journey takes about an hour and a half, all the way up through Poughkeepsie and the Catskill mountains and my mind marvels that such beautiful, deep countryside can exist so close to Manhattan. The view alone makes me, if possible, even more homesick.

The Eleanor Young clinic is on Franklin Street, easy enough to find. In fact, it's more like a small country hotel than a hospital though; totally surrounded by stunning, beautifully maintained grounds.

The hospital itself is small-ish and a brusque receptionist tells me what room I can find Liz in.

'But I need to see your handbag first, before I can let you in to see her,' she snaps briskly.

'My handbag?'

'In case you're smuggling any substances in. It's been known to happen. Drug addicts often get their friends to bring in stash from the outside. It's what drug addicts do; it's part of their job description.'

'Emm . . . sure,' I say, handing over my bag, which she starts to rummage through.

'And don't stay too long, will you? We had to pump her stomach twice and she's still feeling a little nauseous.'

'No, don't worry, I don't want to tire her.'

She seems satisfied enough with the contents of my handbag to hand it back to me.

'OK, room 201. Last room at the end of the corridor, on your right.'

When I do find Liz, I'm utterly shocked when I see her face; something that was there before is now gone. She looks empty and ravaged and it's frightening to see.

She's awake when I get there and when she sees that it's me, tears start to roll down her pale, chalk-white cheeks.

'Annie,' she says in a weak, croaky voice. 'Annie, I'm so sorry.'

'No, honey, don't be. I'm the one who's sorry.'

'I don't know . . . I don't know why I did what I did. There's no reason for it and I've got no excuse. All I know is that you tried your best to be a good friend to me and . . . I was completely horrible to you. I've been lying here, playing it over and over in my mind, all the vicious things I flung at you when you were only trying to help. And I need you to know how sorry I am. Can you forgive me, Annie?'

She sits up slowly and we hug each other and stay like that for a long, long time.

AUTUMN

Chapter Fifteen

Fall in New York and the city is more beautiful than you could possibly imagine. Leaves everywhere, the beginnings of a nip in the air, a crisp coolness to the evenings now . . . but somehow I just can't bring myself to appreciate it. Because there's been a shift in Dan and what's more I can put a date on when it started. It's ever since Jules arrived back in Ireland. I don't quite know what's going on, it's hard to put my finger on, but here are the facts.

These days he doesn't call or even text me late at night to say meet him at the moon any more. All that has completely ground to a halt. And I know he's a free man on his gap year off from me too, and I know there's nothing wrong with this. It's just that I miss all those long, idle, meandering late-night chats with him more than I can say.

A few times, I tried calling him at night and discovered that the Countess Dracula's kids are now answering the phone. No doubt staying over, yet again. And what's more, they treat me like I'm some kind of nuisance caller. 'Mummy? It's that woman on the phone again!' That kind of thing.

When I'm ringing my own home. Bloody annoying, to say the very least.

Then another time Lisa herself answers and gleefully tells me that Dan has agreed to fork out for her and the kids to go to Euro Disney, as a special treat for them.

'He's got so fond of the kids,' she gloats at me, 'it's marvellous to see! And of course, for their part, they just idolise him, particularly Harry. Calls him Uncle Dan and refuses to go to sleep till Dan's tucked him into bed!'

Swear to God, I have to have a lie down in a darkened room after this particular stab of reality.

Then, just a few days after Jules would have got back home, Dan and I had the single weirdest conversation of all. He called and seemed tense and jumpy on the phone, most unlike him. I put it down to exhaustion, but looking back, it was something more than that. Trying to dissect what he said was of no use, because it was what he *didn't* say that worried me.

He'd caught me at a bad time too; the very worst time, in fact. It was just six-thirty in the evening and I was racing down Forty-Fourth Street to get to the Shubert when he called. An unusual time for him to ring, and it was almost impossible for me to hear him properly over the roar of traffic and background noise.

First of all, from the bit of conversation that I could snatch, he went off on a big preamble about how this was my year of freedom and I was to enjoy every minute of it. Then he said something totally out of character for him about how loving someone sometimes means setting them free.

But most worrying of all was what he said before he hung up.

'Annie, you know we talked about meeting up for our anniversary in New York?'

340

'Yes, of course . . .' I said. How would I have forgotten? I was actually starting to really look forward to it. To live for it, in fact.

'Well, I just wanted you to know, that if your circumstances ever changed or if there was ever any reason why you wouldn't want me to come, you know I'd understand. All you need to do is tell me. We're adults and whatever is coming our way, we'll somehow work it out.'

I was hassled and straining to hear him above the din of blaring car horns when we had this chat; all I know is that I hung the phone up with one thought on my mind.

Something's up.

Took me all of four seconds to put two and two together.

Jules. Jules has gone and told him about what happened between me and Jack, before I got a chance to.

Shit, shit and shit again.

Things escalate from there, fast. Next morning, I get an urgent email from Jules, instructing me to ring her mobile at a certain time, when she'll be able to talk freely. Jaysus, it's like something out of a John le Carré spy thriller. I do as she says and am surprised to hear her sounding panicky and upset on the phone.

'Annie, I have to talk to you,' she hisses.

'I have to talk to you too.'

'What's up with you? You sound stressed off your head.'

'Did you mention anything to Dan about . . . well . . . you know, about what happened at the Hamptons that weekend?'

'Emm . . . well, I might have let something slip . . .'

I knew it, I knew it, I knew it . . . oh fuck, fuck, fuck, what do I do now?

'. . . but Annie, there's something far more urgent I have

341

to tell you . . . there's been a development in the last few days and I don't think you're going to like it.'

'Tell me . . .'

Tell me quick.

'Course I wasn't sure, so I wanted to check all my facts before I spoke to you. Just to be certain.'

'Is it your Mum?'

'Sadly not. I *wish*. She's still whinging because all I brought her back from New York was that Empire State snow globe, and I wouldn't mind, but it weighed a bloody ton AND I had to carry it all the way home in my hand baggage . . .'

'Please! Will you just tell me what's up?'

I'm snapping now and I hadn't meant to.

'Right, but you'd better be sitting down for this. And be warned, you won't like it, but I feel it's my duty to tell you.'

'Jules!'

'It seems that while I was away, the Countess Dracula has gone and moved herself and the kids into The Moorings. Lock, stock and barrel. I wasn't certain when I first came home, but now I know for sure. The conniving bloody-minded bitch has rented out her own house for extra cash and is living here now.'

'Hon, it's vitally important that you answer me this honestly; just how much of this is an exaggeration?'

'May I be struck down this minute, not a word of it!' she hisses defensively and somehow, somehow . . . I believe her.

'The Countess Dracula, Dan and the kids are now all officially living together at The Moorings. Like one big happy fecking family. She and Dan are in separate rooms . . . for now . . . but who knows how long that'll last for? She sees a vulnerable, lonely, overworked man and you mark my words, she's moving in on him. Has dinners ready for him on the table every night, no matter when he gets in, does all his laundry for him . . .'

For a second my throat constricts and I have to remind myself to breathe. I can't take this in, it's just too much. Can Lisa really have done that? Taken my place just like that? And I know, just know without being told that her plans include more, far more than staying at The Moorings to save money . . . what if for once, Jules isn't over-egging it? What if the Countess Dracula has her eye on the bigger prize? On Dan himself?

This is it, then. My very worst fears confirmed. What I've dreaded for so long has finally happened and here I am, an ocean away and powerless to do anything . . .

Jules talks on, but I have to tell her that I'll call her back, mainly because my brain has gone into meltdown and I need time to think, to walk, to get my head together, to breathe into a paper bag if needs be.

So I get out of the apartment and start pounding the pavement, praying to God that I won't bump into any of the others and am forced to start acting like there's nothing up with me.

It's a crystal clear fall day, but there's a nip in the air and I came out without a jacket, so after a good half-hour of pacing and thinking, I slip into the warmth of a Starbucks on West Fifty-Third street, grab a tea and a chair with trembling hands and sit in a quiet, dark corner to think.

I trust Dan, of course I do. With my life.

I don't believe for a second that there's an unfaithful bone in his body.

It's Lisa fecking Ledbetter that I don't trust an inch. She's

343

always had a thing for Dan, I've always known that and now most likely the whole fecking town of Stickens knows it too. And now this.

What's stabbing me most of all is how easy all this has been for her. How easy *I've* made it for her. Empty house, newly single man living alone, all she had to do was toss a few heavy hints here and there and now look at what she's got.

Worst of all is the one thought that keeps playing like a loop in my head. I'm not exactly in a position to criticise, now am I? I've played around a bit, so how can I expect Dan not to? But try as I might, I keep coming back to the same, sickening thought.

The Countess Dracula is in my home, living my life and there's nothing on earth I can possibly do about it.

I think back to the last strange half-conversation I had with Dan. All that talk about if you love someone, then you should set them free. Is this what he was hinting at? That I set him free so he could be with someone else? Is that why he's hardly been calling me at all lately? Because he's already moved on with someone else?

And worse still is the thought of what mischief Jules has been up to since she got back to Stickens.

Jules. Much as I love her dearly, I think back to her awful habit of exaggerating tales out of all proportion till they bear only the merest sliver of resemblance to the truth. Knowing her, she's blabbed on and on endlessly about Jack and everything that happened while she was here, with the result that God only knows what Dan must be thinking now.

I don't blame Jules a bit; this is what she does and it's my own fault, I should have known better. I should have got to Dan before she did and I didn't and now I have to live with the fallout.

But one thing is for certain, I can't sit here doing nothing. I won't. I need to be alone with Dan. I need to tell him everything. About Jack, everything. Not that there's much to tell, but God alone knows what damage has been done and there's only one way for me to clear everything up. Worst of all, I need to hear whatever Dan has to say to me about what's going on in his private life. I may not like what I hear, but the very least I need is to hear it from him, first hand.

Right then. There's only one thing for it I decide, even surprising myself by feeling a lightness, a sense of relief once the decision has finally been made.

I'm going home.

Once I've put the wheels in motion, the rest is surprisingly easy. For starters, all of the cast are contractually entitled to one week's holiday during the year's run and I'm the only one who hasn't availed of this yet. Both Blythe and Chris already took their holidays months ago: Blythe travelled home to see her son and to give him 'a few bob' as she put it, while Chris and Josh took little Oscar to Disneyland, Florida during her week off. Meanwhile, Alex went out to Vegas with some pals of hers only a few weeks ago and of course poor old Liz is out of the show now, but for very different reasons. Which just leaves me, with a whole, entire week off that I'm fully entitled to.

I notify the stage director to officially ask permission and he's terrific about it, saying that he can call in my understudy for rehearsal in the next day or two, depending on when I need to travel. As soon as possible, I tell him.

Jack, I know, is back out in LA this week for yet more meetings, but as soon as word filters back to him, he's on the phone to me immediately.

'You're going *away*?' he asks, completely stunned.

You'd swear I'd said I was going off to join an enclosed order of nuns. 'It's my week's holidays. I haven't taken them yet, so I just thought . . .'

'Yes, yes, I know you're entitled to a free week,' he says and even though he's calling from thousands of miles away in Beverly Hills, I can still hear the impatience in his voice.

'But why do you have to go now? And where are you off to?'

'Home.'

'*Home?* Is everything OK? What's going on? Why the sudden mad dash to get back there?'

'Jack, just take it from me, there's stuff going on that I need to be around for. That can't be sorted out long distance.'

'Tell you what,' he sighs like he's cutting me a deal, and in the background I'd swear I can hear the lapping of water, like he's ringing me from some five-star swimming pool in the Chateau Marmont, being served by beautiful cocktail waitresses with PHD's hanging out of their earlobes.

Which knowing him, he probably is.

'If you really have to go home, then do, but how about you just go back to Ireland for a weekend, then come out here to LA for the rest of your week off? You'd love it here – blue skies, palm trees, beautiful people everywhere, I could introduce you to some movie producers . . .'

'You don't understand, Jack. I really have to spend the week at home. It's important.'

I sound irritated, edgy and snappy. And if I'm being

brutally honest, the real reason is because I feel a bit sick at what happened between us. I hate living with it and what's more, I hate that Jack is piling pressure on me now.

'Well, if for any reasons your plan should change, just remember my offer is still on the table.'

It's my last Sunday matinee before I travel back to Ireland and the only person who I've confided the whole story to is Blythe, who's so completely understanding about everything that it would nearly break your heart.

'Whatever is going on back in your house,' she tells me calmly, 'there's one thing for certain – you can only sort it out by being there in person. So best of luck, pet, and keep in touch, to let me know how you get on. And you never know, maybe all your fears are unfounded and the whole thing is just one big misunderstanding. I'll light a candle for you every day that . . . well . . . that . . .'

That what? I can see her thinking. Because what's the right outcome in this mess?

'. . . that the right thing happens for everyone concerned,' she finishes off tactfully.

Light a candle? Make that a bonfire of them while you're at it, I think ruefully.

My flight is at eight-forty in the evening, so I grab a cab for the airport straight after the show at five-ish and arrive at JFK good and early. Back in Ireland, no one knows what I'm at or is even expecting me; this is a covert visit and I'll be arriving by stealth first thing tomorrow morning, surprise being the best form of attack here, I feel.

Not unlike the Normandy landings.

My plan is to call Dan when I arrive at Shannon and say, 'Hey! Guess where I am?' In my head, I have it all worked out; he'll dash to the airport to collect me, we'll have a lovely reunion scene and then . . . the part I'm not looking forward to, we'll go somewhere far from Stickens, far from The Moorings where we can talk. Properly talk. Where he can tell me what's going on in his life and where I'll come clean about mine.

That, by the way, would be about as far as I've got in my cunning master plan; the rest, I figure, we'll just take from there.

Anyway, feeling more cautiously optimistic than I've a right to and with a spring in my step, I clamber out of the taxi, pay the fare and am just about to load my bag into a trolley before heading to check-in, when my mobile rings.

Jules. I answer the phone, silently praying that she won't hear all the airport announcements in the background.

'Hey, love,' I answer, trying to sound perky and sunny while wheeling an overstuffed suitcase to the check-in desk. 'Good to hear from you! What's up?'

'Oh Annie . . .' Jesus, I realise she's almost sobbing.

'You know I promised to keep you posted on any and all developments from this end?'

I say nothing, but my stomach suddenly forms itself into a very inconvenient knot.

'Well, there's more news, terrible news, and you won't like it, but I thought you really should know.'

'Tell me,' I manage to say, sounding hoarse.

'They've all gone to Euro Disney. Earlier today. All of them. Dan took Lisa and the kids, piled them into his jeep and off they drove to Dublin for the flight to Paris.'

My knees start to buckle, but somehow I manage to find my voice.

'Dan . . . went with them?'

'Dan went with them.'

There's three hundred things I want to ask her but a weak, watery 'Are you sure?' is all I can get out.

'A hundred percent. He even put James in charge of the surgery till he gets back. I'm so sorry, Annie, I don't know what else to say.'

I have to tell her that I'll call her back, mainly because there's a good chance I might physically throw up.

Somehow, I manage to drag myself and my luggage to a plastic seat beside the check-in area and sit there for a long, long time. Slumped into the chair and utterly numb. The pain hasn't hit yet, there's just a black hole inside of me, with the expectation of pain.

I call Dan's mobile and it's that long foreign ring tone, the one you only ever get if you're on the continent, abroad. I hang up, not leaving any message and make a silent vow that if he ever calls or texts me again, I won't answer.

So he's really gone to Paris with her then, I think, as the knife of realisation finally plunges in. Dan who has to be physically dragged away from work. Dan who never, ever takes a holiday, for any reason whatsoever. Dan who wouldn't even come to New York for my opening night.

Yet he's no bother going to Euro Disney with Lisa and her kids? My flight is being called and still I just sit there, letting the long line of disgruntled, hassled passengers all walk past me to check in.

What to do, what to do, what to do?

Going back to Ireland now is out of the question. And I'm just way too shell-shocked and weak-kneed to face crawling back to Manhattan, back to all the well-intentioned questions I'd have to face from the others about why I cancelled my week off in the first place. My mind has spiralled off into an agonising whirlwind and right now there's only one person who I want to be with. Someone who'll pick me up and try to put me back together, as she's done before and I know will do again.

I pick up my phone and call my mother. As ever, she comes up trumps for me; I give her an abridged, potted history of what's happened and in the background I can hear her tap-tapping away at her computer keyboard.

Stay calm, she tells me, we'll sort you out. You've got a week off, so let's make the most of it. She finds a flight that's due to leave for Washington later this evening at seven-thirty and books me onto it, coolly telling me to pick up my ticket at the Delta check-in desk.

Moving numbly along, I do just as she tells me, and an hour later, I'm on a flight to DC, where Mum has promised she'll be waiting at the other end for me.

The flight is an hour-and-a-half long and I sob my heart out the whole sorry way.

Chapter Sixteen

It's like fecking déjà vu. Here I am, sitting with Mum, with much wailing, lamenting and gnashing of teeth as I go over and over the whole horrible story of Dan and our sorry marriage sabbatical, with special embellishment reserved for this latest update in the never-ending saga. I'm sitting at the kitchen table opposite Mum, head in my hands, like an old drama queen who's been pulled out of retirement for one final repeat performance, except this time I've scarcely the energy to lift my eyes up to her.

Mum, by the way, is giving me a right dose of tough love now; I'm guessing her logic is that she's being cruel to be kind. The two of us are in the kitchen of her elegant, sophisticated Washington apartment on Wisconsin Avenue, in McLean, DC, the heart of the embassy belt. The décor is typical Mum; she's completely redecorated a modern condo to make it look older, to give it a bit of gravitas and to fit in with all of her antique furniture, collected over years of travelling and haggling at every auction house from Pakistan to Georgetown and back again.

Something she excels at, just like Mum excels at everything.

She's looking at me worriedly now, serving afternoon tea

351

in Hermès and pearls, all neat and groomed with her sleek bobbed hair, ready for business even though it's a Sunday and the consulate is closed.

A completely disconnected thought flashes through my mind: why so dressed up on her day off? In case there might be some last-minute lost passport emergency involving an Irish national? On a Sunday night? But I let it pass – too much else to worry about. She pours tea into two elegant china cups and hands one over to me, although what I'd really kill for right now is a glass of anything alcoholic. No, scratch that; make that a *bucket* of anything alcoholic.

'May I remind you, Annie dear,' Mum says firmly, 'that you didn't so much back away from your life in Stickens as run screaming in the opposite direction from it? Remember last Christmas, how upset you were? Everything about being there was driving you crazy – feeling that you were living in someone else's house, the constant comings and goings of all of Dan's family and colleagues, never seeing him from dawn till dusk . . .'

I nod glumly. I know. Course I remember. All too bleeding well.

'Then this opportunity to go away for a year came along and you were off like a bullet. And as we know, the long-distance relationship thing didn't work because let's face it, they so rarely do, so you both wisely agreed to take a break.'

'I know all this, Mum, I know . . .'

'Excuse me, madam, I'm not finished. The point I'm trying to make is that here you are lamenting a life that you couldn't get away from quickly enough when you were actually living it. And alright, worst case scenario, suppose that Dan has met someone else. Which I'm not even accepting may be the case, because all we have to go on is hearsay. But say he has met someone who may just suit life at The Moorings a little more than you did? Who may even enjoy it? Dearest Annie, don't you see?'

'See what, Mum?'

'That you can't have your cake and eat it. You didn't want that life when you had it, you chose this life instead. You wanted freedom, you got it and now here's the price to be paid. Everything in life comes with a price tag. You're surely aware of that?'

Jaysus. And here I was thinking that coming to DC to see my mother might in some way be soothing and restorative.

Big mistake. Huge.

'Of course,' she says, elegantly anointing a scone with butter, 'if you've changed your mind in any way, if you've now decided that once your year in New York is up, you actually *want* to return home to Dan and to life in Waterford and to simply take up where you left off, then that's very different.'

'What do you mean?'

'Because in that case, you've got to figure out a way to get him back, don't you?'

I lie awake in Mum's spare room that night, channel surfing, unable to sleep. My mobile phone is beside me, but I forgot to pack the charger and so it dies on me.

Which come to think of it is no harm.

I try to watch TV to take my mind off things and find *The Wizard of Oz* on TCM. The part where Judy Garland is clicking her red slippers together three times and saying, 'There's no place like home,' over and over again, while a load of Munchkins look on.

It takes me back to what Mum said earlier. Is that what

I'm like now? A Dorothy who ran screaming from Kansas and who's now slowly beginning to feel, ah sure what the hell, actually come to think of it, Kansas wasn't all that bad really? That there really *is* no place like home? And the irony is that it took the Countess fecking Dracula for me to be able to see this clearly.

And then I realise with a jolt. It's not that this Dorothy particularly wants to return to Kansas, thanks very much.

I just want to be where Dan is. But I'm too late.

When I eventually fall asleep, unsurprisingly, I dream about him. Like I'm somehow flicking through emotional snapshots of happier times.

There he is, still haunting me, even in my subconscious.

Our wedding day

Dan and I don't do perfect, but that day was as close as either of us has ever come. To date, at least. We were ridiculously young, barely out of college, and so determined nothing would stop us, that all opposition and well-intentioned advice against our marrying was a total waste of everyone's time. And believe me, there was a lot of it.

Pretty much as soon as everyone had recovered from the shock of our engagement, all the barneys about the actual wedding day itself started. Audrey and Dan Senior of course, wanted it to be in Waterford, held in the Stickens parish church, followed by a reception in a marquee at The Moorings afterwards, with half the town invited.

As for Dan and me, getting married barefoot on a beach at sunset in the Bahamas with not a relative in sight would have been our dream, but as he kept pointing out time and again, once I turned up to marry him and he turned up to marry me, then nothing else really mattered, did it?

And in the end, it didn't. A hasty compromise was reached and we got married in University Church Dublin, with a small reception afterwards in the Shelbourne Hotel for about forty people. Jules was my bridesmaid and has since destroyed every photo in existence of herself on the day, on account of the fact that she was wearing train track braces at the time and reckoned she looked not unlike Hannibal Lecter in yellow taffeta.

By the day itself, Audrey was barely speaking to me because I'd politely declined her edict that I get married wearing her wedding dress, on the grounds that not only was it about five sizes too big for me, but also came with a giant hoop skirt made of tulle so stiff that I swear it actually stood up by itself. Walking in it made me look and feel like a giant bell, so instead I opted for a simple Calvin Klein white silk sheath dress that clung well and most important of all, that I knew Dan would love.

But in spite of all the tension beforehand, for Dan and me the day itself was pretty close to perfection. Of course stuff went wrong: a pigeon flew into the church and pooed on some friend of Audrey's flowery hat, to great sniggers from the rows behind her. Oh, and when Dan knelt down, you could still see the giant price tag on the back of his shoes.

But none of that mattered. When I walked down the aisle, on my mother's arm as my father had refused to come (which would have been . . . ohh, let me see . . . yes, row number seventy nine), Dan bent down to tenderly kiss me with tears in his eyes.

'Do you know just how heartbreakingly beautiful you look?' he whispered, which of course was enough to start me off sniffling too.

Then as we took our vows and he locked eyes with me, solemnly promising to love me every minute of forever, it honestly felt like I was floating. And when I looked up to him and vowed to love and honour him all the days of my life, he bent down to kiss me again, a long, lingering kiss this time, well before the priest had given him the official nod to.

'I love you, Annie,' he said simply. 'Always have, always will.'

Chapter Seventeen

The week passes quickly, too quickly. I hardly see Mum, but then she's working ridiculously long hours these days and often doesn't get back to the apartment till well past seven or eight most evenings. So I've taken to spending my days alone, dozing or watching TV, thinking about what in hell I'll do when this is all over and the end of the year comes. Because quite apart from everything else, I'll be jobless, homeless and husband-less, won't I? And one of these fine days, I'm going to have to face up to that hard, cold fact and make some kind of contingency plan.

Just not right now. Not today.

Sleep has become my opiate, my drug of choice, my oblivion. Now the days have fallen into a kind of pattern; by the time I haul myself wearily out of bed at about eleven, often far later, Mum will have long gone to work, so that's when I plonk myself down in front of the TV, bowl of Cheerios in one hand, remote control in the other and think, great. Only another two hours till Ellen DeGeneres.

One evening, when Mum comes home to find me still in my pyjamas in front of the TV not having washed myself or even gone outside of the door all day, she gives out to me for allowing myself to wallow, understandably enough.

'You need fresh air and exercise,' she says crisply, dumping down her briefcase on her desk and surveying the mess I've made in the living room.

'I mean it, Annie, you can't go on like this and what's more I won't allow you to. Tomorrow you're leaving this apartment and doing a lovely tour of the city. The Potomac, the White House, Arlington cemetery, the whole lot. Then when you get back, we can have an intelligent conversation, like normal adults do. I don't want to come home again and find you're still here with nothing to talk about except some new diet product you saw on the Ellen Show called Skinny Cow.'

'Ah come on, be fair. That only happened once.'

'I mean it, missy. No more holing yourself up in here like Anne Frank. Tomorrow you're going out and that's final.'

Then she tells me that she's not staying in this evening, instead she's going out for dinner with a colleague and that I'm most welcome to join, if I want to. I pass, pleading tiredness, even though I've been sleeping for sixteen hours most nights. She doesn't try to talk me into it and I have to say, looks really terrific as she heads off for her night out, in a neat black bespoke dress, impeccable make-up and a pair of stunning, red-heeled Louboutin shoes. She's even had a blow-dry today too, I notice . . . and is that a manicure I see?

Something in the way she tells me not to wait up for her begins to rouse my suspicions. Slowly start to put two and two together as yet another memory is jogged. Why was she so dressed up to the nines the day I arrived, even though it was a Sunday, her day off?

'Mum? This colleague you're meeting tonight . . . is this by any chance . . . a date?'

The prim blush on her cheeks tells me everything I need to know.

Don't get me wrong, I'm delighted she's met someone else; Mum has been on her own for so long that no one deserves it more. But as I fall into a deep, troubled sleep that night, one thought keeps rattling round my addled brain.

Sweet baby Jesus and the orphans, is the whole, entire world in love except for me?

Hard to believe, but the following day is my last before I'm due back for work, so I do as I'm told and become a tourist for the day. It's a dry, windswept fall morning, perfect for sight-seeing and as DC is actually surprisingly compact, I cover a lot in the little time I have. Madame Tussauds, the Smithsonian, I even made it all the way up as far as the Lincoln memorial. It's the best distraction I could have asked for and I hadn't realised it, but it's well past seven in the evening by the time I even think about getting back to Mum's apartment.

The lights are already on when I let myself in, which is great – means Mum's home. Then I hear voices coming from the living room and realise she's not alone.

Oh Christ, don't tell me. The new boyfriend?

'Annie dear, is that you?' Mum calls out. 'We're in here. And there's someone I'd like you to meet!'

'Two seconds!' I yell back, straightening myself up a bit in the hall mirror and trying to smooth down the worse excesses of my bushy hair, now even wilder and more unkempt after a day exposed to the elements in the windy outdoors. Why, why, why couldn't I have inherited Mum's silky locks instead of a head of hair that needs a half can of serum dunked over into it to avoid me looking like Side Show Bob from *The Simpsons*?

Two minutes later, Mum is introducing her new 'friend' who, by the way, goes by the highly improbable name of Henry Jefferson the Third. Turns out he's a lawyer who's now working in the White House as a special advisor to President Obama, or POTUS, as he keeps referring to him. He's a bit older than Mum, pushing sixty, I'd guess, and short in height, bald as a coot but with the widest grin I think I've ever seen. Divorced too it seems, with kids a fair bit older than me.

Mum opens a bottle of wine which loosens everyone up and pretty soon, the stories start flowing too. In fact, after a while I begin to see exactly what it is that pulls Mum towards someone like Henry Jefferson the Third. He's sunny and warm and a terrific raconteur to boot, full of funny, anecdotal, inside stories about his job that make me feel a bit like I'm in an episode of the *West Wing*. He's also exuberant and full of fun and seems to bring out a girlish, giddier side to her. In fact, I almost feel like I'm chaperoning the pair of them and I think that Henry is really pulling out all the stops to impress her too.

Can't wait to get Mum on her own later to give her the low down. But most importantly of all, to tell her that, for what it's worth, I fully approve. Because no one deserves a bit of fun in their life more than my mother.

Absolutely no one.

Chapter Eighteen

So this, I suppose, is a happy ending then, at least, a happy ending of sorts. Which, as I've slowly come to learn, is the official American religion. Because, on the surface, everything appears to have worked itself out with frightening symmetry.

First there's Mum and her new man, a definite happy ending there. She waved me off at the airport earlier this morning, hugged me warmly and advised me not to worry too much about Dan. That sometimes things have a way of working themselves out. Hard to believe from where I'm standing right now, and if I'm being honest, it all sounds like something straight out of *Forrest Gump,* but I did appreciate the sentiment.

Then some astonishingly good news: while I was away, it seems Liz checked herself out of the Albany clinic and better yet, she's coming back to work tonight.

She's waiting for me in the dressing room when I get in, with the most massive bouquet of flowers and a card that reads, simply, 'Thanks for being a pal.' I smile delightedly and hug her to bits, genuinely overjoyed to see her back, but if I'm being brutally honest . . . this all just seems a bit, well . . . *sudden.* And it has to be said, she's still looking worryingly thin and with that hollow-eyed gaunt look still etched on her pale, white face. Not what I would have hoped for, not by a long shot.

'So aren't you pleased to see me?' she says, sensing that I'm holding back a bit.

'Honey, I'm beside myself, but . . . what about the clinic? I thought they had you on a programme? That there was a whole course of rehab you had to go through . . .?'

'Oh, babe, you have no idea,' she says, rolling her eyes to heaven and shoving her feet up onto the dressing table. 'You know, being stuck in that kiphole in the back arse of nowhere, surrounded by depressives was only making me, if anything, worse. They made me do group therapy, for feck's sake. Me? In group therapy? Surrounded by a shower of cockheads all droning on and on and on, day and bleeding night. You want to have heard some of them, Annie; truck drivers from Idaho analysing the reason why they drank a litre of Jack Daniel's a day and could it be because their wives didn't understand them? Jaysus, I thought, if I was married to any one of them, I'd drink double that just to drown my sorrows.'

Then she puts on a note-perfect American accent and starts ripping off the psychiatrist in charge of her treatment.

'"Hi, everybody, I'm Dr Goldman and I want to begin today's session by welcoming Liz from Ireland and asking her to tell us her story." No story to tell, I said. "Of course there's a story, Liz: there's *always* a story, so in your own time, feel free to tell the group all about your drug abuse. We're here to love and support you and our little circle of trust is non-judgemental." Then the bloody questions would start, like drill-fire. "So when did you first start using? And how much cocaine would you get through in

362

a day? And what was your lowest point? And why did you do it?" No reason, I said. I just wanted to have fun. "But how are your relationships with your family? Did you have an unhappy childhood?" You should have heard her, Annie, trying to turn me into some kind of fecking basket-case, like the rest of the losers in there. So I lost it. Just stood up and told her straight out that I had perfectly cordial relationships with both my parents and just took recreational drugs purely for the laugh. She told me I was in denial, which is stage one, so I told her to feck off, that I was going outside for a cigarette. And that was pretty much the end of that.'

OK, now I'm *really* starting to worry.

'But, Liz, are you sure it's wise to come back to work so soon? I mean, you've really been ill and to put all this pressure on yourself . . .'

'Oh please, don't you start. There's absolutely nothing that'll do me more good than to get back to work. I had to crawl on my hands and knees to Jack, of course, but like he said himself, who is he to argue with a Tony award winner? Besides, this gig is a walk in the park.'

But there's something about her striding over-confidence that's really setting off an alarm bell in my head. She clocks my anxious expression and pats my arm soothingly.

'Christ, Annie, you're such a bloody worrier! No need to fret about this chick any more. I've gone cold turkey and the strongest drink you'll see pass my lips is Diet Coke. Trust me, the strongest thing going up my nose from now on is a Vicks inhaler. That's a promise.'

And she just picks up where she left off and is as amazing as ever in the show. Not only that, but she apologises personally to Blythe, Chris and Alex too, swears that she's on the straight and narrow from now on and no one need ever worry about her again.

Which is terrific. Which is great. Which is a massive relief all round. I just find it all a bit too good to be true, that's all. That she just snapped out of an addiction and went straight back to work like nothing ever happened. Can it really be so easy? Is life really like that?

Which brings me to a sneaky confession I have to make here. Early the following morning, I call her doctor at the Albany rehab centre, Dr Goldman, who's in a meeting but who eventually does get back to me right before I leave for work. I tell her I hope I'm worrying unnecessarily about Liz, but that I'm just wondering what her take on this miraculous turn-around is? About her checking herself out of the programme so fast, I explain.

Dr Goldman's answer chills me to the bone.

'Annie, I appreciate that you're concerned about your friend. But remember, I can't help those who don't want to be helped.'

And as if all this wasn't enough, on top of everything else there's the constant, sickening worry over Dan. But could it be that he's got his happy ending too? I've become expert at schooling myself not to indulge in the torture of thinking about him and Lisa and their ready-made family unit, but sometimes I can't help myself.

Back from Paris by now, I figure, but beyond that, I don't want to know any more. The minute I got in the door of my little blonde apartment, I deleted every single message on the answering machine, ignoring the whole lot of them. What's more, while I was unpacking, I realised I'd left my mobile in the spare room back at Mum's. Ordinarily, I'd feel like I was missing my right hand, but right now, it's the least of my worries. Frankly, if there's any more bad news from home, I don't need to know and don't want to know.

Occasionally a tiny sliver of hope will find its way into my heart: maybe Lisa drove Dan nuts when they were away, maybe now he sees for himself what an absolute Hammer Horror story the woman is, but then . . . maybe not. For one thing, Dan always sees the good in people, never the bad . . . and maybe now he's found a woman who actually is prepared to put up with a life of never seeing him. And my cross in life is that I'll have to live with the fallout.

Then there's Jack. A part of me is and will always be attracted to him and what's more, he knows it. Knows it and plays on it all the time. A part of me admires him, but if I'm being really honest, there's another part of me that still shrivels up at the tough, insensitive, merciless side to him.

Funny, but if there were ever two sides to a coin, it's most definitely Jack and Dan. Both are gifted at what they do, both are driven almost to the point of obsession, but whereas Jack is ruthless, Dan is kind. And where Jack is unrelenting in pursuit of what he wants, Dan just lets things happen, all in their own good time. Both are strong, but Jack thunders around the place till he gets his way with the full force of his blast-furnace personality, whereas Dan is one of those people that makes you realise what a colossal mistake it is to confuse calmness with weakness. Because calmness often belies huge strength, and so it is with him.

Jack has asked me out on a date tonight, a proper date. After the show, just the two of us, and after much bludgeoning on his part, I eventually give in. Honest to God, it's like he pursued a kind of scorched earth policy:

every time I'd say no to him and explain that I needed time out, he'd plant a seed in my head of Dan in Paris with Lisa, over and over again, till he eventually wore down all resistance on my part.

So I suppose this is a happy ending then.

It just doesn't feel like one, that's all.

And now, here I am, stepping out of a cab, picking my steps through lashing sheets of rain, outside The Plaza hotel. The show's over and the rest of the night stretches ahead of us. Dinner, Jack said, at my hotel. Just dinner, I said firmly, but you don't need to be a mind reader to know what he's thinking. That this will be our first night together. The first time in my life that I'll sleep with any man other than my husband.

I think of Dan in Paris, I think of Lisa, I think of the two of them together in The Moorings right now . . . and all I feel is numb. Anaesthetised. Like I've already worked my way through the A to Z of every conceivable emotion known to heartbroken women till there's nothing left but this cold, empty shell, wearing a borrowed dress and shoes.

If I'd thought we'd be having dinner downstairs, in the Oak Room restaurant maybe, I was all wrong. Jack has everything pre-planned, like a true master of seduction. He's already waiting for me in the lobby, wearing his off duty gear of designer jeans and a jet black cashmere sweater, crisp black shirt peeping out from underneath. He lights up when he sees me, kisses me lightly, then slipping an arm around my waist, leads me towards the elevator bank. No messing around, it would seem, this is a private dinner for two.

The express elevator shoots skywards and all I can think

is . . . can I really do this? Because right now, I just don't know.

I say none of this to Jack of course, instead we talk politely about the show tonight and how great Liz was. He was at the theatre, of course, but some latent prudishness in me insisted on our leaving separately, even though gossip about the two of us has long since died down as everyone, right down to the ushers and the staff who sell programmes at the interval, have all long since assumed that Jack and I are a foregone conclusion. Including, it would seem, the man himself.

Two minutes later, we're up on one of the hotel's private floors, where all the apartments are. His arm is tight around my waist now as he steers me towards the entrance door and inside.

Funny but I always wondered about his living space; Jack struck me as one of those guys who although meticulous about his own appearance would be slovenly about all else. Might even be something we could possibly joke about, to lighten the mood a bit. As usual though, I'm wrong. The apartment is flawlessly tidy, exactly like a hotel suite, but with a few little personal touches, added purely because he's been here for so long. It's a stunning room – if you happen to like the colour grey, that is. Absolutely everything's decorated in shades of it: carpets, furniture, wallpaper, windows, the whole works.

In fact the only touch of actual colour is a painting Jack proudly shows off to me, one he bought from an art gallery in Hell's Kitchen awhile back, of . . . I'm not kidding . . . a red Ferrari. He swaggers a bit as he shows it off to me, smirking at my reaction when I hear the price – more than I'm being paid for the entire run of the show.

Then he proudly takes me to the window to show off the view, which stretches all the way over Central Park. I can see how on a clear day it would be stunning, but right now the rain is really bucketing down, drumming against the windows and we can't see that much. A right storm is brewing, as a gale force wind starts to wallop itself off the building and normally weather like this makes me feel snug and warm and glad to be inside, but not tonight.

A discreet ring at the door and it's room service with dinner. A table for two is set up in the middle of the room and Jack goes to the minibar to crack open a bottle of champagne. Funny, but it's as if he's single-handedly orchestrating the whole scene without actually saying or doing anything. He nods at one waiter and the curtains are drawn, raises his eyebrows at another and the lights are dimmed. He's got this all meticulously planned out, I think detachedly, like he's directing the entire evening. Like it's one of his stage productions.

He hands me a glass of champagne, then guides me to the table. A hefty tip is discreetly slipped to the waiters and we're left alone.

This is it then, I think, no turning back now. From where my chair is positioned, I can see right through to the bedroom: a sleigh bed big enough to sleep an entire family, scented candles dotted around the room, and a bouquet of red roses relieving the dull monotony of the grey.

What in the name of arse am I doing? Why am I here? Out of revenge? To get my own back at Dan? To try and feel something other than the awful emptiness that's inside me?

It's like watching a master class in foreplay, is all I can think, like I'm completely distanced from the whole thing.

We eat, or rather, he eats and I pick at my food; no appetite.

And then, crunch time. He leads me to the sofa, puts on classical music in the background and slowly moves in towards me, arm around my shoulder, lips at my ear. We both know what's coming next and I've run out of excuses to put him off.

His kisses my hand delicately, then stops to fiddle with my wedding ring.

'Why do you insist on still wearing this, my dear? Don't you think it's a travesty? Or do you wear it as a lucky charm to stave off wolves like me?'

'Don't touch it,' I say and it's only when I see his reaction that I realise I almost snapped the words at him.

Then, wordlessly, he starts to nibble my earlobe and I let him, staring straight ahead, completely tuned out. I can't imagine, I am trying really hard not to imagine what's going on at The Moorings right about now. Is someone else kissing Dan too? Is someone else lying beside him, wanting him, making love to him?

Breathing more heavily, Jack moves down to my neck, kissing every square inch of it, his hand moving up the crushed velvet of my dress and cupping my boobs, gently pressing down. Now he's moving up a gear, his whole body is stiffening and his hands feel that bit rougher, as he lays me backwards onto the sofa, stretching me out and caressing up and down every inch of me. He's on top of me now, pressing down hard on me, biting into my neck and expertly undoing the zip at the back of my dress.

And all the time, I'm miles away.

Three thousand miles away. In county Waterford, to be exact. At home.

369

His icy hands are under my dress now, working their way downwards and lightly grazing my thighs as he starts to moan more urgently. It's only when he kisses me full on, slipping a darty tongue in my mouth . . . . and I pull away from him, that he eventually realises something's up. That somehow I can't access that animal attraction to him that was there before. That I'm just lying here, utterly unresponsive. Like a corpse, present in body but not in spirit.

'Annie? Annie, what's up?'

Gone is his sexy toffee-voice, now he's beginning to sound gruff, impatient.

'Answer me. Is something wrong?'

I haul myself up onto my elbows, brushing hair out of my eyes and fumbling to pull the zip of my dress back up.

'Jesus Christ, what are you doing? Where are you going?'

'Jack, I'm sorry, I can't do this . . .'

'Don't be so ridiculous, you're not going anywhere.'

He's on his feet now, cold and angry. I look at him and see all the desire that was there a few seconds ago quickly drain from his face.

'I'm sorry,' is all I can repeat over again. 'I just can't. Not now and maybe not ever. If Dan did this to me, I don't know what I'd do, so it doesn't seem right that I leap into bed with you just to get even.'

'Dan *is* doing this to you, my deluded little idiot, at this very minute possibly.'

'*WHAT* did you just say?'

'Oh please, it's all over the theatre. Your ex has moved on and you're still in this ridiculously protracted mourning period for him? Have you taken complete leave of your senses?'

'I can't explain,' I say, groping to get my arms into the sleeves of my coat. Only the truth too, I couldn't explain if I tried. It's like I'm stuck in this no man's land. I wasn't able to make it work with Dan and now I can't seem to move on either.

Jack is lighting up a cigarette and holding it exactly level with his lips, realising that sex is firmly off tonight's agenda.

'You do know that you're making a huge mistake, my dear?' he says, exhaling deep blue cloud puffs. 'Because walk out that door and I'm telling you right now that you and I are over.'

But I don't answer, mainly because there's nothing left to be said. We look at each other for a long time, like two actors in a play who've forgotten their lines and it's a case of who'll blink first. In the end, I give up. So I just grab my shoes, slip them over my bare feet and wordlessly leave.

I wait by the elevator bank, half wondering whether he'll come after me, but he doesn't. He lets me go and what's more I'm glad of it.

No cabs outside the hotel and by now the rain is buffeting down so heavily it's like a slap in my face, but I don't care.

And when I do eventually get home, drenched right through to my knickers, the temptation to call Dan is so overwhelmingly huge that it hurts.

Chapter Nineteen

The minute I cross the threshold of the theatre for work the following evening, I swear I can practically smell trouble brewing in the air. It's everywhere; it's in the nervous glances the wardrobe mistress throws me when I meet her coming out of my dressing room, it's in the discreet eye-roll the stage director throws me; even the perpetual good cheer of Hayley, Queen of the Box Office, seems to have dimmed a bit this evening. As much as to say, fasten your seatbelts, folks. Tonight's going to be a bumpy ride.

It's only when I throw open the dressing room door and head inside that I realise exactly what's going on. Liz is already here ahead of me and one single look from her tells me just about everything I need to know. The wildly dilated pupils, the restlessness, the agitation, the aggressive energy.

Sweet Jesus, I do not be-fecking-lieve this. She's only twenty-four hours out of hospital and already out of her head. No question. My heart sinks like a stone as the penny doesn't so much drop as fall thudding to the floor. Here's the reason why she was in such a mad rush to check herself out of the Eleanor Young clinic. Here's the reason she wanted her freedom back so desperately, so urgently. So she could get out and start scoring all over again.

Suddenly I feel weak as a kitten. Perspiration breaks out and starts to roll from my armpits down towards my ribcage and all I can think is, what in the name of God do we do now? And how do we get through the show tonight with her like this?

Right then. Plan A: act normal. I start off by playing it as routinely as possible around her, dumping my bags down, flinging my coat off as usual, saying hi, asking how her day was. Faux-casual, even if I'm far from feeling it. Meanwhile she's pacing up and down the tiny room like a maniac, flicking through the script and simultaneously lighting up a fag.

'Ehh . . . sorry, Liz, but you know you're not supposed to smoke inside the building.'

'Feck off,' she snaps, glaring haughtily at me. 'Who asked you anyway?'

'Oookaay,' I say, stepping back at bit, realising just exactly how disastrous this evening could well be. 'Ehhh, just so you know, I didn't actually make up that law. America did.'

A sullen glare from her, like I only said that to get in a personal dig at her and then she flicks the fag carelessly into a used coffee cup. Meanwhile, I have to bite my tongue, as I've had to do so bloody often in the past, and remind myself that this isn't the Liz I know and love in front of me; it's the very worst version of her.

'Emmm, Liz,' I say, picking my words very, very carefully. 'Are you feeling OK tonight?'

'Fantastic. Never better. Why do you ask?'

'Because you don't seem like yourself.'

'Well, as it happens, just in case you're about to go gabbing off to the others about what condition I'm in, I've never been better. Oh and by the way, you know the opening scene in Act Two? I've decided to play it a bit differently. It's boring as arse the way it is, it needs to be jazzed up a bit. Just warning you in advance to be on your toes.'

'But you can't do that! You can't just change the way we've been working a scene for almost a year now, without rehearsing it, or at least going through Jack first!'

'Oh no? And tell me this: how many Tony awards do you have on your sideboard? Just watch me.'

The tom-toms have already gone through the building because the others have copped on that there's something majorly up with her too; you can tell by the panicky looks that are passing between myself, Blythe, Chris and Alex backstage before curtain up.

As for me, my entire digestive system is in one big knot of tension, not helped by the fact that I had to swipe a baby bottle of vodka off Liz in the little bathroom we share not five minutes ago. I caught her slugging straight out of it like a wino, claiming it was for her nerves and somehow managed to wrest it out of her iron grip, to a further string of abuse from her . . . but now I'm thinking, *booze*? On top of whatever she was shoving up her nose all day?

Christ Alive, it's like trying to babysit Sid Vicious.

The show starts and the first scene goes OK. Liz is late in on a few cues, but nothing that could be noticed by anyone other than the rest of us onstage with her. Scene two again, holds up. Liz seems OK, just stumbles over one of her speeches, but recovers enough for the rest of us to semaphore relieved glances across the stage at each other.

The trouble doesn't start till well into the third scene, when we're all onstage at the same time and Blythe throws her a line. Liz ignores her and there's a horrible, horrible pause, while we all realise that she's dried onstage. Completely dried up and forgotten her lines.

I'm too far away from her to be of any use, but Alex, thinking on her feet, moves close to her, fully in character and hisses the right line at her. Still no response. Then realising that her cue isn't coming, Chris covers up and skips on a half page of dialogue, which the rest of us pick up on, leaving Liz looking bewildered on stage. It's a fast-paced scene, one that Jack has consistently hammered into us must be played at rapid-fire speed and now it's just limping along lamely, pathetically.

And then, real disaster. Just as the scene is supposed to build to a dramatic crescendo, and Liz is meant to deliver her most difficult and wordy speech, she rises to her feet, takes a terrifyingly long pause and slowly eyeballs each of us sharing the stage with her in turn. Chris, Alex, Blythe and I are frozen like terrified statues, each one of us dreading what's coming next and yet powerless to prevent it. I feel like someone who knows they're about to die, but who can't guess the method – poison or sword.

OK, now sweat is actually streaming down me and I honestly think I'll have an anxiety stroke if Liz doesn't start her shagging speech and break this awful, charged silence.

She does. Eventually. And somehow she manages to stumble through the first paragraph, except that now she's just line reading, like a first-year drama student reciting a boring poem that they don't particularly like by rote. Like she's just sending this performance in by fax, a million miles from her usual, effervescent, brilliant self.

A part of me is wondering whether the audience can

somehow pick up on the nervousness that's practically hopping off the rest of us as we all watch her, waiting, dreading what's going to come out of her mouth next. They must do. I can see faces in the first few rows exchange glances with each other as much as to say *this* actress is a Tony winner? Ehh . . . *why?*

Seconds start to feel like hours and sure enough, two minutes later, Liz loses it. Completely. Falters on a line of dialogue, then starts to giggle. And doesn't even bother trying to recover from it.

No, what she does is worse, far, far worse. Instead, she continues on, except now her laughs have turned into something more manic sounding and uncontrollable. The rest of us are really panicking now, frantically firing 'do something!' looks across the stage at each other, but it's too late.

And that's when it happens.

Liz turns directly to the audience, deliberately breaking the fourth wall and then addresses them directly.

'Ladies and gentlemen,' she begins and I swear you could hear a pin drop. I can see as far as about row seven and it's as though they're thinking, could this be some bizarre part of the show? Is this meant to happen? From the wings, the stage director is frantically yelling into his headset that something's gone badly wrong . . . and that's when I see Jack backstage, looking coldly out at Liz, his face blank and expressionless, waiting, just waiting like the rest of us to see what in the name of God is about to unfold.

'Sorry to have to do this to you all,' Liz is saying to the crowd, sounding skittish and high as the ceiling, 'but as you've probably gathered, I haven't got a clue of what I say next. So if you'll all excuse me, I'm buggering off now.

I've had enough of this and I'd safely say that all have as well!'

And with that, she strides off the stage, leaving the rest of us standing there like mutes, utterly dumbstruck.

The fallout is horrendous. The curtain swishes down and from where we're all rooted to the spot, we can clearly see Jack urgently grabbing Liz by the arm, almost pouncing on her like a tiger and telling her in no uncertain terms that she's fired. That this was her probationary last chance after the Tony awards fiasco, and that now she's royally blown it sky high. What's more, that she's to collect her things from the dressing room, turn in her ID card, leave the building and never, ever come back.

'You can't fire me,' she almost spits back into his face, 'have you seen my reviews? I'm a Tony winner, for fuck's sake. Do you know how lucky you are to even have me in this?'

'Get her out of here,' Jack commands the stage director and I swear his voice is like vinegar. 'And if she as much as *attempts* to show her face at the stage door again, call the police.'

There's a shocked second where I can see the penny dropping with Liz, that he really means it this time. That it's all over for her. She looks like someone who's just been physically slapped across the face, so that's when I step in, officially unable to take any more.

Shaking, I walk over to her and tell her that I'm taking her home to sleep off the effects of whatever crap she's spent the day putting into her system, then first thing in the morning, I'm taking her straight back to the Eleanor Young clinic. And that it's not negotiable.

'Like fuck you are!' she almost barks at me, shoving me away from her, before turning on her heel, charging out the stage door and off into the night, still wearing her costume.

I think it's the longest night of my life. A few hours later, we're all back home, Chris, Alex and I, sitting up in Blythe's apartment, trying our best to stay calm and all the while just staring at the phone, waiting on it to ring. Hoping that maybe she's OK, that maybe she's just out with her shadowy new gang of pals and that maybe she'll crawl home by herself at some point. Like she would have done on so many nights before. Fervently hoping, although not one of us is really hopeful. We all know that what happened tonight is endgame for Liz.

Because now she's completely vanished. It's almost two in the morning, she still hasn't come back home and she's not answering her phone either. To complicate matters, none of us have contact numbers or even names of the mysterious friends she's been spending more and more time with, although I'm pretty certain she must be with one of them now.

Course she was. Who else would have supplied her?

Chris being Chris as usual takes charge and for once, in my shell-shocked, inert state, I'm glad of her decisive bossiness; glad to have the decisions made for the rest of us. She even tried calling the police, but they said unless Liz was missing for forty-eight hours, they couldn't officially classify her as a missing person.

Needless to say, the show was abandoned after what happened. A brief announcement was made to the audience explaining that one of the cast was 'too unwell to continue performing'. A euphemism right up there with 'tired and emotional' if ever there was one. And of course, we could hardly continue the show with Liz's understudy playing out the rest of it; it would have been beyond weird to have two actresses playing the same part, in the same show. So instead, they've all been refunded their money and offered complimentary tickets for another performance.

But of course that won't stop the story leaking, and already Chris has come in with tomorrow morning's paper, full of it.

Before he left the theatre, Jack coolly announced to all of us that from now on, Rachel, Liz's understudy would continue in the role, till the end of the year. So in one fell swoop, Liz has brought her glittering Broadway career to a crashing end.

It's the weirdest thing – every horrible detail of tonight is still vividly etched sharp in my memory, as though I might need to take a test on it later.

Worst thing of all was Jack's reaction; now that he's written Liz off, it's as though he's barely concerned about her welfare, where she is, who she's with or most frightening of all, what she's doing. It's as though all that matters to him is the sacred cow that is the show, and now that he's eliminated the one person who dared put it in jeopardy, it's all behind him.

I always knew he was cold, just not callous along with it, that's all.

'I've seen it all happen before, you know,' Blythe says sadly, passing round mugs of tea to Alex, Chris and me as we all sit in her living room, unable to sleep, just waiting, hoping for news.

'Seen what?' says Chris, sounding beyond exhausted.

'Great talents like Liz just throwing it all away.'

'Yeah,' says little Alex, curled up on the sofa with a rug thrown over her. 'I know what you mean. People as gifted as Liz often come with a sort of self-destruct button. They seem to cultivate an attitude that rules are for fools and that they're somehow above all that.'

Funny thing about Alex, she has the rare ability to effortlessly put her finger on the pulse of whatever everyone else is thinking.

'Well I'm sorry,' says Chris crisply, 'I'm as shocked at what happened tonight as the rest of you, but frankly given the choice, I'd far prefer to work with someone a little bit less talented than Liz, if it meant that at least they were professional. Give me success without the psychodrama any day.'

Blythe nods sorrowfully, but I know just what Alex meant. God Almighty, to me this is like watching a Greek tragedy unfold. One where Liz is a bold high-flyer who dazzles everyone with her effortless brilliance, only to commit a stunning act of folly. And just when she had it all, too.

We all stagger off to bed at about three in the morning and I fall asleep praying to God, Jesus, Shiva, Buddha, Santa, anyone who's listening, that Liz is out there somewhere, safe and alive.

Then about two hours later, I'm woken up by the phone on the bedside table. It's Chris, oh thank you God, with news. The cops have just called her to say Liz has been found.

'Where is she?' I ask groggily.

'In the emergency room of St Luke's hospital, on Fifty-Eighth Street and Ninth Avenue. She's taken an overdose and . . . oh Annie, it's far, far worse than we thought. You have to prepare yourself.'

'Prepare myself for what?'

'They don't know if she's going to make it or not.'

Chapter Twenty

We've been taking it in shifts around Liz's bedside at the hospital, holding vigil all night and all morning, vowing not to slip off to try and get some rest until someone else comes along to relieve us. Liz is in the ICU at St Luke's hospital, in a tiny, private room, wired up to monitors, drips, wires, the whole works.

She's slid into a deep coma, the doctors have explained to us, brought on by the massive overdose of narcotics that were in her system. Apparently she was convulsing when they first admitted her, her blood pressure was through the ceiling and she was vomiting everywhere. And on top of all that, they've got her on oxygen to try and stabilise her breathing, as well as an IV drip to try and get some hydration back into her.

They're doing everything for her, we're assured over and over again, but the battle is far from over. The chances that she could come out of this permanently brain damaged are high. Or worse still, there's a chance she may not come out of it at all. I try to ask what are the odds of her coming out of it unscathed but I'd forgotten that the medical profession don't deal in mindless optimism. 'We're doing everything we can,' is the only oblique answer I get.

Chris as usual, takes total charge and even manages to get in contact with Liz's family back home in Ireland, to break the news to them. Worst of all are the acres of press coverage that are bound to come out of this, not only about what's happened to Liz, but also about the 'friends' of hers who supplied her with enough coke to get her into this state in the first place.

Already the police have issued a statement requesting whoever dropped Liz off at the hospital to come forward for questioning. Which means at some point, there'll have to be a full investigation, questions asked, charges pressed.

No matter which way you look at this, it's a nightmare.

Chris and I had been sitting up with her all through the night and all this morning – the two of us came here together as soon as we first got the phone call. Then Blythe arrived about an hour ago, white-faced and shocked, so I urged Chris to go home and try to get some rest. I had to; the woman was practically sleepwalking on her jaded feet.

Meanwhile Blythe and I have been told that even though Liz is in a deep coma, that hearing is always the last thing to go and that if we keep on chatting away to her, there's every chance that she might just be able to hear us. Which is what the two of us have been doing non-stop, but we're talking completely inane crap mostly. Nothing that'll get her heart rate soaring again.

Blythe reads out the papers to her, omitting to mention that Liz herself has made page one of the *New York Times* and the *Post* not to mention several TV news shows. It occurs to me that if the Liz I know and love could only hear her, she'd tell her to shut the fuck up jabbering on about current affairs, which never interested her much anyway, and to run out and get her a fag and an ashtray, in that order. So instead, I read out a few bits to her from *The National Inquirer* and *Hot Gossip* magazine about the latest Brangelina break-up rumours; far more up Liz's street.

A few hours later, Alex comes in to relieve us, carrying three polystyrene cups of vending machine coffee, to perk us all up a bit. She brings fresh news: Liz's father has called her to say that he's already on his way to New York and that his flight arrives sometime later today. My heart goes out to the poor man, having to make that long, transatlantic journey, not having the first clue what lies ahead of him.

'Look at you, Annie, you're a complete wreck,' says Alex, handing me over the coffee. 'You've been here all night and you haven't a chance of getting through the show later on unless you manage to get a few hours' kip. Go home for God's sake. Rest now, while you can.'

'Oh yes, love, you should,' says Blythe nodding enthusiastically. 'You've done all you could and more. If there's any change, don't worry, I'll ring you the minute.'

I remember my mobile phone, still sitting in Mum's DC apartment, and for about the thousandth time, mentally smack myself on the forehead for my sheer stupidity in leaving the shagging thing behind. But the others promise to call my landline at the apartment if there are any further developments, good or bad, and so reluctantly, I take my leave.

It's a rare, sunny autumn day and as I hail a cab and give the driver my address, I slump exhaustedly onto the back seat of the car, utterly worn out and so dog tired that my brain is actually starting to pound. So hard to believe that today is only Thursday. Only a few days ago, I think, I was in Washington with Mum. Only a few days ago, Liz was onstage. And only two days ago, I went to The Plaza to have dinner with Jack, but then the less said about that particular episode, the better.

We stop in traffic and I look blankly out at the hordes of shoppers and Japanese tourists with cameras strolling nonchalantly past. Carrying discount shopping bags, snapping photos, doing all the normal sight-seeing stuff. All I can selfishly and irrationally think is, how can they act so carefree? Don't they realise that there are people out there hovering between life and death in ICU units? That right now my best friend is attached to a monitor, clinging onto life?

We arrive at my building on Madison Avenue, I pay the driver and somehow crawl my weary way upstairs to bed, where I'm asleep the minute my head hits the pillow, still fully clothed.

I'm in the deepest slumber imaginable when suddenly the intercom buzzer on my front door goes. Instantly I'm wide awake, sitting bolt upright and already panicking. The digital alarm clock on my bedside table says it's just one in the afternoon. In a second I'm up, my heart walloping off my chest, throat contracted, beads of perspiration already starting to stream.

It must be one of the girls, with news. Has to be.

Jesus Christ, just let it be good news, dear Jesus, just please let it be good news . . .

I nearly fall over, I'm racing that fast to the door and fling it wide open, expecting Alex, Chris or maybe Blythe.

But it's not any of them.

Standing there, carrying a suitcase and looking even bigger and broader and taller than I remember, is Dan.

I look up at his rugged, handsome face, feeling his soft, jet-black eyes urgently scanning mine . . . and I'm in complete and utter shock, as the blood starts to sing in my ears. Then without even knowing how or why it's happening, I find myself sobbing. Big, ugly, uncontrollable tears of exhaustion mixed with shock that he's actually *here*.

Dan, who I thought was back from Paris and now cosily shacked up at The Moorings with feck-head Lisa?

What the hell is going on?

'Shhhhhh, come on, darling, it's OK,' he says, gathering me up into his huge arms and bundling me inside. 'I know what's happened and I know what you've been through and I'm here now and we'll face into it together. If you'll let me.'

'Dan,' I weep straight into his shirt, 'I can't believe that it's you! It's really you . . . you're here!'

He's gently put me down onto the sofa now, lifting me as though I weigh approximately the same as a dead leaf. And now he's right beside me and I can't stop touching him, checking that it really is him . . . his face, all covered in stubble like he hasn't slept in days, his hair, unkempt, like he's been sleeping rough and his hands which are gripping mine so tight it's nearly hurting.

'Am I dreaming?' I keep saying over and over again. 'Am I going to wake up any second now and you'll be gone?'

'Oh Christ, Annie,' he says, moving right in beside me and cradling me in his warm arms, his lips just inches away from mine. 'You have no idea what I've been going through these past few days, the past few months in fact; how completely useless I've been without you. Never in my life will I let you out of my sight again. That's if you still want me. Because I've been tortured . . . I've been to hell and back ever since Jules came home from New York full of tales about this smarmy git who's been moving in on you . . .'

'Jack,' I interrupt him, 'Jack Gordon . . . but . . . oh, Dan, I have so much to tell you, I don't know where to start . . .'

'I have so much to tell you too, darling . . . so much to make up for . . . because I've been such a royal idiot . . .'

We're clinging to each other now, limbs all tangled together, like we haven't done in years. Like this is the Dan of old, suddenly and miraculously come back to me.

Then, the one question that's burning me up. The one I have to know the answer to, no matter how painful.

Inconvenient tears start to roll and I have to really fight hard to get this out.

'Dan? I thought you were in Paris, with the Count . . . I mean, with Lisa. And her kids,' I tack on in a tiny voice.

He looks at me for a long, long time and every second that passes I'm thinking the very worst. That maybe this is the whole reason he's come all this way? To break it to me that he's with her now and that he and I are over? Properly, officially over?

'Yes,' he eventually says, his soul plain to see in his soft black eyes and for a split second I think that my heart might shatter.

'Yes, Lisa did want me to come to Paris. Yes, she was very insistent, said it was a thank you to me for letting her and the kids move into The Moorings.'

He's right beside me now, we're holding onto each other tightly, forehead to forehead.

'Dan, you can tell me,' I whisper. 'Whatever happened, remember that I'm still your best friend. And whatever does happen, I always will be. Nothing is ever going to change that.'

And now he's kissing me. Softly, gently, lightly. My cheeks first, then he moves over to my earlobes. Oh God, is all I think, rolling my head back and pulling him in even tighter, it's been years since he's even looked at me with such longing, such desire.

'There's absolutely nothing for me to tell,' he murmurs. 'Nothing. You have to believe me, love. Lisa went and bought a ticket for me to Paris and I honestly think that right up till the moment I drove her and the kids to Dublin airport, she really thought she'd be able to talk me into it . . . but I'd been a complete idiot. I'd misread the signals all along, I think . . . well, let's just say that I think Lisa wanted more from me than just a shoulder to cry on. An awful lot more. Her marriage had just broken up and I think she figured I was an easy target, living all alone, desperately missing you . . .'

I was right, I think, pulling away from him as a bitter, cold triumph floods over me. She spotted that Dan was vulnerable and had no qualms about just moving in on him. Getting him to step into a ready-made family.

'Dan? Did you . . . did you think about going with her? Did you want to go?'

'For maybe a day or two, but no more. We reached the airport, then I just got one of those road to Damascus moments where I thought, what in hell am I doing here? Have I been unintentionally leading this woman on all this time? Because if I had, it was a rotten thing to do, especially when there were young kids in the picture too. So I told her it would be wrong of me to go away with them all, turned the car right around and headed straight for home.'

'But I called your mobile and it was that foreign ring tone! That's what convinced me that . . .'

'Shhhh love, it's OK,' he whispers, cradling my head in the crook of his giant arm.

'All that happened was that Lisa took my phone with her by accident and she left me with hers. Anyway, I'm bloody glad that I came home when I did because when Jules saw me back and clearly alone, she burst into tears, said she'd made a horrible mistake and that somehow she had to get a hold of you. Which, by the way, both of us have been trying to do for the past week. Frantically. Didn't you get any of my messages? I must have left you hundreds by now.'

I think of my mobile sitting in my Mum's flat in Washington. Out of batteries all last week and now most likely winging its merry way to me via Fedex, with all of those messages that would have saved me all of that heartache. Then I think about when I got back on Tuesday, how I just deleted every single message on the landline. And how my laptop hasn't even been as much as turned on since I got back from DC. For well over a week now I've been utterly incommunicado. And why? All because I didn't want to hear bad news from home.

Let it be tattooed in ink behind my eyeballs. I am the greatest living gobshite on the face of this earth. Officially.

Suddenly, just when I want him to the most, Dan isn't holding me anymore. Instead, he's moved away a bit, but slowly he turns back to me and looks me straight in the eye.

'Sweetheart, I've come clean with you and now it's your turn. Is there anything you want to tell me? The same thing goes – I'm still your best friend and I'll sit here and listen to anything you have to tell me.'

His huge, black eyes anxiously look down at me, waiting for the blow to fall. It's no time for lies or glossing over things, so I come clean and confess all, fed up of feeling like a child caught up in an elaborate complex lie and in a funny way, relieved to finally get it off my chest. And it's painful but somehow I do it, knowing that Jules has already paved the way for me anyway.

Dan physically winces and pulls even further away from me when I tell him that yes, I did kiss Jack and more than once too. I stress that I only even agreed to date Jack in the first place because I thought that he was off in Paris playing happy families with Lisa. And I was lonely and broken-hearted and was just reaching out to someone . . . but to the wrong person.

Next thing Dan has moved right away from me and is now sitting on the edge of the sofa, holding his head in his hands, deep in thought, unreachable.

Say something, I think, looking at his huge hulking frame, so far from me now.

Say anything.

'It's all my fault,' he whispers.

'Dan, no, that's not possible! How could it be?'

I've slid over to him now, and am stroking his thick, black hair, then move down to gently massage the back of his brown, suntanned neck.

'Because I drove you to this. If it was me that made you feel like you wanted another life with another man . . . then there's something wrong with me, isn't there? I mean . . . what kind of a husband does that to his own wife?'

'Stop being so hard on yourself, love, that's just not true . . .'

'Annie, have you any idea what I've been through since Jules came home full of tales of this git wining and dining you both, whisking you off on helicopter tours, taking you up to the Hamptons, all the time moving in on you, on my wife . . . I wanted to get on a plane and come over here and physically cripple him. I wanted to do the guy actual harm. Even allowing for Jules's tendency to exaggerate everything, I thought, if even a fraction of this is true, then I'm in big trouble. So that's when I called you . . . that night when you were on your way to the theatre.'

'I remember. It was a weird conversation and I didn't know what was up with you. I felt something had shifted but didn't know what.'

'I figured . . . I gave you a year of freedom genuinely thinking it was the right thing to do at the time. I knew how stifled you felt back in Stickens, how rough it was on you with me working all the time, so I thought the best way for me to hold on to you in the long term, was to let you go. On the age-old principle that if you love someone, then you should set them free. If they come back to you, they're yours forever and if they don't they were never yours in the first place. God knows, the first few months were rough without you, but then we'd talk on the phone and you just sounded so, so . . . alive . . . in a way that you hadn't done in years. So no matter how much I missed you, I knew we'd both done the right thing.'

'Dan, I . . . well, I honestly thought that you'd barely notice I'd even gone.'

'Don't, love, don't make me feel worse than I already do. I don't think I'll ever forgive myself for driving you away the way I did, I'm still beating myself up over it. Then I'd hear your voice on the phone and you'd sound ten years younger, so happy, so fulfilled and that kept me going for a long, long time. But then when Jules got back and when I heard that this Jack git was so clearly intent on having a full-blown, serious relationship with you . . . I snapped. Couldn't take it. Annie, I've been a mess ever since Jules got back. Couldn't concentrate on work, couldn't sleep, completely useless. I kept thinking, what have I done? What tortured me most of all was that I was the architect of all this, that I'd brought the whole thing on myself. By working so hard all the time, by neglecting you, by not treating you the way you deserved, when you'd given up so much for me. I was in the depths of depression and then all last week when you weren't answering your phone I started to panic and assume the worst. That you were with this guy and didn't want to take my calls. So I called the theatre and they told me you'd taken a week off. With him, I could only presume. My mind was in a pulp, eaten up with the idea of you gone off with someone else, so that's when I just drove to Shannon airport and waited on standby for the first flight they could put me on to New York. I had to wait till today to get a seat, but I didn't care. My plan was to camp outside your apartment till I heard from your own lips if you'd chosen this guy over me. If I'd really lost you.'

I'm stunned into silence while he says all of this, completely speechless.

'Have I, Annie?' he says, turning back to me and taking my hands into his huge bear-like grip. 'Have I lost you?'

'No,' I sob, but through tears of relief and happiness and joy this time. 'No, no, of course, not. How could you have?'

There's so much more I want to say, but the words get stuck in my throat. I want to tell him that we're soul mates, that he and I are something that cannot be split apart, no matter how hard either of us tried to . . .

He moves closer and gently brushes the tears from my cheek with his finger, then pulls me towards him.

And next thing, he's kissing me like the years have just

fallen away and we're back to being two love-struck teenagers all over again.

We're both so rag-tired, heavy-lidded with exhaustion and yet still have so much to talk about, that I'd have gladly stayed snuggled up with Dan on my couch for the whole afternoon. Holding each other, rediscovering each other, reconnecting right back to the way we were a long, long, time ago.

But suddenly the vision of Liz lying in that hospital bed comes hurdling into my thoughts. And so I fill Dan in on the details, telling him that we're all beside ourselves and just how precarious her condition is.

'I should call the hospital, love,' I tell him and he agrees, gently easing himself out of my arms and reaching over to the coffee table to where the landline is, then passing it back to me. 'Good idea,' he murmurs softly. 'Her family must be here by now, so maybe there's something we can do to help them.'

I smile lovingly up at him. Vintage Dan, he's just found his wife again and is already wondering what we can do to help total strangers. Sure enough, when I call the hospital, Liz's dad has just arrived, but there's no change in her. None at all. I thank the registrar and hang up and next thing, Dan's right beside me again, cradling me against him and holding me tight.

'Shhh, don't be upset, love, they're doing all they can for her. And remember miracles happen every day. Hey, look, one just happened to me, didn't it?'

I brush my hand up against his stubbly, rough, exhausted face, thinking God Almighty, he looks like a Johnny Cash song. Then we snuggle up on the sofa together, clinging onto each other like our lives depended on it.

393

We stay like that for a long, long time and I think I must have dozed off for a bit, because next thing I know I'm groggily coming round, still locked in Dan's arms.

'Wake up, Sleeping Beauty,' he murmurs.

'Oh my God,' I smile weakly, 'you weren't a dream, you're really here.'

'Really here and never leaving your side again unless you order me away.'

Then he slowly turns his head down to me, cups my head in his hands and leans in to kiss me. A soft, lingering kiss at first but then gradually becoming deeper and more intense till next thing he's slid his hand down my shirt and is slowly unbuttoning it. I let him, bending down to kiss his hand as he does, loving how warm his touch is against my skin, and never wanting this moment to end. Then I reach up to pull his jumper over his head and he undresses fast, not letting me go, stopping to kiss me all the time.

Two minutes later, we're both naked on the sofa, his huge, deeply tanned, rock hard body clinging to mine as he rolls over me tantalisingly, licking my earlobes, kissing my neck, breasts, everywhere, like an explorer expertly mapping out my skin with his tongue.

Then, as we make love like we haven't done in the longest, longest time, I realise just how much I'd completely forgotten about him. I'd blanked out his taut, toned body, the musky smell of him, the sheer hulking size of him and how tiny and safe I always feel in his arms, how intense and urgent and passionate a lover he is.

How did I forget all this? How could I have?

Afterwards, we lie side by side on the sofa together for a long, long time, stretched out in easy silence.

'I love you,' he keeps telling me over and over again, the

black eyes regaining some of their old twinkle. 'Always have, always will.'

'I love you too. Even when I didn't like you, I still loved you.'

And he laughs and it occurs to me, it's been so long since I've seen Dan really laugh, I'd actually forgotten what his teeth looked like.

Funny but I spent so much time these past few weeks wanting to go home.

But with Dan beside me, his head on my chest, his arms locked tightly around me, I suddenly realise.

I *am* home.

Later on in the afternoon I take Dan to the hospital to keep vigil on Liz. Where there's no change. Her father is still here and my heart goes out to him when I see his pale, shattered face, his whole body bent double with exhaustion. Dan encourages him to go back to Liz's apartment to try and sleep, but he refuses to budge.

'Well, then at least come downstairs and have something to eat,' says Dan kindly.

He agrees to be led down to the canteen by Dan, but stops halfway out the door to thank me and the others too for watching over Liz round the clock.

'Over here, we're like her family too,' is all I can say.

I stay behind and read out yet more gossipy magazine stuff to Liz, hoping, praying that on some level she can hear me. Then I realise that what's been happening of late in my own life might just be of more interest to her than news about Lady Gaga's meat dress, so I tell her everything.

Bring her up to speed on absolutely everything. About

my dinner date with Jack and how I couldn't get out of The Plaza fast enough, about how I'd thought Dan was with someone else, while the whole time he was thinking the very same thing about me. So he hopped on a flight over and now here we both are. Figuring out things.

'But you know something, Liz? This time, I think that he and I might be OK.'

I look down at her, so tiny and thin in the hospital bed, with drips coming out of what looks like every vein on her arm and think . . . *be OK too, Liz. You've got too much to live for to go now. Just open your eyes, that's all we're asking . . . such a little thing to ask for.*

I've introduced Dan to the whole gang now and it's like every time he's out of the hospital room, either Chris, Alex or Blythe feels the need to tell me exactly what they think about him, no details spared.

'Such a good looking man, love!' says Blythe. 'And a real gentle giant too. Far more suitable for you than . . . well, we needn't say any more on that subject, need we? Do you know I went to St Patrick's Cathedral yesterday to pray to St Jude for poor little Liz and I lit a candle for you too that the right thing would happen for you in . . . well, let's just say in your romantic life. And look how well that turned out for you? But then that's St Jude for you. He never lets me down. Patron saint of hopeless cases, you know.'

Much later in the afternoon, I'm outside in the hospital corridor at a vending machine, watching milky tea shoot into a plastic cup when Dan comes rushing up to me, his huge hands gripping me urgently by the shoulders.

'Annie, love, come quick. You need to see this.'

I abandon the tea and race back to the ICU with him,

where everyone else is gathered around her bed – her father, Blythe, Chris, Alex. The whole gang's here.

Dan and I stand together at the back of the room, and I can feel his warm hand slipping around mine. I glance up at him and he gives me a look that says, *it's OK. She's going to be OK.*

'Liz?' her dad says to her gently, 'Liz, can you hear me. You opened your eyes just a minute ago, do you think you could do it again? Try, Liz, please try. Try for me.'

And that's when it happens. Slowly, barely perceptibly, her eyelids start to flutter and I physically gasp. Then she sees us, all of us, gathered around her, watching her with a combination of terror and relief and happiness.

There's no mistake. Liz is awake. For sure. Gradually, she takes each one of us in, then manages to mouth a weak *thank you.*

'You see?' says Blythe triumphantly. 'I told you. St Jude has never once let me down. Ever.'

Chapter Twenty-One

I'm almost late for the show, barely shaving the half-hour call, but for once I don't care. Because not only has a miracle happened to Liz today but Dan is here, beside me. Where he belongs

So he and I grab a taxi to the theatre together and we're still clinging to each other in the back seat, as he softly kisses my neck, ears, cheeks, running his hands through my hair every chance he gets. 'You know, back at your apartment earlier was amazing,' Dan whispers. 'Best afternoon I've had in I don't know how long. Why haven't you and I been having sex more often? We're bloody good at it!'

I grin up at him, still euphoric about Liz being OK and only now that all the worry over her has been eliminated, allowing myself to sink deep into happiness about Dan . . . and next thing we're kissing again, his mouth firm and insistent on mine.

'Honeymooners, huh?' says the taxi driver from the front seat, clocking the pair of us in his rear-view mirror.

'In a way, yes,' I say and Dan smiles that crooked smile that I love so much.

'Actually,' he leans forward to proudly tell the driver, arms tightly wrapped around me, 'would you believe that we've been together ever since we were fifteen years old?'

The driver whistles, duly impressed.

'Well congratulations to you both. Wish my wife and I were as loved up as you guys after all that time. Some achievement, huh?'

We just look at each other and smile.

For love to strike once, I think, is easy. Especially when you're only fifteen. For it to strike twice with the same person is nothing short of a miracle.

Then right outside the theatre box office, he suddenly grabs me and leans down to kiss me all over again, then slowly moves down to nibble at my neck, tickling me. Getting more and more intense all time and it's only wonderful.

'Sweetheart?' he murmurs softly in my ear. 'Love of my life? Heart of my heart?'

'Shut up talking and kiss me some more.'

'Oh I fully intend to, but first tell me, do you really have to go to work? Can't we just go back to bed and continue making up for lost time?'

I break off to smile up at him and realise that the black eyes are twinkling down at me like they haven't done in the longest time.

'Ehhh . . . let me just get this straight. *You* are the one ticking *me* off for having to work?' I laugh, teasing him.

'I know, love, I know I've been a nightmare to live with. But if you'll just give me one more chance, I can tell you that things are going to be very different from now on . . . far more sex in the afternoon I think, for starters . . .'

'Mmmmmmm . . . *very* good idea . . .'

Then he breaks off to kiss me properly again and I'm on tip-toe now, my arms locked tight around him, when next thing I hear a familiar voice from behind.

'Annie Cole, don't tell me you're picking up strange men off the streets now?'

It's Hayley, Queen of the Box Office, almost unrecognisable in a hoodie and on her way into work. Like I should be.

'This isn't a strange man,' I beam at her, eyes shining brightly. 'Hayley, I'd like you to meet my husband.'

'Oh my Lord, you must be the famous Dan!' she exclaims, her face lighting up in instant recognition. 'Ohhh, I'm so glad you two are working everything out! You know for a minute there, I thought you guys were in trouble.'

Dan stays for a full two weeks and now, with the worry of Liz gone, I don't feel guilty about the deep joy I'm feeling any more. Liz, by the way, is doing exceptionally well; she's back at the Eleanor Young clinic having treatment, sticking with the programme this time and every Monday, without fail, the rest of us troop up to Albany to visit her. She's still weak as a kitten but is slowly gaining weight and as Dr Goldman says, recovery is a long process and she'll need just to take things one day at a time. But so far so good . . .

Meanwhile it's like Dan and I are on a second honeymoon. Having spent so long apart, and I'm not just talking about since I came to New York either, now it's as though we can't bear to be as much as three inches away from each other. No matter where we go, in restaurants, clubs or bars, we're like some mythological two-headed, four-legged beast, constantly wrapped around each other, touching each other, snatching kisses every chance we get.

It reminds me of days of old – we've barely left each other's side and it's only magical. We're completely back to that relaxed easiness, that level of familiarity where we can practically hear thoughts dropping into each other's heads. Together we're revisiting all the landmarks we saw here before and instead of feeling a pang of nostalgia, now all I can think of is our future and what lies ahead. And I'm not frightened any more. Not now. With Dan beside me, how could I be?

Jack and Dan finally do meet, late after the show one night, when Dan is sitting chatting to me in my dressing room. Totally unannounced, Jack strides in, ostensibly to give Rachel some performance notes. Each instantly cops on who the other is before I introduce them, but if I thought there'd be any underlying tension, I was well wrong.

Without even realising I'm doing it, instinctively I lean in towards Dan, who slips a possessive arm around my waist as he politely shakes hands with Jack, as much as to say, *she's forgiven me and she's chosen me.* Meanwhile Jack just gives him one of his Jack looks, nods curtly at me, and is gone. The next news bulletin I hear about him is that he's finally been offered a movie script that he's agreed to work on and is out in LA.

Not long after, one lazy afternoon, Dan and I are strolling through Central Park in the warm October sunshine, when he suddenly pulls me down onto a bench beside him and kisses me spontaneously. One of those long lingering kisses that turns into something more intense and I just know that if we were back in my apartment, we'd most likely both have all our clothes off and be diving into bed together round now.

'Mmmmmm,' I say, cradling the back of his neck when we both eventually do come up for air. 'Now what was that for?'

'For putting up with me,' he says, whispering into my hair. 'Like no other woman in Ireland would have. How did you stand it all that time, Annie? With me working, working, working day and night? Jules gave me a right earbashing about it when she got back from her holiday here, you know. Told me in no uncertain terms that I hadn't exactly acted like husband of the year and that if I lost you, I'd only myself to blame.'

'Oh, honey, I knew you had to work as hard as you did. I knew you were only trying to build up the practice and needed the cash to support not just us but your mum and Jules too. It was rough going, I'll admit, but I did understand.'

'All those times I let you down and acted like some work-obsessed shit. Last year's anniversary, Christmas Day, for God's sake . . . I've been playing it over and over in my mind and all I can think is how lucky I am you didn't divorce me.'

'I'll be honest, it certainly wasn't easy . . . but that was then, and this is now.'

He laces his hands around mine and is playing with my wedding ring now.

'You know, I've been thinking, love.'

'What's up?' I ask.

'When your contract is up here and the show is over . . . I don't want you coming home to The Moorings with me and then you and I falling into the same old pattern again; me gone all the time while you struggle on alone.'

I don't answer him straight away. Mainly because while I've been dying to finish work and get back to my life with Dan again, I have to admit, the picture he's just painted isn't an appealing one. Because, the God's honest truth is, I just don't know if I could go back to that life again. Maybe all would be well for a time, but for how long? And would the same old problems start resurfacing?

'So, what do you think we should do?' I ask him tentatively. 'I mean, there's your mother to think about and Jules too.'

And Lisa fecking Ledbetter, I add bitterly in my head. Who's still living in the house, kids and all, most likely claiming squatters' rights by now. Wouldn't put it past her.

No, definitely not a pretty picture.

'Sweetheart,' he says, slipping a warm arm around my shoulder. 'If it's one lesson I've learned the hard way it's this: what matters most is you and I. Our marriage is my number one priority. So would you just trust me for the next few weeks? I've got to get back soon, but by the time I come back to you this December, I promise you, things will be very different.'

'You'll still come back in December?'

'Course I will. I made you a promise, didn't I? And will you trust me to sort things out at home before you get back?'

'I'd trust you with my whole life.'

'That's my girl.'

We kiss again, more deeply though and next thing his warm, eager hands have somehow slid under my jacket and jumper, cradling my breasts, brushing his thumb over my nipples, touching me all over, making me want him so much that it's making me dizzy and my breath is coming in short, panting bursts.

'Annie?'

'Don't stop . . . whatever you do, don't stop . . .'

'I've no intention of stopping . . . I was wondering . . . do we have time to get back to your apartment, before you have to go to work, I mean?'

'Oh, there's always time.'

Two weeks later and I can tell by Dan that although he's sad to go, still a huge part of him needs to be back at work, doing what he loves best. We hug at JFK airport and he brushes away my tears and tells me that he'll be back for me before I know it.

'I'll ring you as soon as I get home, love,' he calls out to me as he races for the gate, about to miss the final boarding call. 'I'll meet you at the moon!'

I blow him a kiss and wave till he's out of sight. And as I watch him stride away towards the boarding gate, I think back to when I sat here by myself, not so long ago, howling crying because I thought he was with someone else. What a change a few weeks can bring, I smile quietly, walking away with a spring in my step.

Funny, but as I count the weeks down to when I'll see him again, I often think of that hazy parallel life that I might have had, with Jack. Because who knows what would have happened if Dan had ended up with Lisa? Or if I'd given up on him and chosen a whole other life instead?

Maybe I'd have moved out to LA with Jack . . . maybe we'd have stayed together . . . maybe a whole lot of things.

As I say, I sometimes think about that other, distant

parallel life that shimmered like a mirage on the horizon for a brief, shining moment. From time to time, I play it out in my mental theatre and wonder what if . . . but never, ever for long.

I push the thought away and now it's all about the future.

WINTER

Epilogue

Dan is as good as his word and the following December, he's back, in time for our anniversary. Bearing hot news too; when he was back in Ireland, he had to attend a conference up in Dublin . . . where . . . wait for it . . . he was offered a new job.

It's at a busy practice in the city centre, but I can see the proud gleam in his eye when he tells me all about it. But as for me, I'm ecstatic! Because this is exactly like an action replay of our old happy life in the city. Before we moved down to Stickens, before all our problems started.

'So Mrs Ferguson,' he rolls over and says to me on a chilly, lazy afternoon just after he's arrived, when the two of us are tangled up naked in bed together. But then, ever since he walked through the door, we've been doing an awful lot of making up for lost time.

'What do you think of that, then?'

'It's amazing, honey . . . but . . . what about your mother? And The Moorings?'

I want to tack on and the Countess bleeding Dracula too, but manage to bite my tongue in time. Don't want to even invoke her name during our romantic reunion scene, plenty of time for that later.

'You know what? They'll all do perfectly well without us. After all, when I was here with you back in October, everyone managed just fine. The practice was fine, my mother was fine . . . the world continued to revolve without me being there . . . it all worked out. If it's one thing I've learned this past year, it's that I'm not indispensable. Besides we'll only be in Dublin, just a drive away, that's all. And my mother has a full-time nurse now, so I don't worry about her as much as I used to. Then Jules is starting her creative writing course in Cork . . .'

'Good,' I nod, and he smiles. 'She'll be their star pupil.'

He grins and pulls me in closer to him.

'And then the practice will still keep on running without me. I've taken on a new intern who's only fantastic, so he can stay up at the house and keep an eye on the place when we're gone . . .'

Oh sod it anyway, I can't resist asking . . .

'But . . . well, won't Lisa and the kids be there too?'

'That's what I've been trying to tell you, love. No, they won't. I didn't want to tell you this over the phone, but ever since I got back from seeing you last time, it seems that she's been actively trying to patch things up with her husband. So she told me that by the time you got back, she and the kids will already have moved back to London, to be with him. Best thing really,' he adds kindly. 'Harry and Sue were really missing their dad. They were slowly starting to turn me into a kind of surrogate father and it was all wrong. Those kids need to be with their real dad.'

I have to slump back against the pillows, unable to take in all of this good news.

In fact, I nearly feel like bursting into a chorus of *Ding*

Dong the Witch is Dead from *The Wizard of Oz,* but somehow manage to restrain myself.

And we're moving back to Dublin too! Where we were once so happy. Where we'll be happy again. I just know it.

And now it's my turn to tell Dan something else too.

Some big news I've been keeping to myself. Something that I didn't want to tell him over the phone either.

'Course, you know, sometime in the future, the time might come when we may seriously think about moving back to The Moorings,' I tell him, lightly, teasingly.

'What are you talking about, love?' he says, leaning over me now and looking me full in the face, puzzled.

'Oh, you know, I'm just saying, maybe one day you and I might just need a bigger house, that's all. When a bit more space may just suit us. Like for instance . . . oh, I dunno . . . a house with a nursery, like The Moorings has? Say if I were having a baby, for example? If I were to ever . . . find myself pregnant?'

'Annie . . .?' He pulls me up to him now, his whole heart in his warm black eyes.

And that's when I tell him. The news I've been secretly carrying around with me since not long after he left in October. That he's about to become a dad. And that I'm only eight weeks gone, but that I've had a scan already and that everything seems absolutely perfect.

It was torture, keeping it from him all these weeks, but I had to see the look on Dan's face when I told him, I just had to. And oh my God it was *so* worth it. Worth all the morning sickness, the nausea, the soreness, the constant tiredness and worst of all the secrecy; worth it all just to see the way he's looking at me right now.

Worth it all, worth more.

For a second I think he might pass out with shock, but then as the realisation dawns on him, his whole face bursts into that lovely, wonderful, crooked smile, that I love so much. He hugs me over and over again and in all the time I've known him, I don't think I've ever seen Dan, my Dan, this blissfully, overwhelmingly happy.

He kisses me so deeply that it takes my breath away and all I can think is: how lucky are we? If all the great love stories are about loss, how lucky are we that ours was so short lived?

Because love turned upside down is love for all that. And if marriage is all about falling in love, then my life lesson has been this: a long and successful marriage requires falling in love with the same person, not just once but over and over again.

That night, we go back to the Rockefeller Center, scene of so many romantic scenes between us and now the scene of another one. We don't skate, just snuggle up on the benches looking down at the swarms of skaters swirling away beneath us. It doesn't snow, like it conveniently did for us the night we first got engaged another lifetime ago, but I know just sitting here that this is a magical moment for us, one I'll be replaying on a loop in my mind for years to come.

We've come full circle, Dan and me. Somehow, against the odds, we've made it.

'I love you,' Dan breaks off to whisper to me. 'Always have, always will.'

And suddenly, just like that, our whole future unfolds in front of us like a rolling red carpet, as far as the eye can see.

Read on for Annie Cole's
(Unofficial) Guide
to New York

Annie Cole's (Unofficial) Guide to New York City

Shopping

OK, just to be clear, New York City is *the* shopping capital of the world. Period. In fact, let's face it, NYC is to shopping what Cheryl Cole is to fake tan; you just can't imagine one without the other. So for what it's worth, here are a few 'must-dos' for your NYC itinerary.

1. Century 21

Located downtown on Courtland Street, right beside where the Freedom Tower is now well under way.

Anyroadup, as any visitor to the city will tell you, one of the worst problems – particularly with a short visit to NYC – is the dreaded jetlag. Now trying to deny jetlag is a bit like trying to deny gravity, and lying in your bed wide awake, staring at the ceiling at 5 a.m. is par for the course, worse luck. Trouble with New York though is that none of the major department stores open until 10 a.m., which leaves you stomping round empty streets for hours on end, gazing forlornly at the steel shutters down outside Macy's and not having the first clue what to do with yourself.

But this is why Century 21 is such a minor miracle for tourists, because it opens at 8 a.m., and is far and away the city's best kept secret. Believe me, you'll find designer dresses at knockdown prices; and by knockdown, I mean reduced from four figures down to a staggering sixty dollars or so.

And the shoe department...oh dear God, the shoes! I know a pair of those glossy little Chanel pumps in Europe cost upwards of three hundred Euros, and may I be struck down this minute, but I got a pair in Century 21 for forty bucks. Yes, you read that right. *Forty.* Trust me, allow yourself at least half a day for Century 21, because you're going to need it.

Best for: shoes and handbags.

To be avoided: if you can't handle crowds of fellow bargain hunters shoving their elbows in your face. It's designed for the hardier shopper, not for the faint-hearted.

2. Daffy's

Located on Herald Square and 34th Street, though mind you, there's a bigger, better one at Lexington Avenue and East 57th. Another discount store with the enticing slogan, 'Dress in Prada for Next to Nada.' Dontcha just love it? Well worth checking out, particularly for kids' clothes and household stuff too.

Best for: absolutely anything and everything. Something for everyone, really.

To be avoided: if you're a heterosexual male, and therefore have to be chloroformed to be dragged within a ten foot radius of a department store.

3. Lord & Taylor

Located at 484 5th Avenue and 38th Street.
Oooh, you'll thank me for this one. A New York shopping institution popular among locals, and astonishingly, for such a well located store…nearly always tourist-free.
Best for: anything from work clothes, to mid-priced stuff, all the way up to seriously trendy, catwalk-clobber altogether. You know, the sort of street-smart chic outfit you really only ever see on SJP, then wonder where she went to buy it. Here, more than likely.
To be avoided: by no one I can think of. Even blokes will like Lord & Taylor, mainly because in spite of its central location in the dead centre of 5th Avenue, it's always lovely and quiet. No queues, no crowds, no hassle. *Ever.* Oh, and another tip? Bring your passport along with you to guarantee yet another ten percent off your final price.

4. Just about anything beginning with a 'B'

By which of course I mean the mighty triumvirate of Bloomingdale's, Barneys and Bergdorf's. Fabulous to stroll around and go people watching in, even if you don't buy. Because trust me, these stores are priiiiiii-ceeeey. That aside, honest to God, you've never seen so much mink fur on such taut, pulled-back faces. What is it about plastic surgeons that makes everyone over the age of seventy in this town ultimately wind up looking like Joan Rivers?
Best for: seeing how the other half live. And shop, of course.
To be avoided: unless you've just happened to cash in on the winning Euromillions lottery. Put it this way, Jackie Kennedy did all her shopping at Bergdorf's. That should tell you everything you need to know.

Eating Out

1. The Rockefeller Café at the Rockefeller Center

Just gorgeous and overlooks the ice skating rink in winter. Very reasonable too. And who knows, maybe after a few drinks you might think to hell with it, slap on a pair of ice skates and try your hand at becoming the next *Dancing on Ice* star. But let me know if you end up falling on your bum with half the restaurant gaping out at you, like I did.

2. Raoul's Restaurant, 180 Prince Street, Soho

A French bistro, with – trust me – the best French fries in the city. This place always has a great buzz about it and there's even a fortune-teller outside the ladies room, so while you're queuing for the loo you can pass the time being told you'll meet a tall, dark, handsome stranger...

3. The Tribeca Grill, 375 Greenwich Street

Fab restaurant, mid-priced, and owned by none other than Robert De Niro himself. Great for movie buffs as there's all sorts of memorabilia from his films plastering the walls, so you'll find yourself eating your burger with *Raging Bull* glowering back at you. Be warned though; just because De Niro owns the place doesn't necessarily mean he'll be checking in your coat and asking you how you're enjoying your stay. A mate of mine did actually think that, and ended up deeply disappointed.

4. Blue Fin, 1567 Broadway and Times Square

If you're a *Sex and the City* fan, you might remember a scene where Big and Carrie meet for lunch and he tells her he's getting married to Natasha. She then loses it and storms out as fast as her Jimmy Choos will carry her, and really, would you blame the girl? Anyway, that was all shot here in Blue Fin.

Achingly cool and full of be-suited, moneyed-types at the bar who can be found checking out the talent, particularly on a Friday night. Great for singles but not so great if you're on a date, mainly because there's a high chance you could meet someone else at the bar while you're there. After all, this is New York, and anything is possible...

Touristy Must-Dos

1. The Staten Island Ferry

As the name suggests, this connects Manhattan with nearby Staten Island. The ferry goes from the Whitehall terminal in downtown Manhattan to the St. George terminal on Staten Island approximately every half hour, so you're never waiting for too long. It's been called one of the great short journeys in the world and it's easy to see why. Not only do you get to see the whole sweeping skyline in all its soaring majesty, but you get a fantastic view of the Statue of Liberty too. By the way, there's now a massive fundraising campaign on to restore the statue and their slogan is, 'the grand old lady, who welcomed millions to America, now needs a little help herself.' Break your heart, wouldn't it?

2. The Empire State Building

Need I say more? Familiar to us all, and particularly anyone who bawled their way through *An Affair to Remember* or *Sleepless in Seattle*. Best done on a clear night, when the city spreads out beneath you like a magical, starry carpet. To be avoided if it's cloudy, or else trust me, you'll barely be able to see your own hand in front of you.

3. Central Park

Great for a Sunday morning stroll to see where real Noo Yowkers go to unwind, jog, walk their dogs, and even ride horses. Check out Strawberry Fields, a shrine dedicated to John Lennon, not far from the Dakota Building where he lived. In the summer, you can catch some world-class outdoor theatre when Shakespeare in the Park season starts, and in winter there's nothing more romantic than a meandering carriage ride around the North Meadow. So what's not to love?